* * *

QUEST FOR THE TRUE CROSS

QUEST FOR THE TRUE CROSS

The Templar Series: Part One

Non Nobis Domine

TONY MCMAHON

First published in 2015 by Tony McMahon
262 Camberwell New Road
London SE5 0RP
http://www.questforthetruecross.com/

A CIP catalogue record for this book is available from the British Library

ISBN: 0957272014
ISBN 13: 9780957272019

ABOUT THE AUTHOR

Tony McMahon is a London-based author, former BBC producer and history buff. Previous books have included a no-holds-barred biography of boxing champion Errol Christie – *No Place To Hide* (published by Aurum Press) – which was shortlisted for the best sports biography of 2011. He also wrote the biography of Neville Staple - *Original Rude Boy* – who was the vocalist in 1980s legendary 2Tone band The Specials.

ACKNOWLEDGEMENTS

Richenda Todd, leading copy editor in the field of historical fiction and my copywriter Jane Donovan. Thanks to two history teachers in my family for their assistance – Professor João Leite in Porto, Portugal, and Kevin Murphy. Among museum staff I badgered for answers, I would single out Meriel Jeater at the Museum of London, Stuart Ivinson at the Royal Armouries Museum and the staff at Castelo São Jorge in Lisbon. Also in that city, the very helpful people at the Fabula Urbis bookshop.

An honourable mention goes to Paulo Alcobia Neves at the Municipality of Tomar. In Israel, I relied on Ehud Harpaz to take me to all the relevant sites in Jerusalem, Tiberias, Acre and Caesaria. My mother and father, Peter and Alice McMahon, for drawing on their work in the mental health field to explain the psychiatric condition I allude to with my main protagonist. Mike Dent, a sub-editor by trade, who was forced to have chapters read out to him. Miguel Moorcraft and José Joaquim Silva for helping out with Portuguese translation.

Part 1

CRUSADER DOMINIONS
KNOWN AS OUTREMER

Christmas Day, Anno Domini 1144
Monday 28 Jumaada al-THaany 539 Anno Hegirae

Prologue

TEMPLAR CHURCH,
EDESSA

The priest clasped at his assailant's tunic as he struggled for air. Besnik lessened the pressure on the old man's windpipe yet his grimy hands remained firmly round Father's Jean's neck, leaving unsightly purple bruises.

"You should have found a linen box to crawl into and hide," the Romani mercenary cackled.

"I beg you not to do this, my son," the priest gasped.

"I'm not your son."

This cannot be how I meet my end, Father Jean thought. Surely this creature is capable of some decency. Nobody can be devoid of all compassion. If I can only find some common ground between us, I will see the sun rise tomorrow.

"We are … we are both men of the book. Children of Abraham." Father Jean took a faltering breath. "Only our view of His Son truly divides us."

His assailant was unmoved.

"I'm neither Saracen nor Frank," Besnik sneered at the priest. "Don't waste words about your useless God on me."

Time was marching against Besnik and his accomplice Giyassedin. Outside the city was falling to the Seljuk Turks. An immense Saracen wave had crashed over the seemingly impenetrable fortifications. The Christian forces had been scattered and their control of this great Syrian city was very much at an end. It wouldn't be long before the Turks found this church and ranksacked its riches. The two thieves had to work fast.

Besnik's hand gripped Father Jean's throat once more. The Romani derived a sadistic thrill from tightening his fingers around his victim's windpipe. The priest grabbed at the mercenary's hand but it was locked in position and squeezing. He lifted Father Jean off his feet, the priest kicking at Besnik in a futile defence.

"I ... I ... I ... know ... nothing ..."

His hold was so tight that the cartilage in Father Jean's throat crackled. Eyes bulging and face reddened, the black-robed cleric writhed as Besnik calmly and methodically throttled him.

"I told you he wouldn't talk," Giyassedin observed from the side of the altar in a matter-of-fact way. "He'd rather die than tell us."

Besnik dropped the priest in a heap on the floor. His patience had worn thin. He resumed beating the old man with his fists. Blow after blow rained down on the cleric's bloodied face. Feebly, the old man raised a hand to defend himself but Besnik pushed it away. A strong punch closed the priest's left eye as he groaned for this brutal torture to cease.

"Where is it?" Besnik yelled at Father Jean.

"I ... I cannot ... I must not say."

The mercenary drew his dagger from its leather sheath and grabbing the priest by the few grey hairs on his head, severed an ear with one rapid slicing action. Father Jean clasped his head and screamed. Besnik repeated the question.

"Where ... is ... it?"

His senses dulled by agony, the priest involuntarily allowed his one good eye to dart leftwards for the briefest instant. That was enough for Besnik. He now knew where to find the treasure that he and his accomplice sought. Leaving Father Jean in a pained heap on the flagstone floor, he moved over to the stone pulpit.

"Help me move this," he barked at Giyassedin.

"Are you sure?"

"Positive."

The two thieves pushed at the block of stone surmounted by a carving of an eagle, the symbol of John the Apostle. With a grinding sound, the pulpit yielded its secret inch by inch. Beneath it was a crudely dug hole in the floor. Besnik thrust a flaming torch into the darkness, revealing a small hill of human bones. A skull stared back mournfully at the mercenary.

"Good," Besnik announced.

Father Jean looked on in horror.

"What have I done?" The priest wept on his knees, too weak to stand.

Father Jean had never wanted to be a martyr – that was for braver and saintly men. But this creature had no God, he was sure of that.

"Kill me! In God's name … kill me," he whispered.

Convulsing in agony, the priest looked up at Besnik. Scum of Christendom! The lowest of God's creatures! One of that accursed race of men who had fashioned the very nails driven into the hands of Christ in return for base coin. Everybody knew of the perfidy of the Romani people, stealers of bibles and relics, friendless and condemned to wander the earth. And he had delivered up a great Templar treasure to this devil.

Those great knights of the Temple of Jerusalem will never forgive me.

"You – you dog!" the priest spat. "You're more vile than a Saracen!"

Besnik grabbed the cleric's chin, shoved it back and ran his sharp dagger blade across Father Jean's throat as if he were killing a pig on market day. A crimson jet spurted out across the grey flagstones. In the warm evening air, the blood soon congealed around the prone body.

Giyassedin blithely ignored the murder. There was a robbery to commit after all. He'd always found that a rope came in useful when despoiling churches and he removed the length wound across his torso. Fastening one end to a pillar, Giyassedin threw the remaining length through the exposed hole. Being slighter than Besnik, he knew it made more sense for him to shin down into the darkness below. In no time, he'd disappeared from view.

Besnik threw a torch down.

Sitting away from the priest, the Romani pondered his next move. If they found the Templars' magic symbol, the Atabeg would pay them handsomely. It would be a vast reward!

A beautiful palace! Beautiful women! Everything I've ever wanted.

Besnik had hoped that the war would prove extremely lucrative but the pickings so far had been very meagre indeed. Like carrion birds, he and Giyassedin could only loot after the soldiers had taken their share and they were so greedy. Nothing left for hard-working professional thieves! But for now, they had beaten the soldiers to this place.

Down below, the Seljuk stumbled among the bones of bishops and knights, waving his torch in all directions. It had to be here somewhere. Any moment there would be a glint of gold, a sparkle of some jewels and he'd have found the church's greatest possession.

Giyassedin wasn't just thrilled by the prospect of riches. Besnik's accomplice was also revelling in the victory his people had achieved that day. The Seljuk Turks, led by the Atabeg, had swept away all the infidel crusaders ranged before them.

Those Frankish dogs can go back to their cold kingdoms in the North!

Foolish Edessa, Giyassedin mused. Foolish to resist our glorious Atabeg Zengi, ruler of Aleppo and Mosul, son of Aq Sunqur al-Hajib, faithful disciple of Allah and conqueror of a thousand kingdoms. A man who liked to adorn himself in a splendid cloak given to him as a bribe by the Emperor of Constantinople as that Greek Christian infidel desperately sought peace terms.

Once the Seljuk army had stormed into Edessa, they'd moved as a killing tide from house to house, cutting down all who stood in their way. Even the city's Archbishop had been trampled to death as his own flock stampeded before the Seljuk scimitars.

Allah has guided my people to great victories!

Giyassedin smiled to himself.

This city will now belong to men like me!

Suddenly Giyassedin's torch picked out the large glittering reliquary, propped against a wall.

"I think I've found it," the Seljuk shouted up.

Besnik closed his eyes, his thin lips drawn into a leer.

"Are you sure?"

"Yes." Giyassedin gulped in awe. "It's very beautiful."

"Never mind its beauty," Besnik rebuked him coldly, "don't get too attached to it. Tomorrow we will dine like caliphs when the Atabeg has rewarded us."

Giyassedin shook with excitement at such a prospect and lunged through the gloom to grab the treasure and bring it to the light. From above, Besnik watched as the face full of childlike wonder emerged from the murk of the crypt holding the jewel-encrusted object.

"Tie the rope around it," he ordered his accomplice, "I will bring it up slowly. Mind how you do it. We don't want it damaged."

Kicking aside a skeleton, Giyassedin fastened the end of the rope to the reliquary and then watched as it bobbed in the air before being slowly manoeuvred out of the hole above by Besnik.

The mercenary held up the reliquary. The biblical scenes depicted in paint and enamelling meant nothing to him. Like a scavenging rodent, his eyes darted all over the sacred cross looking for a jewel that wasn't prominently displayed – some sapphire or pearl that was tucked away from view.

Finding a jewel he didn't think would be missed, Besnik took his dagger and gouged it out. Then, hurriedly, he ripped a velvet cloth from the altar and wrapped up the treasure as if putting swaddling clothes round a newborn baby. Once concealed, he surprised himself by hugging it fondly, quite overcome with emotion. The Romani had never embraced a human being with such affection.

"My friend," the Seljuk's voice called from the crypt, "have you forgotten me?"

Besnik stopped. There was a single line from the Qur'an he'd once heard and had saved it in his head for a moment like this.

"Whomever Allah wants to deceive you cannot help."

Giyassedin had learnt his Qur'an by rote and was startled by the Romani's knowledge of the sacred book. He cheerfully yelled up the rest of the verse learnt at a madrassah as a small boy.

"Allah does not want them to know the truth because he intends to disgrace them and then torture them."

Having correctly completed the quote from the Prophet, the trusting Seljuk looked up in confusion and then terror as the illuminated hole above his head closed like an eclipse.

Why is this happening? There must be some mistake!

"No! Please – Besnik! My friend! Don't do this to me!"

But the mercenary ignored him. He was bored of the Turk's relentless cheeriness and had no intention of sharing the reward with him. With one last push, he restored the pulpit to its original position. Giyassedin would be entombed with the bones of the Templars for all eternity.

"That is the problem with you Seljuks," Besnik observed dryly as he placed the reliquary under his arm. "You know that book of yours off by heart but you have no idea what it means."

Chapter 1

JERUSALEM

The Franks cowered in terror behind the shutters of their houses as the miserable procession of blood- and filth-stained mantles snaked through the narrow streets. Any thought of celebrating the birth of Christ faded fast as this macabre spectacle materialised before them. The sight of a ruined army and the overwhelming stench of carnage and slaughter stifled all hope of seasonal cheer.

Our greatest knights reduced to this.

Defeated warriors trudged towards the great temple platform built by Herod countless centuries ago, crowned by an aurulent dome shimmering in the baking sun. The stone mass of the platform and the battlements ringing the city had once seemed impregnable to Saracen attack – as defiant as the great walls of Constantinople. But no longer! The pathetic sight of these bloodied crusaders signified doom for the Franks.

God has turned His eyes away from us.

Many years before, the crusaders had breached the ancient walls of Jerusalem. What a victory that had been, the sacred crucifix supplanting the crescent of Islam! After four centuries under the rule of a caliph, Jerusalem had returned to being a Christian city. The knights had slain so many of the heretics that their stirrups were splashed in blood as their horses galloped through the streets. Or so the chroniclers had claimed.

Now the tables were turned. The enemy, once so decisively vanquished, menaced Jerusalem from beyond the city walls. The Franks, as the Saracens termed the city's Christians, knew what they could expect if the Muslims stormed through the gates. There would be no mercy shown to those who had hammered a cross into the top of the golden dome, raising Christ above Allah.

Why is God favouring them? Shouldn't we be rewarded by heaven for what we did?

A short distance away, in the fields and deserts beyond Jerusalem, the sharp scimitars of the enemy glistened in the afternoon sun. Those ornately inscribed blades would soon feast on Frankish flesh, cutting down men, women and children in their wake, ignoring their pitiful cries. Churches would be despoiled and all trace of the infidel crusaders would be swept away. A great cleansing would take place.

A Frank clutched his son as if it might be for the last time. Soon we will both be walking into heaven or hell. Our souls will be weighed in the balance and our fate decided for all eternity. Either the angels will carry us aloft or the devils will fix hooks in our flesh and drag us to the scorching fires below. Not that you're old enough to have committed any great sin, he thought, looking down at his son.

The forlorn father surveyed the file of battered and broken men below and shook his head in disbelief. The Knights Templar had suffered an ignominious defeat. It was surely a portent of what lay ahead for the city. These once seemingly invicible Templars would be powerless to stop the Muslims swarming over the battlements and slitting every infidel throat.

Christ abandons us to our fate!

Nearby the markets still heaved with dates, sabra fruit, figs and almonds — the teeming produce of the fertile lands around them. Delicious wine was brought from the North, chilled by snow collected in the mountains of the biblical land of Canaan. Exquisitely patterned textiles, brought from lands so distant they had never been visited, were haggled over.

The Christians had got used to such glorious abundance and luxury. Their houses were beautifully tiled and gurgling fountains cooled spacious courtyards. Silk gowns adorned the bodies of the Franks and turbans covered their heads. What a contrast this had been to the roughness of life in the West, wearing coarse wool garments as protection from the biting cold.

Now it was time to get away if you could. Bid farewell to the good life. Under cover of night, pack whatever you could carry and bribe a gatekeeper to slip out of the city. Flee along ancient roads to Jaffa or Acre and hope there was a ship that could sail you back to France or Aragon, England or Flanders. The alternative was too gruesome to contemplate.

You have failed us, Templars.

The Templar dead stared expressionlessly up at the sky from the carts that trundled past. Carrion birds pecked at the lifeless knights, their bodies turning rancid in the afternoon heat. They were the lucky ones. Better to be beyond life than the wounded, groaning and shrieking, their limbs hacked and torn by Saracen scimitars. In a few hours, most of them would breathe their last.

Their laments were drowned out by the mournful clip-clop of hundreds of horses and the chaplains muttering their useless prayers for salvation. What was the point of their pleas to God now? He'd favoured the Saracens and damned the Templars. Maybe it was true what was furtively claimed about these knights: the stories of them bowing down before a devil's head, the rumours of unnatural love and the blasphemous initiation rites. Could God be punishing Jerusalem's Frankish Christians for the transgressions of the Templars?

The whole sorry mass continued to edge ever closer towards the heart of Jerusalem – the commanding and holy Temple Mount.

"Have you seen my master? Sir William de Mandeville?"

An Easterner wove through the mounted warriors searching for a knight he'd last seen many hours before. His torso was encased in gold lamellar armour. A conical helmet covered his head with a red-and-white striped turban round the base and a strip of material down the back of his neck. His skin was noticeably darker than the crusader Franks and his hair as black as ebony. He pulled at his goatee and his eyes darted about feverishly.

"Have you seen my master?"

A Templar knight held his hand flat over his pierced eye socket and ignored the strange man buzzing round him like an insistent fly. Pathros moved on from this dazed figure to the Marshal, who still carried the black-and-white piebald standard of the Templar Order under his right arm. Only when this standard was lowered could a Templar squadron retreat. It hadn't been lowered for many hours that day. This was the Templar way; first into battle and last out. But that day they had paid a high price for their courage.

"My master, I cannot find him. Sir William de Mandeville."

The Marshal turned to glance disdainfully at Pathros. Filthy Syrian, he thought. A lowly turcopole! One of those disreputable and untrustworthy men hired from among the heretical Eastern Christians. Or perhaps he was an Islamic apostate who had changed sides for a better life. Never to be treated as an equal! Good with a bow, of course, as were all Turks and Syrians, but always to be viewed as lesser men. They could never hope to be a knight and wear the sacred white mantle of the Order. Pathros looked pleadingly at the senior Templar officer.

"Get back into line!" the Marshal barked. "*Now!*"

Pathros skulked away but he wouldn't give up his search. William was alive; he knew it. But he hadn't seen the knight since the confusion of the morning fight. At some point, the English Templar had charged once more into the fray, his helmet recklessly discarded. Pathros had watched helplessly as that familiar blond mop of hair had disappeared amidst the murderous throng and clanging of swords.

My master is not dead, I am sure of that.

Pathros turned from the gloomy crusader mass around him and stared ahead to the Herodian stone platform, once the supporting structure for the great Temple of the Jews burnt down by the Romans. The Dome of the Rock sat at the centre of the platform, a mosque built by the first Muslim invaders and indescribably beautiful. Though he wasn't a follower of the Prophet, Pathros felt a slight twinge of pride that people of the East like himself had created the patterned mosaics and intricate trellised windows that adorned the octagonal structure as well as the gold dome hypnotising all those who gazed on it.

The Franks will surely pay dearly for what they have done, Pathros thought. But I will suffer more for being in league with the Templar enemy. The Saracens would regard Pathros as an apostate and his crucified body would hang alongside a pig and a dog. He could protest all he wanted that his family had always been Christian and never converted to Islam. They had been Christian since the days of the Roman emperor Constantine. So how could he be an apostate if he'd never read a word of the Qur'an or accepted its message?

Pathros felt as if he'd slipped between two worlds: that of the Frankish Christians and the Saracen Muslims. I'm not good enough for either of them, he often mused. My family was Christian when the Franks and English were still worshipping trees and rivers. Jesus was one of us – he'd often quip to an irritated William, who imagined the saviour to be tall and blond like him. And Syria was my family's land before those Muslim armies stormed out of the desert with their mysterious creed. We Syrian Christians are the rightful owners of these lands. We have been here longer than anybody.

Pathros hurried towards the Herodian platform.

Please don't be dead, William. Please, for me, live!

Inside the Dome of the Rock, the crusaders had whitewashed the mosaics with their heretical pronouncements in Arabic that had been placed there merely a few decades after the death of their prophet. How dare these heathens claim that Jesus Christ wasn't the son of God! How dare they defile Jerusalem with their satanic creed!

To purify this place of all traces of Islam, the crusaders had erected an altar to Saint Nicholas in the middle and renamed the building, the Templum Domini. Yet no amount of incense, holy water and candle smoke could erase the fact that very soon the Saracens would be back to claim what was theirs.

Nearby was the House of the Augustinians, where the holy canons lived – a structure the Saracens would demolish in the blink of an eye when they returned. Rising up behind that was the Temple of Solomon, an impressively solid edifice supported by giant Corinthian pillars. Islam claimed this fine church as the Al-Aqsa mosque but the Templars had sworn it would remain in Christ's hands for all eternity. They truly believed it was the very temple of the great Jewish king and had made it their headquarters. In the secret and mysterious tunnels underneath lay treasures yet to be discovered including – it was whispered – the Holy Grail itself.

The defeated squadron moved up on to the stone platform of the Temple Mount. One figure had ridden ahead, driving his horse forward at a hellish pace.

Blood trickled down the side of his head and sweat covered his lightly bearded face. He flung himself from his steed and, not bothering to tether it, stumbled like a drunk up the steps of the Temple of Solomon.

As he burst through the main doors, he sent a small group of Augustinian canons scattering behind the pillars. They hid and watched nervously as he ranted and raved and tore at his mantle. One of the canons whispered frantically to another.

"What is he saying?"

"I cannot tell."

Flailing like an untamed stallion, the deranged knight pushed over a statue of some or other saint then tumbled to the tiled floor of the nave, kicking and punching at invisible assailants. Standing again, he drew his heavy sword from its scabbard and slashed in all directions, his eyes screwed up. Incoherent cries fell from his lips as he hacked at phantom bodies.

The canons, hiding from this fearsome figure, strained to make out his garbled words. Something about a monster that had entered his soul and how Christ must rip this creature out of him. Then he knelt and sobbed while his gloved hands tore at his white mantle emblazoned with the scarlet eight-pointed cross of the Templar Order. It was as if the demon within was striving to remove the sacred garment from his body.

The young knight was strongly built with a thick chest and muscular arms from carrying a heavy shield and sword in battle for hours on end. The canons were sure that with one flick of his wrist he could send them all flying. So they stayed where they were, observing.

"*You!*" The knight pointed at the crucified Jesus over the main altar. "Take this devil away! His words are like daggers. I can't —" He gasped, as if in pain, and crouched low, gripping the chainmail coif that covered most of his head. "No, I won't serve you. Leave me, Basilisk. I won't bow to you!"

The Augustinians glanced at each other in horror.

"Fetch some of the knights," Dom Mathias, a senior canon, whispered to the others. "And bring the reliquary of Saint Anastasius."

The knight cried out, his face a picture of agony.

"Your father betrayed you! Mine didn't. You can't win me over with that talk!"

Dom Mathias inched round the pillar behind which he'd been hiding. Once, the Augustinian had witnessed the Bishop of Poitiers lay hands upon a possessed man and the Devil had fled from his mouth. Saint Radegund had likewise freed many women of demons simply by laying her fingertips on the face of the afflicted. Winged creatures flew from out of their victims, shrieking and howling.

But Dom Mathias was sure this knight wouldn't respond to such gentle measures. Something much more drastic would be needed to cleanse this possessed soul. Satan had found a strong house within which to dwell and it would have to be made to shake before the Evil One quit.

Down the nave clanked a group of five knights, still in full chainmail, carrying swords, maces and daggers. The first, Ralf Devereux, laid a hand on the shoulder of the tormented knight.

"Come on, Will. Less of this, eh?"

For a heartbeat William de Mandeville didn't seem to hear his one-time friend. Then he whirled round, shaking off the hand and glared. He struck Ralf full in the face, sending him reeling. With that, the other knights lunged on to their fellow Templar. William fought back but they were too many and he subsided, exhausted. Rubbing his swollen cheek, Ralf helped the others lift William and take him to the small infirmary alongside the church.

Dom Mathias ran to the baptismal font and scooped some water into his hands then carefully followed the group of knights. The priest knew mere water wouldn't suffice for the task ahead but it might cow the demon momentarily. The Augustinian steeled himself for the grotesque operation he'd soon have to perform.

The adjoining building had once been a mosque. The Order had deliberately blocked the mihrab where the imam used to address his flock with a thick wall and subdivided the prayer space to create living quarters and rooms for secular purposes. William was carried into one of these rooms and fastened with cords to a simple bed.

Dom Mathias sprinkled the knight with the holy water. This caused William to revive and he began struggling furiously against the bonds, which only got tighter, cutting and bruising his arms and legs.

The Christian warrior's powerful body wrenched forward as he addressed thin air.

"You no longer resemble your father! Show me your power then," he cried out. "Bring down these walls … rain fire from the skies and I will fall before you as a supplicant!"

William's face was covered in beads of perspiration and his light blue eyes stared intently at the ceiling. His comrades gathered round the bed, distraught to see such a great fighter for the cause of Christ reduced to this miserable state. Behind them, the Templar physician Brother John and his assistant prepared some herbal remedies. But Dom Mathias shook his head and exchanged glances with the other canons. Scented leaves and sprigs wouldn't repel the Devil. They knew what had to be done.

Brother John leaned over the Templar knight, observing his flickering eyelids and half-open mouth. His patient had the broad jawline of fine Norman stock complemented by high cheekbones and a noble brow, glowing skin and strong teeth. William had been bred for knighthood and nothing else. His strong body had been rigorously trained for the arts of war, with endless drills and weapon practice.

"We mustn't lose a warrior like this," Brother John addressed the other knights, who nodded vigorously in agreement.

He let a small amount of blood from William's forearm and tasted it. There wasn't a hint of bitterness. It was sweet to the taste. That was a good sign at least.

"What is it you see, brother?" the physician asked his patient but William appeared unable to hear him.

Brother John shouted back to his assistant.

"Get that poultice ready!"

A Templar serjeant dressed in the distinctive black mantle of his lower rank crammed a small muslin bag full with curative herbs. There was comfrey used by the Saracens to alleviate pain; coriander was added, well known for its ability to cure plague; then a tiny amount of belladonna and monkshood, being the magical ingredients that would break the demon's hold. The sack was held over a glass container of water boiling over a flame.

Dom Mathias watched this procedure with contempt. He'd seen William's behaviour in a house of God, mere herbs wouldn't expel the Devil. One of the canons handed his superior a sharp metal instrument. The experienced cleric glanced down at the sharp drill in his hand that glistened in the faded light of the infirmary. This was how to cast out Satan, not brewed-up leaves and twigs.

"He was at the front all the time," Roger, one of the five knights, muttered in a listless tone. The battle was painfully fresh in all their minds. "I never saw his sword drop, not even for a moment. Cut down one of those bastards after another."

The ambush outside Nablus had been a hideous surprise. The knights had been travelling north to link up with other Templars to relieve the city of Edessa from a Turkish siege. Edessa was a jewel in the crusader crown, a great metropolis they needed to retain if their mission in the Holy Land was to succeed. But then, out of nowhere it seemed, a Saracen force had descended on the crusaders. Maybe these Saracens had ridden from Damascus or Aleppo but wherever their origin, they were deep inside crusader territory.

"Lost his wits, the poor sod!" Roger's friend Thomas watched William as his head turned from one side to the other, burbling sacrilegious nonsense. "Seen it before, good men driven to madness by so much death."

"But not William." Richard, the fourth knight, would have none of this talk of possession. "This is a passing thing."

"It's nothing of the sort!"

Dom Mathias edged forward.

"You must use this!" He thrust the metal drill-like object at the physician. "You know what needs be done! Take it and use it ..."

"I cannot," Brother John remonstrated.

"You will answer to a higher authority if you don't! This man has conversed with devils in a house of God. We must release the evil ... you must use it!"

The physician's hand trembled as he reluctantly accepted the frightful instrument. Dom Mathias pulled back the chainmail coif from William's head, yanking it down to his shoulders. In the small windowless room, lit only by torches, the knight's golden-blond hair shone even though matted by sweat and the filth of the battlefield. The canon gestured and the physician placed the sharp point against William's skull.

The Augustinian raised his hands.

"*Exorcizo te, immundíssime spíritus, omnis incúrsio adversárii, omne phantasma, omnis légio, in nómine Dómini nostri Jesu Christi eradicáre ...*"

The unused poultice steamed away, filling the air with a stifling aroma. Priests and knights wiped the sweat from their brows as the temperature rose in the small space. Very soon, the demon would be released from the knight's head and God's holy will would have been done.

Outside on the Temple Mount, Pathros still frantically sought his master, unaware of the horrific fate about to befall him. As he passed a Templar knight on horseback, the unfamiliar figure turned on the turcopole.

"You the one who fills Will's head with idiotic stories!"

He spat on the ground. Turcopoles were to be seen and not heard but this one was always jabbering his supposed wisdom to his master. Everybody knew about him. The weird turcopole who either had his head stuck in a book or was talking heresy to his master.

"Sick to death of hearing him repeating your nonsense to the lads. That kind of pagan talk is what we don't need round here."

Pathros bowed his head in an act of false contrition.

"Poor old Will might be impressed with your Turkish chatter but we're not. You hear me? Keep babbling to him the way you do and I'll cut your damned tongue out!"

Pathros was filled with rage. My family has more nobility in one little finger than you do, Frankish dog, he mused angrily. Once more, the proud Syrian was transported back in his mind to his father's sumptuous dwelling in Aleppo. The young Pathros attended by servants; taught by a Greek tutor and dressed in fine fabrics. His skin scented with the olive oil and bay leaf soap from the bathhouse. Pathros had cut quite a dash as a fourteen-year-old and it was expected would one day make the family even richer.

But then the dark times had come.

The great earthquake hadn't just brought the walls of their house crashing down, it had set the majority population against the Christians, who were purged from all high offices of state. After all, somebody must be blamed for the earth moving in such a destructive way. Why not the Christians? Pathros had watched his family plunge into poverty. With tears in her eyes, his mother had begged her eldest son to leave and find his fortune anywhere – even with the Franks. And that was how he'd ended up in the service of the Templars.

The abusive knight rode off. Under his breath, Pathros cursed the man, hoping his horse would trample him underfoot and his death agonies would be slow and protracted. But then he stopped and wondered if the knight had a point. Had he filled William de Mandeville's head with too much exotic thinking?

Pathros loved to share his voluminous knowledge of Greek, Roman and Persian medicine and philosophy. All that childhood tutoring had stuffed his mind with so much erudition and yet he often felt it had nowhere to go. What was the point of having read so many great works when none of these crusaders seemed to appreciate his learning? Except for William – his master and dearest friend. He had an untypical curiosity. Unlike his uncouth comrades at arms, the English Templar seemed to enjoy picking the Syrian's brain.

The evening before the ambush at Nablus, the knight and his turcopole had watched the last glow of the evening sun together. William was impatient for more stories. His Eastern servant seemed to know all the mysteries of the Saracen lands. It was certainly true that Pathros had journeyed far and wide through the Dar al-Islam and William yearned to see through his eyes the wondrous things he had beheld.

"Tell me about Abraxas again," William insisted.

"The creature with snake coils for legs," Pathros stroked his goatee apprehensively. "Some of my people believe that he is more powerful and omnipotent than God and the Devil combined, maybe that he is older than both of them. They say that he has existed before time itself was created and his power stretches far into the void."

William grappled with the idea but it was too fantastical to comprehend.

"Are you seriously saying it was something that lived in the great darkness before there was any light? I can't imagine it. It … it just seems too incredible."

"I do not believe it myself."

"Mmmm …" Something was on William's mind. "I think some of our knights venerate this creature. I'm sure of it, in fact."

"How so?"

"I was at our fort in Tiberias and talking with some of the brothers. One of them was an odd chap – a bit unnerving, in fact. He seemed restless and ill at ease. We talked about our homelands … people we had left behind … and as he spoke, he rubbed the ring on his forefinger over and over. The gemstone had something carved on it and I waited for his other finger to move away. Then I saw it. Abraxas! Don't you think that's strange? One of us Templars carrying a symbol of a devilish being?"

Pathros said nothing for a moment. He'd seen many knights dabble in the cults of the East.

"It does seem … inappropriate, my friend, for a Christian." The turcopole ran his finger across his lips. "Maybe we should not speak of these things."

"Why not?" William retorted. "Think this stupid Frank can't possibly understand stuff like that! I may not be as educated as my older brother, but I get everything you're saying, every last word of it! And anyhow," the knight smirked mischievously, "I forbid you to withhold anything from me. I'm your master, after all."

Pathros snapped out of his reverie. On the Temple platform, he continued his desperate search for William. At last, an archer claimed he'd seen the knight.

"Where did you see my master?"

Laughing, the impudent English serf pointed towards the Temple of Solomon.

"Went in there, he did. Lumbering like a drunk, sobbing like a woman." He clearly enjoyed witnessing his social betters at a low ebb. "Never seen such a thing in my life."

Pathros charged into the church.

Within the same building, in its largest room, a stormy council of war was in progress. The glum-faced leaders of the Order of the Temple in Jerusalem crammed round an illustrated map of the crusader kingdoms of Tripoli, Antioch, Jerusalem and, crucially, Edessa. Had the city held out against the Saracens? Nobody knew. No word had come from its besieged people.

The Grand Master, Robert de Craon, traced the tip of his index finger around the walls of the city of Edessa depicted on the parchment.

"They will never break through," his voice crackled with age and sickness.

The map didn't portray the terrible truth yet to reach this council of war: the Seljuks had successfully stormed the fortifications. Even now they were mopping up any Frankish resistance and looting anything of value. Nobody had been able to escape and spread the news of the city's fall.

"Edessa's walls will never yield to the Saracen ... of that I'm sure."

"With all due respect, Grand Master," the Seneschal barked, "we cannot be sure what's going on at Edessa." The Order's second in command was itching for the top position. Any opportunity to discredit the old fool was gleefully seized. "And our relief force got nowhere near after being ambushed at Nablus. So you'll pardon me if I don't share your unbridled optimism."

Another Templar officer piped up.

"Traitors everywhere! Saracens must have journeyed days to ambush our boys at Nablus but none of our scouts saw a thing. Personally, I don't trust a single Muslim, Christian or Jew in this city!"

"Quite," the Seneschal agreed.

The Grand Master's blood boiled.

"Enough!" He breathed in short, insistent gasps; his limbs ached with every movement and his sight was growing ever more blurred. "Edessa is safe so long as our most sacred of relics is within the city. You think God would disown a people who have the True Cross in their possession."

The Seneschal bit his lip. The Grand Master's decision to send the Lignum Crucis – the very wood upon which Christ was crucified – to Edessa had been a grave risk. A foolhardy gesture of support to the city! Who knew where it was now?

"If Edessa falls," the Seneschal began haltingly, "and any other cities including this one topple to the Turks then our Order is utterly finished. Especially if Christians throughout the world find out that we have delivered Christ's cross into the hands of the Saracens ..."

"It's safe, I tell you!" the Grand Master bellowed. "I won't be questioned any further about this. The Lignum Crucis was needed in Edessa and I would have made the same decision a thousand times. I'm sure brave Father Jean and his priests have hidden it securely away. And wherever the True Cross is, its powers will envelop the city and protect it. Of that I'm absolutely sure!"

Back in the infirmary, William's whole body seemed to lift from the sweat-soaked sheet beneath him as he struggled against his bonds. Dom Mathias urged Brother John on to perform the necessary operation. Once the skull had been drilled into, the evil spirit could be expelled.

"Don't be weak," Dom Mathias insisted.

"It will kill him," Brother John quivered.

"Do it! Think only of his immortal soul. Drive the metal into this poor boy's head and make him a good and holy man again!"

"I can't!"

"You will! You must!"

Pathros had followed the trail of blood to the door of the infirmary and pushed it open as the drill point pricked William's skin. The turcopole sprang to the bedside and pulled Brother John's arm away.

"Stop! What is this Frankish barbarity?"

"Get out of here, turcopole!" Dom Mathias sneered angrily. "This isn't your place. You'll be severely punished for this. Leave now!"

But Pathros stood his ground.

"You will not do this. Only I can cure my friend! I have read the works of Avicenna and Galen the Roman," he pronounced to the shocked canons and knights. "I have studied the great Greeks and Persians and I am the only man who can heal my master."

Without pausing, Pathros reached into his large leather medicine bag and produced a vial full of a brightly coloured elixir. Holding William's nose, he poured it down the knight's throat. After a little choking, the liquid went down. And within a minute, the Templar knight had begun to doze, even snoring slightly.

"There!" Pathros announced triumphantly.

In his half-sleeping state, William smiled. Once more he stood in a field in Vézelay. The French town contained the basilica to Mary Magdalene, revered by pilgrims throughout the continent. She was a fallen woman but knew how to intercede for the common people with God. Through her, the prayers of the peasants with their base requests would be understood and answered by the divine Creator.

The ground beneath William's feet had been churned to mud by thousands of devout folk pushing and shoving to see the strange man preaching on the hilltop. This bedraggled figure raised his hands high and exalted the multitude to take the Cross and fight the Saracen.

"Can you sit in your homes while the pagans desecrate our holy places!"

Serf and noble alike were swept up in the fervour inspired by Bernard, the saintly Abbot of Clairvaux, as he railed at the sinful atrocities committed by the non-believers against the Christians.

"All sins will be forgiven. All wrongdoing erased from the divine record. Take the Cross, take it now and with your sword and shield make haste to Outremer. Defend our pilgrims! Defend our faith!"

Who could fail not to heed that call? Bernard had scarcely finished rousing the crowd to action when a tall figure bounded towards him. William de Mandeville knelt before his mentor and demanded he sew a cross to his mantle. With a heart fit to burst with pleasure, Bernard affixed the symbol to the knight's chest.

"Clever words won't vanquish the Saracen," Bernard whispered to William that day, "but bloody deeds surely will." He'd placed his hands on William's broad shoulders. "You don't kill men on crusade, you kill evil. For doing that, my son, your soul will remain spotless and pure."

Bernard regarded this flower of valiant Norman manhood before him and implored the Lord for a thousand more that day.

"Great times call for great people and you are such a person, Brother William. In your eyes, I see nothing less than the radiance of the Holy Spirit."

William turned to the multitude and raised his heavy sword high above his head, its blade glinting in the afternoon sun. Mothers and wives toiling in the villages wept, knowing their menfolk would be lost to them for many years. So many followed the Templar knight's example that the abbot was forced to cut up his own monastic garments to fashion a myriad crosses.

Turning on his bed in the infirmary, William found himself facing a forbidding granite wall. The sheet beneath his face was moist with sweat and the holy water Dom Mathias had sprinkled. His forehead throbbed and his body ached from so many fits and convulsions but he refused to be despondent or defeated.

I will be well again, he assured himself.

I will be well.

Chapter 2

A SHIP BOUND FOR ENGLAND

William stirred from the briefest of sleeps but wasn't yet fully awake. Beneath closed eyelids, the sky was an orange glow streaked with scarlet lines, as if the heavens themselves were bleeding. Below this curved lid covering the earth crashed a beast with countless heads and hooves pounding towards his squadron of Templars. It bellowed in a deafening roar yet only William could hear its voice.

I am the one that entered into paradise and spoke with Eve the things my father had told me to say.

Its arms ended in sharp blades with which it sliced through human flesh, uttering blasphemous growls as it did so. The air around William vibrated to the monstrous bellowing of this creature while his fellow Templars remained silent as one after another succumbed to its awesome power.

I am he that hardened the heart of Pharaoh against the children of Israel.

"Be silent!" William commanded the beast.

The Templar turned to see if the Order's piebald banner had been lowered to signal the retreat from such an unbeatable foe but it remained resolutely high. Obediently the Templar jabbed his spurs into his destrier but the poor animal stared back with wild and terrified eyes, its quivering hind legs edging backwards from certain death.

I caused them to fashion a golden calf and prostrate themselves before it.

"Leave us! I command you," William wept, rocking backwards and forwards and gripping his head, "I order you to go! Return to where you came from!"

Suddenly great shafts of light illuminated the battlefield and the heavens blinded both sides with its bright light. Something had broken through the sky and floated triumphantly above the clouds. A rupture in the dome above the earth had admitted a divine presence.

"Save us," William moaned, "please save us."

His hand above his eyes, William tried to make out the nature of this wondrous apparition. Gradually he beheld the haloed and winged figure standing in the sun with the sword of righteousness in its right hand.

With his other hand, the archangel pointed defiantly at its wicked brother and as it did so, a great fire scorched the blaspheming beast and its many heads, causing them to gnaw their own tongues in terrible pain. It screamed out loud.

I am the poisonous son of a poisonous father!

The many eyes ran down its cheeks and the beast's skin charred and blackened. Beneath the thousands of hooves, the ground opened up and consumed the hellish creature into the raging fires from whence it had come.

William awoke with a start.

Up above, Pathros was hunched over a small metal tripod on the deck of the ship. It supported a glass crucible that was being heated gently by a small flame underneath. The pale liquid within bubbled as the turcopole sprinkled a little poppy seed into the infusion.

The sailors slouching on deck watched him closely, but it was with well-disposed curiosity rather than hostility. This extremely wise Saracen had cured a virulent outbreak of stomach sickness. The vomiting, bleeding and swelling had spread fear among the crew, who suspected an outbreak of plague. Two men had already been thrown overboard, either dead or damned near close.

Despair had gripped the crew: they wanted to live and see their homes again. Plague, though, was like an invisible hand that touched you and then you fell into a fever and after days of suffering, gasped your last. Ships had been known to drift for years with nobody on board after King Death had wreaked his havoc.

Pathros had been dispassionately surveying the progress of the illness among the crew. It wasn't plague, he was convinced of that beyond any doubt. The idiot Franks think every cramp and twinge is plague, he mused. As they docked at a port in the kingdom of Aragon, the turcopole darted away into a market and returned with a large sack of liquorice roots.

"Every man must chew on these!"

They had obeyed the Syrian without question. The tubers tasted noxious but sure enough, they banished the ailment. A grateful sailor approached Pathros, thanking him, a bit awkwardly, for what he'd done.

"Them black sticks got a strange magic in them."

"No, they do not. They are medicine."

"Oh, right." The sailor found the Syrian's haughty demeanour somewhat unnerving but continued. "Got something to ask you … if you don't mind, like. You being a man of the world, it seems."

Pathros looked up from the hot glass crucible.

"Yes, my friend."

The sailor hunched down and lowered his voice till it was barely audible.

"I got a problem with my wife."

Pathros eyed the man's groin.

"You are not able to please her?"

"*No!*" The sailor was quite affronted. "Thing is, see … last time I was back from Outremer, some two years ago … I swear she was different."

"She was older?"

"Not older as such … no." He lowered his voice conspiratorially. "She wasn't the same person."

"I am not understanding you, my friend. Either she was your wife or she was not."

"Ain't so easy as that. You should know, with being a magician and all." Pathros made to object but then gave up. The sailor continued. "I'm sure that Tom the Mason has taken my wife to be his wife, see, and put a changeling in her place. Looks exactly like my dear, sweet Hilda … but it's not her, I tell you. It's a changeling, sent by him to fool me."

The turcopole endeavoured to hide his derision.

"That could happen, I suppose, my friend."

"Oh, it's happened alright. And when I get back … I'm going to slit Tom open from his chin to his bollocks."

"I'm sure that will teach him a lesson," Pathros turned back to his crucible just as William appeared from below deck. He rubbed the sleep from his eyes and squinted as he acclimatised to the daylight. The sailor tugged his forelock to the great knight then made himself scarce.

"Getting to know the crew?"

The Syrian smirked: "They seem to have taken a liking to me. I'm finding it very unusual for Franks to regard me as something above a dog."

"Don't get too used to it," William told his turcopole, "we'll be in England soon. I can't guarantee you a friendly welcome."

The Templar gripped the single mast to steady himself as the vessel tossed and turned. He rubbed the side of his forehead to feel again the indent where Brother John had nearly bored into his brain. His legs still felt weak beneath him. His chest twinged from a minor battle wound. But worst of all, his pride was crushed.

William sighed to himself.

I have failed as a knight. I am nothing.

Reports of his erratic and blasphemous behaviour in the very Temple of Solomon had been relayed by the Augustinian canons to his superiors. Those gossipy eunuchs in cassocks, William fumed. The Templar command had immediately ordered his return to England. A knight who conversed with the Devil, smashed the image of a saint and mocked Christ in a church wasn't fit to be on crusade.

I was the bravest fighter in battle! This isn't fair!

The clinker-built nef heeled in a wave but instinctively Pathros anticipated the movement of the sea and raised the glass crucible in his gloved hands. William eyed the liquid in the vessel.

"Don't lose any of it!"

"I won't," Pathros answered.

Pathros poured the elixir from the glass crucible into several small vials and placed small corks in each, then placed them in his bag. The Templar suddenly grabbed Pathros' wrist as he went to put the last vial away.

"I need one now."

"My friend, you rely on this too much."

The turcopole knew he was overstepping the mark. If his master wanted a poppy infusion, then he had no right to deny him. But William was a friend as much as a master.

"Give me it!"

The turcopole acquiesced and handed over a vial. This had been going on for months – long before Nablus. Only after that ambush had everybody witnessed William's growing madness. Pathros had seen it many times. It cut him deeply to see such a fine human being brought so low.

William gulped the infusion down. Yes, it was shameful to be reliant for one's wits on potions but it was the ony way he could find inner peace. Within moments, a warm glow enveloped his mind. He exhaled slowly.

Pathros observed the tranquil expression on the Templar's fair-bearded face, his eyes half-closed with contentment. The turcopole reached into his hefty, leather medicine bag bulging with herbs, glass containers and ancient medical texts. He fished out an illuminated manual by the Persian alchemist and doctor, Rhazes, and began thumbing through it.

"Do you ever stop reading?" William murmured.

"No, my friend, it is my greatest comfort."

"I wish I had such a comfort."

Pathros nodded awkwardly.

"This great man writes that all religion is old wives' tales founded on contradictions that confuse the simple and foster dogmatism."

William shrugged: "So he thinks we're all fools."

"Well …" it was hard to disagree with that summation. "He doesn't really believe in God. He thinks those of us who do are like children who have yet to grow up."

"You should be careful what you say." The knight gazed at his extremely clever servant. "In England, you might find yourself standing on a heap of burning wood with some priest screaming at you to recant and kiss the crucifix. And I won't be able to help you."

"I shall bear that in mind, my friend."

William rose unsteadily, gripping the gunwale of the nef. He made his way towards the stern of the boat, where a red-faced, burly captain, wrapped in ram skins, steered the vessel.

"Greetings to you, captain!"

"And to you, Sir William!"

The Templar looked out to the horizon. In a few days, England's white cliffs would announce his premature homecoming. He'd have to trudge back to Pleshey Castle and explain to his father, Geoffrey de Mandeville, Earl of Essex, how he'd spent the last three years.

There would be plenty of tales of battle glory and Saracens put to the sword. How the Earl would love that! William would delight his father by recounting how he'd smashed his mace into a pagan's skull. 'Spilt his brains on the field, I hope,' the old man would roar. Then he'd beg his son to get on horseback and display his improved combat skills.

Show me how you butchered those Saracens! Did you remember everything I taught you? Were you the best warrior in the field?

"I didn't let you down, Father," William would say, "I gave my all for the crusade, as I promised when I took the Cross." It was what William had been prepared for throughout his youth. His father used to take the boy, barely in puberty, out to the forests and force him to wield a great sword that more than equalled him in weight.

Over and over he sliced at sacks of grain suspended from branches, intended to represent enemy cavalry. As the grain poured on to the ground, his father would cheer William on.

One day that will be Saracen blood gushing!

The knight couldn't wait to be back with his father, the Earl of Essex. They had been hewn from the same block. Both built for war – proud of their brawn and always scoffing down great hunks of meat together to build themselves up for the fights that lay ahead. What a contrast William presented to a slightly built and malevolent figure that always observed the Earl and his favourite son from a distance.

Edward despised what he was seeing. What a pair of mindless idiots, he seethed. What complete dullards! The older son had never shown any interest in martial display or the endless drills much beloved by William and their father. Edward couldn't lift a heavy sword and had never once tried to aim and shoot an arrow. "That's why we have serfs," he'd sneer from the safety of the castle.

"My brother is built like a horse," he noted to their mother – the Countess Rohese. "But we don't need a horse to run an earldom. A well-tutored mind is what's required to survive in England. The ability to anticipate the next move of a fickle king and to make sure you end up on the wining side in every twist and turn of court politics. As if my brother would ever be capable of playing such a subtle game of politics."

Every so often, the Earl of Essex would catch sight of the brooding face in the distance: the weakling destined to be the next earl. Once he turned to the more impressive figure next to him.

"Your mother is rearing a fine student of philosophy there. Just what England needs, eh, boy? More philosophers."

"He studies hard and means well," William responded, showing his brother due respect.

"He studies alright," the Earl replied. "But he doesn't mean well. I'm afraid he embodies some of the worst and meanest vices of our people."

The Earl meant the Norman aristocracy of England, of which they were a part. Two generations had passed since the greatest of battles that had overwhelmed the Saxons. The new nobility still sat uneasily in their new saddle, speaking a different language from their subjects. And they fought among themselves as much as they did against their hate-filled subjects.

"You're on good terms with the King?" William asked his father.

"Of course!"

"He'd always stand by us?"

"Absolutely! The King knows that in me he has no firmer a friend. I'd never betray him. Never!"

The Earl surveyed his castle with pride, once a rotting wooden motte and bailey but recently converted to a fine stone keep and freshly dug moat. It was one of several such fortifications his father before him had built to ensure his grip on their domain was firm and unshakeable.

"Your grandfather had some tempestuous times with the family of William, the Great Conqueror. But with Stephen, there is the strongest of bonds between us. I've sworn him countless oaths to protect his life. He knows the de Mandevilles will never be traitors. And I think our family will rise higher then ever before, with Stephen on the throne. You mark my words."

William broke off from daydreaming about the Earl as a wave crashed against the side of the ship. The captain seemed to be struggling against the elements and he resolved to give him a helping hand. He climbed the steps that took him above the aft-castle and joined his hands to those of the captain on the steering oar.

"No need for that, sonny. I know what I'm doing. You fight wars and I'll steer this beauty!"

William removed his hands. The captain was an odd sight; the ram skins tied haphazardly to his body made him look, from below, like some curious woolly beast with a red face. But as the wind picked up and chilled the Templar to the bone, he grew to understand why the man was so curiously attired.

"How does England fare?"

The Templar was eager to converse and to know how things were back at home. But the captain didn't reply at once. His mouth opened and shut repeatedly as if finding the right words was causing him some discomfort. Eventually he blurted out the truth.

"Your Saracen told me you been away three years in total."

"My turcopole," William corrected the ship's master.

"Whatever you choose to call him. Well, things haven't been good in England. Good order turned upside down. All on account of King Stephen being cast from his throne by that bitch Matilda."

"The daughter of the old king – Henry?"

This couldn't be true. Stephen was the family's greatest ally but now a dangerous rival had usurped his throne. The de Mandevilles might be in dire peril from this woman who wouldn't look kindly on friends of the defeated monarch. William knew who Matilda was. Every noble in England was aware of the Empress Matilda — wife of the Holy Roman Emperor and only rivalled in her burning desire for power by Eleanor of Aquitaine, the Queen of France.

"What has happened to our rightful king?"

"Oh," the captain continued, "he escaped from the prison she put him in. Matilda couldn't hold him for long. Got the good men of England together and sent that evil cow packing. Even London put a flea in the bitch's ear and told her where to go. She scurried off with her devil tail between her legs, back to wherever she came from."

"Oh … good." William was visibly relieved.

"Yes," the captain agreed. "It all ended well."

"And to think all this happened since I took the Cross!"

The captain nodded, reaffirming the incredible turn of events.

"One moment she was queen and we were all done for. England was under the spell of a she-witch. God had forsaken our country. Damned us all, it seemed. Turned His back and looked the other away. But we should have known better. He was still with England. Sent the Devil away. And Amen to that, I say."

William thanked the captain and climbed down the steps to re-join Pathros. Grappling with the steering oar once more, the captain watched him go. There was one bit of information he hadn't imparted. Something fearful about the young knight's family he couldn't bring himself to utter. Better that Sir William find out for himself when he returned. It wasn't his place as a mere ship's captain to relay such unfortunate tidings.

The Templar strode back down the deck. At some point his father would find out why William had left Outremer. These things couldn't be kept secret forever. The knight vexed over what words he'd find to explain his conduct. It would break the old man's heart.

Chapter 3

THE PLAIN BEYOND EDESSA

Besnik was still smarting from the way he'd been treated in the Atabeg's tent. Bastards, he thought. I would kill them all if I could. How dare they humiliate me as if I was a speck of dust, a grain of sand? I got their damned Templar Cross and they wouldn't have found that magic talisman if it hadn't been for my cunning.

"I'd crush them all if I had the power."

His eyes watered with rage as he relived the moment he'd taken the True Cross to the Atabeg's tent, still wrapped in the velvet altar cloth. Besnik had burst in, maybe a little too hastily. A guard had struck him to the ground, thinking he was an assassin come to slay the great leader. Another had drawn his sword to plunge its blade into the Romani's gut.

But then all eyes had fixed on the True Cross, revealed for all to see. Goblets and jaws dropped at the sight of such rich beauty. Shafts of golden light shot in all directions as the candelabras in the royal tent illuminated the countless jewels and precious metals.

At the Atabeg's side lounged his Frankish eunuch slave Yarankash, who regarded Besnik with complete disdain, as if one of the camp dogs had inadvertently strolled in.

I will have this stinking Romani whipped after he leaves the tent.

Zengi's eyes widened as he greedily scanned the rubies, garnets, sapphires, amethysts and pearls. Besnik turned the small key at the centre of the cross and opened the little door made of ivory. Inside was the sacred object that this huge reliquary had been made to contain. The Atabeg couldn't resist a closer look and, leaping from his cushions, pushed the doting Yarankash aside, picking out the tiny relic with his thumb and forefinger.

He held up the small piece of decaying wood to his courtiers.

"We have been told to fear the Brothers of the Temple of Solomon but this is their magic. This pathetic piece of wood! What barbarians! What creatures of superstition!"

Zengi plopped the relic back into the reliquary. Then he leant back in brooding contemplation. The grandiose reliquary would be a pleasing addition to his treasury but he didn't really need it. The Atabeg was beating the Frankish scum without the need of their magical talismans or gilded crosses but the same couldn't be said of his cousin, the Taifa of Badajoz.

Many miles distant, in the westernmost reaches of the Muslim caliphate, the crusaders were winning a titanic struggle between Christian forces and the armies of Islam. On the coast of the Atlantic, infidels from the North threatened the dazzling city of Al-Usbuna.

The Atabeg had been inundated with pleas for assistance from his beleaguered cousin: these beasts will demolish our great mosque and turn it into a cathedral. They will make us all convert to their lies. I stand at the walls of my city and see them camped on every hill around me. Demons! Beasts! Do not leave us to be slain. They will exterminate all of us. I pray to you, cousin – help us!

Zengi resolved on a truly altruistic gesture, one that would surely win the favour of God. It would be a magnificent act of generosity – a great-hearted and munificent gesture. Something that would show he was the true leader of the Muslim world.

"I have no need of a lucky charm but my cousin and brother in Allah, the Taifa of Badajoz, he is in need of good fortune. Take it to him."

With that, the True Cross of the Knights Templar was spirited away. Yarankash begged the Atabeg to kick the insolent Romani out of the tent and ignore his impertinent demands for a reward.

"You dare ask for gold as if anything in Edessa is yours to sell to our omnipotent Atabeg? Please, my lord, have him whipped and cast out of the camp."

But Zengi had relented. It was only honourable, he pronounced to his courtiers, to pay this man who had gone to such great lengths to find the Templar magic. With that, he'd put a sack of gold coins into Besnik's eager hands. Bowing all the way, the Romani had paced backwards out of the tent, mounted his horse and galloped out of the Seljuk encampment.

He now found himself on a sandy plain on a night where the sky was coated in millions of stars. In one hand, he held the reward and in the other a slice of lamb wrapped in yufka bread that an old woman had offered up to him earlier within the camp.

She thought the food was being handed to a warrior who had fought bravely and selflessly that day. Instead it was feeding a man who had committed two murders that night – Father Jean and Giyassedin.

The palm trees of a not too distant oasis swayed in the light evening breeze. He could easily make it there in the next hour and quench his thirst. The horse would be tethered and Besnik might sleep a while. But before he reached the oasis, the mercenary began to doze off, swaying precariously in the saddle.

Suddenly he awoke with a jolt. His horse had come to an abrupt halt. Besnik's eyes opened and he immediately sensed he was in trouble. Three mounted men in Seljuk military dress with blazing torches blocked his path. Their heads were covered with close-fitting steel helmets surmounted by sharp spikes and their elaborate weapons and horse trimmings showed they were of senior rank.

"Everything in Edessa belongs to our great leader," one of the stern trio informed Besnik. "Nothing belongs to you."

"I don't know what you mean," Besnik trembled.

Another Seljuk circled him aggressively.

"Thief."

"I am no thief."

The three Seljuks laughed but there was no joy, only menace in the sound.

"We know what you did in that church. Our men found the Frankish priest slain on his altar. Now the Christians think we committed that act. You have sullied our victory at Edessa with your barbarism."

"You are mistaken," Besnik pleaded. "Whatever you are talking about, I am innocent of it. I know of no priest. I have killed nobody."

Had Giyassedin talked? No, he couldn't have. He'd surely be dead by now. *I must get away. My life is in danger.*

The third Seljuk rode forward with his hand outstretched.

"The Atabeg demands the return of his coin. All of it."

Besnik was dumbfounded.

"No, you cannot have it. It is mine, my reward. This is a mistake."

The men drew their swords and trotted round the hapless figure, prodding his torso with the tips of their blades. Over and over again they insisted he hand over the gold and he repeatedly refused.

"Good men, great warriors, the Atabeg has the wealth of the world. What does he need of this?"

One of the Seljuks brought his blade under Besnik's chin.

"It is not for you to ask what moves the spirit of the great conqueror. You are nothing, you are less than nothing."

Another Seljuk jabbed at him.

"Off your horse!"

Besnik shook his head, refusing to dismount. No good would come of it. But suddenly, he was violently shoved and fell to the ground. The bag in his hand fell open and the gold coins spread across the sand. The three Seljuks jumped down and pulled the hapless mercenary over to a large rock.

"What are you doing?" Besnik squealed.

It was Yarankash who had sent these men, he was sure of it. That vindictive eunuch could only relieve his own sexless misery by imposing cruelty on others.

"The Atabeg would not want you to hurt me. He knows I am a loyal subject."

At this, the Seljuks guffawed. Then one grabbed Besnik's arms by the wrists and stretched them out in front of him. At the same time, another held him by the waist and pulled him in the other direction. The third Seljuk brought his scimitar down and cut through both forearms in a second, striking the rock beneath so hard it sent up splinters of light. With the hot flame from a torch, they cauterised his stumps while Besnik screamed an incoherent plea for mercy.

"The Atabeg condemns you as a thief," a Seljuk pronounced, "and removes your hands as the law demands. But he also desires that you should not be tempted to commit this crime again. He commands us to remove the cause of temptation — your ability to see things that glitter and glisten. Things you might want to steal."

One of the men rolled his torch in the sand to extinguish the flame. The other two held the mercenary still. The pulsing ember was then plunged into Besnik's left eye. It felt as if a sharp knife had been thrust deep inside his skull. The Romani struggled to resist the inevitable.

"No ... *no* ..."

A Seljuk gripped his head firmly in place. With his remaining good eye, Besnik watched helplessly as the misty orange light returned and condemned him to eternal darkness.

"Your tongue," one of the Seljuks noted, "the Atabeg has decided you can keep to beg for food and water."

Foraging through Besnik's bag, one of the Seljuks retrieved the jewel taken from the True Cross. Yarankash had examined the reliquary and in seconds had noticed the small omission.

The soldiers grinned at the pathetic animal before them, howling on all fours in horrifying anguish. Besnik had been reduced to the dog that Yarankash believed him to be.

Chapter 4

THE COAST OF ENGLAND

The nef skirted the shoreline of England with its undulating band of white cliffs and lush green meadows and grasslands beyond. The cliffs made William shudder. He'd once seen a serf accused of theft cast off the edge and his brains dashed on the rocks below. There had been no trial. The townsfolk of Dover had rounded on this poor creature and called their brutality an act of justice.

What cowardice!

It was one thing to kill on a battlefield for Christ but quite another to gang up on some alleged malfeasant and murder him on the say-so of a villager who might have nursed a grudge or mistakenly accused the wretch. William hated such deeds: they were ignoble and base.

If I was earl, he mused, there wouldn't be this kind of mob justice. I'd rule fairly. Even the basest man could make his voice heard. But that was unlikely to ever happen. His brother Edward, being the eldest son, would inherit Essex on their father's death. William shuddered at the thought.

God help the people of Essex!

The knight turned away from the chalk cliffs. The men on board were glad to see shore but William felt nothing but foreboding. He'd have done anything to be looking on to the port of Acre in the Holy Land and stepping on to hot, parched sand, making his way through a bustling souk with the cries of Eastern merchants ringing in his ears.

The departure from England three years before had been a thrilling day. William and the other crusaders had been so hungry for glory against the Saracen. Young warriors full of boldness, they longed to cut down the pagans in the hundreds and liberate the holy places from the grip of the Islamic caliphate.

On board ship, William struck up a friendship with another youth drawn from the same noble stock. They recognised in each other the same kind of person: drilled from childhood in the arts of war, on crusade to find a purpose and identity, glad to be leaving home for an adventure in Outremer. Robert St Jacques was as sturdily built as William and fair-skinned too, though his hair was a dark, oak brown in contrast to his new friend's brilliant blond thatch, half-covered by his chainmail coif.

Both were certain they had found their battlefield companion and pledged loud oaths to protect each other from Saracen scimitars. The two fresh-faced knights were cheerfully oblivious to the sullen crew around them. These men had plied the waters between England and Outremer many times. They had seen countless youths in chainmail filling the air with their mindless bravado, only to return home broken and twisted by the horrors of war.

"How old are you, William?" Robert had asked as the cog ploughed through foamy waves, rocking violently.

"Nineteen."

"Have you ever been with a woman?"

William cast a cheeky sideways glance at Robert. Back in Essex, he'd been with a couple of the villagers who had been only too willing to show the Earl's handsome son a few tricks. Far from disapproving, his father the Earl had cheered on these indiscretions. It was good to see William was virile and manly, unlike his elder son who showed a disturbing lack of interest in the sin of lust.

"If he stays a virgin much longer," the Earl had once thundered to William, "I'll take that skinny bookworm to a Southwark stew myself and get him deflowered by some Winchester Geese!"

The "Geese" were women who plied their trade in brothels on land owned by the Bishop of Winchester. Ignoring scripture, the wealthy prelate taxed his Geese with gusto and recorded the amount in his parchment rolls. "If only all of my tenants could be so industrious," the good Bishop often complained.

"We're celibate now, of course," William remarked. "Surely you remember our vows?"

Robert had a sinful twinkle in his eye.

"How could I forget? But you know, what we do in public and what we do behind closed doors can be two different things. I'm sure God just wants us to be discreet – don't you think?"

William was tempted by this dubious notion but it was too relaxed a reading of the Templar Rule. In fact, it was an outright breaking of the Rule. He had pledged to Bernard of Clairvaux – the saintly patron of the Knights Templar – that in spite of being every bit as manly and hot-blooded as any secular knight, William de Mandeville wouldn't stray. He'd be the very epitome of a warrior monk. "I will be an example to others like me," he'd rashly promised. This had pleased the saintly Bernard enormously and William didn't feel ready to betray that great confidence in him.

"I'm going to obey my vows. I won't weaken, you'll see!"

"For now," Robert chortled. "Wait till you see the raven-headed beauties in Jerusalem. I fully intend to empty my sacks. More fool you if you don't!"

William tried hard not to like the sound of this. He ran his hand across his stubbly jaw to hide a lascivious smile and struggled to suppress a rather dirty chuckle. But catching sight of the eight-pointed cross on his pure white mantle brought him up short. Ashamed, he privately apologised to his Maker for the thoughts he'd just entertained.

Arriving in Acre, the two men had been greeted by another dock much busier than Dartford and enveloped in a blazing and suffocating heat. Knights in full armour sweltered under an unforgiving and relentless sun. Those who had been in the Holy Land for a long time were used to these conditions, but at least one fair-skinned Templar knight didn't make it to the gangplank before fainting in a heap. The white-skinned freckled youth would have a miserable time getting used to the new climate.

For weeks, Robert and William were stationed at the preceptory at Acre. One moment it was military drills and the next it was intense prayer as the Templar Rule demanded. From Lauds in the morning, through Terce, Sext, None, Vespers and Compline last thing at night, these young men were never allowed to forget they had taken a monastic as well as a military vow. And if there was no chaplain to lead them in prayer, as they weren't themselves ordained as priests, then they had to stop wherever they were to recite the the Lord's Prayer over and over.

A bellicose commander barked numerous warnings at his youthful charges about the temptations and perils that lay ahead.

"You will walk through Jerusalem and see men you think are Saracens but they are Christians. They came here looking exactly like you – but they were intoxicated by the foul airs of this land. They took to wearing fine silks, keeping dancing girls, chewing on dates and almonds all day and even shunning the eating of pork. Some hire local cooks too so they may feast on heathen dishes from sunrise to sunset."

Robert winked at William. This was exactly how he wanted to end up.

The commander changed tack, telling his young charges that there was something even worse than these effete men of Jerusalem: another band of warrior monks that dared to assume they were as chivalrous and brave as the Templars, if not more so.

"Hospitallers! Punch one in the guts for me! You can tell they're inferior because their knights dress like our serjeants. On the battlefield you wouldn't be able to tell them apart except that our serjeants fight better."

This got a big cheer. All young men loved the thrill of competition and being pitted against the rival Order of the Hospital spurred the knights on in their training and war games. As each day passed, William and Robert mastered new ways to kill the Saracens and defend their brother Templars. They became expert in the many uses of the lance, mace and sword. Very soon, they yearned to put these lessons into practice.

One morning after the hour of Terce, Robert and William had, unusually, some time to themselves, chatting and kicking up the sand around them in the hot arid air of the Holy Land. Robert pointed to a well about a hundred yards distant, an inconsequential stone structure with a wooden bucket hanging from a pulley.

"Race you there!" Robert challenged the other knight.

The two men removed their armour down to their linen shirts and leggings. William had never been beaten in any race. Towering over most other men, his long legs had always powered him to the finishing line first. But Robert suddenly belted off without a signal.

"Cheat!" William shouted as he bounded after him.

The searing heat bore down. William panted and sweated as he strove to catch up with Robert. Only a few more steps and he'd overtake him. But then he tripped on a rock and crashed down on to his face. Quickly getting up again, he resumed the race but he was winded and had lost all momentum.

"Damn!"

It was too late. Robert was leaning nonchalantly against the well, beaming with pride. As William approached he lazily lowered the bucket inside the well and held the vessel over his head, mouth open, letting the cooling water pour over him and into his mouth.

"You will excuse my manners," he grinned. "The loser needs water as well."

"Very amusing." William scowled, never a good loser.

Robert leant over the rim of the well and lowered the bucket once more. But instead of hauling it back up and quenching William's thirst, he let it drop to the bottom. It splashed in the cool refreshing water below. For a few moments, he continued to look down into the well, saying nothing.

"Stop fooling," William said, "give me some water."

"No," Robert replied. Slowly, he turned to his friend and slumped to the ground. "I'm dead, my friend."

"You look very alive to me," William answered, a little puzzled.

Robert pushed the young Templar away from the well.

"Don't touch the water."

This was one of Robert's silly jests. William reached for the rope and began pulling up the bucket. But he froze as something caught his attention in the dark rippling liquid below. For a moment, all he could see was the shimmering surface of the water bubbling up from a desert aquifer. But slowly a grim form became visible. Lying at the bottom was the half-rotted carcass of a sheep, a bulging eye staring back from the remains of its head. Their commander had warned them of this dirty Saracen trick and here it was: the poisoning of wells with dead animals.

"If you go to the infirmary …"

Robert raised his hand: it was over, and he knew it. The poison would already be doing its work and within two days, the desert sand heaped on his body, a small wooden cross placed over it.

"I'm dead."

"Don't say that! I won't hear it! Come on, Robert, we can get you to the infirmary and the physician will put you right."

"It's useless."

"Come on, you can't give up so easily!"

"Stop this, Will!" Robert straightened himself and began walking back towards the preceptory. "If you want to be a friend, take this back to my mother." He unfastened a charm from round his neck and handed it back to William, who followed behind him. "And dig my grave deep so my body won't be a feast for the jackals."

In complete silence, they continued to the infirmary. Within a few short hours, Robert's belly was on fire and his throat had turned a dull yellow. The chaplain and serjeants struggled to hold him down while William bleakly registered each twist and turn of his friend's death agonies. The jerks and writhing weren't too dissimilar to the way thieves danced on the gallows. The friend he had hoped to ride alongside in battle was being devoured by Saracen poison.

A physician in a long ankle-length striped gown and tight white cap forced Dwale down Robert's throat. The sedating mix of henbane, hemlock, mandragora and ivy calmed the patient. There was nothing else they could do. At the end of the bed, a chaplain read prayers for the sick and dying while ringing a small brass bell intermittently. The physician turned to all present and threw up his hands in despair.

An elderly serjeant piped up that he'd once seen a poisoned man cured by having boiling water poured down his throat. It had cleansed the demons within and he'd been right as rain within a few days. With all other remedies exhausted, everybody agreed to this drastic course of action. In no time, the serjeant approached the bed with a pot of steaming liquid. But as he was about to pour it down a funnel into Robert's throat, a bronzed hand clasped his shoulder.

"No, my friend. That will only ensure he dies."

"Get your filthy hand off me, turcopole!"

But Pathros wasn't prepared to see such a torture inflicted on a young man.

"His throat will close up and he will simply die quicker. I insist you do not do this."

The exotically armoured stranger took William aback. Who was he? Nobody had heard him enter the infirmary. Nobody had been aware of his presence until this moment. Yet here he was, interfering in matters that had nothing to do with him.

"Re-join your fellow turcopoles outside. We've no need of you here!"

"Please," he insisted, "I can help."

Wiliam was exasperated.

"Look, I don't who you think you are ... you're just a turcopole."

The Templar resolved to report this insolent servant to the Turcopolier, the man in charge of these local mercenaries. He'd punish him for this transgression.

"Put the hot water down his throat!" William yelled. "We must save him, we can't let him die!"

The turcopole tapped the distressed Templar on the arm.

"I am Pathros. And I do not wish to see your friend suffer more than he has to."

"You're a turcopole," the young Templar shook with rage. "You shouldn't be here. There must be tasks for you to do outside. Preparing saddles! Cleaning boots! Just go away!"

Instead of obediently making an exit, Pathros stood his ground. William noted his armour and ornate scimitar. For a Syrian or Turk in the service of the Templars, he was very expensively attired. Most of the turcopoles were simple desert Christians, even Saracens on occasion, that served the Order so they could eat and survive but this man's bearing and dress suggested that in his society, he might once have enjoyed high status. Despite his initial haughty reaction, William found himself becoming slowly intrigued by the Eastern stranger.

Could he really have some knowledge after all that would save my friend?

Calmly, Pathros opened a large leather bag swung over his left shoulder and produced a small vial of liquid. He removed a small cork stopper from the vial.

"This will make his parting easier, he will merely slip away. That is for the best."

"You can't save him?" William shot back.

"Maybe if I had been there at the moment he was poisoned but it is too late now, my friend. That hour has long passed."

William found the turcopole's over-familiar style of addressing him unsettling. A Syrian referring to him as a 'friend' — that was too strange. So far in Outremer, William had simply barked orders at the local servants as any normal Frank would. But this turcopole clearly aspired to be treated as something more than just a cleaner of boots.

The Templar looked back at Robert. He couldn't be saved. His prospective battle comrade was lost to this life. Why prolong the agony?

"Alright, give my friend your potion," William instructed the stranger.

The physician blustered and objected to an Easterner getting involved in such matters. Their hands shouldn't touch our knights in such a way. They are sorcerers. This is sinful — magic. I will report this to the Marshal. The remonstrations droned on but William had blocked his ears. He watched as Pathros poured liquid from a vial down Robert's throat and his friend fell into an eternal sleep. As his last breath escaped from his lungs, Robert's face seemed almost peaceful.

He regarded his lost comrade. Robert had departed this life without ever striking a blow against the Saracen. William would soon be charging to battle with his Templar squadron, yet, in spite of riding alongside his brother knights, he'd be alone in spirit. He hated to admit it, but he badly needed a companion, a confidant and a friend in this foreign land. With Robert dead, he had no one.

If that wasn't bad enough, William didn't even have a squire or a decent horse. His shield had been badly dented in battle practice. His sword bore a worrying fracture down the middle. William was sure it would shatter at the first real blow. Worse still, his mantle wasn't as pure white as it should be; instead it was covered in muddy stains and torn.

The Templar had never really had to fend for himself. Brushing his horse and preparing any food were chores that taxed his abilities. He was beginning to realise how sheltered a life he'd led at home, surrounded by castle retainers and eager-to-please serfs.

William turned to the turcopole.

"Will you serve me?"

Pathros bowed, a little unconvincingly, William thought.

"With pleasure, my friend."

Chapter 5

THE DESERT IN OUTREMER

The dark-skinned ragged figure heard a goat bleating and then children playing. A village? His throat burned with an indescribable thirst. A village would have a well and people who would show him charity. A little bread perhaps and a cup of water. Then he'd be on his way as he was never welcome for long, wherever he stopped.

Carefully, he moved forward, trying not to fall. The stumps of his arms were already coated in dried blood from many tumbles on to the sand or rocky ground. Over and over he muttered a poem he'd been taught as a child. It was just doggerel but its endless repetition gave him some tiny comfort.

He knew the village was getting nearer as the children's voices grew louder. He almost skipped with joy at the thought of some nourishment after what had seemed like an eternity under the scorching sun. For a despondent moment, he tried to remember the last time he'd eaten. It had been some village or other; a kindly soul had offered him a small bowl of stew. It might have been yesterday or days ago, he could no longer tell.

The only way Besnik knew if it was light or dark was when it was hot or cold. At sunset, the temperature plummeted and he shivered till dawn. The frozen air prevented him sleeping except in small random snatches. In between time he wandered aimlessly, caked in his own filth, his mind fraying. He barely knew who he was anymore.

Suddenly, a sharp jabbing sensation caused him to turn to the right. That was his forearm stinging. Then another hit on his cheek, which drew blood. And now one after another like huge hailstones showering down on him. This was accompanied by the cruel and heartless laughter of wicked children. The little beasts were pelting him.

"Stop!" He put his stumps up in front of his face. "I only want food. Then I will go!"

But the shower of stones didn't halt. In spite of all that had happened to him, Besnik didn't want to die. Not like this anyway. He pulled his rags up around his head but this left his legs and midriff exposed. The jagged projectiles grazed his abdomen and thighs. He fell to his knees and with a final groan of resignation, let his arms fall and begged the end would be swift.

But then the children stopped. Not one more stone was thrown. They were still there – he could hear their breathing – but something had caught their attention. Besnik cocked an ear to the emerging sound: a thunderous pounding of hooves growing ever louder from behind him. He guessed at ten or maybe twenty warriors on horseback.

The Seljuks had come to finish him off. Yarankash had sent them to bring back his head. Good! Finish the job, he thought. I do not wish to be left like an animal in the desert.

Wield the scimitar and slice through my neck.

To die by the hand of a soldier, Besnik thought, that would at least give my ending some honour and dignity. I do not wish to die of hunger like a dog, feasted on by ants and flies till only dry skin and bones are left.

The horses stopped. The children ran screaming in a local Aramaic dialect to their parents, warning them of the strange visitors. Besnik bowed his head and bared his neck for the blade. He could hear the snorting of horses and the clanking of swords and shields. One of the men dismounted, his spurs jangling as he landed with two heavy feet on the ground. Then the footsteps pounded towards him.

The Romani took a deep breath hoping that in the next life his lost sight would be returned to him. There was no God Besnik felt he could pray to. Just let me return me to the earth, he intoned to some unknowable deity, so I may take my vengeance on those who reduced me from a human to an animal. Let me come back and tear them limb from limb, rip out their tongues and put out their eyes. Then let me watch them scurry in the sand for *their* food and drink.

A mailed hand reached under his chin and raised his head up.

"Who did this to you?"

The man spoke in Arabic but he was no Saracen.

"The Atabeg," Besnik replied meekly.

"Why?" the man asked.

Besnik leered, unable to hide the hatred he'd nursed through all those days and weeks of roaming in darkness. His blackened and rotten teeth tore at his cracked lips.

"I ... I took a jewel out of his cross." The Romani felt a flash of indignation. "The cross I stole for him. Me, I stole it. I earned the reward. He would not have it without me."

The mailed hand withdrew from his chin. The warrior turned to the other mounted figures and exchanged a few words. Besnik listened intently and his stomach turned as he realised they were conversing in one of the Frankish tongues.

"Who are you?" The blind Romani asked. "Do you mean me ill?"

The talking stopped and the warrior paced back to Besnik. His mailed hand grasped the Romani by his long, straggled and unkempt hair and dragged the emaciated body, still aching from the stones flung by the children, towards the horses. Then he was flung across the back of one of the mighty steeds. The warrior mounted and took the reins with one hand and held Besnik in place with the other. The group broke into a canter.

"Who are you?" the Romani repeated the question, feeling that at any moment he'd fall to the ground and be trampled underfoot. A commanding voice boomed back at him.

"Templars."

Part 2

ENGLAND

Chapter 6

TEMPLAR PRECEPTORY
PARISH OF ST ANDREW OLD BOURNE,
OUTSIDE THE CITY WALLS OF LONDON

From a window in the Great Hall, the two senior Templars watched William walk through the walled orchard. The taller man, Hugh of Argentine – the English Templar Grand Master – ran his index finger pensively round the rim of the maple cup half-full of red wine. At any moment the young knight would chance upon the garden's appalling secret.

I am truly sorry for what you are about to see, William.

There was nothing Hugh could do about it. The law of church and king dictated that this object had to remain in place for who knew how long. It had to remain below heaven and above hell, in some indeterminate realm.

Hugh's patrician face was a picture of dread anticipation but Brother Wulfric found it hard to resist a sadistic smile as he watched William edge closer to what would surely destroy any vestige of arrogance within him. The tough old fossil of a Saxon had a shock of white hair and a slightly beaked nose, giving him the appearance of a wizened, malevolent eagle. Go on, he thought to himself, keep moving towards that tree. You will soon see what your family amounts to.

Your pain will fill me with pleasure.

Wulfric gleefully considered how he'd soon have William back under his control and the many ways in which he'd drain him of all self-confidence and esteem.

That Norman puppy will suffer an unending purgatory of humiliation and I will be its gleeful architect.

The Master of England drained the cup dry.

"See if you can find it in your heart to be kind to him. His father was a childhood friend of mine. That's the only reason I placed my cloak over him."

Wulfric bristled at Hugh's request.

"*Kind,*" he snapped in his usual resentful manner. "Son of a traitor, that's what he is."

"You speak true, of course, brother Wulfric – but the son is surely not to blame for the sins of the father."

"Indeed." Wulfric trawled his mind for a more unforgiving line of scripture. It didn't take him long to find one. "Doesn't it also say in the bible that the iniquity of the father shall be visited upon the children unto the third and fourth generations?"

Hugh winced at the old man's habitual bile. He understood why Wulfric was so twisted within. The de Mandevilles and families like them had swept away the old Saxon elite and Wulfric still nursed a deep grudge that went back three generations. Even his position as preceptor of the rich Templar estate of Cressing Temple in Essex was insufficient compensation for what Wulfric felt his forebears had lost to families like the de Mandevilles.

"What about the Saracen?" he growled.

"He won't stay," Hugh answered. "We'll send him back to Syria. He can fend for himself among his kind."

William padded through the grass in full armour, his turcopole following dutifully behind. His white mantle emblazoned with the scarlet Cross Pattee of the Order gleamed in the spring light. It was the time of rebirth, with Lady Day gone and winter's deathly reign finally ended. Fields were being ploughed and villages celebrated with traditional dances.

The sun streamed through the pink and white apple blossom and William reached up to pick a small flower.

"I was dreading coming back but now I realise there's things I missed about England." He turned to Pathros. "It's a good land, you know … a blessed land."

"Really?"

"Don't be so cynical, Pathros."

The turcopole shivered and stared up bleakly at the grey, leaden sky. The sun had become a stranger to him since he'd set foot in this land and he wondered if it would ever show its face.

"It's very different, my friend – not quite as I had expected."

Pathros listened for a moment to the infernal din not far from the orchard. Hawkers and fishwives ceaselessly yelled and carts trundled to Cheapside, the great market within the walls of nearby London. Massive water wheels turned in the rivers Fleet and Thames. Herders were driving their livestock up to the smooth field by Saint Bartholomew's Priory to see if a good price could be fetched in the meat market.

"Quite a racket, isn't it?" William chortled. "That's why I love this orchard. It's an oasis of calm from that all that din and filth. You don't have to worry about what you might tread in or what's going to land on your head."

"Very reassuring," Pathros replied. Then he looked around at what should have been pleasant and agreeable surroundings. "Why are we here?"

"We've been told to come," William replied. "I'm just obeying our superior."

And I hope he'll let me go back to Outremer. What happened in Jerusalem that day shouldn't be held against me. Not with my fine record of fighting.

Pathros was unnerved.

"The serjeant at the door ... he told us not to bother attending the prayers at Sext ... not even to trouble ourselves with the obligatory Paternosters." Pathros frowned. "You don't think that is strange, my friend? Or are the Templars here less concerned with God than in Outremer?"

William shrugged off the turcopole's concern.

"You're always suspicious ... too much thinking in that Syrian head of yours. Never happy unless you suspect something monstrous is about to happen." The young Templar watched a blackbird swoop from a branch and tug a worm out of the ground. "I'm sure the Master will be here to greet us shortly." He glanced at Pathros' medicine bag. "Do you think I need another elixir?"

"No, my friend."

"You're probably right."

"Everything in moderation, my friend."

William had expected to be plunged into gloom in England but instead he was full of cheer. He felt, once more, every inch the warrior. His great sword hung down from his waist and beside it the sharp dagger used in close combat. His shield was still strapped to his back and its weight didn't encumber him. A heavy chainmail hauberk covered William's body down to his knees and over it hung a mantle and cloak. Under his arm, he clasped the steel helmet that had deflected so many scimitar blows it still bore innumerable scratches and dents.

I will be back in Outremer soon. My superiors here will agree that's where a man like me should be.

"I owe you a great debt, Pathros – I hope you realise that."

The Syrian had been a great support in so many ways: the medicine he administered for William's tormented mind, caring for his equipment and being such an interesting, if slightly curious companion.

"It pleases me to see you ready for combat again."

Yes, William pondered, I'm able to fight for Christ once more. When Hugh appeared, the young knight would admit his faults in Outremer but point out that it was a passing sickness – something any soldier might suffer from, given the brutal circumstances of war.

Before the possession, he'd been a resolute slayer of Saracens. Nobody could question his record. And William felt sure the Master would pack him off on the next cog out of Dartmouth, bound for Acre. Once more, he would thunder out on to the battlefield alongside his brother knights and cut down the enemies of the Cross.

The turcopole felt a great sense of unease.

There is something wrong in this place. I can feel it.

"Will you see your family while we are in England, my friend?"

"Of course," William replied. "I haven't seen them for three years."

He wondered how they would all look now. The Earl's nose might be a little redder through drinking way too much. His mother would be fermenting another scheme in her mind to advance the family's interests with the King. And his brother ... well, he'd be staring resentfully from an arrow slit in the castle without a kind word for anybody in this world.

"What is that?" Pathros had glimpsed a strange object through the branches of the trees. Partially obscured by the leaves and blossoms, a long grey object swung in the breeze. It was suspended about two feet off the ground and appeared to float in mid-air as if held up by an invisible hand. Pathros squinted hard to make sense of it.

"I don't know," William replied.

From the window of the Great Hall, Hugh crossed himself. Then, tapping Wulfric on the shoulder, the two men made their way towards William. As they did so, the young knight advanced towards the lead casket tied by ropes to a thick branch that groaned under the weight of its unnatural cargo. William's lips trembled as he began to make sense of what he was seeing.

"Father!"

I know it's you. They have killed you. They have taken you from me.

Hesitantly, he ran his fingertips across the familial crest embossed on the surface of the coffin lid.

"This can't be!"

William's heart thumped angrily. He stumbled back in shock. Then in blind fury, he drew his sword and swung it behind his head. With one blow he'd slice through the ropes. Then a burial plot would be dug and his dead father placed in consecrated ground.

Suddenly, a stern voice interjected.

"Stop! You'll leave it there!"

Hugh of Argentine glowered at William.

"Do as I command you!"

William thrust his sword headlong into the ground, burying the blade several inches in fury.

"What have you done to my father?"

"I did nothing," the Master answered calmly. "Your father brought this on himself."

William placed the palms of his hands on the coffin and wept.

"He counted you as a friend."

"I *was* his friend."

"What kind of a friend does this? This is monstrous. He can't stare God in the face while you leave his body like this ... you know that! How could you do this to my father?"

Hugh of Argentine regarded the coffin. Slumped within was a bloodied and mouldering cadaver covered in bloody arrow wounds. One shot had been fatal while the others had been for the amusement of the archers. If the Master hadn't intervened and cast his cloak over him, this body would have been dismembered and its limbs displayed over the gateways of many castles in Essex.

"You think this sight pleases me?" the Master asked William. "I'd bury my old friend if it were permitted but it isn't."

He could see the young Templar was still minded to disobey him and cut the ropes.

"Why?" William pleaded.

Hugh felt overcome with sorrow at the thought of recent events.

"Your father was ever a gambler, that was the ruin of him. Played dice with the basest sorts, even the serfs and slaves." William knew this was true. He could hear the Earl's jolly cackle as he won yet again at some or other game of chance. "Trouble is, he treated this calamitous war between Stephen and the Empress as just another gamble. Another throw of the dice! A turn of the card! Going with one side and then the other. I warned him repeatedly of his folly, but he persisted in switching from the King to the usurper Matilda with the ease of a man changing his shirt."

"He wasn't loyal to our king?"

"Sometimes he was, William, and sometimes he wasn't."

"I can't believe that!"

"Believe it! Eventually, Stephen regained his throne. The tide of war moved decisively in his favour. He'd no need or wish to tolerate the capricious behaviour of nobles like your father. And he struck out at them — even those who had once been held in the highest esteem and dear to his heart. He pursued them to their death."

"My father would never have rebelled against the King," William was consumed with confusion, "A more loyal friend ... he'd never have betrayed the King ... he loved the King."

"That may have once been true," the Master replied, "but England's grievous state these last years drained the goodness out of many. Your father was swept up in the great evil of our time." Hugh's heart felt heavy as he recounted what happened next to the Earl. "That's why he ended up an outlaw, a wolfhead. Any man, as you know, could strike him down with the King's favour."

"He didn't deserve this."

The Earl's body was being deliberately suspended between heaven and hell. It couldn't enter consecrated ground until King and Church permitted it. Until then, the Earl would hang from the branch of an apple tree, the very tree from which the Devil had tempted humanity.

"He despoiled abbeys, William! He robbed cattle——"

"To stay alive, I'm sure ..."

"— a good man stays on God's path no matter what is thrown at him. We are tested by the Almighty and tempted to commit sin. But we resist. You should know what, you're a Templar. And that's why you must accept that your father will remain excommunicate and unburied for as long as it pleases the King and his church."

"There's nothing I can do?"

"Nothing!"

"Then I want to return to Jerusalem!"

The hot tears streamed down William's cheeks. His father was dead, his family was in disgrace, but he could still fight for honour and glory. Even at that moment, he'd have raised his sword and slain a thousand Saracens without tiring. Such was the young Templar's fury he could have slain a thousand Saracens without tiring.

I don't believe what they're saying about you, Father. But I can restore our family name. You would expect that of me.

"There's no reason for me to stay in England. I will sail for Outremer in the morning with my turcopole."

"You will do no such thing!" a familiar rasping voice froze William to the spot. "Cressing Temple has missed you and that's where you're going."

The young knight and the old Saxon exchanged bitter glances.

"What's he doing here?" William asked Hugh, refusing to acknowledge the malevolent figure by his side.

"You must go back with Brother Wulfric to Cressing," the Master replied. "That's where you began your training as a Templar knight and it must be where you resume that training until you're fit to fight once more in our ranks."

This was like being cast headlong into hell's satanic deep while still very much alive. William had spent a miserable first apprenticeship at Cressing when he'd first entered the Order of the Temple. Wulfric had thoroughly enjoyed those months spent taking a young scion of the de Mandevilles down a few pegs. Now he could repeat the experience indefinitely.

"I won't go." William protested, while Hugh glowered at his insubordination. "I won't swill pigs or milk cows. I'm not a haywarden or a shepherd, that's not what I was brought up to be …"

"Aah," Wulfric exclaimed, "still the full-of-himself Norman puppy!"

"Peace, Brother Wulfric." Hugh would get his way. "You will do as I command, William. Some humility will calm your soul and will drive the Devil out of you."

"The Devil has gone!" William slammed his sword into the ground. "I swear it."

"I fear He hasn't," Hugh persisted.

He was right, of course, William admitted to himself. The Devil was still visiting him, haunting his mind and filling his thoughts. Only Pathros' elixirs offered some relief, an escape from this malign fiend.

"I'm better than sweeping floors. Please don't reduce me to that."

The Master was deeply antagonised by William's derisory attitude towards the humble work of hundreds of preceptories from Scotland to Aragon. Cows and sheep put food in the bellies of warriors. The milk and wool from these estates bought the lances and shields, horses and food for crusading brothers in the East. Every member of the Order was a small cog in a well-designed and efficient apparatus. Each had a task to perform no matter how trivial it might seem.

"Sweep floors, milk cows, shear sheep. Do all those things, William! The Devil will find your labours tedious and leave you. It is for the best. I'm not

QUEST FOR THE TRUE CROSS

trying to make you miserable, I'm trying to save you from yourself and the creature that would try to own you."

The Master had seen many crusaders succumb to the machinations of the Antichrist, particularly those sworn to obey the Rule of the Temple. The angel cast out from heaven was forever plotting his return from and he sought out those minds that were weakened and susceptible to his wiles. In William, Satan had found an all too willing accomplice.

"We need no imbeciles in Outremer who speak with the Devil," Wulfric sneered before turning to Hugh. "As if things weren't bad enough out there. Edessa now in Saracen hands and he wants to go back and scream his fevered blasphemies again." The Saxon's cold eyes fixed on William. "I heard about the things you said while possessed ... abominable ... To think such damnable words could be uttered in the very city in which our Lord once lived and breathed. You should be ashamed of yourself. And yet instead you arrogantly demand to go back!"

Pathros had been silent in the company of these knights but something Wulfric had just said forced him to speak, in spite of his official lowly position.

"Edessa has fallen?"

Wulfric could scarcely believe that some Eastern dog had the temerity to speak in their presence.

"Shut that creature's mouth!"

"He's not a creature," William retorted. "That's my turcopole and companion, Pathros."

"I don't care what he is," Wulfric reproached the young knight, "he doesn't foul the air about me with his breath!"

"You have something to say, Pathros," William turned to the turcopole, "then say it and don't fear any reprisal. Especially from him," he sneered at Wulfric.

The alien and exotic figure in black and gold stepped forward stroking his goatee, in deep thought. Just before they had ridden out and been ambushed at Nablus, Pathros had been party to some gossip. It had been something he'd kept to himself up to this moment.

"Standing by the camp fires in Jerusalem and listening to the idle talk of the Franks," Pathros explained, calmly avoiding Wulfric's glare, "I heard that the True Cross, the most cherished relic possessed by this great Order, had been taken to Edessa. I was simply wondering, good sirs, whether it is still in safekeeping." He paused as Hugh gasped audibly in disbelief that such information was known beyond the war council of the Grand Master in Jerusalem. "If it is now in peril then surely my dear friend Sir William, whom I serve most loyally and obediently, could sail back to where we have come from and rescue it. In this way, great gentlemen, he could retrieve his honour and that of his family."

Hugh strode over to Pathros and looked deep into his dark brown eyes.

"Why does any of this concern you? You go back to Syria and find another master. Forget William de Mandeville ever existed. Is that understood?"

"I care for my friend," Pathros replied coolly.

"He's not your friend, he's your master."

Wulfric turned to William.

"You've been too familiar with this Saracen. Now he thinks he can converse with us as an equal."

William was suddenly lost in a train of thought: the True Cross was in peril. It might already be in Saracen hands. Here was a perfect reason for him to return to Outremer.

"Let me journey to Edessa!" William exploded at Hugh. "I'll get the Lignum Crucis back and place it myself in the Church of the Holy Sepulchre! You know I'm the man to do this. I won't rest till I've got it safely in my hands. And then," the young Templar eyed the lead casket swaying gently in a light breeze, "I can restore honour to my family name and bury my father, the Earl."

Hugh of Argentine seethed.

"Our True Cross is completely safe."

"You can't be sure."

"Don't question my judgement, William. I'm the head of this Order in England – not you."

"The arrogance!" Wulfric muttered.

"You really think," Hugh bristled, "that our great leaders in Jerusalem, including the Grand Master, would allow the most treasured and sacred relic in Christendom to fall into Saracen hands?"

"Impudent," Wulfric chimed in.

Hugh cast his cup away.

"Leave now as I've commanded. Return to where you began your training as a Knight Templar. This rude turcopole can remain with you if that makes things easier."

Utterly crushed, William surrendered to his fate. He was being condemned to never-ending servile drudgery. A gratified Wulfric pondered whether he'd make the cocksure knight swill the hog pens first, or lay marle on the fields for a few hours till his back was bent in pain. The only emotion he'd allow the young de Mandeville to express would be sheer tedium.

"Bring your Saracen, if you must," the preceptor of Cressing snarled as he made for the stables. "But we leave now." Wulfric fumed loudly as he went, directing his venom at Pathros. "Damned Easterners ... can't tell truth from lies ... right from wrong ... left from right ... light from dark. No souls and no morals. On the same level as rats in my view."

"My turcopole is as much God's creation as you ... more so!" William whimpered, now forced to follow the old Saxon back to Essex.

This outburst was too much for Wulfric.

"Never tell me," he jabbed a bony finger in the direction of Pathros, "that this creature looks anything like God. If you ever suggest it in my presence again, you can explain your heresy to a church court. Then you and your foreign cur can join the flames together. Quite a sight that'll be!"

William fell back to join his much-maligned turcopole. Pathros reached into his medicine bag.

"Don't worry about my feelings, my friend," Pathros handed the knight a vial of the curing elixir, "I have enough of these to last at least twenty days."

The knight gave the turcopole a despairing look. Twenty weeks, months or years — who knew how long he'd be condemned to that dreary hole in Essex?

"And," Pathros added, "they are lying about the True Cross. I am certain of it. Trust me, we will back in Jerusalem soon enough."

"I hope you're right," William answered. Then a thought occurred to him. "Pathros ..."

"Yes."

"Don't think I'm just keeping you here for the ..."

"I know, my friend. The medicine is just one of the many valuable services I provide to my master."

"Your company," William replied, "will be as valuable as your medicine in the times ahead."

At the stables, Wulfric greeted a mute and sullen retainer. Behind this man were two despondent mules ready to take their luggage. With a sprightly bound for a man his age, Wulfric leapt on to his horse and beckoned everybody to follow his lead. They needed to make progress before sunset.

"We will cross the River Fleet and go through the city then leave by the Ealdgate and up into Essex."

William cast one last glance in the direction of the suspended coffin. Wulfric couldn't resist adding to his charge's anguish.

"Your family certainly made a name for themselves while you were gone."

"You've no right to speak of my father," William snapped back.

"Oh, but I do! And I will. You will be made painfully aware of every sin and slight your father – and now his oldest son – has inflicted upon us while you consorted with Satan in Outremer."

Wulfric tried not to let the sides of his mouth curl upwards.

"My servant Daegmund will take your chests. If he gives you the evil eye, don't be too surprised. Your father killed his brother, a monk at Ramsey Abbey. Killed all the monks, in fact, while he went about robbing the place."

"My father was a good man," William shot back.

"You'll think differently soon enough," the preceptor responded. "And the new Earl is much like the old. Worse even. Quite a talent for inventing taxes nobody can afford to pay. Then he tortures the poor souls who tell him they have nothing more to give." Wulfric beckoned to the retainer. "Show William your feet, Daegmund. I can see in his face the young Norman doesn't believe me. Thinks I'm making it all up about his accursed family."

Propping himself against the stable wall, the servant unbound one of his feet. Great blisters covered the reddened and badly bruised skin while two of his toes seemed entirely burnt away. Defiantly, Daegmund held out the mutilated appendage to the knight.

"Are you saying my brother did that?" William asked.

"I could reduce the blisters …" Pathros made for his bag of medicines.

"Keep your Saracen sorcery to yourself!" Wulfric snapped at the turcopole then answered the knight. "Oh yes, I'm saying exactly that. You think my tongue is false. Well, may God strike me as dumb as poor Daegmund here if I tell a lie. Your brother's men did this – they call it de Mandeville law in Essex. Mark it well. Remember this sight." William regarded the remnants of the retainer's foot. "Because you won't find a shred of love for you and your family where we're going."

Chapter 7

PLESHEY CASTLE
SEAT OF THE EARLS OF ESSEX

This was a climb Edward de Mandeville dreaded, up the seemingly endless winding staircase made more miserable by the sharp cold wind trapped in the shaft and stabbing at his face. Pleshey had been built after the conquest of England as a motte and bailey, a great mound surmounted by a wooden palisade. Stone had eventually replaced wood as the de Mandevilles had prospered, making it more defensible. But as a place to live, Edward found it woefully lacking in any comforts.

"Damn!" he yelped, momentarily losing his footing on the narrow and slippery steps.

The newly created Earl's elegant and finely stitched fur-trimmed boots paced ever upwards. Through the narrow slits in the walls, Edward de Mandeville, second Earl of Essex, could have chosen to survey his vast lands, but nothing would have depressed him more. The earldom he'd so long prepared for had transformed into a burdensome yoke around his young neck.

At a familiar point, a dark exit beckoned. It was the second highest level, above which was the exit to the battlements. Edward darted through, finding himself in a damp corridor bereft of tapestries, shields or any ornaments. It was one of the bleakest stretches inside the castle; only some patches of moss offered any trace of colour. Then the Earl stood before a familiar heavy door. With a cursory knock, he entered.

A wholly different scene presented itself. Church-sized candles blazed in tall and chunky iron stands. Their flickering light illuminated the walls covered in rich silk hangings and a wooden ceiling painted with fantastical creatures and heraldic signs. Overseeing this riot of colour was a Parisian-sculpted statue of the Virgin, smiling serenely in dazzling marine-blue robes and a halo of gold stars.

The flagstones of the floor were strewn with a heady mixture of English lavender, fresh hay anointed with various Eastern aromatic oils and other scent-bearing flora. The Earl struggled to breathe this intoxicating miasma but appreciated it was there to mask the stench of approaching death.

"Mother."

A four-poster bed dominated the centre of the room with an occupant obscured from view by heavy damask drapes.

"Mother?"

She was still alive. From behind the damask, a wheezy and insistent breathing could be heard defying whatever forces were trying to tear her soul away. The Earl wasn't altogether convinced that these forces were angelic and that his mother was destined for eternal bliss. More likely, hell's invisible sentinels were clawing at the dying woman, impatient for the Countess to breathe her last.

The Earl peeled back the damask to reveal the whitened corpse-like face of Rohese de Vere, first Countess of Essex. The colour had disappeared completely from her once sparkling eyes like extinguished torches. Her lips moved almost imperceptibly as Edward hovered over her.

"What ... do you want?"

Even though his mother resided in the same castle, Edward wasn't a regular visitor. But today, there was something very important to impart to the old buzzard. Even her jaded, world-weary senses would be pricked by his news.

"He's back."

Rohese didn't need a further explanation.

"Are you sure?"

Edward nodded.

"They say he had a sickness of the spirit. Even that he might have been possessed. They say," the Earl moved closer to his mother's expressionless face, "that he was ordered to leave the Holy Land. What do you think about that, Mother?"

The Countess turned her face towards her eldest son but looked over his shoulder to the fireplace with its painted hood bearing the arms of the earldom. There was no fire but the grate was reassuringly full of ashes.

"That boy ... was always a fool," Rohese wheezed. "Inherited the weakest parts of your father."

Edward turned to eye the grate.

"You burnt it?"

"Yes ... with my own hands. As I said I would."

But the new Earl still felt terribly insecure.

"Will he find out?"

"Who would tell him?"

The Countess' grey eyes examined her fretting son. All the stupid boy ever seemed to do was worry. Her husband had committed one last foolish act in a vain attempt to save his soul but the Countess had made sure this act would never see the light of day. The document had been rightly consigned to the flames. As for the executors, the three witnesses to this act of supreme folly, they had all met unfortunate ends, along with the two monks who had written the document.

Thomas Draper, Ben Mercer, Richard Cooper, brothers Odo and Alfred ...

She recited their names in her head to reassure herself that anybody who knew of the will had been wiped from the face of God's earth.

"Why would he reject me?"

"Your father?" the Countess asked.

"Yes, my father. Who else?"

Edward paced over to the fireplace and poked miserably at the ashes under the iron fire stand. Then he slumped on to a stool adorned with carved and gilded lion heads. On the table next to him sat a portable altarpiece, a small ivory triptych showing scenes from the life of the Virgin Mary. Rohese had been told by the local Benedictine abbot that she was required to pray before this in her last dying days but the Countess had given up, believing her sins couldn't be so easily expunged.

"I never wronged him," Edward continued.

"You never pleased him either," his mother coldly pointed out. "You couldn't help it ... not every son can be a warrior."

Edward stared at the fireplace, not wishing to show his mother the tears in his eyes.

"He didn't want me to be earl! He thought I wasn't fit!"

"Keep your voice down," his mother hissed. "He wasn't in his right mind being pursued by the King's men like a common thief. Got the idea into his head to make your brother earl. Utter stupidity, of course."

The Earl turned back to his mother. In spite of her shrunken and deathly state, she still showed no signs of inner weakness.

"He hated me."

"Yes, he did. Just didn't understand you as I do."

The Earl rose abruptly to his feet. "I hope he rots in that tree."

Even the Countess felt a momentary pricking of her conscience. She tried to imagine the grim scene, as she would never glimpse it with her own eyes. A casket bound by ropes in a Templar orchard forbidden burial in consecrated ground.

Rohese had supported and counselled every twist and turn of her husband's political journey until the last few months. She'd made her peace with the King and resigned herself to the inevitable: her husband would be killed. Not for Rohese a life on the run, living on nettle stew, hiding in bushes.

"Dead men must look after themselves," Rohese whispered, "it says so in the bible." The Countess eased herself up against the bolster to sit upright and breathe more easily. "The late Earl can explain his conduct to the Devil but we, the living, have work to do. So you must bend William to your will, force him to accept that you're the law here now. And he must bend his knee to you."

Edward very much doubted his soldier brother would do any such thing.

"He's proud, Mother. And he's a Templar."

The Countess wished she could summon the power to rise from her damask prison and strike her son about the face until he showed some courage. She clutched at the sheets with her skeletal fingers and struggled to speak as her aged heart pounded heavily.

"I don't give a damn about his Templar rubbish. You're the earl!" Her anger flushed two red cobwebs of blood across her cheeks. "You're everything I've fought for! All of me I've poured into you."

Shaking with fury, Rohese glowered at the eldest son nurtured so long to rule.

"Make him obey you!"

Chapter 8

THE TEMPLAR PRECEPTORY
CRESSING TEMPLE,
ESSEX

William approached the huge barley barn with dread in his heart. A great crushing weight seemed to bear down on his chest as he gazed once more at that mighty timber structure that spoke volumes about Templar wealth and industriousness on the land. The box frame building loomed mightier than many cathedrals and could have matched the great pyramids Pathros had told William of in the land of Egypt. Yet William wasn't impressed: he felt the building drawing him closer with a malign magnetic pull, as if it resented him ever leaving its presence.

Dotted in the fields round the preceptory were hundreds of sheep whose precious wool kept faraway garrisons in arms and provisions from Acre to Edessa and Tripoli to Famagusta. There were also well-tended bullocks; draught oxen, geese and hens, while the fields were sown with wheat, peas, beans and drage. The common people of Essex who farmed these lands owed their whole existence to the Order of the Temple.

Wulfric, erect on his horse, surveyed his domain with pride. No serf or villein keeled over in these fields, broken from famine, as they did on the

Earl's demesne. God's fields yielded a great bounty while the Devil's fields were barren.

Which field will I make the puppy plough first?

He could picture the knight bereft of sword and shield and chainmail and reduced to wearing a shabby tunic and plain leggings covered in dung, his spine throbbing pain as he was forced to bend and plant seed throughout the daylight hours.

God in heaven, I thank you for delivering the proud puppy back to me!

As they drew closer to the great barn with its many outbuildings, William could make out the figures of serjeant-brothers in their black mantles and red crosses buzzing round like the bees in one of Cressing's many hives. Laymen serfs also ran about urgently, seeing to the day's many tasks. Life in the preceptory was one of constant labour interspersed with prayer.

William saw the great hall, the dovecote, the chapel to the Blessed Virgin Mary, the windmill, watermill and cider press and finally the sad little cemetery for brother knights when they were called to leave this life.

I shall not die in this place, he vowed to himself. I shall escape and my last moment on this earth will be with a sword in my hand, slaying the Saracens in battle. The young knight was shaken from his bitter thoughts as Wulfric suddenly halted. Frozen and motionless, the old man stared ahead.

"What is it?" William asked.

"Silence," Wulfric responded.

Something was amiss: Cressing Temple wasn't its usual busy self. The frenetic activity was one of chaos and turmoil not the humdrum daily toil. Injured men were being lowered carefully from horses and mules; a serjeant of the Order was gripping a bloody wound to his face. Strained voices cried out for assistance. Riderless horses charged round loose. Wulfric dug his spurs into his steed and set off at full pace.

"Follow me!" William shouted to Pathros as he charged after Wulfric.

A horse bolted past as they entered the vast complex of farm buildings and places of prayer. A burly figure lay on the ground being tended to by a physician. Pathros immediately dismounted and went to help.

One of the younger farm hands ran up to William and grabbed the reins of his steed to direct it towards the stables. Running alongside the horse, the young boy gabbled breathlessly.

"Good to have you back, sir. Sorely missed. Want to hear your battle stories, sir. Reckon you killed a few of them Saracens. You heard about Edwy? Badly wounded, sir. Over there he is – being seen to."

"What happened?"

"Grain wagons, sir. They were attacked. Men without God did this. Took three carts. Reckon they were wolfheads myself. Matilda's people maybe."

Many of those who had supported the Empress in her attempt to take England now roamed England as dangerous adventurers but Wulfric knew who had committed this and jutted a bony, accusing finger at William.

"Your brother!" His horse wheeled round. "This is your brother's work!"

"You have no proof," William remonstrated.

"Devils, that's what you de Mandevilles are," the preceptor blustered, furious to see the Order's wealth seized so brazenly. "You'll tell him when you see him that we're not here doing honest and godly labour just to pay his debts. Mark my words well, I'll get back what he has taken a hundredfold and he'll face the full wrath of our Order!"

There was something empty about Wulfric's threat. It felt to William like bluster with nothing to back it up. The old Saxon was huffing and puffing to no avail.

The preceptory's physician was leaning over the supine figure of Edwy, who had a broken arrow sticking out of his cheek. The arrowhead was embedded several inches in his head. As the Templar doctor began digging into his face with a blunt instrument resembling a spoon with a serrated edge down one side, the serjeant regained consciousness and let out a full-throated scream.

Pathros tapped the bungling physician on the shoulder, then barged him out of the way. There was no time to waste on Frankish stupidity. The turcopole smeared a pale blue paste onto the wound that would, as his favourite book on medicine instructed, "kill the tiny demons which cause grave infection". The Cressing physician tried to intervene again but Pathros was in charge and in no mood to tolerate his backwardness.

"I will cure him! Take your superstitious spoon away!"

The physician remonstrated with serjeants and knights standing around but they were now absorbed by the turcopole's urgent activity over Edwy's head. Pathros applied more of his magic liquid and massaged it into the injured serjeant's cheek. The physician argued loudly that the standard procedure was surely to pull out the wooden shaft and then let pus form round the arrowhead. Hopefully, that would allow it to be pulled out in six or seven days.

"Please help me to treat this man," the physician shouted at the Cressing Templars, who were now gathering in greater numbers to watch the operation being performed on the muddy ground. "This is most irregular. This man has no right …"

But they all ignored him. His record on saving lives hadn't been an impressive one and the Templars of Essex were more than happy to let the exotic foreigner have a go instead. Edwy was a popular figure and nobody wanted him to die.

From his bag Pathros produced small pieces of wood wrapped in linen to which he applied rose honey and began pushing them into the facial wound till he'd ascertained the position and size of the arrowhead.

Then he brandished a curious metal implement resembling tongs with a screw running down the middle. This he dug into Edwy's face and, with his free hand, began turning the screw. The serjeant passed out in shock as, slowly but surely, the turcopole withdrew the arrowhead from deep inside his head.

"White wine!" Pathros shouted and a Templar serjeant dutifully ran off to find some.

The turcopole applied more honey to the slowly closing wound and then poured the wine over Edwy's cheek. Next, he applied a plaster packed with herbs and bandaged it to the man's head. As he completed the operation, Edwy came round and gazed into the turcopole's bronzed face.

"By Saint George … I have been brought back to life by a Saracen."

Pathros permitted himself a wry smile.

"That must be very disagreeable, I realise," he said.

William swelled with pride at the handiwork of his turcopole. The Templar knight permitted himself a broad, beaming smile but it was soon wiped off his face as he turned to find Wulfric glowering at his side.

"You tell him ..." Wulfric, shaking with rage, pointed at Pathros, "... no more sorcery here. You tell him to keep his potions away from our people ... because so help me ... if I so much as smell heresy or magic from that Saracen, he'll dangle from the end of a rope."

Chapter 9

THE GREAT HALL
CRESSING TEMPLE

The atmosphere was stifling. In complete silence, the Templar knights sat round a great oak table and shared a modest meal of mutton. Cresset lamps, stone holders adorned with simple carvings of crosses and filled melted animal fat from the kitchen, gave the hall a dim and dreary light.

Some brothers ate off trenchers, large slices of stale bread that would be distributed to the village poor once they had been saturated with mutton dripping. Their relentless chomping was the only sound permitted during the evening meal.

Hocktide was approaching when the English celebrated a great massacre of the Danes. Nobody could really recall the facts of this bloody event but Wulfric always made sure it was well marked. His ancestors had slain these unwelcome arrivals from across the sea, in the hundreds if not thousands, and secretly he prayed that one day the Normans who now ruled in England would suffer the same spectacular fate.

William scanned the forlorn specimens around him as he hunched over his meal, his broad shoulders squeezing two elderly Templars seated on the same bench to either side of him. Not a single knight in this hall is fit or capable of raising a sword in combat, the young knight thought. It seemed laughable to even refer to these ageing or infirm creatures as knights. William surveyed their slobbery, toothless mouths wrestling with the tough meat in front of them, the flickering flames from the cresset lamps lighting up their silvery, grey hair and lined faces.

He glanced at his own still powerful frame. Would he remain in this preceptory till he was like the rest of these brothers? Was Wulfric to get his way and sap the very life force out of him? Years of backbreaking toil would gradually reduce him to one of these worthless wretches. All because in a moment of weakness he'd let the demon enter his mind. He was beginning to wonder if God had forgotten his good service on the battlefield.

You treat me unfairly, Lord. I am still your most obedient of servants.

As the knights sat and chewed the indigestible mutton, the Draper stomped officiously behind them, checking the condition of their armour, habits and cloaks. The Rule stipulated how a Knight Templar was to present himself down to the shortness of his hair and the trim of his beard. An ageing knight sitting opposite William had his white hair pulled sharply between the Draper's thumb and forefinger.

"Cut it!" the Draper hissed into his ear.

Wulfric sat at the head of the table. Every so often he'd look up from his bowl to survey the Templars sat in rows before him. God had given him authority over these men and as preceptor, not a flicker of insolence would be tolerated. As the knights slid into their customary evening torpor, Wulfric suddenly slammed his hand down on the table.

"Brother William, bring your bowl here!"

The knight hesitated.

"Your bowl! Here!"

Slowly, he rose from the table, holding the miserable meal in his hands and advanced towards the old Saxon. He towered over the preceptor as he stood by him. With one rapid downward slap, Wulfric sent the bowl clattering across the floor, leaving the meat on the flagstones.

"Continue eating, Brother William."

"I won't eat off the floor, I've done nothing wrong."

This was the punishment for minor infractions of the Templar Rule. A humiliation for those who were late for prayers or whose eyes had strayed lustfully to the village girls.

"Eat your meal."

"No."

Wulfric jumped up, sending his wooden chair crashing to the floor.

"Eat!"

"I won't! I've done nothing wrong!"

The preceptor's jaw jutted out defiantly.

"Eat, damn you!"

"Never."

Wulfric turned to the others, who stared back in horror at William's defiance.

"None of you ... none of you even dare to mimic the impudence of this Norman puppy!" The old Saxon was going to relish this moment. He was about to put William firmly in his place. "Satan lives in his mouth and speaks for him. His isn't the voice of a Templar. His is the voice of a man possessed of a demon."

William's face flushed crimson. That pleased his tormentor, who rose from his seat.

"You all know, of course, about our brother's possession ... how foolishly he conducted himself in Jerusalem, blaspheming and attacking Christ and all the saints. Sullying the name of this preceptory among the leaders of our Order."

William made to interrupt but Wulfric only raised his voice further.

"Not even in our mystery plays in Witham has the Devil been so well portrayed as our brother acted his part. But then, my fellow brothers, he wasn't acting. This was no play. The Devil was truly inside him. And to my knowledge," he dug William in the chest with his bony finger, "he has yet to depart."

"You've no right to say these things!"

"I have every right, Norman puppy!"

The knight would have relished pummelling Wulfric into the ground until he could speak no more. A wave of almost uncontrollable aggression pulsed through William but he knew that to lash out at the old Saxon would bring an end to his time in the Order.

He won't drive me out of the Templars — that's what he wants — but I will not let him have that satisfaction.

"If you weren't the Master of this preceptory …"

"But I am, Brother William …" – the two men circled each other – "… I am. And I will always be the Master of Cressing Temple so long as you're here, which will be a very, very long time."

"You should remember who I am …"

"I do," Wulfric paused, "I never forget who you are: the son of an outlaw who despoiled our abbeys and killed our monks. The brother of a thief who attacks our grain wagons and leaves one of our serjeants grievously wounded and close to death."

William turned to his brothers. They believed Wulfric; it was written all over their faces. All the great battles fought in Outremer and the selfless devotion shown at all times to the Order meant nothing now. All these easily misguided men had heard about was his descent into madness and possession by the Basilisk – a manifestation of Satan.

"I ask all of you to remember that I've slain more Saracens than any of you here. These arms have wielded the sword against our enemies till they ached with such great pain. I tell you all, brothers, I slew pagans from sunrise to sunset without stopping to quench my thirst. There's no greater fighter for Christ's word in this place."

Wulfric snarled at such an arrogant claim.

"This man lies about my family," William continued. "He holds me responsible for things that happened between Saxon and Norman so long ago even the oldest people in our villages can't remember. I tell you, in all honesty, the de Mandevilles aren't what he says we are."

The knight registered the universal lack of sympathy for his plight. No man present bore any love for the ruling family of Essex. Most of them were of Saxon stock. William decided to give some ground to their feelings.

"Alright, I can see you all believe what this poisoned and rabid dog says — very well then. I promise that when my brother next holds court in Witham, I'll go to him and prove Brother Wulfric has a mind that's twisted and malformed. I'll challenge my brother directly in front of the common people about the things that have been alleged here. You'll see that my family are innocent!"

The preceptor leered: "He holds court tomorrow!"
William paused, not expecting this news.
"Good, I'll see him then! I'll prove you're wrong."

Chapter 10

OUTSIDE THE CHURCH OF SAINT NICHOLAS, CHIPPING HILL, WITHAM

If a villager had blinked, they would have missed the small figure soar past as he fled the angry mob behind him. The hue and cry had gone up. The yells of 'Thief!' and 'Stop him!' filled the air. It was every subject's duty to chase the evildoer until they were caught and brought to justice. In this case, the boy could expect a whipping at the very least, if not the noose if the Earl presided over the next assizes.

Nicholas scarcely had time to pant as his skinny legs powered him forward. He bit into the apple. The juice filled his mouth and trickled down his throat. It had been worth it. One more bite. His teeth dug into the skin of the fruit as he continued to run. With some regret, he threw the remainder away but he was already hatching an idea for his next meal.

The adult villagers soon tired themselves out and their cries receded. Nicholas dropped behind a slate wall and caught his breath. He laughed. Then he stopped laughing. They might have recognised him. Everybody in the village knew the urchin and his larcenous ways. Maybe this time he'd gone too far: stealing the apple in broad daylight. He pictured himself tied to the pillory and his back coated with red stripes as the lash thwacked against it.

"Just a stupid apple," he muttered.

He rested his head on the jagged slates. The hue and cry had definitely given out. Lazy, mule-headed villagers, he thought.

Can't out-run me. Want to tie me to a post and beat me? Have to catch me first. That's never going to happen.

Nicholas pulled at the grass. The thrill of the theft was subsiding and once more, he felt very alone. His father had vanished into thin air or so it seemed. Taken the cross and gone to fight in the Holy Land; never to be seen again. Maybe he became king of a far-off land? The boy pondered. He might be like our earl here in Essex, all covered in furs and with a crown on his head and serfs working for him.

The boy couldn't have conceived of the reality of whitened bones on a desert battlefield, long picked clean by the carrion birds. Or of a rotting, half-dead prisoner in a Cairo dungeon with no chance of a ransom ever being paid on his miserable head. His only way out of prison would be the executioner's rope or to be sold as a slave and to die under a landowner's whip.

Nicholas had no idea how much time had gone by since his father had left – the sun had risen and fallen countless times. In his absence his mother had struggled to put food in their bellies. She'd hired herself out to perform the most demeaning tasks on the land and was soon barely distinguishable from the slaves still traded by the Saracens and Greeks.

Day by day, her face seemed to shrivel like tree bark and the light in her eyes was steadily extinguished. One winter evening, Nicholas found her lying lifeless on the earthen floor of their hut.

Dragging her cold corpse by the wrists outside, he'd buried her in a shallow grave in the woods. No villager in Witham cared enough to ask what had happened to the woman.

The urchin looked up. He was sitting within the churchyard of Saint Nicholas, after whom the boy had been named. A small group of villagers were arriving for the last service of the day. One held a loaf of rye bread in his hands. The boy's eyes fixed on the food. As the peasant entered the church, he tossed it a few feet away. Nicholas knew exactly why he'd done this.

Crouching on all fours, he crept like a wolf towards his target. Slinking between the gravestones, Nicholas focused on the object of his desire. Already, he could taste the bread in his mouth, the texture of the coarse crumbs and his belly no longer feeling the twinges of hunger. Only one obstacle lay in his way.

The leper had turned away from the squint in the church wall. The sound of the bread thudding on the ground was very welcome. Slowly, on what was left of his limbs, he dragged himself towards the food. All the time, he thanked God for the charity of those who had once known him as a whole man. He'd been the village haywarden, maintaining the hedges that separated the fields, but that was before the disease had gnawed relentlessly into every part of him.

One fateful day, the parish priest had commanded Jake to appear before the entire village. He was placed under a black cloth. Then the rite of leprosy was read out to him and he was asked repeatedly whether he understood what was happening: Jake was to separate himself from all others. The priest had raised his arms high in the air.

Be thou dead to the world but alive again unto God!

He was to shun the markets, touch no other person and drink only from his own cup.

And know that when you die you will be buried in your own house unless it be, by favour obtained beforehand, in the church!

Nicholas bounced on his toes with remarkable agility towards the leper. The ball of rags had his back to the boy. His decayed arms reached out towards the bread but as they were about to touch and contaminate the bread, Nicholas swooped over Jake and lifted the food from his grasp. The leper let out a moan from his tongue-less mouth.

As he hauled himself up, his hood slipped back to reveal a face so badly gnawed by the leprosy, it scarcely had a distinguishing feature. Skin like a hog's hide and a dry hole for a mouth. Nicholas gawped at the creature. Like a man and a lizard, he thought. Then he saw what was left of Jake's feet.

"You're not shod!"

It was forbidden for lepers to walk barefoot.

"You're not shod and that's forbidden. It's against the law, Jake. You know it."

Now Nicholas was feeling a little better about taking the bread. Jake was breaking church law. And so had to be punished. Even the priest would probably approve. Yes, he deserved to lose the bread. Not covering his feet, that was wrong. Everybody knew that.

But the leper continued to moan and wave his arm towards the rye bread.

"No good doing that, Jake." Nicholas bounded over to a gravestone, leant against it and started tearing pieces of the bread. "I got my whole life, Jake. You're about finished, I reckon. Doing you a favour not feeding you. That'd keep you going for longer."

The leper began to sob.

"Don't go doing that, I hate men that cry. Not right." God has cursed Jake, Nicholas thought. I must have done something right in my life that I'm young and agile and fast on my feet. Jake must have done something fearfully wrong to be like this now. "I got my arms and legs, Jake. I got my tongue. I need food to grow and be strong."

The leper beat the ground over and over again. Ignoring Jake's distress, Nicholas ate over half the loaf and ended up feeling very full. In fact, the boy thief was better fed than he'd been for a long time. He eyed the pathetic creature grovelling before him and began to relent.

"I suppose you're hungry too. Here, you can have what's left."

Chapter 11

THE BARLEY BARN
CRESSING TEMPLE

William went in search of Pathros but he couldn't find the turcopole anywhere. He paced from building to building without luck; then suddenly he spotted a light in the cavernous barley barn. Through its huge doors, a small fire had been lit.

As he drew nearer, two figures could be seen in very animated dialogue followed by the sound of a glass vessel breaking on the ground. William froze. One of them was Pathros. But the young knight could scarcely believe his eyes. The other man, jabbing the turcopole in his chest, was Wulfric.

With a final curse, the preceptor stormed away. The young knight, obscured in the darkness, was thrown into confusion.

What is Wulfric doing there? Why would he want to address Pathros?

With the preceptor gone, William entered the barn. The turcopole seemed disconsolate.

"What's been happening here?" William asked. "What did Brother Wulfric want with you?"

Without catching the Templar's eye, Pathros sighed then responded.

"He took me to task, my friend, about the use of my medicine. Said it was magic. That I must never use it again."

That's very odd, William thought. It was highly irregular for a preceptor to talk directly to a mere turcopole instead of going through his master. Wulfric must have specifically sought out Pathros to have this exchange – but why?

"This is the only time he's spoken to you?"

"Yes."

On the ground were glass fragments and a piece of twisted metal. Wulfric had kicked the delicate metal tripod over and stamped on it, breaking a round glass flask as well and sending its medicinal contents into the dust. William gazed forlornly at the lost elixir.

"Don't worry," Pathros assured the mentally weakened knight, "I can prepare more."

"Good."

William sat on a small stool by the dying fire.

"You dined well with the serjeants?"

"Your sense of humour has not departed you, my friend. They said the meat was mutton but I swear it was dog."

Pathros looked up and registered the misery all over William's face. The first dinner at Cressing Temple had been an ordeal and there were plenty more to come. The turcopole tried to cheer up the knight.

"We will be out of here soon, I am sure of it. Fate has not condemned you to this place, I can sense it."

Something was preying on William's mind.

"Why do you care if Edessa has fallen?"

"I am Syrian. And I am Christian. There are Syrian Christians in Edessa – my brothers and sisters in the faith. What happens to them concerns me. I feel it greatly, my friend."

"Mmmm ..." The knight murmured. "You never told me you knew the True Cross was in Edessa."

Pathros was sensing a hint of distrust in these questions but was obliged to answer his master.

"Being with the lowest ranks, the cup bearers, attendants and slaves as well as the serjeants, I heard everything. The scum of Jerusalem have the biggest ears, my friend, they listen to everything their masters say then share these secrets like booty; it is the only riches they have."

"We knights knew nothing," William replied. "It seems only our superiors and their cup bearers knew the True Cross had gone. Knowing that the Lignum Crucis was safe in Jerusalem gave us a reason to fight. You've got to understand that. Christ was crucified in Jerusalem and we were defending the very wood upon which he died. It meant everything to us to stop the Saracens getting it. And now I find out the Lignum Crucis had been spirited off on the whim of our ageing Grand Master to Edessa and who knows where it is now. It also turns out my turcopole is better informed about all this than me."

"I apologise for not sharing this cup bearer's gossip with you earlier."

"Do you think the Saracens have taken it?"

"Beyond a doubt. Or robbed by thieves."

William rubbed his hands by the fire.

"Hugh of Argentine was certainly furious when you mentioned what you knew."

"Because it's the truth," Pathros smiled. "And because I gave you a reason not to be in England anymore. Here is a quest you should go on to clear your family name. I think this Hugh of Argentine knows you of all Templar knights could find and retrieve this great object. Only his pride and that man who has imprisoned us here stops you from going, my friend."

William was lost in thought for a moment.

"So why would Hugh of Argentine lie to me about this matter — saying it is safe when you say it's probably stolen?"

The turcopole pulled at his goatee.

"He knows you desire, above all else, to be back on crusade. So he deflects your attention, my friend, by falsely claiming all is well. But I have read much about the way to read a man's face. The great scholars have informed me how to know when somebody is lying. And Master Hugh, I must say, is not a very good liar."

Could Pathros be right?

William felt a thrill at the thought he could ride out in search of the Lignum Crucis — the True Cross. Only he would be able to find it and return triumphant with the relic nestled in his strong arms. Then he could bury his father and bring honour to the family name. In the meantime, he was stuck in Essex. It was time for Pathros to take him on a mental journey to raise his spirits and transport him from his current surroundings.

"Pathros, let's imagine that we are back on the Temple Mount. The golden sun would be setting. The markets would be full of din and music. Knights would be reflecting or telling boastful stories about the day's fighting."

The turcopole said nothing at first. Instead, he produced a vial of the usual elixir from his medicine bag — one that Wulfric had been unable to destroy in his rage. Knocking it back, William let the infusion tingle in his veins and soothe his mind. Now he was truly transported back to Jerusalem and egged the turcopole on to tell him the stories he loved.

Pathros obliged with tales of the worshippers of Zoroaster who tended a flame that never went out. Then he described the hawk- and cow-headed deities that made the River Nile flood and brought pestilence to the enemies of Pharaoh. As the Syrian's silky voice floated like incense smoke in the night air, the Templar felt as if he was present in the fantastical places the turcopole described.

He stood with Pathros before the Sphinx, a great stone beast built by Ham, son of Noah, in the lands given to him after the flood. By the turcopole's side, he then sailed up the treacherous River Gihon, which had once encircled the Garden of Eden and whose source was located many thousands of miles away, deep in the Kingdom of Prester John.

He conversed with Prester John, the Christian priest-king whose kingdom was so deep in Africa that all contact with civilisation had been lost. It was said this mysterious monarch possessed the Fountain of Youth and in William's daydreaming, he offered the two visitors the required three short sips to remain young forever. Then he showed William and Pathros the magic mirror guarded by three thousand men, in which he could see all that was happening in his kingdom.

William rose to his feet unsteadily, intoxicated once more by Pathros' stories of the East and the potent content of the vial.

"We must go to our dormitories."

Gathering his medicine-making instruments, the turcopole followed. William headed to a larger outbuilding where the knights slept and Pathros to the serjeants' sleeping quarters.

In the shadows outside, a figure had remained listening to the two conversing. Under his breath, the old Saxon preceptor muttered an oath to himself.

"By the bones of Saint Barbara, I'll cut out that Saracen's tongue then stretch his neck at the end of a rope!"

Chapter 12

WITHAM CASTLE

Edward was the very epitome of French good taste in a purple mantle lined with squirrel fur, tight leggings and slightly pointed shoes. He watched from the top of the curtain wall as yet more wagons trundled in under cover of night, laden this time with the bounty of the Benedictines. The Earl's steward advanced awkwardly along the battlements, his thumbs hooked in his low-slung belt and so unhealthy in appearance that he looked to Edward like a walking cadaver. He reported back, with little enthusiasm, on the success of their mission.

"We cleaned out their tithe barns, sire. Not a scrap left."

"You look the very picture of remorse, Ageric," the Earl trilled sarcastically.

The other man didn't share Edward's indifference to divine wrath.

"I worry about taking the possession of the church, sire. They say the Abbot once cursed a thief who stole a bible from them of great value," the steward bit his lip fearfully, "and very soon after, the man came back with it, begging forgiveness as the book had turned into a serpent and bitten him."

Edward's shrill cackle rang through the night air and his chamberlain, Blacwin, joined in the mirth obsequiously – anything to score a point against Ageric, his rival for their master's attention.

"You're an ignorant man," the Earl watched the piles of grain disappear through the gate beneath him, "but then I suppose you haven't had the benefit of proper schooling."

Edward was very proud of the education he'd received at the knee of Peter Abelard, the finest scholar in Christendom and mortal enemy of the ascetic fraudster Bernard of Clairvaux, whom his brother William idolised. Abelard, the wisest man in Paris, trained young nobles for leadership in the church and kingdom while Bernard puked into a sick bucket and mistook his repulsive self-denial for true holiness.

Bellatore, Oratore, Laboratore.

There are those of us who must rule, Edward mused. Then those like the Benedictines and Cistercians who are ordained to pray. While the scum toil as God has willed and being base creatures they contrive at all times to deny me what is rightly mine. The cunning serf claims he can give no more in taxes and service but squeeze him hard and something will always drop out.

"The Benedictines will fill their barns again soon. God commands the people to pay their tithes. I only wish he was so obliging to me."

Blacwin snorted at the blasphemy while Ageric was scandalised at such words but kept his counsel. The Earl surveyed the lands beyond his castle shrouded in darkness and began to almost like his demesne. This inheritance had been nothing but a burden after his father's untimely death, but raiding the indecently rich Benedictine monks and Templars had improved his finances considerably. Or so it seemed.

"I assume we can make our next payment to the King," Edward turned to Blacwin. The chamberlain's face contorted as he tried to find the right words.

"We're not quite there yet."

"Explain."

"Sire, your creditors in Norwich ..."

"The Jews!" Edward slammed his fist down on the cold stones of the battlements. "Damn! How obscene is it that I have to go on bended knee to the likes of that dog Eleazar or Abraham Mokke who dares to eye me scornfully like some common debtor!"

"They are protected by the King, sire, we are powerless. They are collecting from you what is owed to him. Our lives would be forfeit if we ever struck out at them."

He was right, of course. The Norman kings had outlawed any attack on a Jew subject to the direst of penalties. The Sheriff of Norwich, John of Chesney, had taken his responsibility to heart so much so that his literate enemies had dubbed him 'defensor judaeorum'. Even the Bishop of that city, a Cistercian called Everard of Calne, had afforded them his support. Men keen to show how loyal they were to King Stephen after the great anarchy of recent times.

"You know," Edward recovered his composure, "in France and Flanders, I have heard tell of children being abducted by the Jews and their blood drained in gold and silver vessels for the devilish rituals of these Hebrews. Their little corpses have been found in a gross mockery of our Lord's crucifixion." The Earl turned to his chamberlain and steward. "And I must tell you, the reaction of the common people has been ferocious towards these foul murderers." The last of the wagons trundled under the gate. "All of the Jews have been killed in some towns and everything they own taken."

Blacwin latched onto his master's meaning immediately: "It would be terrible if something like that were to happen here, sire."

"It would be an affront to God and all decent people," Edward agreed. "Tell me, Blacwin, how wealthy is Abraham Mokke?"

"Exceedingly," the chamberlain replied. "Beyond our wildest dreams."

Ageric closed his eyes and took a deep breath.

Chapter 13

THE GOLGOTHA TAVERN
WITHAM

Nicholas found himself in the company of thieves. These were older men scourged by the lash, locked in the stocks or disfigured by the branding iron. One man had no ears while another had the letter 'V' for vagabond burnt on his upper arm. They were an inspiration to Nicholas – adventurers who had done great things in this world!

He listened to the endless series of tall tales being recounted around the large oak table, while waiting for the Kingston-ware jug brimming with frothy ale to make its way round for his turn at a hearty slurp. To his back, a huge log fire crackled in a vast hearth. Above it a cauldron full of some indescribable stew bubbled angrily. The smell of several days' leftovers filled the tavern with a pungent stench but to Nicholas it seemed heavenly.

The big man across the table drained the jug, to Nicholas' disappointment. But another jug soon arrived. The Earl's steward had rewarded these thieves well for the raid on the Templar and Benedictine wagons but the coin was being spent rapidly in the tavern. Very soon they would need another criminal task to fill the ale jugs.

"Would you like a story?"

"Aye," the whole company replied.

John the Tanner had just come back from fighting the Muslims, though not in Outremer. He'd been in some strange land that Nicholas had never heard of before. Not in the East where Nicholas' father had disappeared but in the South. A place John pronounced as "Al Anderlooz".

"Let me tell ya how I met the hunchback ..." The glassy-eyed cutpurses and cutthroats leaned forward in anticipation of a good tale. "Long time ago, longer than I care to remember, I went to a Christian kingdom they called Aragon. Made out I was a crusader, taken the cross and out to avenge the many sins against our holy church." The group guffawed at such nonsense. "But there were Templars everywhere. Meant I couldn't do an honest day's work."

Another roar of laughter!

"So I upped sticks for another kingdom nearby called Castile. Less Templars there! I could go about my business unmolested as it were. And in no time I met a man with the same interests as myself: the hunchback. Ugly as sin and stank to high heaven but an appetite for sheep and cattle." John raised the ale jug and winked. "Other people's sheep and cattle, of course."

He paused as if recalling this far distant memory.

"With him, I rode deep into the lands of the followers of Mohammed – right to the very heart of Al Anderlooz. And we're stealing all their cows and sheep. No pigs, of course, on account of their views of such meat."

It seemed the Muslim caliphate of Al-Andalus was heaving with treasures compared to the Christian kingdoms of Aragon and Castile to the North. This pagan domain had more loot than any man could dream of. And the women, John noted, were as dark as a black Madonna but with the morals of Satan – a perfect combination!

"Just imagine how poor Moustafa felt when he woke in the morning. Finds out his animals have all gone and his good lady wife has been given a good seeing to." John grasped his groin in case anybody didn't get his meaning. "That hurt those pagan bastards the most. To know we had our way with their women!"

Sancho the Hunchback had an uncanny knack of knowing where all the best cows and sheep were to be found in Al Anderlooz, as well as plenty of gold and silver and pretty ladies.

"Them followers of Mohammed got so angry with us they start whining to the Christians. Oh, come and save us, they wailed. Abu Barcada – that's what they called the hunchback in their language – he's a monster. He's a devil. We should join together to destroy him." John took another slurp. His audience was hanging onto his every word. "Well, them Christians out there agreed with their Muslim neighbours. They all banded together. But the hunchback just laughs about it and says, damn them all."

John then recounted how the hunchback mounted his most daring raid yet. Ignoring his enemies, he marched his band of thieves on to the great Muslim city of Córdoba – mightiest city in Al Anderlooz. Bigger than Seville even – or Al-Usbuna! A glittering paradise with a great mosque entered by huge golden doors that the hunchback said we would take away on our carts.

"Those Muslims quaked behind their walls and watched as we took fifty thousand of their sheep and two thousand cattle, herding them across a great river," John referred to the Guadalquivir. "What a sight to behold! But the Moors had had enough. We had pricked and poked at them too much. Now they rode out with their curvy swords and shining steel helmets shouting fearsome stuff at us."

Nicholas imagined dreamily how rich every one of those men stood to be if they got away with their booty. But things weren't looking good for the hunchback in John's story.

"Sancho realises we are outnumbered. He shouts to the skies above that God has cursed him with a big hump on his back since the day he was born so he expects nothing from the Almighty. Tells us all to fight like lions if we ever want to see our loved ones again."

John was getting to the climax of his story when he noticed a tall, gaunt figure enter the tavern. The general rowdiness subsided at the sight of Ageric, who looked around for the Tanner. Seeing him in the corner with his band of thieves, he beckoned him over. Disgruntled but trying not to show it, the Tanner put down the ale jug and went to join the steward.

Nicholas quickly grabbed the jug and began glugging for all he was worth, but was stopped as another man wrenched it from his small hands.

"Mind yourself there, boy."

"I'm a man."

The company laughed.

"Not yet you're not!"

The Tanner returned from his chat to the steward, ashen-faced. He pointed to two of his drinking partners to leave with him. One was Hunrith the Gong Farmer, whose job was to clean the castle latrines. The other was Aylmer the Blacksmith, who had become quite merry by this stage. He was in no mood to depart.

"What does he want now?"

"Best not ask," John replied to Aylmer, "we must pass your forge first. Iron nails, three of them. I take it you have nails made."

"Hundreds of them."

"Good." John reached for the jug. "We'll need strong stomachs for this, lads." As he drained the last of the ale, the Tanner caught sight of the bailiff, the village law enforcer, entering the tavern. "What in God's name does he want?"

Nicholas tried to hide behind the broad back of the blacksmith but it was too late, he'd been spotted. The bailiff bounded over with great purpose and in no time was binding Nicholas' hands behind his back. The thieves now stood back or quietly melted away from the boy. The bailiff spat into his ear.

"You little shit!"

Chapter 14

THE KNIGHTS' DORMITORY, CRESSING TEMPLE

Their hauberks removed but swords lying by their sides, the knights slept as if prepared for battle on top of simple beds and hay-stuffed mattresses. Around them, tallow candles burned to keep the room in semi-brightness and drive out any impurity of thought or deed, as the Rule stipulated.

Tired by the exertions of the day, they had all fallen into a fitful slumber. Mouths agape, they snored their way to the first dawn prayers.

As William's eyes closed, he was transported back to what could have been one of many battlefields in Outremer, moments before the clash of two armies. Slamming their swords into the ground, he and the other Templar knights knelt and, gazing upwards at an expectant sky, implored the Almighty to deliver them a victory against the Saracen.

Then in a cloud of dust, their horses charged on to a plain ringed by fiercely high mountains that imprisoned the two armies, one fighting for Christ and the other for Allah.

In all directions, swords and scimitars, maces and daggers rose and fell rhythmically in the air, striking and slashing without ceasing for a moment's pause. William's white steed reared in terror while the knight brought his sword crashing down with full force on the turbaned head of a Saracen warrior. His habit was smeared with blood and sweat poured down his face. William watched a fellow knight, now on foot, plunge his sword through the chest of a Muslim warrior. The man looked up, beaming at his bloody handiwork, but he paid for this moment of hubris as a Saracen drove a curved blade into his back.

The ground was coated with the bodies of the slain who had fallen where they died, arms still raised to defend themselves, eyes staring wide at their assailant and mouths hideously contorted. The earth quaked under the weight of soldiers' feet and horses' hooves as a knight bearing the Templar standard thundered past and rode headlong into the Saracen force to the cheers of the crusaders who followed close behind.

William woke with a start, jolted from sleep by a sudden noise. The door to the dormitory appeared to have opened but nobody had entered and none of the other knights had awoken. Yet he sensed a presence within the room.

"Who's there?"

The candle flames wavered and then stilled.

"Speak, now."

William lay flat on his bed, not daring to rise. Suddenly the creature reared up before him.

It is I.

The beast's scaly body extended the full length of the dormitory. Its bull-sized head bore down on the Templar as it had often done in Jerusalem.

With a revolting hiss, it extended the cobra-like hood behind its hideous face. Out of its head grew a fleshy, scarlet crown that pulsed with its heartbeat. It had once been a creature of perfect beauty, but vanity had condemned it to this form.

"I left you in Outremer!"

You can never leave me. No distance is too great. I am everywhere and anywhere.

"I want you gone. I won't serve you! Just leave me alone!"

The monster hovered above the Templar, baring its fangs to drip a translucent poison over William's face. He knew it could kill with its bite or simply a glance from its yellow eyes but, so far, it had chosen to spare him. The knight could hear its voice in his head though the basilisk's mouth made no movement.

Eli. Eli. Lama sabachthani. Father, you have betrayed me.

"You betrayed your father," William responded, "but my father didn't betray me."

Really! He could have made you Earl of Essex but he gave that to your brother.

"He's my older brother, that's the law."

Great men make the law and can un-make it. He betrayed you. But I will never betray you. Be mine. Worship me. I will make you the most powerful man in the world. All will bow down before you!

The Templar hoped one of the other knights would stir but all of them were mired in deepest sleep. Had they been bewitched into that state? The monster, unholy brother of Michael, Gabriel and Uriel, conjured from fire and ruler of hell, drew closer to William then pulled away again.

Its glittering eyes blazed like comets. Its mouth was like a vast dark cave leading deep into the underworld and a million cursed souls. Its long silver tongue vibrated and its fangs retracted and elongated with each pungent breath.

My father betrayed me again and again. He moulded clay into flesh and said it was his son. How do you think I felt about that? Then he lied, saying this mortal son had co-existed with Him for all time. But I am He who co-existed with the Father. I — who was not fashioned from base clay.

Satan wanted to convince William that they shared the same pain. Both their fathers had spurned and cast them down. But William would have none of this. The love between him and his father had never died. They had been as one in life and only an accident of birth prevented him from being earl. Satan had rebelled and sought to overthrow his father. But William had always been the loyal and dutiful son.

"Leave me, Basilisk."

I was His favoured son! Not the Galilean. You know that to be true.

"I will have no more of this."

I cannot leave you, Templar. You are mine. I will return.

Slowly the head of the beast sank as the body shuffled back out of the door, vanishing into the dark night beyond.

Chapter 15

THORPE WOOD
EAST OF THE CITY OF NORWICH

In the chilly and still night air of Thorpe Wood, Samuel could only hear an owl hooting and vermin scurrying in the undergrowth. He'd emerged from the dense woodland and into a small clearing, where he now crouched, completely motionless.

Before long, in the full moonlight that bathed the forest, giving it an eerily magical aura, the twelve-year-old boy spotted his prey. With the swiftness of a wild animal, he fell on the rabbit before it could leap to safety and broke its neck.

Then from his jacket pocket, Samuel produced the skinning knife given to him as a young apprentice. If he was to make the grade as a skinner, he needed all the practice he could get and so he set to work on the dead animal in the semi-darkness of the moonlit wood.

As he'd been taught, Samuel pressed his hands down on the rabbit's belly to squeeze any residual urine out of its bladder. With its back legs splayed open and facing him, the contented boy made a first incision, slicing open the abdomen up to its neck, making sure his knife travelled at a shallow depth lest it burst the rabbit's guts open and splattered blood on the precious fur.

Peeling the pelt back as far as it would go, Samuel opened the gut and turning the rabbit over and shaking it vigorously allowed the intestine to fall out, then pulled it with his hand till it fell to the ground: food for the foxes, rats and birds.

So absorbed was the apprentice skinner with his nocturnal practice of his future trade that he was unaware at that very moment of being watched. Every so often the moon would pick out one of the five pairs of eyes like glass beads but William saw none of this. Neither did he hear anything as the hooded figures crept forward silently.

The rabbit's heart and kidneys Samuel put in his jacket pocket to throw in the pot and flavour the following day's stew. Then the animal was turned over for the second incision across its back after which he peeled the fur from the top half of the rabbit with the rapidity of someone becoming well versed in this technique.

A twig snapped nearby.

The boy was momentarily startled but then thought nothing of it. A boar or a young deer passing by that would cause him no bother. He was more concerned that his older cousin with whom he lodged in Norwich would notice his absence and tan his hide in the morning.

The rabbit's ribcage cracked in his small hands as he pulled the skinned top half in one direction and the fur on the bottom half away from himself. It was hard getting the fur detached from the ends of the legs without damaging it and he carefully cut with his knife to remove it. Then Samuel stopped suddenly.

Amid the rustle of the leaves he heard a voice.

"Must be imagining things."

He sat with the long, thin, pink torso of the rabbit in one hand and the fur in another but was now distracted from the animal by a shadowy object moving between the trees.

"Who's there?"

No response. Could it be the King's men come to enforce the Forest Law where to so much as disturb a deer could result in blinding as a punishment and to fire an arrow saw the miscreant's hands severed? Samuel peered hard at the nearby trees but saw nothing.

He picked up the rabbit carcass and put it inside his jacket. It would be a job to explain to his cousin how he'd come by it and the nervous man would fret over any likely penalty. But then the two would eat it. Food was food after all. Meat wasn't to be thrown away in these hard times — even if it did belong to the King. Samuel stuffed the fur into his jacket pockets and prepared to leave.

What was that noise?

He was frozen to the spot.

Samuel's eyes were wide open in terror. A hooded figure loomed before him, about twenty feet away. The boy circled round to find four more malevolent figures at an equal distance from each other, completely silent and their faces obscured. He realised he was surrounded and very much alone.

"What do you want of me?"

They said nothing. It was then that he noticed that one had what appeared to be some nails in his hand, the silvery metal occasionally catching the moonlight. Another carried a small bag firmly in his hand, the contents of which were impossible to know. A third carried two large pieces of wood under each arm.

Samuel was in no doubt that these men bore him no goodwill.

"Kind sirs, I beg you ..."

Each man took a couple of steps forward and the boy knew they were about to rush him. While there was still a decent gap between them he bolted like a hare and avoiding their grasping hands, darted into the woods in the hope of losing them. His heart racing and body shot through with fear, he kept moving at a furious pace, knowing instinctively that his very life was in danger.

"God help me. Please. Help me!"

The pounding footsteps behind crunched through the layers of leaves relentlessly while he leapt over logs and roots to escape them. He had no idea what direction he was headed as the branches seemed to conspire to block his path and the ground threw up unexpected obstacles.

He tripped and fell, grazing his hands, then hurriedly got up and continued to belt through Thorpe Wood, wondering when the forest would end and if he'd be any safer in the fields. Their determination to catch him suggested not.

Samuel had no idea who was bearing down on him but their panting and hoarse curses were audible as they persisted. One man was very close as the young boy's legs began to weaken so he ducked through a small opening in some dense bracken and fought his way through several feet of thorny bushes.

Scratches now covered his arms and legs as he struggled to escape.

Reaching another opening and beneath a huge oak, the boy paused. The voices were more distant and moving away. He stood in one spot without making a sound and waited. Turning to look behind him, Samuel couldn't see any of the men.

I'm safe. They've gone. What did they want? I need to get home.

Then a huge hand clamped his wrist and he found himself staring up at a face as big as the moon. It grinned. A big ruddy black-toothed grin surmounted by huge, bulging and bloodshot eyes.

"Goodness me, Sam," John the Tanner exclaimed, gazing upwards at the branches of the oak and wiping his sweat-drenched brow with his free hand, "that's quite a chase you gave us there. Wherever did you think you were going?"

Chapter 16

WULFRIC'S STUDY

Wulfric couldn't sleep. He was far too happy for slumber. This had been his first day with the Norman puppy back under his supervision and already he'd begun to break him. Chuckling, he relived the moment over and over again when he threw William's bowl to the floor: the look of anguish on the young Templar's face; the full realisation that he was no longer the great crusader and that years of humdrum humiliation lay ahead.

"I will do it every night and he will eat like a dog if it's the last thing I see in my life."

Wulfric was slightly tipsy from the wine he'd been knocking back in the privacy of his study. The other brothers weren't permitted to see this sin of drunkenness. It wasn't for pleasure, he assured himself, but medical necessity. The old Saxon's body was riddled with twinges and sharp stabbing pains that only the product of French Templar grapes could soothe.

In his hands Wulfric read the letter handed to him by Hugh of Argentine, very much for his eyes only. It was deemed important enough to have been written on vellum and bore the seal of the Grand Master.

Having pored over it once, Wulfric did so again and again – the words never losing their power.

"So it has gone," the old Saxon muttered.

The blind and crippled Romani had confessed to the crime with no need for torture. Besnik had been only too happy to divulge the whereabouts of the True Cross and then babble on incessantly about his unfair treatment at the hands of the Atabeg.

Poor, poor William.

The preceptor smirked. If the Templar knew that Christendom's holiest relic was in the hands of the Saracens, he'd be impossible to keep within the walls of Cressing Temple. The impetuous and volatile Norman puppy would scamper away in seconds.

But that was never going to happen.

He devoured the contents of the letter one last time then held the expensive vellum over the candle flame. Slowly a black scorch mark spread across the surface and then it burst into flames.

"Pigs and cows," Wulfric said to himself. "That will be your crusade, master William. Pigs and cows."

And before next Hocktide, I will have your turcopole burned in the square at Witham as a heretic.

Chapter 17

THE MARKET PLACE,
WITHAM

Crammed into the tiny, hive-shaped, single room of the jail, Nicholas and about ten other accused criminals were awaiting the Earl's warped idea of justice. The leg irons chafed the boy's legs and cut into his ankles whenever he moved, but he was irrepressible. Somehow he still believed the full force of the law wouldn't be brought down on him. He turned to a depressed figure sitting nearby.

"What you here for?"

The man didn't answer but Nicholas continued anyway.

"I know who you are – Aedelbald the sapper. You dig holes under castles. That must be exciting!"

"Shut up, boy," a hugely fat man, markedly short of breath, gasped. "Can't you see he wants to be left alone?"

"I'm a man, not a boy," Nicholas responded. "Oldest man in my cottage."

"Cottage?" Another prisoner joined in. "I know where you live. If that's a cottage, I live in a castle." He began screeching with laughter. "I'm the King of England if you live in a cottage! Listen to that boy's nonsense. Cottage indeed!"

But Nicholas wasn't to be crushed so easily.

"They won't hurt me," he opined, twiddling a piece of filthy straw between his fingers. "I'm too young, no beard on my chin yet. So they'll let me go, I'm sure of it."

The sapper now turned to Nicholas, his eyes sunk deep through despair and hunger.

"You don't know the Earl, do you, boy? Brand his own mother if she didn't pay her tax."

"If she didn't brand him first!" the fat man chimed in.

This gave the band of prisoners a laugh. They had all known the intimidating Countess in her prime. A tough old bird, to be sure. But unlike Edward, she had won the respect of the villagers. Her eldest son in contrast attracted nothing but a visceral hatred.

"You'll get what we get from the Earl." The sapper leant across to Nicholas, hissing: "He doesn't give a damn about the likes of us, we're just vermin."

Nicholas looked at the group around him; legs and arms slumped across each other in the close confines of the cell. Their faces spoke of despair and resignation because they knew that as the sun set, some of their bodies would be silhouetted on the horizon hanging from the gallows. Or they would be staggering away minus a limb or branded in the face.

Riding past the jail and entirely ignorant of its occupants, William and Pathros made their way towards the Earl's party. At least four years had passed since William had seen Edward. One brother had been on crusade while the other was studying in Paris. William's heart felt heavy as he approached his older brother. This wouldn't be a joyful reunion.

The Earl and the Bishop sat, preparing to administer justice, on a raised dais above the village throng. Stallholders below provided refreshments or sold produce while mud-covered pigs, having smelt the food, came trotting out of the woodland to roll around in the mud of the market square.

Every social rank had come to see the King's tenant-in-chief pass judgements. Foresters, stablemen, toll collectors and cellarers rubbed shoulders and exchanged views and gossip. Petty disputes over scraps of land were argued about and news sought as to what was going on in Chelmsford or further afield in London.

A ripple of excited anticipation already gripped the crowd with the presence of Aylmer the Blacksmith. He was busy heating up an iron bar. But this was no ordinary iron bar: it had been placed on the church altar overnight and blessed by a priest that morning. Very soon, this sanctified piece of metal would be white hot and then one of the malfeasants would have to carry it for several paces in a trial by ordeal – a grisly but entertaining spectacle.

The Earl watched his long absent brother approach. He pretended to be engrossed in discussion with the Diocesan Bishop, a very finely dressed prelate who was there to give Edward's punishments the sacred seal of approval. Out of the corner of his eye, all Edward could focus on was the scarlet eight-pointed cross coming ever closer.

The big Templar knight has come to show me up – but I'll show him who's in charge now!

William dismounted, leaving Pathros to tether the two horses. He could sense his brother was avoiding eye contact. Edward had always done that as a child when he had something to hide. And he always had some or other secret to conceal. Forever scheming and plotting! Lacking any physical prowess, Edward mistook cunning and backstabbing for mental prowess.

The Earl pretended to have only just noticed William arriving.

"Will!" Edward flung his arms round the Templar and hugged him close. "I'm so glad you're back."

"It is good to see you too, brother," William regarded his fine robe and baron's crown. It sat uneasily on his head whereas it had fitted their father's head perfectly.

William tried to smile.

"You look every inch an earl. Mother must be very proud of you."

"She is," Edward responded. "Very much."

The two young de Mandevilles sat down. Even though Edward's throne was deliberately set higher, William still towered over and dominated his brother's much slighter frame. This was irksome, to be upstaged by his younger brother in front of the entire village. The Earl sat bolt upright, trying to match the Templar warrior in stature, but his effort was in vain.

The two young men found it hard to look the other in the face and instead regarded the blacksmith below. Yellow sparks spat out intermittently from his brazier.

"Well," Edward strove to break the ice, "you a Templar, eh? That's quite something. Father would have been so pleased to see you like this. All covered in chainmail and a heavy sword at your side. You were always the soldier, William. Not me, I'm afraid. Born to rule these ungrateful swine instead." He patted William on the knee. "Think you got the better part of the bargain, brother."

William gave a bleak nod.

"Templars!" Edward continued. "To be part of that rich web whose silken threads extend from Syria to Scotland." He turned to his chamberlain. "You know, Blacwin, they have a thousand preceptories between here and Antioch – all of them sitting on piles of bullion."

"Not all, brother," William corrected him. "Some of our communities of brothers are quite poor. They've got next to nothing. Only their faith keeps them going."

The Earl was unconvinced.

"Oh, come, come, brother, everyone knows you Templars are richer than Croesus! He was an ancient Greek, by the way. I know your friend the Abbot of Clairvaux doesn't approve of us studying the pagan ancients." Edward was glad to have been tutored by the Abbot's rival, the ever more worldly Peter Abelard. "No, be serious, you Templars may swear a vow of poverty but there it ends. A mountain of gold under your feet!"

He turned again to his chamberlain, Blacwin.

"They have this intriguing parchment, you know. A knight may travel with just the clothes on his back from here to Jerusalem and he merely hands in this parchment with coded symbols on it to another Templar in the Holy Land and receives an agreed amount of gold livres. The rest of us must carry our wealth round in caskets and boxes and be robbed on the highway. Very clever! I admire how clever you Templars are! Really, I do."

A watchman dragged the first prisoner from the jail. It was the fat man. He had taken the Lord's name in vain very loudly while drunk. This was his third similar offence. The Diocesan Bishop whispered to Edward that this time exile from Witham would be preferable to a fine. But the Earl wasn't about to forsake any amount of money.

"Fine him."

He turned back to William, though not before registering the positively obscene size of the gem on the Bishop's ring.

It's like a sheep's eye!

That alone would contribute a few hundred marks towards my outstanding debts if only the Bishop would obligingly fall down a well. Maybe that would need to be arranged.

"I also hear that nobles have left their estates to the Templars while they go on crusade. Such trust! Such a reputation your Order has, Will. Yet here I am, sitting on thousands of marks of Father's debt. Quite a contrast, eh?"

"I'm sorry that Father left things in such a bad way," William replied. "But then you're the Earl. You've inherited this great title, brother. It's your responsibility now, not mine. I'm just a simple knight who swings a sword around and cuts down Saracens."

"Quite so." Edward pulled at his robes, rearranging them. "But you can help me."

"How?"

"We are brothers, William. Aren't we? We share the same bloodline. As Mother always says, if you don't have family then you have nothing – surely you would agree with that?"

The Templar remained expressionless.

"Will," the Earl seethed through clenched teeth, "don't force me to beg like a dog. I'm the Samaritan by the roadside, broken and bleeding, and you're the good man, the Templar, who can ease my suffering. All that money you people have and I'm here struggling every day to keep things afloat."

William pulled down his chainmail coif and ran his fingers through his hair.

"The Good Samaritan, that's interesting." The Templar pictured the pitiful sight of Daegmund, Wulfric's silent and sullen servant. "Remind me how that story goes in the bible, you being more learned than me. Does the Good

Samaritan tax the local peasants and then burn their feet when they refuse to pay up? Did he raid Templar grain wagons? I may be getting some of this wrong …"

"And so what," Edward hissed, "if you're getting it right! The only interest you ever had in our serfs was the women you could bed. So please, take your pious demeanour somewhere else."

"This isn't the way Father would have wanted you to rule."

Edward ran his finger down the fur lining of his robe.

"I don't need a lecture in kingship from Father's hunting companion. You should remember, William, you're nothing but the spare brother. If I'd died in childbirth, the family would have had a use for you. But I didn't. And here I am, earl. Not you, me."

The sapper had now been brought out and was whimpering, hands clasped and begging for forgiveness. He'd killed a deer in the King's forest. But the Bishop reminded the Earl of the man's sterling service as a sapper in the crusades and for King Stephen in the recent war against Matilda. A villein like this was always useful in a siege, digging tunnels under castles and bringing down their walls, but Edward was having none of it: William had darkened his mood severely.

"This human mole knows the punishment for eating the King's deer!"

Screaming for mercy, the sapper was dragged off to have his right hand removed.

Edward turned back to William and tugged at the white Templar mantle covering his armour: "We both know why you wear this thing. The spare brother needs a cause to fight for – Christ and the Kingdom of Heaven. But it seems Christ didn't want you in Jerusalem. Oh, you look hurt now! Yes, I know about your little fit of madness, that's no surprise to me. My mind was always the stronger, the better trained – yours was impetuous and buffeted this way and that by any whim. Your heart has always ruled you William and that's a fatal flaw in any man."

Nicholas was now led out struggling between two watchmen. His crime was so heinous that the crowd had no compunction in throwing rotten produce and the filth from beneath their feet in his direction. To rob poor Jake who had nothing in the world was beyond contempt. They looked forward to seeing the wretched urchin swing.

"He pleads innocent, my Lord," the Bishop gestured to the boy.

"I did nothing. That Jake, he never liked me. Makes things up. I'd never do that to him!"

The iron bar crackled nearby and Nicholas saw the blacksmith from the Golgotha Tavern. The same man he'd sat at the table with and listened to tales from their mutual friend, John the Tanner. Nicholas tried to acknowledge him but he looked away sheepishly. The boy had no idea that his tavern companion was about to disfigure his hand.

"Ordeal!" Edward yelled to the delight of the villagers. The Accused's right hand was forcibly outstretched to receive the white-hot object. Nicholas could already feel the pain shooting up his arm even before touching it. He tried to break free from his captors, kicking and punching but to no avail. Then he spotted the tall, striking Templar on the dais – a stranger he'd never seen before – and gave William his most pleading look.

The Bishop calmly explained the procedure.

"Place it in his hand. You, boy, will walk nine steps from where you are to the trough over there and then you can release it. Bind his hand afterwards. If after three days it has healed, the boy is innocent of the crime. If his hand has not healed, he will hang. *Dominus vobiscum.*"

The blacksmith had the blazing iron bar gripped in a pair of tongs and slowly edged towards Nicholas. Edward watched his brother's face contort with horror at the spectacle. Always wanting to help the underdog, always taking the side of the weak.

That's your problem, William – always siding with the weak against the strong. But it's the strong that always win.

"I could stop this, you know," Edward whispered. "But you must help me with father's debts. I ask for only a small fraction of what your Order has. And you're a de Mandeville, you owe this to your family."

"My friend," Pathros chipped in with this medical opinion, "this child's hand will be ruined. I have nothing that will cure it."

The Earl smirked.

"Listen to your Saracen monkey, William. The boy's hand will soon be nothing but a fleshy clump." Edward suddenly jabbed William in the chest, beaming from ear to ear. "Do you remember all those years ago, brother, when you were so appalled at those villagers in Dover who threw that man off the cliffs? My goodness, you went on and on about how terrible it was and I just said, 'Forget it, William, this is what the rabble are like.' But you'd have none of it. Even Father couldn't understand why you were making so much fuss."

William watched the hot iron bar intently.

Because I'm human! Because this is wrong!

In a few seconds the fiery ingot would attach itself to the pathetic small palm outstretched to meet it. Layers of skin would be stripped off and the fat and muscle would bubble and cook beneath. All that would be left of the hand would be charred skin and exposed bone. Nicholas could feel the heat of the bar on his face as the hulking figure of the blacksmith grew ever nearer.

"Give me twenty thousand marks, William, and I will set the boy free now."

I'll give you nothing and the boy will not be harmed.

The Templar flashed a look of undiluted hatred at Edward.

"I will take my leave of you now, brother."

With that, William leapt from the dais, seeming to fly through the air. A single kick of his metal boot sent the hot iron bar hurtling towards the watching crowd. Punching one of the watchmen square in the face, William grabbed Nicholas under his arm like a bundle and belted for his horse. Pathros followed in loyal and joyous pursuit. In no time, the two men were riding out of the village with the juvenile thief.

Chapter 18

PLESHEY CASTLE

Edward pounded into his mother's room to recount the morning's events in Witham only to find her fully dressed and being attended to by two maids. She dismissed them curtly and addressed her son.

"What is this I hear about a boy being killed in Thorpe Wood?"

The Earl's face went a deathly white.

"I've heard nothing."

Rohese didn't believe him.

"They say his hands and feet had been nailed to a wooden cross in imitation of Our Lord – revolting!"

"It is a blasphemous crime, Mother. And I hear the Jews did it ..."

"That's odd. You knew nothing about it a moment ago."

"... I forgot at first. But now I remember."

Rohese's eyes narrowed.

"I'm the one who's forgetful here – not you."

Surely her son wasn't capable of such a deed? It was one thing to be ruthless as a ruler, but that should never tip over into cruel and blasphemous acts. They had their immortal souls to consider after all. To slay a child in mockery of Christ's death ... The Countess shuddered.

"You've always been a strange and unhappy boy."

"I'm not strange at all, Mother." Edward paced across the flagstones. "And I'll enquire further about what happened in the forest. I'm sure we'll get to the bottom of it."

"When you do find out who did it," Rohese remarked caustically, "don't crucify them as well, eh? One horrendous act of blasphemy is enough for any lifetime. Don't make a habit of it."

"I haven't crucified anybody, Mother … and never will do."

Edward needed to change the subject.

"Look, I came here to talk about my brother. I don't know why but I think he knows about the will. I could see it in his eyes."

"What did you see in his eyes?" Rohese inquired derisively.

"You're going to think this sounds ridiculous," Edward paused, "but I saw Father in his face. As if he was looking at me through my brother."

"Well, he wasn't. Your father is in no position to look at you or anybody else." Her eyes swivelled towards the hearth. "William knows nothing. What once existed has been consigned to the flames and that's that. I burnt it with my own hands.

Edward then told his mother what had happened in Witham: his brother's refusal to find any Templar money to alleviate his onerous debts, the comments that he was an unfit ruler and, worst of all, riding off with the boy thief who was about to be put to ordeal. The Countess was beside herself at these tidings.

"He spoke to you like that in front of the scum?" She slumped back onto the bed, lying back on the bolster. "My womb was wasted creating that idiot!" The Countess' body might have been frail but her eyes burnt with an intense rage. William had no right to undermine the dynasty she had striven to create. If the people saw the house of de Mandeville divided, they would cease to respect the family.

"Maybe he must die."

"Mother?"

"I'm serious, my son."

She gazed at the hood over the fire grate with the crest of the Essex earldom emblazoned on it. That was all that mattered. The de Mandevilles had come so close to losing everything in the recent anarchy. At one point King Stephen had even stripped them of their castles and lands. Only through humbling herself, pleading on her knees for the King's mercy, had she held on to their domains.

"He's disloyal," Rohese smouldered.

"What do I have to do?"

"Strike at him, my son. He could undermine everything." Her throat constricted in anger and she arched forward to catch her breath. "He's no son of mine … he's no brother to you … he should be treated like a traitor. A wolfhead! A vagabond! An outlaw!"

Edward bent low to speak into his mother's ear.

"But to get to him now, I'd have to attack the Templars. He will be tucked inside that fortified preceptory with all his little Templar friends. And they won't surrender him to me without a struggle. Whatever they think of William, those Templars always stick together."

Her ancient lungs had once more run out of air but she managed to hiss with a final wisp of breath: "Kill them all!"

Chapter 19

THE TEMPLAR PRECEPTORY
CRESSING TEMPLE

The young serf ran across the fields as fast as his legs could carry him. "The Earl comes! The Earl comes!"

He was caught in mid-flight as an arrow whistled into his back, cracking his spine and felling him in an instant. Edward and the hundred-strong band of armed liegemen on foot and horseback hurtled towards the preceptory. Their hooves trampled over their first victim as they bore down on their target.

The serf's cry had been heard and the menacing host spotted. Now the alarum bell rang frantically, summoning the Templar knights and serjeants to their stations. The ageing knights heaved into their chainmail and picked up their shields and great swords. They hadn't expected to ever see battle again. This preceptory was a place for living out final days, not embarking on fresh combat. Leave that to the younger Templars out in the Holy Land.

Edwy, the serjeant brought back from the dead by Pathros, watched from the window of the great hall, a long bow by his side. His cheek was still covered in a heavily applied medical paste mixed by the turcopole and the wound had healed well. Pathros joined his new Frankish friend. He looked out at the advancing enemy.

"You English really are a violent people."

"Never thought I'd see this." Edwy shook his head. "An earl of this realm attacking us. Unthinkable. Ungodly. He'll go to hell – beyond a doubt, I'm telling you."

The Templar serjeant couldn't help but notice the exotic bow Pathros was preparing to use. He'd seen such devices used by the Seljuk Turks in Outremer during his service on crusade and fancied himself as a bit of an expert on Eastern weaponry.

"Ox-bone handle, that" – Edwy gestured towards the Turkish bow – "nice workmanship. Correct me if I'm mistaken, but that bow has several types of wood bound together to create the right tension. Saw Saracens making bows like that when I was out in Outremer."

"That is exactly how it is made." Pathros answered, not at all bored by Edwy's showy display of knowledge. "For a Frank, you seem to be very learned."

"I'll take that as a compliment."

Edwy still regarded Pathros' bow with a hint of jealousy. He looked at his own plainer but much larger Welsh bow, made of elm. Though always true to its mark, it lacked the sophistication of the turcopole's weapon.

"Dare say you think that fancy weapon of yours can kill more of our enemies today?"

Pathros raised an eyebrow.

"You wish to compete, my friend?"

"Pah!" Edwy dismissed the challenge.

"I will surely win," the turcopole boasted.

The serjeant had to rise to that challenge.

"You're on, Saracen. I'll make you eat your words and more."

There was a flurry of activity behind the great hall. The secret treasury of the Templars was being hidden, just in case. A line of serfs passed objects of inestimable value carefully from one pair of hands to another.

At the end of the line a knight was disappearing off with each object through a dark entrance carved into a small mound covered in turf. This was a sacred space where only those wearing the white mantle of the Order could enter. Everyone else was strictly forbidden.

Down stone steps hewn out of the rock the knight stumbled with a precious cargo, emerging into a bell-shaped cave carved entirely by Templar hands. His lit torch revealed walls covered in scratched images, whose meaning was known only to the Templar knights. The confusion of lines and circles depicted the martyred saints most venerated by the Order. One series of intersecting lines with a stick man at the centre showed Lazarus tied to an iron griddle, his body being burnt over a fire.

In front of a simple altar, boxes and caskets were being piled up. They were full of relics, holy vessels and bullion. Another knight entered the manmade cave and placed the head of Saint Polycarp on the altar. Covered in peeling sheets of blackened and desiccated skin, it seemed to grin malevolently in the semi-darkness. In front of it, on the ground, was the black-and-white piebald standard of the Templars. Wulfric had no intention of honouring this skirmish with the Earl's rabble by employing the standard. Instead, it would be hidden away with all the other preceptory's riches.

Above ground, Wulfric rode out, blazing with fury, to parlay with the Earl's steward. Ageric watched the old Saxon eagle approach.

"Not enough to burn and rob Ramsay Abbey when you were in the service of the old earl," Wulfric began speaking before his horse had come to a halt, "you now wish to desecrate this place. Not enough to rape and murder for the traitor rightfully shot through with arrows, you come here to sin against God for his son. What are you, Ageric? A bonded slave to the de Mandevilles?"

"Hand over the boy thief and the Earl's brother and we'll go," Ageric answered. "I know you hate that William de Mandeville as much as we do. Just give him to us and he'll be our problem."

"No."

You're not here just for William and the boy; you want our wealth. Your master — another de Mandeville — wants to take everything I have built here.

"Your master thinks I will help him pay the King's debts," Wulfric bristled. "It wasn't enough for him to raid our wagons, now he wants our land and possessions. But we won't yield, Ageric, mark my words well. You'll find no soft compliant Benedictines here. Take one step further and I'll run you through myself."

Ageric listened to the preceptor's bluster but knew that behind Wulfric was a motley band of clapped-out knights who would put up a poor fight against the Earl's younger liegemen. Both sides would take casualties but Edward de Mandeville would prevail. By the end of the day, fresh plots would be filled in the Templar cemetery.

"Give them to us."

"*No!*" Whatever Wulfric thought of the thief Nicholas or William, he'd never let the likes of Ageric or his master dictate to the Templar Order. No layman would tell him what he could or couldn't do. Only the Pope and Hugh of Argentine had jurisdiction over this preceptory. "Out of my sight and take your rabble with you!"

Ageric returned to Edward, who was within earshot, lurking in the cemetery with his men, ready to begin the attack. The Earl knew the stubborn old Saxon wouldn't give way and that was exactly what he wanted. It was time to show these Templars that this was his domain and not theirs. If they defied his writ, they would all be cut down or strung up.

Edward ran his index finger over his signet ring bearing the family seal. He was the law in Essex and nobody else. I'll make an example of my own brother, he mused. I'll show everybody here that not even blood ties can excuse a traitor or a rebel from the gallows.

The humiliation in Witham had to be avenged and in such a way that villages for miles around would speak of this day for generations. Hit your enemy and hit hard, he'd been taught in Paris. Now that theory would guide his decisive action.

Every last coin, chalice, sheep and cow and even the stones and timbers of this place would be shipped away to pay off his debts and restore his authority. But first, he needed to soften up his enemy's minds – weaken their resolve.

"Dig up the Templar graves – all of them!"

"My Lord?" Ageric was astounded by the request.

"Dig them up and line their bodies along the wall in full view of those decrepit old knights in there."

Edward gestured to the Great Hall.

This will scare the old fools.

"I want them to know I've got no mercy in my soul, no compassion, no love. I want them to understand exactly what I'm capable of. Dig them up!"

Wulfric thundered back like a dark cloud. William watched and waited for the inevitable verbal onslaught.

"This is your fault."

"You wanted me to see my brother," William remonstrated.

"Yes – to prove he stole our produce – the thieving de Mandeville! But I didn't ask you to go rescuing thieves, this boy here!" Nicholas slid behind William. "Now we've got your brother and his thugs at our gates."

"Don't let them take me, sir," Nicholas piped up to William. "I'm hardly worth the bother, really I'm not. Just a boy! No hair on my chin, not one." He felt his chin just to make sure. "That Jake never liked me, even when he was whole. Always had it in for me. And them apples, they were rotten to the core. Tasted horrible."

"Tell that infernal boy to be silent!" Wulfric barked.

"How was I to know the apples weren't to be taken?" Nicholas whimpered.

"Be quiet!" William placed his hand on the urchin's shoulder. "Brother Wulfric, we've only known hatred between us and I can't pretend to feel anything but bitterness towards you still, but you were right about my brother. I spoke to him. I saw the evil in his face and from his own lips. And I understand now that I was wrong. He tortured Daegmund and many more, I'm sure. So I'll fight alongside you today to put matters right. And if necessary, if the moment presents itself, I"ll split my brother in two with my own sword."

Wulfric found this small hint of warmth towards him from William rather unsettling.

"I've never liked you either. Came here with a big head when you were a kid, saying you'd be the best knight there ever was. Well, every preceptory from here to Antioch knows what happened when you went to Outremer. You made an ass of yourself – but not just any ass. No, you had to be an ass that got possessed by the Devil. Now you're back here, and look what happens."

"I'll deal with my brother this very day, I promise."

The old Saxon shook his head.

"I don't believe you. Don't expect me to soften my heart towards you, brother William. It turned to stone long ago."

Suddenly Edwy cried out.

"They are digging up the bodies, Brother Wulfric ... lining them up against the barn."

The Templars gathered round the windows of the Great Hall and watched the ghoulish scene unfolding. One after another, the mouldering remains of those who had gone before were exhumed and propped up. Earth-covered, half-worm-eaten corpses now stood to mock attention along the side of the barn.

"To arms!" Wulfric screamed. "All of you!"

Knights, serjeants and able-bodied men in the preceptory ran in all directions in a frenzy of activity. The clatter of shields filled the air as they were slung across the backs of warriors and fastened by guiges. On some were scrawled the motto of the Order: *Sigillum Militum Xpisti*. The Seal of a Soldier of Christ!

Unadorned swords, deliberately plain as laid down by the Rule, were hung from leather belts and steel helmets were slid over their heads, some with apron visors obscuring the face entirely while others had just a nasal guard. From a wooden rack, maces and lances were retrieved as the monastic warriors swung into full battle action.

Mounting their horses, the less-than-fit knights were transformed into fierce visions in their glowing white habits and steel helmets. Wulfric gave them some final rousing and uncompromising words.

"Today we are outnumbered but that counts for nothing. We fight base types with base motives. We know what de Mandeville truly seeks but he will take nothing from this holy place. We fight till they are defeated or we are all cut down! Draw your swords!"

As they exited the Great Hall, the whoosh of a crossbow bolt rooted everyone to the spot. By the window, Edwy had breathed his last, his heart pierced by one of the Earl's finest shots. He crashed to the wooden floor, his longbow by his side. They heard a cheer go up from the Earl's men.

Pathros knelt by the big serjeant. Edwy's eyes were still wide open, either in shock at the mass exhumation or the surprise of the bolt smacking into his ribcage. With the palm of his hand, the turcopole closed them for all eternity.

"Sleep now," he whispered.

His medicine had brought Edwy back from the dead once but he could do nothing more. God had wanted this soul very badly and the moment of the opinionated serjeant's death had merely been postponed. The only one of these boorish English who has ever shown me a shred of respect, the turcopole thought, and now he is taken.

Serjeant brothers now fired endless volleys of arrows at the ox carts behind which the Earl's liegemen took cover, biding their moment to attack. One man screamed as an arrow tore his forearm open, cutting into bone and sinew. Wulfric urged on the knights; they had no alternative than to move forward.

They rode out with shields raised but lack of youthful vigour could be sensed in their sluggishness. Younger knights would have hurled themselves at the enemy but these Templars cantered cautiously, their nerves obvious.

"Look what they did to your dead comrades!" Wulfric yelled at the knights, "can we permit this? Cut down all of them!"

William looked at the decaying corpses his brother had exhumed and then to the ageing knights riding by him. Wulfric was right: he'd brought nothing but ill fortune to Cressing Temple. So it fell to him to rouse these old warriors into action, to prove that a de Mandeville could fight for virtue.

"Brother Wulfric speaks true!" the young Templar shouted, trying desperately to enthuse all those around him. "Come on, you are all great knights! Raise your swords. Victory or death!"

It was as if he'd cast a spell over this infirm and elderly host. Horses sped to a gallop, swords were held high. A new determination gripped these Templars who for years had known nothing but farm work.

Some spark of martial valour came alive and now the Earl's liegemen faced worthy opponents. In no time they were fleeing in the face of the Templar advance.

Hooves stamped contemptuously on the backs of these rogues and blades slashed across their backs. Seeing his men in a disorderly retreat, Edward ordered out his knights to charge on the Templars. With a din of yells and clashes of shield and sword, the intensity of the skirmish increased to something more like a battle. A mace crashed downwards and the first Templar knight fell to the ground, mortally wounded. Edward screamed threats and curses at his own side. Defeat would mean floggings and fines so they pushed forward against the Templar onslaught.

Steadily the old knights of Cressing were edged back. Wulfric found his sword arm tiring and with a first flash of fear wondered if this would be the day he'd meet his end. William continued to cut and thrust but with no support from those around him as they wearied, he too had to retreat gradually. Seeing the beginning of a rout and sensing Templar bullion was within his reach, Edward egged on his men ever more excitedly.

Within the hall, Pathros picked up his bow, regarded his dead companion of just a few days, and plucked an arrow from his ornately decorated quiver. He dispatched his shafts in rapid succession. They whizzed through the air so fast they were invisible to the naked eye. One by one, liegemen shrieked in agony as they clasped an arm or their face and fell or retreated. Then even the horses sank to their knees and keeled over as if struck by a mysterious force.

The battle was suddenly turning in the Templars' favour. Wulfric stared back at the Great Hall disapprovingly then resumed fighting. The turcopole's arrows seemed to be guided by an invisible hand as they cut down or maimed one after another of the Earl's fighters. Edward watched in horror as his force was gradually decimated.

"Fall back!" the steward commanded before Edward could countermand him. "Back, I say!"

The men on foot scurried to any shelter they could find while the reduced cavalry rode back into the cemetery and re-joined the Earl.

"They'll be back soon," Wulfric muttered. He turned to his knights and serjeants. "Good work, my brothers. God was on our side." He beckoned to William. "Come with me."

The two men rode back to the Great Hall. The preceptor dismounted and strode into the building. Opening a monk's bench, he pulled out two encoded pieces of parchment. There were symbols on the document that any preceptory in the Templar network would understand; William could present the letters in exchange for the coin he needed.

Wulfric removed his helmet to reveal an elderly face now streaked with sweat and blood.

"Go back to Outremer." He hesitated, so unwilling to say the next words. "God clearly doesn't want you here in Witham, that much is plain to me now. I thought you could be fashioned into a better Templar ... have some of that insufferable arrogance knocked out of you ... but in everything happening now, I see God's hand. He wants you gone, I'm sure of it." Wulfric glared at Pathros. "And by the way, your turcopole fights dishonourably. Shooting at horses, that's a Turkish trick. I don't like it."

In spite of his desperation to get away from Witham, the young Templar didn't agree this was the right moment.

"I must stay and fight with all of you."

"Just go, leave here. I never wish to see you or your Saracen or this little thief again!" The trio regarded Wulfric, dumbfounded. "Now follow me!"

With that, the old Saxon led them towards the mysterious mound behind the Hall. No knight was normally permitted to enter the space beneath but Wulfric was in no mood to stand on ceremony. He ushered William, Pathros and Nicholas through the concealed entrance and in no time the boy thief's eyes were wide as plates as he found himself surrounded by gold bullion and relics coated in jewels. Wulfric then pulled back a thick curtain behind the small stone altar to reveal a roughly hewn door, which he unlocked.

Behind it was a murky void.

"A tunnel," the preceptor explained. "Goes a long way. Here, take this," he handed William his flaming torch. "It'll bring you out at a stream by White Notley. From there, you take the Roman road. There's a stable nearby and you can have any horse you want."

Pathros didn't need a second invitation and bound into the tunnel. William and Wulfric fixed each other in what they knew would be their final encounter.

"You were right about my brother."

"I was right about your family."

William shook his head. "I will prove you wrong on that. I will show you there is honour in the name de Mandeville."

With that, he disappeared while Nicholas followed behind. As the boy was about to enter the tunnel, Wulfric grabbed his wrist in a vice-like grip.

"Give it back."

"Don't know what you mean."

"Now!"

Fumbling in his breeches, he brought out a small gold trinket holding the thumb bone of some long-deceased saint. Gingerly, he placed it in Wulfric's other hand. The preceptor relaxed his grip.

"Once a thief, eh, boy?"

Chapter 20

PLESHEY CASTLE

The Countess of Essex had been carried down from her room high up in the castle to the Great Hall, where she was propped up on a daybed by an arrangement of cushions. She looked through colourless eyes at the men before her: John the Tanner, Aylmer the Blacksmith and Hunrith the Gong Farmer, who had taken the unusual step of washing himself especially for this meeting. She was unaware that these men had crucified an innocent boy in Thorpe Wood but she knew they were capable of dark deeds – for which she was prepared to pay.

"Don't return,"– Rohese gasped a few short breaths –"until you have my son with you. You can chase him to ends of the world if needs be but I want him back." She gestured to some sacks of coins. "You can see that we will give you all the money you need. All I ask is that you don't return empty-handed, because I will make you regret it very deeply."

They bowed.

"Pardon me, my lady, but do you wish him to be returned alive?" John the Tanner asked.

Rohese shrugged and closed her eyes.

"Leave me now."

Edward signalled for the men to go. He gazed at his mother, whose skin was like paper. Her body was now so wasted away with illness and age that it could barely be made out under the bed coverings heaped on to keep her warm. The Countess was dying; her last day wasn't so far off.

Rohese looked back at the Earl.

My son, we must do terrible things to hold on to power. But if you had that innocent boy crucified, I will have to destroy you or my soul will be damned.

"How did William escape?"

Edward clasped his hands.

"He fled like a rat before we took the preceptory. All we found were some decrepit creatures that laughably call themselves knights. They're languishing in our dungeon right now." Edward slurped his wine loudly. "And they can stay there till they rot."

But Rohese had no interest in the imprisoned Templars. It was William who occupied her thoughts.

"Are you sure he'll flee to Clairvaux?"

"Oh yes, Mother. He'll look for answers with the fraudulent holy man who recruited him to the Knights Templar. I know my brother, he's really quite predictable."

"What does he see in that madman?" Rohese referred to Bernard of Clairvaux, viewed as saintly by so many in Christendom.

"That piss-stained abbot!" Edward snorted.

I am worldly, Edward mused, while my brother is a zealous simpleton. The philosopher ruler against the boneheaded Templar! How fortunate I was to have been tutored by Peter Abelard, the greatest philosopher in Paris and foe of Bernard of Clairvaux. Edward grinned. He counted himself truly blessed that such a brilliant mind had shaped his thoughts while his credulous brother clawed at the filth-covered cassock of Bernard.

Abelard had instructed his young charges not to be impressed by the ascetic posing of the fraudulent Abbot of Clairvaux, who only impressed the foolish and stupid of all classes. Starvation and denial weren't the paths to truth; engagement with the real world was a surer route. Those who ran kingdoms and commanded armies were the real heroes, not ranting clerics who rolled in their own dung.

Let Bernard spew his ignorant bile while we debate the Greek and Roman philosophers in refined surroundings, Abelard told his students. Any charlatan can tear his garments and posture like an Old Testament prophet. It was a pathetic trick, a meaningless posture! Only the simple could possibly be impressed by this display of tawdry piety.

Edward had listened to these wise lectures while sitting next to future kings and popes. But little did Abelard realise the lengths to which Bernard would go to silence him. He had powerful friends; the Templars were on his side. They harassed and plotted and schemed to break the great teacher of Paris; they insulted him in church councils. Pagan! Godless! Heretic! They wore my great teacher down, Edward reflected, till they drove him to his death.

A crime against learning!

Bernard and his Templar thugs couldn't let Abelard lecture in peace. For this act alone, Edward vowed he'd always hate the Abbot of Clairvaux and the white-mantled monsters that had killed his teacher.

"What does he see in that man?" Rohese croaked.

"He thinks a priest that never washes must be holy. Abbot Bernard is covered in boils and sores so my dear brother deludes himself that the swamp frog of Clairvaux is a saint."

The Countess gasped in disbelief.

"Your brother is a simpleton. An ass in the field has more wisdom."

"Indeed," Edward agreed.

Chapter 21

ROAD TO CHELMSFORD

On the horizon about ten or fifteen of the Earl's liegemen galloped in William's direction. They had been in hot pursuit since the trio had fled Witham. It seemed as if they'd never shake their pursuers off.

William swung his horse round towards the Roman Road and dug in his spurs. The palfrey whinnied in terror as its hooves sunk into molehills and slipped on the wet muddy ground.

"Come on ... move, damn you!"

Nicholas clung to the Templar's belt, sharing the same horse. His nose was running almost constantly and his eyes itched all the time. With his dirt-caked fingers he rubbed them constantly till they went quite red.

"Closing in, sir, they're going to get us!"

Already the voices of the liegemen could be heard behind them, urging their steeds forward. But they faced the same problem of the soggy terrain. William cajoled the poor animal beneath him. The Roman Road was just one big leap away and Edward's men hopelessly outnumbered them.

"Come on!"

With one agonised bound, the harried horse bounded on to the firmer surface followed by Pathros and his steed. Now they broke into a rapid gallop to make good their escape. William's white mantle and the turcopole's black cloak flapped behind them as they charged towards Chelmsford.

The riders sped across the River Can, past a small hill bearing a gallows that groaned under the weight of rotting corpses. William had no doubt now that they were serfs and even men of higher birth unable to pay his brother's onerous taxes.

Suddenly a shepherd appeared with what seemed like a never-ending stream of sheep blocking their path. Nicholas bobbed up and down impatiently, wiping his runny nose with his sleeve.

"We can leap over these sheep. Big horses, these! One big jump! Come on, sirs, don't want to get caught." He glanced at his hand. "They'll make me hold that hot iron bar if they catch me. Make these horses fly!"

Pathros sighed.

"Horses cannot fly."

"I heard of one that could."

The turcopole gasped at yet more Frankish idiocy.

"Did you see it?" he asked Nicholas. "With your own eyes?"

"No, just heard – down the Golgotha Tavern. Learn a lot of things there."

Nicholas was starting to take a dislike to Pathros. Never talks to me very nice, he thought.

Like I'm a baby. Master William has a kind face but this Turk is all proud and full of himself. Nasty little pointy beard as well. And smells of flowers!

Out of the corner of his eye, Pathros was forming his own less-than-flattering opinion of their new companion. He smelt like a pig and sniffed like one too. Most probably he had never washed, which was why he kept scratching himself. He was certainly illiterate too. And even by the low intellectual standards of the Franks, this boy was a damned imbecile. My friend William is always attracted by the novelty of the new, Pathros thought, but this jabbering sparrow will not amuse him for long.

In the hours that followed, the horses pounded along the decaying, ancient road along which the armies of the Caesars had marched. Then the road petered out.

The fields and forests of Essex gave way to noxious marshes – an evil terrain where the earth belched out sulphurous fumes and a man struggled to see his hand before his face. Wisps of mist encircled the horses' hooves and seemed to form white chains binding them to the spot.

Their pursuers halted, not daring to go any further, and Pathros watched as the ignorant, superstitious liegemen skulked away.

What dullards and savages these Franks are!

The three travellers pushed on, eager to be away from this ungodly quagmire.

"Where are we?" Pathros enquired.

"The River Thames, near the sea," William answered.

The turcopole looked round, confused.

"I see no river."

The Templar knight glanced down.

"You're in it."

The broad estuary was just inches deep where they stood. There was barely any tidal movement as the water struggled to negotiate huge clumps of colourless vegetation. The air was filled with a curious gurgling sound and all around, toads and newts slithered and small biting insects buzzed. Nicholas swatted his face repeatedly and glanced down at the dead mosquitoes in the palm of his hand. He wiped them off only to have to kill another one as it landed on his cheek or exposed forearm.

"What are they, my friend?" Pathros pointed to blurry figures somewhere in the distance.

Their voices could be heard, muffled by the foul air and swallowed up by the vast expanse of nothingness. William could just make out that they were digging up clods of earth and piling them in mounds. Were they trying to clear the marsh and make the river more navigable? Surely the immensity of the task made their activity utterly pointless.

"They're struggling against God's will, I think," William replied.

As they approached the group, a small tumbledown wooden jetty revealed itself through the smog. William remembered being in this place before when he'd boarded a barge from the village of Tilbury to Gravesend on the other side. Sitting on the wet ground and waiting were a couple of pilgrims.

Both stood up as a large raft emerged from the ether, looking as welcoming as the ferry across the River Styx. It was a big enough craft for Pathros and William to remain on horseback while the pilgrims huddled close to them, although their fellow passengers muttered about the weight of the steeds, fearing they would sink the vessel.

The barge eased away. The ferryman, a powerfully built ox-like man, pushed a huge pole deep down into the riverbed to propel the raft through the marshy waters. Already the vessel had picked up three other passengers: a young serf curled up on the floor, a stout woman with a wicker cage containing a hen and a Benedictine monk, who sat cross-legged with his hood pulled down over his head.

"Why's he shaking?" Nicholas pointed to the young serf. "Reckon the Devil's got him. Getting worse too. Devil is shaking him good and proper."

Sure enough, the young serf was convulsing and shivering. The stout woman became defensive about her sick son.

"Marsh fever, sirs. Nothing more than that! We all got it. Comes and goes, it does."

All of a sudden, the Benedictine monk jerked into life. With long white fingers he pulled back his hood to reveal a rodent-like face and a cadaverous grin, with teeth that were uniformly blackened and rotten. His eyes were milky and could barely see. Through his semi-blindness, he made out the cross on William's mantle.

"Aaaah, Templar."

"Yes," William replied.

"Not so proud now, are you?"

William was unnerved by this unpleasant figure. His almost sightless eyes seemed to bore into the knight. And the putrid smile never left his face.

"What do you mean, brother?"

"You know what I mean."

The mustard-coloured mist swirled round the seated figure as if he was exuding this hellish smoke.

"If you've got something to say, then say it plainly."

The smile disappeared.

"You know perfectly well what I mean. The True Cross, the Lignum Crucis! Entrusted to you damned Templars. That was a mistake! Of course you lot are trying to keep what's happened a secret but I know everything about your less-than-holy Order."

William slid off his horse, causing the ferry to rock perilously. But he ignored the frightened protests around him. Instead, he brought his face close to the Benedictine.

"How would you know anything about the Lignum Crucis?"

"Oh, you Templars! Think you're the cleverest and smartest Order in Christendom. Rest of us are fools in your view. Well, we Benedictines have our network too. We share our information from abbey to abbey and church to church. And we know all about your True Cross and what's happened to it. Damned Templars!"

"Well then," William tried to appear almost disinterested, "impress me with your knowledge. I'm sure I'll be amazed at what you know about us."

The Benedictine cackled.

"You're too low-ranking to have been told the truth by your superiors."

William lowered his voice.

"How would you like to go for a swim?"

The monk regarded the gloopy swamp and became more forthcoming.

"The Saracens have it, don't they? You know that. They've stolen it. The wood upon which our Saviour died is now in pagan hands and it's all the fault of you Templars."

"Are you sure of this?"

"Surer than I am of anything." The monk drew his hood back over his head. "God will punish you proud knights. You've lost His Cross. And rest assured, Templar, you'll never retrieve it from those Saracens."

William contemplated the haunting figure before him.

God or the Devil sent you to me, foul monk. Whichever it is, you have made my quest as clear as day. I must find the Lignum Crucis.

Chapter 22

THE PORT OF DARTFORD,
KENT

Whitsuntide had come round with its yearly excuse for drinking, feasting, wrestling and – to the astonishment of Pathros, falsely thinking nothing the Franks did could shock him – some kind of bloody sport involving cudgels. Tamer amusement was derived from lowering painted wooden doves, or real ones, through the Holy Ghost holes of larger churches in memory of the Pentecost.

The vast jostling crowd left Nicholas dazed, as they entered Dartford. This was the furthest he'd ever ventured from Witham and never before had he witnessed such a press of humanity: hawkers, cutpurses, pilgrims and seaman. Not only the language of the Kent English but the guttural strains of Flemish and lilting tones of Lombard merchants could be distinguished through the hubbub.

"Never seen so many people. Must be the biggest city in the world, I swear it. Can't be a bigger one."

Pathros was browsing a medical manuscript as he rode along and scoffed loudly.

"So," the turcopole addressed Nicholas while intently scanning his learned tome, "you think this village dwarfs Damascus, Baghdad or even the great Constantinople, queen of all cities."

"Never heard of them. Made up names, I'm sure."

"They are not made up," Pathros felt his throat constrict at this boy's stupidity. "These cities are very real, I assure you."

"Still never heard of them."

This exchange was interrupted as a group of local Templar serjeants barged between William and Pathros' horses, trundling a wagon heaped with sacks of flour. It had been ground at several of the Order's mills located along the River Darent. The serjeants acknowledged William while ignoring Pathros, too base to be given any recognition.

"Find out where we can get palfreys for the journey to Clairvaux," William instructed Pathros. Their present horses were built for war; they needed thicker-set animals that could endure a trudge of many weeks. "And find a cog we can board. Any ship will do, so long as it's bound for the coast of France."

Pathros had already spotted a small wooden vessel bobbing on the quayside as if impatient to sail. The cog was slamming angrily against the oak revetments, wooden walls built by Dartford's carpenters to keep the sea in its proper place. At one end of the dock, masons were already replacing wood with stone. It was fortunate the cog wasn't slamming against the new wall or it might have smashed itself to bits.

"And you, Nicholas" – William landed a soft, playful punch on his cheek – "go find some provisions. We'll need food." The knight handed him two bronze coins. "That should be enough."

With his two companions assigned to their tasks, William chased after the Templar serjeants. The words of the strange Benedictine monk on the raft were reverberating over and over in his head.

Could Hugh of Argentine really have lied to me about the True Cross? Can I return to Outremer with a quest, a purpose and a chance to bury my father?

William needed to get in front of Bernard of Clairvaux again, the esteemed cleric who had recruited him to the Knights Templar. He had to obtain the holy man's absolution for his sinful behaviour in Jerusalem and permission to go back on crusade. Bernard could overrule all opposition to his return. And William needed to know from Bernard's own lips whether he still had what it took to be a great Knight Templar.

I'm sure he will know where to find the Lignum Crucis.

William passed a wagon loaded with flour and rode alongside a ruddy-faced serjeant. He was surprised and a little embarrassed to find himself being addressed by such a fine knight as William de Mandeville.

"Serjeant," William broached the subject delicately, "how are things here in Dartford?"

"Very well, sir – we're prospering, as you can plainly see."

"Indeed! What news have you heard from Edessa?"

The serjeant coughed.

"Fallen, sir. Holy Land is a right mess, if you ask me. I was there two-year back and we were firmly in the saddle, so to speak. But them Saracens have got new fire in them. I reckon it's those Turks – evil bastards, they are. Reckon things could get very ugly, sir. Very ugly indeed as it goes."

"Yes," William agreed, "And what about the True Cross? I'd heard it was in Edessa … that we sent it there to give the city hope in its struggle."

The serjeant shook his head.

"I know nothing of such things, sir. And neither do I ask. That's matters for the likes of you, not us ordinary folk. You hear rumour – loose tongues saying hateful things they ought not to. But you ignore it, sir. Put it out of your mind."

"Mmmm … loose tongues. Terrible! People really oughtn't to gossip. Still, what have you heard?"

"I'd rather not pass on such things as I have—"

"Please," William interjected, "tell me. You won't get in any trouble, I swear it. I won't mention this conversation to our superiors."

The serjeant went beetroot purple in the face.

"Well, my goodness! Just so long as you know I give no credence to this," he stammered, "but I had heard from somebody who is just back from Acre that he heard from an archer who fled from Edessa that the Cross had been taken. The Saracens somehow got it. Can't be true, can it, sir?"

"No," the knight agreed, "as you say it's merely chatter among the men."

William turned his horse away. So Hugh really had deceived him. The Benedictine monk was right: the Saracens had seized the most holy and sacred relic of the Order of the Temple of Solomon.

It had to be somewhere. They wouldn't have destroyed it — the cross was too powerful a symbol to just crush or burn. They would hold onto it and use it against the Templars when the situation demanded. Where could it be?

I must get it back … I must be the one who retrieves our holiest relic!

Bernard of Clairvaux would tell him how to get it back. He'd absolve him of his sins and wipe away the stain of his possession by the demon. All William had to do was get to the modest abbey in Burgundy, fling himself at the old man's feet and beg for his help. Bernard's heart would melt and he'd help his favourite young warrior deliver his quest.

A commotion had broken out near a tavern. At first, William took it to be a fight between drunks but soon the shouts became more distinct and alarming. His heart sank as he heard one word repeated by the furious swarm of people now heading in his direction.

"Thief!"

At the head of a hue and cry was Nicholas, with bread and cheeses under his arms. His legs could barely be distinguished, they were moving so fast. William broke into a rapid gallop and, leaning down, scooped up Nicholas then rode towards the cog. Pathros was beckoning as the captain wished to put to sail immediately. The tide had turned in his favour and he was eager to catch it there and then.

William's horse knocked over a pilgrim who was kissing the well-worn feet of a statue of Saint Christopher bearing the infant Jesus through treacherous waters. He shouted obscenities after the knight but William was oblivious as the mob bore down on him. With no time to dismount, his horse leapt over the wooden revetments and onto the deck of the cog.

Pathros pulled at the gangplank as the enraged townsfolk approached.

William swung his sword at their faces and forced them away from the ship. Slowly it departed from the quayside while angry market traders yelled their vengeance at Nicholas.

"Getting food and stealing food," Pathros lectured Nicholas, "you do realise there is a difference?"

Nicholas held out his ill-gotten gains, unrepentant.

"Good cheese, this. Wasn't enough money to buy it, Master William, but I had to get it. Only the best for a great man like you."

The knight wanted to admonish the boy but instead he was more than a little flattered. He tore off a piece of bread and was about to pop it in his mouth when Pathros pulled it away and threw it into the water. William was shocked by the turcopole's insolence.

"What the hell is wrong with you, Pathros?"

"I must speak with you alone."

"Always having a go at me," Nicholas interjected, scratching his scalp then wiping his nose, "Turks are devils ... You are, for sure ... Evil eyes you got. I found food for Master William and you're just causing me trouble. Trying to make my master hate me ..."

"Please," Pathros begged William, "we must speak, just you and me."

Perplexed, the Templar accompanied Pathros to the other end of the small cog.

"Why are you tormenting that boy?" The Templar was close to severing all ties with this unruly turcopole. "You've taken against him from the moment we met the poor child. I've always been kind to you when all around despise and detest you, why can't you give the same kindness to Nicholas?" William was boiling with rage: "And never knock bread out of my own mouth. Came that close to running you through!"

"I had to." Pathros held up his medical book. "It's the boy."

"The boy, the boy, the *boy*! You're making yourself look very petty. So much for your Eastern wisdom!"

"My friend, you must leave him behind in England and embark on this quest with me alone." Pathros thumbed to a page and showed it to William but it was in Persian and the Templar was stumped. "This tells you why he must not come with us."

"It's gobbledygook – what does it say?"

Pathros pulled harder than ever at his goatee.

"Do you not notice, dear friend, that he is always having excretions running from his eyes, his nose and scratching and itching?"

"He's not the cleanest boy I've ever met – but he's typical of Witham."

"My friend, my dear friend, *the boy has leprosy*."

Chapter 23

ARMARIOLUM, CLAIRVAUX ABBEY, VALLÉE D'ABSINTHE, BURGUNDY

The monk nodded to the jailer, who opened the door of the subterranean cell and hauled out the filth-covered and misshapen clump bound in chains then dragged him up the steps to meet the abbey's visitors. The prisoner's feet trailed behind him, his blood-stained knees bouncing off the edges of the steps as he groaned and whined unintelligible words.

In the armariolum above, Bernard spoke to his former pupil.

"I know why you're here and I have something to show you."

The saintly ascetic gripped his phlegm bucket. He coughed blood into it. His lungs burnt with a rage from years of fasting and sleeping on the cold ground. No pillow had touched his head nor blanket covered his body for many years as he mortified his sinful flesh.

Pathros made for his medicine bag but William stopped him, as he knew the old abbot had no wish to be relieved of his suffering. But this self-inflicted ordeal wasn't to the turcopole's taste and he left the musty and dank room to pace the cloister outside, powerless to cure a cleric bent on his own destruction.

The room Bernard chose to sit in was the place where the monks returned their borrowed books. He knew the dust and smell would heap more pain on his weary chest. The very air was thick with the pungent odour of stale parchment and ink. Even a healthy young knight like William found the acrid miasma choking.

Bernard, Abbot of Clairvaux, had renounced the wealth of his family and glorified in this life of self-imposed poverty and pain. He'd even persuaded others of his own rank to join him in this voluntary misery. It was his aim to set a new standard for monastic abstinence. Through their denial of all worldly temptations, Bernard and his followers would shame the comfort-seeking Benedictines in the eyes of the faithful.

This was a life of ascetic mortification that Pathros had witnessed in the East and as he breathed the fresher air of the cloister, his mind was taken back to those strange hermits in the deserts of Syria. For centuries, saintly men had clambered to the tops of pillars and sat there for months and years till their legs were consumed with gangrene through lack of motion.

His parents had taken the young Pathros to see one of these holy men and from the base of the pillar, the rich and poor alike shouted up their requests and prayers. But on the long journey home the inquisitive child had only asked questions about the ascetic's physical condition and not a word about His Holiness.

How does he sleep, Father? Do his bones wither inside him? These and many more enquiries had been met with disapproving glances from his father, whose faith ran in his veins. A bureaucratic functionary of the Saracen rulers, he clung to the beliefs of his ancestors, refusing to convert to Islam as a more ambitious man might have done.

As he daydreamed about his childhood, Pathros looked through one of the cloister arches to the fields of Burgundy beyond. It was at that moment he saw three ungainly men riding towards the abbey, almost equal in size to the nags under them.

One man had a distinctly unpleasant-looking mace he'd crafted himself, all jagged edges, while another wore a necklace of rings that Pathros assumed had been wrenched from the fingers of his victims. One of them was singing.

"When that maiden caressed me
I swear she undressed me
Now I has the pox ... the pox ... the pox
A burning ... a burning
For I'm never learning
To leave them fair maidens alone ..."

They weren't merchants, pilgrims or soldiers.

"What do men like that want here?" he whispered to himself.

But in an instant, Pathros was distracted by the distressing commotion from the small room off the cloister. Bernard had resumed his coughing fit with such intensity that his face turned an alarming scarlet and veins throbbed as if they might burst.

The Abbot glanced up and his eyes met Nicholas.

"Who is this?"

"A boy. His name is Nicholas."

Bernard reached for a bible behind him and tossed it over to the young lad. "Open it."

Nicholas obeyed but he didn't see the words of scripture so much as a jumble of shapes that swam before his eyes.

"What do you see?" Bernard asked but Nicholas shrugged. "If you cannot answer that, what do you *not* see?" Again the boy had no comment to make on such lofty matters so Bernard answered: "No mermaids. No men with heads in their chests. No griffins or goblins grinning at you off the pages. Nothing but the untroubled word of God, pure as the day it was recounted by the Apostles. Now what do you think of that?"

Nicholas raised his eyebrows as if to indicate he was impressed by the strange man's words but hadn't the faintest idea what he was getting at. The finer points of theology were beyond the ken of a village pickpocket.

"Teach him to read the bible," Bernard ordered William. "Bring him back when he can. I would like to hear the boy read the psalms in my church. As I tutored you now, you must tutor him. That is how the truth is passed from one generation to the next."

Bernard rubbed his chest to ease its constant pain.

"I want to go back to Outremer," William said.

"You can't."

"I must."

"No – you can't. I know what happened out there. It's inconceivable you could return."

William was totally crestfallen.

"You said you knew what I wanted And now you deny me what I want. I'm beginning to wish I hadn't come here."

"Oh," Bernard coughed, "don't wish that! I've got something far more important than that to discuss with you."

"More important than the True Cross?"

"No," Bernard spat into his bucket again. "You seem to think that finding the Lignum Crucis and going back to Outremer are one and the same thing. They are not; they are quite different. The Holy Cross is nowhere near Jerusalem."

"How do you know, great father?"

Bernard grabbed a thick wooden staff leaning against the wall and banged it loudly on the flagstones beneath his feet.

"Because of this."

A figure in manacles and leg irons was dragged into the armariolum and dropped onto the floor, his hair matted about his heavily bearded face, his body emaciated after months of imprisonment.

Bernard stared gloomily at the figure.

"You will not return to the Holy Land, William, but you will go on a crusade – the most important of crusades for your great Order." The abbot gestured to the wretch before them. "This creature calls himself Besnik, by the way." Bernard tapped the prisoner's head with his foot. "Tell us what you did at Edessa."

His lips almost touching the ground, the Romani mercenary remained motionless. But then he began to recite in halting words the account of his discovery of the True Cross. As ever, he omitted all mention of murdering Giyassedin, whose body remained entombed in the ossuary.

"Where is our most sacred cross now?" Bernard asked.

"Al-Usbuna. The Taifa of Badajoz has it. The Atabeg laughed when I gave him the treasure. Said he had no need of Templar magic. But his cousin, the Taifa, he said he needed such magic."

Bernard's expression darkened.

"He always misses the bit out where he murdered Father Jean, a chaplain I knew very well. There are few saints in Outremer but Jean was one of them. I won't forgive this devil so he and I will rot together in this abbey until we both expire. Take him away!"

While Besnik was dragged back below ground, Bernard rose and clasped William's shoulder. He gestured towards the cloister where Pathros had gone to get some air and the two now followed his footsteps.

"That foul thing took our Lord's cross to the Saracens." The abbot looked approvingly at the simple arches of the cloister uncluttered by the expensive ornamentation beloved of the corrupt and venal Benedictines from which his Order had quit. "They haven't chosen to boast yet of their gain but they will, be sure of that. And it will damage the standing of the Knights Templar among Christians everywhere."

They continued to make their way round the cloister with William supporting Bernard, who shuffled like a man beyond his years. The saintly ascetic had never been possessed of a cheery disposition but William detected a new bitterness that unnerved him.

"I know in my heart why the Saracen lord of Edessa has sent the Lignum Crucis to his cousin in this accursed Mohammedan fleshpot they call Al-Usbuna. Deep down, they know its power though they deride it before their own people."

Bernard wiped his mouth on his sleeve and continued.

"While the heathens are tasting victory in the East and our forces suffer, God has favoured us in the West, where we are triumphing, William. Each day another town falls to Christ. I do not understand why the Almighty is pointing us towards the end of the world but he clearly wants us to take our swords into those realms. And so we must take Al-Usbuna."

The abbot took a few deep but rattling breaths as if his chest was full of small stones.

William had come to Clairvaux expecting to be pushed back towards the East but Bernard was pointing the other way. He was speaking of some city that William had never even heard of and which had no holy significance. To defend the streets and paths where Christ's feet had once trodden was one thing but to be sent to fight at the world's westernmost end made no sense.

"There is a great danger, William, because of what this mercenary scum we hold here has done. When our warriors arrive in full armour before the walls of Al-Usbuna, I believe the Saracen will display the Cross to destroy the fighting spirit of our side. Imagine the sight of that atop the enemy's battlements and the cries of despair that will fill the air from our armies. Brave and hardy men will drop their shields and swords and quit the battlefield never to return."

Bernard coughed violently, having spoken too long but then tapped William's hand and winked.

"But they could not do that if they did not have it. That is why you will not return to the Holy Land. You will join a curious but brave people called the Portuguese, who wish to take Al-Usbuna to be the capital of their new kingdom. I have arranged for you to meet their leader, a man called Dom Afonso, who, it so happens, is a cousin of mine. His father was a Burgundian noble and as you know, this is a small world here."

"I've never even heard of this kingdom. Couldn't imagine where it can be found."

"You'll find it, the Holy Spirit will guide you." Bernard's tired eyes fixed on his student. "God cries out for vengeance, William. There is no mission more important than this one that I am entrusting to you. This new kingdom," the abbot confided to him about the emerging realm of Portugal, "will strike like a dagger into the western flank of the Saracen realms. It will mortally wound them from the direction they least expect and you can be a part of that. Journey through Castile and Al-Andalus, meet Dom Afonso, stand with him shoulder to shoulder, fight with him like a true brother in Christ and ..."

The abbot jolted forward as if he'd been struck in the chest and began to convulse with a bronchial fit.

"... recover the Cross, William. The Holy Spirit will guide you to where it is. But get it back!"

The monk who had retrieved then led Besnik away reappeared to announce that three men had arrived, asking about their guests. They had business with William and needed to speak to him in private.

"You know these men?" Bernard asked.

"No, but I know who sent them," William replied.

"They mean you ill?"

"They mean to take me or my head back to my brother in return for a bounty payment."

Bernard pondered this dangerous situation.

"We will feed them and their horses and tell them they may join us for the evening meal where our three guests will also be with us, but you, my friends, will be long gone."

Chapter 24

PLESHEY CASTLE

Rohese was dying. Her breath had reduced to short, anxious gasps and her face had assumed a corpse-like pallor. Edward bent down low as if to kiss the Countess on the cheek but instead he murmured close to her ear.

"I suppose I should tell you, Mother ... You were right ... I did have that child killed in the forest. And if I'm a monster, Mother, it's because I was born of one. Monsters, generally speaking, beget monsters."

Edward rose and barked at the physician.

"How long?"

"The apoplexy has gripped her," the medical man answered, referring to the loss of movement and total inability to speak she had suddenly experienced the day before. "Not much time left, sire."

"Can you be sure?"

The physician held up a cup of Rohese's urine, which was almost white in colour. This was the sure sign of age and a cooling of the body prior to death. Every half-decent man of healing knew that.

"Yes, the Countess is nearing the end."

But Edward was finding his mother's prolonged dying somewhat tedious and changed the subject.

"I hear they denied you a bishopric," he said to the physician, who was also an abbot. "Your proximity to women and their discharges displeased the learned prelates."

"In my line of work, sire, I have to look at what passes from the body and take samples of blood, as the great and wise doctors have advised. My proximity was inevitable."

Edward watched with detached interest as the physician-cum-abbot's assistant bled the purple vein on the Countess' left arm to assess the balance of the humours. On the table nearby was a range of medical instruments including a pestle and mortar for grinding herbs and an astrological chart from the day that Rohese was born. This chart helped the physician pinpoint when to administer the Countess' medicine for maximum effect.

"I'm impressed that a man such as yourself puts his true passion above mere advancement in the Church," Edward flattered the abbot. "However, don't try too hard with my mother …"

"I'll try not to."

"… she's had a long life. If this is her time then don't keep her dithering around here. Hell can't wait forever, you know!"

The Earl left the room. As he did so, Rohese revived. Her brow furrowed and eyelids flickered as if she were in some kind of trance. Gripping the physician's forearm, the old countess cried out.

"Stop those men!"

"*Which* men?"

"Ooooh, have mercy, God! Have mercy on me, a villainous soul … a blackened heart … Have mercy," she turned to the physician, deranged and possessed to his reckoning, "… those men … get them back … They mustn't kill my son, William."

She paused as her feeble heart pounded against her ribcage.

They should kill Edward instead! Edward — a murderer of children!

Chapter 25

THE LAND OF THE BASQUES
KINGDOM OF NAVARRE

Nicholas couldn't remember when this journey had begun. But he certainly wished it would end soon. When they had left Dartford, it had seemed like such a great adventure and an escape from all those who had hated him back in the village. Those mean and spiteful peasants who had never so much as tossed a crumb at him and his mother as they had starved in their hut.

Master William had rescued him from the blacksmith — a man he'd mistaken for a friend. They'd sat round the same table in the Golgotha Tavern and yet the burly brute was prepared to destroy the boy's hand with a blazing-hot iron at a cursory signal from the Earl.

I can't trust anyone. Only kind Master William who rescued me.

Nicholas sat astride a mule that the Templar knight had bought for him. "One day you'll ride a proper horse but not yet," William told the boy. Nicholas didn't mind — he was still amazed at the generosity of the Templar. However, while his affection for the knight grew so too did his suspicion towards the turcopole. It was a shame they had to tolerate his company. Nicholas secretly hoped that soon they'd be able to get rid of him.

As they had approached the city of Bordeaux, one side of Nicholas' face swelled up. Nicholas tried to keep the pain a secret. He knew what the blacksmiths did with their pliers; there was always a good turnout in Witham to watch a tooth pulling. Nobody was going near his teeth! He'd say nothing and just pray to Saint Apollonia for a cure. She'd look after him.

However, Pathros had noticed the boy's worsening condition. Dismounting suddenly, he pulled Nicholas off his mule, threw him to the ground and forced open his mouth. The element of surprise was vital when extracting the teeth of a young, feisty and rather dim Frank. The boy lashed out like a wild beast but with Pathros kneeling on his arms, his resistance was in vain.

The turcopole applied some poppy paste to the infected gum but Nicholas refused to gargle on a mixture of brine and crushed henbane root to numb the mouth. So be it, Pathros thought with malicious glee, so much more painful for the little Frankish thief.

Barely able to conceal a somewhat malicious grin, Pathros produced a pair of pliers, one of several medical instruments he'd acquired in the souks of Syria. Plenty of screaming and cursing ensued as he got to work. After some yanking, Pathros flourished the blackened tooth in the jaws of the pliers.

"You are now cured."

"You bastard!"

As the boy hollered his abuse, Pathros couldn't help but notice the woeful state of his ears: they were full to the brim with wax. No wonder he seemed so stupid all the time, he couldn't hear what was being said. Determined to clean them, Pathros produced a small metal pipette from his bag and squirted some droplets of horse nettle infusion into Nicholas' ears before wiping them out with a rag.

I hope to God I do not catch his leprosy, looking after him.

"Heathen bastard!"

"You are most disrespectful," Pathros pretended to be offended.

"Saracen dog!" Nicholas continued.

The Golgotha Tavern had been a good place to pick up insults.

From Bordeaux, the three travellers had spent countless days, possibly even weeks, passing through the land of Gascony, whose Occitan dialect steadily gave way to the Basque language of the mountainous Pyrenees. They'd have to cross this great ridge before beginning their journey across the vast Iberian plain to the new kingdom of Portugal. But as they neared the forbidding peaks of the Pyrenees, the last few Gascons they met warned against going any further.

"It's the route taken by pilgrims on their way to the shrine of Saint James the Apostle at Santiago de Compostela," one priest informed them, "but many never make it. Those mountains are full of bandits and murderers. Many of them are Basques, who hire themselves out as guides then slit their throats during the night. If they make it across to the other side, then they're put to death in a most fearful manner by the Iberian Muslims. I'd stay here. Or go home!"

"Over there" – a Gascon innkeeper pointed to the Pyrenees – "they eat like hogs and bark like dogs. Don't close your eyes in that man's company" – he gestured to the Basque guide William had decided to hire in spite of the warnings – "not even for a second."

Hours later those words echoed in the knight's head as they trotted in pitch dark along a treacherous mountain path with a vertiginous drop to one side. The stillness was interrupted by the sound of a rock fall. The occasional heap of rags only added to their unease. These were the stolen and discarded clothes of dead pilgrims.

Nicholas didn't like the look of Izani, their Basque guide.

More evil-looking than that Pathros!

The man's hair was coated with some foul-smelling oil, his green eyes shone eerily in the starlight and his mouth was an unpleasant thin line. Never smiles or blinks, Nicholas thought. He wasn't to be trusted and Nicholas resolved not to sleep one wink until they had exited these mountains.

Pathros sank his teeth into some salted fish and baby squids, all of which proved impossible to chew. It was hard to believe there were a people who ate even worse than the English, he thought. Forlornly, the turcopole cast a glance at the lakes so far below, which the Gascons said teemed with trout. Glancing at Nicholas, he spied the lad chewing on a piece of smoked ham.

"Where did you get that from?"

"Found it."

"You have been stealing again."

"Have not. I found it. Suppose you want some."

Pathros regarded the piece of dried squid in his hand.

"No." He forced the inedible morsel into his mouth, "I do not want or need your food."

William observed Izani closely. The Basque sat tall and lean and silent, bolt upright in his saddle, quietly registering every sight and sound in the dark mountain valleys. Around his neck was a curved horn on a metal chain and he clasped two small javelin-like weapons called auconas firmly in his left hand.

Would he kill us with those little spears if we dared to sleep?

It was going to take a good three days or more to negotiate this endlessly hilly terrain. In the distance an owl hooted. Then Izani did the oddest thing. William was startled as he suddenly mimicked the owl sound.

"Why did you do that?" William asked in French.

Izani did not respond but in the middle distance, another hoot sounded.

"Who are you conversing with?" the knight persisted, now reaching for his sword.

These were no owls but Basques communicating with each other.

The Gascons were right — they're going to kill us!

These mountain people had a fearsome reputation, having never been tamed by Roman, Goth or Saracen. Izani's ancestors had even killed the legendary Roland, the greatest ever knight, immortalised by troubadours. But they wouldn't kill William de Mandeville quite so easily.

The Templar removed his sword and swung round to face the guide, placing the blade tip under Izani's chin. The Basque raised his head but showed no fear or any feeling at all.

"Who is out there?" the knight demanded.

A more distant owl hoot could be heard far off in the distance, insisting on a reply. Izani's green eyes flashed at William and his right hand moved towards the horn around his neck.

"Don't touch it!" William shouted. "You're not going to murder us. Because in a second, I'll detach your head from your body! And I'll dispose of your friends too. Now answer my question. Who's out there?"

Izani dropped his hand.

"I must answer them," he said in a heavily accented French.

"Why?" William asked.

"You are being followed. Strangers. We do not know who these people are, but they are looking for you. They are hunting you like animals."

William dropped his sword. The bounty hunters sent by his brother had followed them all the way down to the Pyrenees. He thought they'd shaken them off at Clairvaux. But clearly not!

William nodded at Izani, who resumed his nocturnal hoots.

"They are almost here – on the path above us. We must hide."

As if on a cue, an unwelcome sound echoed through the valley. It chilled William to the bone. A tuneless and bawdy song belted out by the gruff voice of Hunrith the Gong Farmer broke the stillness of the night. Pathros had last heard it at Clairvaux.

"When that maiden caressed me
I swear she undressed me
Now I has the pox ... the pox ... the pox
A burning ... a burning
For I'm never learning
To leave them fair maidens alone ..."

The sound grew ever nearer. Nicholas shuddered as he heard the clip-clop of hooves and the jingling of stirrups and reins. William and Pathros were as immobile as the trees and rocks around them.

"Hide!" William ordered Nicholas.

"Let me challenge them from the front," Pathros whispered.

William agreed. The turcopole bounded down the hillside with the agility of a young deer fleeing its predators. Soon he was on a lower stretch of path, where he'd wait for their would-be assailants.

"And you?" the Templar asked the guide.

"This is your fight – it's nothing to do with me."

With that, Izani rode off into the trees. That was the way of his people, swift to attack anybody who threatened their independence but unwilling to become involved in other people's wars.

William dismounted and took up a concealed position with his sword still drawn and held firmly, ready for combat. He briefly caught sight of Nicholas cowering in the undergrowth and gave the boy a reassuring wink. Nicholas smiled back weakly and hurriedly scoffed the rest of the smoked ham he'd stolen from the Gascon innkeeper. It might be his last meal after all.

The bounty hunters conferred among themselves hurriedly as they found two horses and a mule blocking their path. They glanced around to see where the riders had gone and then, hoping the travellers might be sleeping nearby, they hushed each other and rode slowly on, expecting to chance on the dozing trio at any moment.

"Where are those dogs?" one man hissed.

Nicholas clasped one hand to his mouth as he recognised the voice and saw the face picked out in the moonlight: it was John the Tanner from the Golgotha. And behind him was Aylmer the Blacksmith. Not surprisingly, Aylmer had the finest weapons as he'd crafted them himself. Next to him was Hunrith, but Nicholas didn't know him by name. He was a serf who lived and worked in Pleshey Castle and was rarely seen in the village.

His first impulse was to cry out and claim John and Aylmer as drinking friends, but then he remembered again how Aylmer had been prepared to reduce his hand to a fleshy clump with the spitting hot iron bar. A real friend wouldn't do that, Nicholas thought.

I thought they were my friends but they weren't. Well, I'll show them now! Master William will run them through with his sword.

"Where's that Saracen cur?" Hunrith grumbled.

Pathros leapt from his hiding place into their path, holding his bow taut with an arrow carefully aimed.

"I am here."

With swift calm, he unleashed the barbed projectile at John the Tanner. The arrow embedded itself in his chest with a dull thud and the serrated tip shredded his muscle and lung. John fell from his horse, slamming onto the ground below. Aylmer the Blacksmith quickly glanced at his hefty comrade gasping for air like a fish out of water then turned to the turcopole.

"No quarrel with you, Saracen. Your master is who we want! Stay out of this and you can be on your way. Back to wherever you came from."

"I am not a Saracen," Pathros responded calmly, knocking another arrow onto his bow.

"Turkish dog!" Aylmer dropped all pretence of politeness. This silver-tongued Easterner deserved to have his brains dashed out. The blacksmith raised the mace fashioned at his forge in Witham. He'd rip this insolent Saracen to pieces.

Digging in his spurs, Aylmer made for Pathros.

"Prepare to die, Saracen!"

Pathros tried to move but his boots were stuck in the mud. He caught sight of the vicious instrument in Aylmer's hands. One blow from such a weapon would kill him outright.

Ditching his bow, Pathros drew his scimitar from its scabbard with a lightning flash. He barely had time to raise it before Aylmer swiped the mace towards his face. The curved blade of the turcopole's scimitar carved a bloody line across his attacker's forearm.

"Jesus!"

Aylmer shrieked in unspeakable agony. The tendons in his right arm were severed, leaving his right hand hanging uselessly from his wrist. Seeing his two comrades unable to fight, Hunrith decided to escape as William bounded towards him on foot. The Templar had a murderous look on his face. Capturing him was clearly not to be so easy as the bounty hunters had hoped.

Hunrith fled with Aylmer galloping behind, holding onto his now useless arm. His mace with its many hooks and studs lay in the mud. A few feet away, John the Tanner writhed on the ground. His breath had been reduced to an unpleasant gurgle as his lungs filled with blood. Nicholas knelt by his face.

"We could have fought together, you and me. Just like you did with Sancho the Hunchback. We'd have killed loads of them Saracens." The boy watched John struggling to live. "Why'd you do this? Chase us to kill us. I thought you were a good man and …"

The bounty hunter shook his head.

"You babble too much, young leper thief ... what do you know about goodness?"

"More than you," Nicholas flushed with anger. "Better than you, I am."

William gently nudged the boy to one side.

"Did my brother send you? Is this Edward's doing?"

John's mouth opened. At first William thought he was catching his breath but then he cackled, a final malicious laugh that filled his mouth with blood. His last words would wound the Templar. That at least was some comfort as he departed this world.

"Brother?" he gurgled.

"Yes, my brother. He sent you, did he not?"

William bent low to hear the response he spat out venomously.

"Not ... your ... brother. Your *mother*!"

Chapter 26

A VILLAGE ON THE IBERIAN PLAIN

"Run ... the Almohads!"

A bearded farmer bolted down the main path in the village, screaming. The satanic creatures weren't far behind him.

"They are coming! The Almohads!"

Suddenly, he snapped upright, his eyes looking heavenwards, and fell to the ground with blood pouring from the back of his head. His mounted assailant calmly reloaded his catapult and took aim at another of the villagers.

The crudely plastered houses of the village huddled around a dilapidated mosque, which had the most cursory attempt at a minaret. Next to it was an even smaller church and in a room above the only baker in the village was a tiny synagogue for the two Jewish families that lived in this isolated settlement.

All around these modest dwellings stretched the vast plain; it afforded no escape, shelter or hiding place. The villagers had no time to bring the shutters down over their shops or gather their livestock as their persecutors descended on them.

"*Allahu Akbar!*"

The villagers of all faiths fled together along the main path leading south but suddenly changed direction like a frightened herd as another group of riders emerged from that direction. Men sheltered their women and children under their arms. Some kicked down the doors of their neighbours' houses vainly hoping the Almohads wouldn't spot them.

"*Allahu Akbar!*"

Shards of pottery exploded in the air as the Almohads smashed the jugs, ewers and amphorae hanging up in rows. Many were filled with the wine, which enraged these men of the book yet further. In a voice parched from abstinence and heat, one of the zealots cried out.

"Drunks! Apostates! Sinners! There is a devil in every berry of the grape!"

Seeing his precious produce destroyed, a cowering Andalusian merchant stretched out his hands, imploring the Almohad to stop.

"Please ... this is all I have ..."

But the man on horseback looked down at the false Muslim with eyes of hate.

He thinks he is a Muslim but drinks like a dhimmi. He lies and cheats his way through life with this trade in alcohol.

The Almohad, like all of his kind from the deserts of Africa, phrased his thoughts in Qur'anic verses and the hadiths or sayings of the Prophet. Today this sinful man pleading before him would drink scalded water like a camel and eat of the thorn tree but never satisfy his thirst or hunger. And he'd live like this for an eternity in the place where the sinful are condemned to dwell for all time!

"Please ... you can have anything. Take whatever——"

Without bothering to reply, the Almohad sliced the merchant's head open like a watermelon. The split skull slid off his sharp and polished scimitar.

Sobbing uncontrollably, the dead man's wife started towards his bloodied body. Disgusted, the Almohad roared:

"Cover yourself!"

Fearing for her own life, she quickly pulled her head veil across her face and stepped back into the darkness of the family home. The Almohad leader yelled to his fellow zealots to round up the surviving apostates, Christians and Jews.

"Take them to the water trough over there!"

They trembled like fearful animals before the butcher's knife. The Almohad leader, clad like a prophet from head to toe in robes of deepest black, addressed them all.

"Woe to you. This is your day of doom. A day of anguish for all non-believers." He rode up and down before the condemned. "Maybe you think a magician or a wizard will appear to save you?" He shook his head in answer to his own question. "This is the hour of parting when agony is heaped on agony and affliction on affliction. Breathe the air of this land one last time and prepare yourselves."

Then at his signal the transgressors were wiped out.

Chapter 27

THE KINGDOM OF CASTILE

The landscape around them had changed dramatically in the days since they had left the Pyrenees. A gently rippling plateau stretched out as far as the eye could see, replacing the green and soggy terrain of the Basques. The kingdom of Navarre sweltered under a relentless heat. The further south the trio went, the more tedious they found the mixture of sun-scorched yellows and browns punctuated by anaemic strips of scraggy trees that divided peasant holdings.

Every so often, they would encounter a band of pilgrims on their way to pray at the tomb of Saint James the Apostle. Many had left from Paris or Cologne and had ridden or even walked for months. They had scallop shell badges on their chests, wore wide-brimmed hats to shelter from the sun and carried long staves to ease the suffering of their feet.

They recounted the story of how many centuries ago the Bishop of Iria Flavia, an old Roman town in the northwest of Iberia, had found the sarcophagus of the apostle in a field, having been guided to the spot by heavenly music. This had happened when the Christians had been persecuted into submission all over Iberia by Muslim invaders.

In that darkest hour, the apostle came to save us, the pilgrims claimed. He appeared on horseback in battle and split so many Moorish heads they'd fled like the dogs they are south of the rivers Duero and Ebro, where they cowered to this day.

Pathros listened to this ignorant talk in astonishment, though even he had to concede that the Moors were nowhere to be seen. Where they once ruled in the northernmost regions of Iberia, Christianity had been restored. But the churches being built by the victors looked more like fortresses than places of worship. It was as if the monks and priests weren't wholly convinced that the emirs and caliphs had given up their claim to these lands.

They crossed the River Ebro. Across the old Roman bridge was the kingdom of Castile. It had taken two weeks to get through Navarre and Castile yet this scorched plateau seemed never-ending. How many weeks or months would it take to reach the kingdom of the Portuguese?

Pathros suddenly stopped.

"What's the matter?" William asked him.

"Something is wrong, my friend," he replied, placing his hand to his brow and peering over the shimmering plain to the far horizon.

"Something's always the matter," William smiled knowingly at Nicholas.

"Is he afraid of the bridge?" Nicholas asked, wide-eyed. "They say creatures live under bridges that grab on to you and drag you down into a watery grave."

"No," Pathros sighed, "I am not afraid of the bridge. Look out there!"

William and Nicholas stared intently out over the yellow mass of bleached corn and dusty roads punctuated by the occasional village that rose up from the plain like a termite hill. The shimmering heat obscured the horizon but gradually they made out what Pathros had already spotted. It was like a gigantic ink stain! The ominous blackness spread out over a hillside and moved towards the river.

"Like a swarm of bees!" Nicholas cried out. "What are they, Master William?"

"I'm not sure."

"If they are bees, we should ride away fast! I knew somebody in the village got stung bad by bees. Took her days to die, all swelled up and horrible."

"They are not bees," Pathros snapped. "They are people."

The trio remained in place, transfixed by this great dark movement across the plain. As it grew closer, the distant humming became a deafening wave of lamentation, a sea of sobs and cries. Thousands of carts and wagons rumbled along pulled by oxen and horses laden high with the belongings of families. At the front, a lone Templar in his white mantle led the way. He was fully bearded and his complexion was weather-beaten but he held his lance and shield high as all around him bowed their heads and wept.

As the huge throng edged closer, William rode out to meet his fellow brother.

"God be with you," he said in French, surveying the huge mass of people.

"I am not sure he is," the Templar replied in the same language, but with a Castilian accent.

"How so?"

"Are you blind?"

The other man might have been middle-aged but the rigours of his journey had sapped the vitality out of him. His cheeks were sunken and his eyes surrounded by black rings of tiredness. He told William how they had trudged for weeks from Toledo and the Templar preceptory at Calatrava. They had barely stopped. Nobody had wanted to stop and sleep, not after what they had seen.

"What are you running from?" William asked.

"You don't know?" The Castilian Templar was incredulous. "Behind us, brother, comes a locust storm that is always hungry. A host of black wolves that attacks without any mercy! The Almohads!" He paused at the very mention of the words. "They massacred my brothers at Calatrava and let me go so I could warn the world not to resist them." He looked at the refugee army he was directing. "It was my duty to rescue all these people. After all, brother, wasn't that why we were called into existence? To help the weak!"

He was right: nine brave knights sworn to protect pilgrims from marauding bandits and Saracens had indeed formed the Knights Templar decades before.

Nearby, Pathros was talking to a figure in a funnel-shaped hat and red cloak clasping a golden seven-branched candelabrum to his chest.

"We had synagogues in Toledo and lived in peace with our neighbours," he told the turcopole. "Until they came! Devils from Africa! They killed us – and their own people. I tell you, I've never seen such a lust for blood. I took my young boy here" – he put his arm round his son – "and my wife and we fled. There is nothing for us back there."

"Who are these assassins?" Pathros asked.

The man's son answered with surprising confidence: he could only have been ten or eleven years old.

"Almohads. They have come to overthrow the taifas." Pathros looked confused. The boy continued: "You are clearly not from these lands. I can see that from your armour."

His father beamed. "Clever boy, he knows so much."

The lad pretended not to hear the compliment and continued as if reciting a book he'd recently read on the subject.

"Once the Muslims were united under one Caliph in Cordoba. You have probably never heard of that city, it is magnificent. They say it is the biggest city in the world. But the last Caliph was overthrown and the caliphate was divided among many taifas. The Almohads say they are corrupt and godless. They wish to murder all of them and unite Islam again in Iberia."

"And you?" Pathros asked. "The Jews?"

The father shrugged.

"They want to murder us too."

"They want purity," his son interjected, "they want one faith and one caliphate. Then they will take back all the lands they have lost to the Christians. This is Dar Jihad. I don't suppose you know what that means."

"I know," Pathros said, amused by the precocious boy's learning and wishing he were their travelling companion instead of the thieving ignoramus they had picked up in Witham. The child reminded Pathros of his own young self. "The Dar Jihad means this land is where all the faithful are commanded to come and make war against the infidel."

"And you see that?" The boy pointed at a jagged ridge of mountains in the distance. "They used to call that the Tugur – the teeth. It was supposed to divide the Christian kingdoms from the caliphate. But the Almohads do not respect this. They do not recognise any boundary when serving their God. You will see that soon enough."

"You are a clever boy." Pathros extended his hand in friendship. "What is your name?"

"My family call me Moshe Ben Maimon. When I had Moorish friends …" For the first time the high, confident voice faltered and he bit his lip to hide his hurt. "… they called me Musa Ibn Maimun. But I have no friends among them now. Our Christian neighbours called me Maimonides. You may choose whichever you like – they are just names."

"You look like a Maimonides." Pathros nodded at the child and turned to leave. "I am sure you will be a great man when you grow up."

Nicholas had meanwhile been circulating among the refugees and looking in amazed greed at the possessions piled high on the carts: silks, floor and wall coverings, great chests, finely made tables, silverware, ornaments, dresses and cloaks. These had been prosperous people in Toledo. To Nicholas, they still looked prosperous.

With imploring eyes and rubbing his tummy, he extended a hand out and begged for any food that was going. Unable to speak Castilian or Arabic, or even Latin or French, he simply relied on his own charms, and mime, to win over the adults around him.

"Bad men" – he pointed towards William and Pathros – "never give me anything to eat."

A rotund Christian lady from Toledo patted him on the head. She told him he could journey with them but Nicholas had no idea what she was saying. He simply grinned, nodded and held out his hand in her direction. She obliged with a small piece of bread, which he crammed into his mouth.

William was taking leave of his brother Templar.

"Where are you taking all these people?"

"I don't know," the Castilian Templar shrugged, "we'll just keep walking till we find somewhere far from the Almohads. There is nothing else we can do."

Chapter 28

KINGDOM OF CASTILE

"You use a sword like this." William wielded the heavy steel above his head then brought it down on an imaginary enemy. "And if you drop your sword, you grab your mace." He took the studded Turkish mace from his belt and with both hands swung it at the invisible foe. "And if you drop that, you still have your dagger, or your shield to slam in his face."

"What if you got no weapons?" Nicholas asked.

William raised his fists.

"Use these!" He grimaced as some very violent imagery crossed his mind. "I've even seen men tear into their opponents' flesh with their own teeth. Some knights file them down to spikes so they can draw blood that much easier." He smiled, baring healthy white teeth. "Not something I've ever had to do."

"That boy's teeth would fall to pieces if he tried," Pathros harrumphed.

Handing Nicholas a wooden stave, William began teaching him some sword thrusts and parries, which the Templar knight suspected he might need to know in the quest that lay ahead. So preoccupied were they that both jolted with surprise as a large group of Benedictines rode towards them.

At the centre of this group of monks on horseback was an enclosed carriage with only two tiny windows to admit daylight. As it passed, a shutter opened and a disdainful face peered out, seemingly an abbot.

He was dressed in fine vestments, white gloves and a jewelled episcopal ring. In a split second, the rich cleric closed the shutter. Behind him came mules groaning under the weight of sacks. The whole party seemed to be moving as fast as it could.

As the afternoon wore on, the knight reached beneath his mantle and pulled out a short, rectangular piece of cloth that was placed above his heart. An identical piece of cloth hung over his back. The devotional scapular bore woven images of the Virgin Mary and child.

A mother who loved her son! Unlike my mother, who would plot to kill me.

He placed the scapular back under his mantle.

Once more, Pathros suddenly halted.

"Now what are you seeing?" William asked, more than a little exasperated.

The turcopole had caught sight of something in the distance – like a black wisp hovering above the ground. There it was again – a curious ebony shape, and then another one.

"I am cursed by good eyesight."

"Are you sure there's anything there?" The knight strained to see. William didn't like to admit that the horizon was always a slight blur to him whereas Pathros had the eyes of a hawk. "What is it?"

Pathros turned to William.

"The devils are coming, my friend."

The crow-like forms became steadily more visible. Bright sunlight made the gold leaf on the handles of their scimitars and their horse bridles glint and flash. Tightly bound turbans covered their heads and faces, leaving only a slit for their eyes.

Muffled words in the Berber language drifted towards the trio; even from this distance the tone seemed ominous. There were four warriors in black from head to toe. Pathros knew what he was looking at.

Almohads!

Nicholas watched in blind terror as they moved closer.

"Can we talk to them, Master William, and be on our ways?" The boy wasn't ready for a fight to the death yet. Under the burning heat he felt weak and woozy. He didn't have the strength in his arm to battle grown men. "I reckon if we just ride past them fast nothing bad will happen ..."

William took his mace and handed it to Nicholas. It felt heavy. The weapon slipped a little in his palms, which were sweaty with fear.

"Remember what I taught you," the knight said calmly to their young companion. "Use this well and, if all else fails, use your feet, your hands and … yes, use your teeth. Never stop fighting, not even for a moment."

As the knight turned to face the Almohads, Nicholas trembled.

Through misty eyes, he could see King Death circling him on his bony charger, a skeleton in a moth-eaten cape and crown waiting to tap the boy with his finger. All around this ghastly apparition a foul smoke arose and King Death leered at the boy expectantly. This phantom was incapable of mercy. A tireless reaper of souls that cut short lives with pestilence and war – the harbinger of desolation and terror.

When he touches me, I'll drop down into hell.

Nicholas imagined he could still see the figure drawing closer. If only I'd been good, even for one day. Taking Jake's bread – that alone will send me to the Devil. Too late to repent now! I'm done for.

Pathros momentarily took pity on the boy.

"The mace is a crude and simple weapon. You should have no problem using it."

The four Almohad fighters halted. Their eyes fixed on the white mantle of the Templar: the eight-pointed scarlet cross above William's heart was the badge of the worst kind of infidel. Nothing more needed to be said. Without another word exchanged between them, they drew their scimitars from their scabbards. But the Templar was ready for them.

Determined to strike the first blow, William charged. He swung his heavy sword high over his head as if it was light as a feather and sliced through the shoulder of one of the Almohad. The heavy steel cut through him, almost effortlessly, till it sliced his heart wide open. Blood gushed like a torrent from the cavernous wound. With his mantle drenched in scarlet, William was forced to release his foot from his stirrup, place it on the dead man's chest and push the Almohad off the blade.

Another Almohad turned to slash at William with his scimitar but finding himself caught between the Templar knight and another of his fellow fighters, he was unable to hack at him. William speedily circled his horse round to face this new opponent. The two clashed swords repeatedly as Pathros attacked the third Almohad, who struggled to keep up his guard against the Syrian's ferocious onslaught.

The fourth fighter caught sight of an easier target. A petrified Nicholas tried to turn his mule and flee, but the obstinate animal flung him to the ground and then cantered off, wanting nothing more to do with this skirmish. The Almohad dismounted and pulled a dagger from his belt. He seized Nicholas by a clump of his hair and made to slit his throat.

The boy saw the emerald-encrusted dagger handle move towards him, its blade glinting in the sun. But he still had the mace in his hands. With all the power in his body, he swung it upwards. He could see nothing but sensed the sharp studs embed and then rip through flesh. Grabbing the handle firmly, he pulled it down. There was a tearing sound and the grip on his hair loosened.

Nicholas jumped to his feet.

That'll teach you to fight me!

The Almohad clutched his face with both hands, trying to keep two bloodied slabs of flesh together: the boy had cut his face in two. From the gaping rift, blood poured down both his arms. He fell to the ground, writhing in agony. Nicholas wasted no time and brought the mace crashing down on his skull. Then he repeated the action in a frenzy till he found himself laughing as the weapon pulverised the man's head.

"You'd have done the same to me!" The mace smashed the man's lower jaw. "How do you like that then?"

Before he could deliver another blow, Nicholas found his wrist in a vice-like grip.

"Drop it! *Now!*"

He turned to find William standing over him.

"I did my best, Master William. I killed him good and proper."

"You did very well." The knight retrieved his gore-covered mace and examined the mess. "And you say you've never killed a man?"

"Never, sir. Killed a horse once. Reeve paid me to do it. Broken its leg in a ditch and he didn't know to do. So I bashed its head in."

"But never a man?"

"No."

William was impressed.

"Well, this one made a mistake thinking you'd be an easy opponent."

The Templar regarded the bloody remains of the four Almohad fighters littering the road.

"It seems they are not so invincible, my friend," Pathros said.

The Templar resisted such hubris.

"I think we were lucky this time."

Part 3

THE KINGDOM OF THE PORTUGUESE

Chapter 29

MOGADOURO,
THE REGION CALLED 'TRAS-OS-MONTES'
KINGDOM OF PORTUGAL

Three months had elapsed since they had left England. William, Pathros and Nicholas had advanced far into southern Europe. The summer heat beat down with a ferocious intensity during the day so the trio chose to ride in the cooler dark of night. It was under a starry sky that they slipped into the kingdom of the Portuguese.

Pilgrims on their way to the great shrine of Saint James the Apostle at Santiago had told William that when the land rose upwards, the plateau disappeared and great boulders appeared everywhere as if hurled by a demented giant, then he'd be in Portugal.

Rising up ominously from a jumble of stones were the bleakly defiant walls of the Templar preceptory at Mogadouro. The full moon and stars illuminated the uninviting keep. It looked completely deserted. This wasn't as they had expected. Templars in neighbouring Castile had told William that Mogadouro was a bustling Templar community of knights and serjeants, about fifty strong. But there was no sign of life.

"Don't like this place," Nicholas whined, "we should turn away while we can."

"It's alright," William calmed him, "there's nothing to fear. Though it would be nice to see some signs of life."

"Devil lives here," Nicholas continued, "or maybe Jack O'Lantern."

Nicholas was particularly frightened of Jack O'Lantern. He was an angry old curmudgeon condemned by the Lord to roam the earth with a lamp made from a hollowed-out turnip. Heaven wouldn't have him because he was too miserly and hell barred his way for playing tricks on the Devil.

The numb pain Nicholas had begun to feel in his fingers intensified at the thought of Jack and the things he might do to them.

This is one of his big houses — we should leave before he gets us.

"Master William — I beg of you we should ride fast from here. He's a bastard once he gets his claws into you."

"Who is?" Pathros enquired disdainfully.

"Jack O'Lantern," Nicholas snapped back, "or I suppose he doesn't exist where you come from."

"No, he does not," the turcopole rolled his eyes, "another of your Frankish superstitions."

"Pathros is right, Nicholas." William patted the boy on the head. "There's no evil here. The night makes this preceptory look like a bad place, that's all. But we'll go inside. You'll see there's nothing to be frightened of."

They needed to rest. There was a rickety wooden staircase that barely clung to the stonework of the tower. William placed a foot on it and the whole structure seemed to quiver. But there was no option except to climb.

The decaying steps led to a small arched entrance halfway up the wall and the knight pressed on, with Pathros and Nicholas following. With some relief, William got to the door that was so rotten he wondered if it would disintegrate at his mere touch. He pushed and it opened grudgingly, scraping the stone floor within.

The three travellers walked into a room so thick with darkness, it choked. Worse still was the suffocating stench that hit the backs of their throats and had the trio clasping at their faces. William had smelt nothing like this since he trudged past rotting corpses in the deserts of Outremer. Pathros hadn't believed that anything could reek worse than Nicholas, but this topped it.

There was the sound of something shuffling. They froze.

"Jack O'Lantern is in here!" Nicholas clutched onto William's mantle.

Sure enough, there was the unmistakable sound of breathing. The Templar placed his hand upon the pommel of his sword and prepared to strike down any assailant that was hiding within. Pathros strained to see but his eyes refused to acclimatise to the dark.

"Who are you?" William yelled out.

"The preceptor of Mogadouro," came an answer in Latin.

"Where are the other brother knights?" William asked in the same language.

"They have gone to fight in *nullis diocesis*."

"Where is that?"

"It is a land where there is no ruler – no king, no prince, no bishop. It is a savage and lawless realm between the Christian north and the worshippers of Mohammed in the South. One day a village there is under our control and the next, it is under the Moors." The crackled voice paused and the preceptor drank to quench his thirst. Then he chuckled. "My brothers found life here a little ... how should I say? Boring. Those who have survived Moorish scimitars might be yearning for the dullness they left behind. *Nullis diocesis* is a land of death and hunger."

"Is that where I'll find Dom Afonso Henriques?"

"What business do you have with our king?"

William wondered for a moment if he should share the purpose of his quest with a stranger – then took the plunge.

"I seek the True Cross, the Lignum Crucis."

The preceptor's feet scraped the ground as if this imperceptible figure was suddenly ill at ease. He drank again, this time in bigger gulps. Then drummed his fingers on top of a table.

"Why here?"

"Because here is where it is. Bernard of Clairvaux himself has assured me it is in Al-Andalus. The Moors," William used the name given to the Saracens in this part of the world, "have it and hope its power will ward off our attacks on them. I need ... I must rescue it and restore it to its rightful place."

"Its rightful place?"

"Edessa ... Jerusalem ... the Holy Land. I must get it back to Outremer."

"You are on a fool's errand then," the preceptor responded, "there is no True Cross in Al-Andalus. Bernard is misinformed. He is far from here and he has been told baseless stories. Now go … you can sleep in the stables. I am tired. I need some sleep."

Disheartened at these words, William made his way back down the steps. In the morning, he'd question the preceptor further. There was no way Bernard was wrong; he couldn't be! The saintly protector of the Knights Templar knew the whereabouts of the cross and he even had the man who'd stolen it in his custody.

So why is this preceptor lying?

Why was the entire senior leadership of the Order misleading its own knights? There was the Grand Master in Jerusalem spiriting the cross away to Edessa without telling Templars like William. Hugh of Argentine had claimed it was safe when it patently wasn't. And now this malodorous Portuguese preceptor was proving to be just as mendacious.

William turned to Pathros.

"I'm going to stop taking the elixirs. From now on, in this land of Portugal, I'll need to keep a clear head. It's clear we're going to be lied to all the way in this quest so I need to have my wits about me. Need to see who's telling the truth and who isn't."

The ramshackle stable near the preceptory keep turned out to be a very uninviting resting place. There was no straw on the ground, just churned-up mud. The trio abandoned the idea of sleep. As it was, they were distracted by the sound of a strange melody wafting towards them. Almost as if hypnotised, they rode off towards the noise.

Skirting the base of a hill, they saw a sparkling vision in the valley: torches moving in all directions; women were singing in high-pitched voices, there were drums and a strange whining music.

As William, Pathros and Nicholas drew nearer, they made out a great crowd of villagers. Many of them were wearing gigantic costumes of straw, causing them to resemble haystacks. They twirled and jumped as if possessed, moving to the incessant sound of an Arabic bagpipe, a gaily coloured wooden instrument played at hip level, connected to a leather bag under the player's arm which blew air into the finger pipe.

The droning cacophony pounded inside William's head but he was determined not to ask Pathros for one of his elixirs. However, the music was making him feel light-headed. Trying to make sense of what was going on, he looked for saintly effigies or statues of the Virgin but there were none. This festival didn't seem to mark a religious occasion at all.

William's eyes flickered as the glowing torches sailed past him.

Maybe I should have an elixir. I'm still weak. I don't like what I'm seeing.

The torches blurred yellow, red and orange hues. The shimmering heat seemed to scorch his face.

I must leave. I should never have come here. Something is happening to me!

The crackling of burning wood transported the Templar back to Outremer. Suddenly he imagined a rebel village being sent up in flames. Whirls of smoke everywhere and the sobbing pleas of womenfolk in Aramaic as their husbands and sons were rounded up. Baking kilns were smashed and animal pens broken open. A Saracen youth who'd yelled obscenities at the attacking crusaders lay lifeless on the ground. His mother stared up at William and cursed him in a harsh desert tongue.

May the Devil never leave you!

It's not my fault, William had thought. Your men attacked and robbed a group of pilgrims. They were defenceless. We're teaching you a lesson. You've got to understand.

Suddenly, he jolted with a start as Nicholas' voice rang in his ears.

"It's like Michaelmas back home! Can we join them?"

"No, it's better we don't." William advised. "We don't know what they're celebrating."

The turcopole agreed. This festivity was like nothing he'd ever seen.

"Whatever this is, my friend," Pathros opined, "I don't think it's Christian or Muslim. It is some form of ancient barbarism."

Children now joined the bizarre dance, dressed as wood nymphs, and behind them came a spectacle that took the trio's breath away. Creatures appeared, bounding around like apes, their arms flailing angrily. Their costumes were green, yellow and red and they made guttural grunting noises at the other villagers, who recoiled in horror if they came too near. Their faces could not be seen as they were covered in leather masks with the narrowest of slits for eyes and hooked noses like bills. As they cavorted, small cow bells tied all over their bodies jingled.

Suddenly, one of these hellish animals grabbed a young village girl and began beating the backs of her legs with a stick. William had seen enough and rode forward. Dismounting, he strode towards the colourful ape and struck him with full force. The leather mask flew off and revealed a child, barely the same age as Nicholas. Clearly on the verge of tears, he retrieved his leather mask and ran off.

"Why were you beating her?" William remonstrated. The music stopped. The villagers regarded the Templar with angry suspicion. "He was beating her legs! You all saw that but you did nothing." The young knight was now craving an elixir. His head was swimming. "I'm sorry that was just a child I hit, but he was striking a woman. I didn't know he was so young." William felt as if the world was closing in on him. "Are you even Christians? Can't you speak? What saint's day are you celebrating here? Somebody answer me!"

"We should leave, my friend." Pathros put a hand on William's shoulder but it was curtly shaken off.

"*No*! I'll get to the bottom of this."

Disobediently, the villagers resumed their strange frolics. The music began again, and then the dancing. The colourful apes and wood nymphs chased each other round the small stone houses and the village square. The haystacks twirled and seemed to float off the ground as William watched. His eyelids fluttered as the whining bagpipe sound stabbed at his senses.

"Stop this – all of you! Stand still. I command you! Why are you dressed as sprites and you people over there like dryads?" William staggered. "This isn't right. You're Christian people, not heathens. Stop this, all of you."

Pathros put his hand on William's shoulder as his friend clasped the stones of a wall to balance himself.

"Let us leave."

"*No!*" William shouted, pushing the turcopole away. From behind a water trough he could see one of the nymphs crouching and spying on him. "It's wrong. I must stop this, in God's name. I'm a Templar … I'm a Knight Templar … I must stop this."

From the well in the square, a hand now appeared at the rim as somebody or something crawled out from within. The villagers turned to watch as the figure painted entirely in green with strands of ivy wrapped around him emerged from the underworld.

He had come to rule his kingdom once more: the ancient god of the earth who must be appeased if he is to push the crops out of the ground. If he was angered for any reason, he'd pull the crops back down and famine would stalk the villages.

"They worship the Devil," William sobbed as he fell to his knees and held the hilt of his sword to his throbbing forehead. "I came to this land looking for the True Cross and I've found people worshipping the Devil!"

William prayed intently.

The Lord is my rock and my fortress, and my deliverer, my God, my strength, in whom I will trust, my buckler, and the horn of my salvation and my high tower.

The green man bounded into the middle of the haystacks and begun to spin around in the opposite direction, his arms folded across his chest, while the nymphs hailed his arrival with cheers and joyful chanting. William outstretched his arms like Christ on the crucifix and turned his face to the skies above.

"I will do your work here, Lord. I will save these people."

Nicholas didn't like seeing Master William behaving so strangely. What was happening? Pathros had seen this once before: in the Temple of Solomon when William had been held down by his fellow knights and the Augustinian canons had wanted to drill into his head to release the demonic power. But the knight had ordered his turcopole not to administer any more elixir and Pathros was dutifully obeying. Unbeknown to him, however, a small thieving hand was rummaging through his medicine bag.

As the green man accepted gifts of bread and meat from the villagers of Mogadouro, the music became ever louder and more discordant. William's face was full of the madness Pathros had witnessed in the infirmary in Jerusalem. The knight seemed fixated on the green man whom the villagers welcomed joyously.

"You're a false god!" William yelled.

But the green man ignored him.

William groaned as the scene before him became a nightmarish blur. He held his hands to his eyes as the chaos made his heart beat as hard as it had done during the fiercest clashes with the Saracen in Outremer. His mouth opened and closed as if he wanted to say something but the words wouldn't come. Then he whimpered:

"Stop this ... please, stop this."

As William looked up, the green man had his back to him, but as he span round once more, his head had transformed into something very familiar to the Templar. There amidst the straw men was Basilisk, laughing at him. Its great scaly jaws gaped wide and its fangs descended; its bloodshot eyes mocked the Templar's pretensions to be a holy warrior.

God the Father has forsaken you as he did me.

The ground seemed to shift under the Templar's feet as the entire square, commanded by Basilisk, began to revolve. Then a creature, like a giant spider, leapt onto William's back. It held his nose with its right hand and as his lips parted to breathe, Nicholas poured the elixir he'd taken from Pathros' bag down William's throat.

"That'll sort you out!" the boy thief shouted.

Chapter 30

TOMAR
NULLIUS DIOCESIS

The Benedictines of Tomar were making good their escape from nullius
diocesis.

"Faster!" the abbot screamed.

Every chalice, reliquary, monstrance and glittering casket had to be stuffed
into sacks and loaded onto the backs of mules. In all directions, the monks
scurried to retrieve their treasure and save their skins. The Moors were coming.
Not just the usual raiding party, this time it was a colossal mass of warriors – or
so the scouts had reported.

The abbot had heard about the Almohads. Every so often another wave of
zealots crashed out of Africa and into Iberia, trying to stiffen the backbone of
the caliphate. Their methods were always the same: executions, savage murders
and pillage.

I'm not waiting here to be killed by those fiends.

"Come on, faster! Or I'll leave you brothers behind."

Within the hour, the monks set out. As they crossed the small square at the
centre of Tomar with its pillory at the centre, they found themselves confronted
by some serfs. They were like walking husks. War had bred starvation and
famine; they no longer cared very much whether the Moors or the Templars
triumphed in this cursed part of the world.

"What do you want?" the abbot addressed the rabble.

"Father," one of them croaked, his voice broken by hunger, "where are you going?"

The villagers couldn't help noticing that the Benedictines were miraculously well fed. God had certainly favoured them. One woman looked at the skin hanging off her arms and contrasted it with the fine, if slightly flabby bodies of the monks, whose mules sweltered under their heavy load.

"Is that food?" a woman asked.

"None of your concern!" the abbot snapped. "Out of the way and let us pass!"

But the serfs stood impassively.

"You can't leave us," a boy whimpered.

If the monks were leaving, then it was a sure sign they were doomed. A woman pushed forward with a grey-skinned excuse for a baby in her arms, not destined to live another week.

"Please, Father," she begged, "something for the child. A loaf of bread or some dried beans we could cook."

The abbot was fed up now. What impudence!

"We have nothing to spare——"

He broke off in alarm as a thundering of hooves filled the air. Dear God, no, the abbot thought, we are to be slaughtered by the Moors. He heaved a giant sigh of relief as a group of Templar knights entered the square, like steel giants on horseback, their faces hidden by round helmets and only a slit of a visor to see through.

Great swords hung from the Templars' sides and their shields bore the scars of regular battles and skirmishes in nullius diocesis against the Moors. They seemed barely human as they approached. More like creatures from a fantastical realm.

The abbot was sure that Master Gualdim Pais was among them. He found the irascible Templar commander highly objectionable. His attitude to the Church was distinctly contemptuous. But he'd clear these serfs away and let the Benedictines leave.

"It is alright, my brothers," the abbot addressed his fellow monks, "we are safe now."

The Templar knights halted — about twenty of them, the abbot rapidly counted. They showed no sign of wilting in the searing heat, while the monks constantly mopped perspiration from their brows.

"Pax vobiscum," the abbot greeted them.

But the Templars said nothing. One cantered forward and removed his helmet. The abbot nodded, recognising the master.

"Brother Pais ..."

The Templar commander pointed with his mailed glove to the sacks weighing down the mules.

"You're leaving us, Father?"

The Benedictine abbot didn't like his tone of voice.

"We are defenceless, Master Gualdim — unlike you soldiers of Christ. As men of the cloth, we'll be killed when the infidel arrives. You know that. We must retreat somewhere safer. I am, after all, responsible for the safety of my brother monks—"

The woman with the baby interrupted him.

"They are taking food when we are starving."

"This is not food." The abbot gestured to the sacks. "It's our property."

Gualdim Pais regarded the serfs of Tomar and pitied them. They were the meek. Those who would one day inherit the earth, as the Lord had commanded. While these Benedictines were like the Pharisees who knew their gospels but not how to practise what they preached. Poverty was for others and not for them.

The Templar trotted round to the side of the wagon and drew his sword. With one determined slash, he cut through one of the sacks and a river of gold and silver coins poured onto the ground. The villagers stared down at them and saw the money of the enemy. Dinars and dirhams minted in Cordoba and Seville covered in Arabic script.

"That was given to us by the King of Leon," the abbot fumed.

"Money he extorted from the Moors," Pais responded.

"I know nothing of that."

"Oh come, Father, you know all about it," the Templar said, trotting round again to face the Benedictine. "I'd rather fight and vanquish the Moors than take their bribes to stay away from the battlefield."

"Master Pais." When would this upstart Templar allow him and his monks to leave? "We are, as you know, men of prayer and not swords."

"And the princes of Leon and Aragon and even our own king pay you generously to pray for their souls. That must be a lot of praying, Father."

The abbot began to feel very apprehensive. Was Pais a secret Cathar? Was he a heretic? He was certainly talking like one. Maybe being in *nullis diocesis* for so long had touched his mind.

"You're surely not denying the Church its share of the reward our brave leaders extract from those Moorish dogs?"

Pais looked at the dinars spread on the ground. They would never expel the Moors from Portugal so long as Christian priests were prepared to handle their gold poison. The Benedictines had benefited from Moorish bribes paid to Christian princes to encourage them to sheath their swords. These monks constructed their ornate and vainglorious abbeys with Moorish gold while the Templars were left to fight the source of their obscene wealth. He glanced at the dinars.

What dogs would accept this gold?

"You Benedictines would have taken thirty pieces of silver from Judas to build your abbeys."

"Outrageous!" The abbot blustered. "You let me pass! You hear me! I don't have to explain myself to any bastard here!"

Gualdim Pais urged his horse forward till he towered over the quivering monks. The abbot found himself staring into the horse's nostrils. When he got away, he assured himself, he'd report this whole incident to a church council. Pais would be tried for heresy. It would be his life's mission from now on to light the kindling under this rogue Templar's feet and watch his body burn. But at that moment, the abbot had to endure more insults.

"I have always despised you Cluniac whores." Pais spat on the ground before the abbot's feet. "You hide behind our shields and swords with your own daggers always primed for our backs. I spurn you. I spurn all of you Benedictines."

Then turning to the villagers, Pais cursed the avaricious monks.

"This wealth you see here was created by your hands, not by these fattened creatures. Every line and wrinkle on your worn faces is an ounce of gold in their treasury. You have sweated and toiled to make them rich. And now ... now, they would leave you to your fate."

The villagers grasped their crude farm tools in a way that disquieted the abbot. Their faces no longer showed deference to church authority but unbridled hatred. The other monks looked nervously at their abbot.

One of the serfs took off his cap and addressed Pais.

"Master, we need food, not gold. We've not eaten for days. We have nothing to put in our stews except grass. Our children are dying."

The woman with the baby pointed at the abbot's mule.

"Leave us that, Father."

"I will not!"

The abbot sat bolt upright in the saddle. He'd no intention of walking. Nor was his mule ending up in a peasant cooking pot.

Damned peasants — I hope they all starve! And their filthy broods!

Pais looked out to the horizon from where the Moors were coming. He was confident that no matter how great the force hurtling towards them, the Templars would repel it by God's grace.

"You need enough food to last you till Assumption Day," he informed the famine-stricken serfs. "By then we will have driven back the Moors."

"But we will be dead by then," the woman with the baby pleaded. "We are always forgotten. You fight your great battles. You win them. But while you do that our fields go unploughed. Our livestock die. And we all die. We cannot wait any longer, master. We must eat."

Gualdim Pais gazed at the scorching sun above. For a moment, he was certain he glimpsed an impression of the Holy Spirit upon its surface. A dove with wings outstretched. A sign that the global kingdom of virtue the Templars were destined to create would come to pass very soon.

The rule of corrupt monks and bishops was coming to an end and the Church would be exposed for the Babylon it truly was. Pais felt as if the Holy Spirit was entering into him. He was its cipher on earth, through which its divine will would very soon be realised.

He spoke once more to the villagers.

"I put it to you that there is livestock in this village that you have fattened and fed till their bellies groaned with food. Animals with no productive use at all! You could salt and preserve most of them for the weeks ahead. A couple, I would say, are ready for the pot now. Enough for all of you to feast on this very day."

His meaning wasn't immediately clear. But then the serfs began to view the Benedictines in a whole new light. Gripping their farming implements, they moved towards the tasty specimens.

Pais signalled to the other knights.

"Move on."

Without a further word, the Templars rode out. From the village square there came a series of squeals followed by strangulated cries. It was as if rather large pigs had been hung up from the stone pillory and had their throats cut.

Chapter 31

MOGADOURO

The bounty hunters sent by Rohese were closing in on her second son, having lost his trail across the vast Iberian plain. John the Tanner lay dead and rotting on a path in the Pyrenees but Hunrith and Aylmer had persisted with the lure of the Countess' reward uppermost in their thoughts. The bounty hunters had acquired new companions in Castile who knew the landscape and the language. They were mule traders by profession.

These men were called Maragatos, a nomadic tribe that criss-crossed the vast plains selling their pack animals. The Moors hated them for the base and undignified nature of their trade. The Christians loathed them for the poor quality of the merchandise. They were loyal to nobody but themselves and they would stay with these two Englishmen so long as their bellies were filled.

Unhappy at having to rely on the Maragatos but pleased they were finally closing in on William, the two bounty hunters exchanged knowing grins. Hunrith then burst into his customary, lascivious ditty.

"When that maiden caressed me
I swear she undressed me
Now I has the pox … the pox … the pox
A burning … a burning
For I'm never learning
To leave them fair maidens alone …"

Unaware of this threat to his life, William pounded up the feeble wooden staircase in the light of day bent on confronting the preceptor. With one kick, he all but booted the rickety door off its rusting hinges and bounded into the windowless room that was still dark. But there was sufficient light for him to see the filthy and unwashed preceptor locked in an amorous embrace with a generously proportioned peasant woman.

"Well, now we know why your hospitality was so poor," William snarled. "You might also want to explain why you let those villagers worship pagan gods? Have you forgotten your Templar vows?" He eyed the ample lady before him. "Clearly you have."

"You mean you are never tempted!" the preceptor growled back.

"I'm tempted. A lot. But I've resisted. What's the point of being a Templar knight if you throw your vows out of the window?"

The preceptor's monastic hood fell away from round his neck revealing a large growth to the side of his throat. It was perfectly round and alarmingly large. Nicholas, who had followed William, pointed at the protuberance.

"What's that?"

The preceptor was glad to have a distraction and employed the English he'd picked up on crusade as he answered Nicholas.

"They call me Apple Throat in the village. I ate an apple whole without chewing and it got stuck" – he indicated – "right here. So always eat your food properly, boy."

Pathros eyed the cancerous malignant growth on the man's neck and reckoned he wouldn't last till the next spring. William sat down on a small stool.

"Well, we might as well all get to know each other for a very short while. I'm William de Mandeville, this is my turcopole Pathros and he is Nicholas. And you …"

"João de Silva. The preceptor here."

"And your friend?" William probed sarcastically.

"I am a Donata," the woman answered as they were now speaking in Leonense, "I have given myself to the Order."

"So I see," William took a deep breath. "There is only one thing I want to know and then I'll leave. Where is the True Cross?"

"I told you, it's not in Portugal. Who knows where it is … but it's not here. Do not get me wrong, I respect Bernard of Clairvaux — we all do. But he is wrong on this. The cross is far away. Cairo, maybe; Constantinople. Who knows?"

This angered the young Templar.

He is lying. I'm tired of lies.

"I'm journeying on to meet the King of Portugal. And I'll no doubt meet our Templar superiors. I don't want to tell them what I've seen here. The scenes of lust and debauchery that have frankly shocked me."

"You are not shocked!"

"I am," William lied. "I resist the temptations of the flesh and I'm not even in charge of a preceptory. But you are a senior figure in our order — given great responsibility." William had to stifle a grin. All that this preceptor ruled over was a rickety tower. "You should be an example to younger knights and yet you've sunk deeply into sin."

"Hah," Apple Throat scoffed, "An example to you, eh? You mock me. I have no knights here, only this lovely woman to keep me company. I have every right to have a little happiness. God would not deny me that."

"Well …" William rubbed his stubble-covered chin. "I'll explain your view of our most sacred vows to our superiors. And I'll throw in for good measure your lax attitude to pagan worship on your doorstep. I'm sure they'll understand."

Apple Throat shook visibly at the thought of being kicked out of the Templar order and the only place he had for a home. He began to be somewhat more forthcoming. First, he explained to the trio what they had seen the night before. The preceptor was not encouraging heresy. No — this was all harmless fun. The colourful creatures hitting the legs of the girls were called Caretos. They were reminding the women to be modest and chaste. As for the green man, he was indeed a pagan god but with the Moors menacing this land, now was not a good time to deprive the serfs of their primitive and comforting beliefs.

William was fed up with Apple Throat. He needed some information.

"You've forgotten what it means to be a Templar! We might as well hand over these godless people to the Saracens and wash our hands of them. You've failed to keep them with Christ. Admit it, you have no interest in what they believe or even if their souls are saved." William stood up, towering over the preceptor and his lover, and continued to berate. "You can redeem yourself by telling us what you know about the True Cross. My turcopole has taught me how to know when people are lying. And you, João de Silva, are a truly terrible liar."

The preceptor scratched the lump on his neck.

"Yes ... yes, it is here," he relented, "somewhere in the Moorish city of Al-Usbuna. Though who knows where exactly! The place is a maze of streets, they say. I have never seen this city with my own eyes. But I have heard it is vast – maybe as big as Cordoba or Seville." Then the preceptor's mood changed. "But what damned business is it of yours anyway? When we get it back from the Moors, it is ours – it belongs to our new kingdom of Portugal. Why should we let some Englishman cart it off? We need it here."

"I need it too."

"Your need cannot be greater."

"I assure you it is."

Suddenly, Nicholas yelped. Coming down a nearby hillside were two familiar figures. One holding the viciously crafted mace and the other wearing the necklace of rings prized from the dead. Behind them came a group on mules, also carrying weapons. The charmless ditty reached the ears of those in the keep, freezing them to the spot.

"When that maiden caressed me
I swear she undressed me
Now I has the pox ... the pox ... the pox
A burning ... a burning
For I'm never learning
To leave them fair maidens alone ..."

"It's them ... from Witham," Nicholas peered out of the small doorway.

"Get back inside," William ordered him. "It's dark enough here for us to hide against the wall and not be seen. You," he gestured to Apple Throat, "just get rid of them. Don't let them enter or I can't vouch for the safety of your Donata."

The knight, his turcopole and the boy thief slammed themselves against the wall by the door. William drew his sword ready for use and Pathros readied his scimitar. Nicholas was given a Turkish mace to swing as wildly as he could if they entered. Outside, they could hear the fragile staircase creaking more than ever under the heavy footsteps of Aylmer the Blacksmith. The rest of the company waited below.

Apple Throat went to the door and the Donata followed him. Together they could block the doorway and hide their guests. Aylmer had reached the top, puffing from the minor exertion of his climb, beads of perspiration dotting his forehead. His cheeks were flushed red and he struggled for a moment to speak.

"You seen an English Templar round these parts?"

"No," Apple Throat responded meekly.

"Sure about that?"

There was a moment of hesitation before the preceptor answered again, which Aylmer noted.

"Quite sure. We have seen nobody today."

"We'll be on our way then."

As Apple Throat placed his arm round the Donata and guided her back into the keep, the blacksmith slammed his dagger through the preceptor's spine. Apple Throat collapsed, grasping at the growth on his neck, not knowing what was killing him. Before the Donata could scream, the same knife slashed her throat. Aylmer kicked both bodies into the room and slammed the door shut. He turned to Hunrith and the Maragatos below.

"Looks like we just missed them."

Chapter 32

THE CITY OF PORTO
TEMPLAR PRECEPTORY

The first sighting of the bounty hunters and their curious new band of followers forced William to veer away from Porto and into the Minho, a lush and verdant region dotted with many villages trading in fresh vegetables, salted fish and wine. The people seemed strangers to famine and were welcoming and generous. As winter would see no military campaigning, William let Nicholas enjoy what Christmastide had to offer in the Minho. That seemed to involve him eating his own bodyweight for days on end. Far from infuriating the local peasants, they were pleased to satisfy Nicholas' voracious appetite, treating him as if he was their own son.

But would he see another Christmas? Pathros might have been wrong about the boy, William thought. The Templar had seen many lepers in Outremer, where some even continued to fight the Saracens as knights in the Order of Saint Lazarus, until they succumbed to their ailment. Their pain and suffering was held to be a blessing, a sacred agony that placed them between heaven and hell while still alive and on this earth. William prayed that Pathros had been mistaken and so far, there had been no further signs of this curse descending on Nicholas.

As the spring came, they followed the coastline down to Porto, keeping an eagle eye out for the bounty hunters and their hired thugs. Once within the city walls, William made for the preceptory to withdraw much-needed money. Hugo Martins, master of the Order in Portugal, watched the treasurer take William's credit note and hand the Templar knight a bag of coins secured against the same amount held at Witham. The treasurer inscribed a coded symbol onto the parchment that only his equivalent in other preceptories would understand. It would inform them how much credit William still had.

Martins looked like a man for whom being the head of the Templars in the kingdom of Portugal was a heavy burden. His dark eyes seemed permanently troubled and his face was fixed in a frown. Aged around fifty, his beard was grey and twirled at the ends. As he walked towards William, Pathros noted his limp – a battle wound that had never healed properly.

"Follow me."

He beckoned to William while Pathros and Nicholas filed dutifully behind. They rode up a steep lump of granite on top of which was the citadel. A large hunting dog ran obediently alongside Martins' horse. "Comes with me into battle," the master explained, "always knows when I am in danger.

"Be useful though if it told me when those scheming clerics are close by. Hey, Aleixo! Give me a bark when you sniff a bishop!"

The dog gave its owner a guilty glance as if aware that it was failing in its duty. Martins eyed William.

"Do your churchmen in England connive against us as incessantly as they do here? Ours hate us Templars! They would drown us in our own blood if they could. We show them up, you see. Here we are beating the Moors with a bible in one hand and a sword in the other. What are they doing? Counting the money they have extorted from their congregations? Not exactly noble, is it?"

"Bishops are the same everywhere," William agreed.

"Not that I want to overthrow them,' Martins responded nervously, "I am not some damned heretic. But trust them? Never!"

Martins' face contorted as he imagined what he'd like to do to some of those prelates.

"The thing is," Martins tapped William on the arm, "they want Portugal to belong to them, not to us. But we still have to do all the fighting. Our blood gets splitt! Not theirs!" His voiced rose and veins throbbed. "Damned clerics hide behind their thick church walls and quake with fear until we have run through every Saracen. Then they come out demanding the spoils. Bastards!"

"But King Afonso …" William interjected

"Oh, he likes us Templars. Absolutely! Like his mother, the late Dona Teresa — may she rest with the angels in heaven! We embody everything he wants Portugal to be. Tough. Full of fighting spirit." Martins jutted his chin out. "Masculine! Not like those old women in skirts who sit on bishops' thrones — dripping their poison into the ears of courtiers."

William wanted to ask about the True Cross having journeyed long to be in Portugal. Instead he was getting worrying insights about the disunity on the Christian side of the battle against the Moors of Al-Andalus.

"But these bishops don't pose a real threat to us, surely?"

"You think not?" Martins responded brusquely. "Then you better see something … a sight that will fill your heart with dismay." He hurried his horse on and the trio followed. As they neared the top of the hill, he gestured towards an ebony canopy held by four deacons. "There he is. Even Aleixo hates the sight of him." On cue, the dog's lip seemed to curl. "Pedro Pitões, Bishop of Porto. Loathes us. Would strangle all of us Templars if we had one neck."

William regarded the man that Martins loathed with such intensity — a skeletal figure with ivory-white skin. He looked so physically puny that a gust of wind could have blown him over. Bishop Pitões seemed to be directing some kind of operation down the other side of the hill and invisible to the Templar. Figures scurried up to him, accepted new orders and then disappeared again in a hurry. William could hear his voice, a reedy and unpleasant sound with a waspish sting to it.

Looming behind Pitões was his fortress-like cathedral with arrow slits instead of stained glass windows and towers built for catapults as much as bells. These were the great walls behind which Pitões could flee if the Moors were to appear on the horizon.

Martins gruffly explained, with little sympathy, that the Bishop couldn't bear the rays of the sun on his skin. It was as if they burnt into him. So he wore a black clerical cap pulled round his ears, long gloves and remained under the shadow of his canopy.

"Wait till you see what this monster has brought to our shores," Martins said to William. "You will think your eyes are deceiving you."

They drew closer to the Bishop, who addressed Martins without bothering to turn to greet him.

"As ever, I feel your anger, Brother Hugo, before I see you."

Martins could barely resist the temptation to cuff Pitões round his covered ears.

"You have emptied every stew and tavern in the world and brought them here!" he thundered back. "Cutthroats and vagabonds, that is what they are! They will leave us empty-handed. They will rape our kingdom before they depart!"

A thin-lipped smile traced across Pitões' marble-white face. William noted that his eyes were the palest green and devoid of any warmth.

"This is my dream fulfilled, Brother Hugo," the Bishop said triumphantly, "I shall remember this as the day your Order's stranglehold on our king came to an end."

William was dying to know what the pale and bloodless prelate was referring to. He walked past Pitões and glanced down the other side of the hill. The sight that greeted the Templar was entirely unexpected.

"Dear God ..."

"You are impressed, young man," the Bishop cooed.

A steep rocky gorge led down to the estuary of the River Douro. All over the hillside, Pitões' servants streamed like lines of ants carrying baskets of bread and meat, taking them to the dockside. At the river's edge, countless barrels and jars of wine were lined up ready for the host that Pitões had invited to descend on Porto. He had brought a great foreign mass that would assist the King of Portugal in his noble cause thereby diminishing his reliance on the Order of the Temple.

The armada that Pitões had summoned coated the river estuary and the sea beyond – so densely packed together that the water was almost obscured. There were hundreds of ships bearing the flags of every kingdom and duchy from Burgundy to Cologne and Flanders to England. Nicholas put his hand to his mouth.

Could there be any ships left anywhere else in the world?

Great princes and knights on their way to crusade in Outremer had been invited by Pitões to dock at Porto with the promise of lavish hospitality from the city. Every animal would be slaughtered and the kilns wouldn't cease baking until the fleet moved on again.

But once the ships had docked, Pitões had no intention of letting this great military force depart for Acre and Jerusalem: they had to stay. The calculating cleric had a more immediate use for these secular knights – a chance for them to win glory and riches much closer to home.

They would help Portugal take the great city of Al-Usbuna!

Ten days' ride to the South was the start of the caliphate – the Muslim realms that stretched from the Atlantic to the Indus. This was the westernmost point of the Islamic world. For hundreds of years the emirs and sultans had conquered previously Christian lands on the Iberian peninsula. But the determined crusaders of Portugal, Castile, Leon and Aragon were slowly pushing the Muslim domains back. What had once been tiny pockets of resistance had now become independent kingdoms. The caliphate, though, wasn't about to surrender four centuries of control over this part of the world. It was fighting back!

Towns and villages constantly changed hands between Muslim emirs and Christian princes on yearly, monthly and even weekly basis. The tug of war between two great faiths was constant, bloody and unrelenting.

A bold move was needed to push the Moors back decisively. Pitões believed he had made such a move. This crusader army, drawn from so many kingdoms, would deal the decisive blow. And Al-Asbunna would be their prize.

And the Templars will not be able to take the credit.

Pitões looked on with glee as the first vessels edged close to the quayside and the city's people rushed forward, offering freshly slaughtered meat and the best wines from the vineyards of the Douro as their bishop had commanded. Church deacons then directed the soldiers up the hill, where Pitões waited to greet them. A swarm of lances, pikes, spears, longbows, springalds, spears and axes moved towards the Bishop, who clasped his hands in excitement.

"You will regret this, Pitões." Martins was shaking with impotent rage.

"No," Pitões' voice rasped with pleasure. "I will regret nothing. Behold the end for you and your damned Templars!"

Martins would have severed Pitões' head from his shoulders if William hadn't wheeled his horse round to face the Portuguese master.

"Surely we must rally our brothers, master."

William's intervention got Martins to see sense.

"You are right. Well said, English Templar."

The two cantered away from Pitões.

"We're the only force that can really beat the Moors," William reassured Martins, "God's on our side. Like you say, these knights are here for their own gain. I've seen so many men like them in Outremer – mercenaries, pirates, thieves – but we're different. We're Templars! We fight for the love of God. And we've got to advance against the Moors before that massive army does."

"Yes," Martins agreed, not realising that William's motive was as much to do with getting to the True Cross first as it was defending the honour of the Order. "Let us leave this place."

As they sped to a gallop, the air around them resonated to languages and dialects from every part of Christendom. Pitões gave a benediction with his gloved hand as the knights, bearing their kite shields and swords, began to fill the hilltop in front of the cathedral. They held large hunks of meat they chewed voraciously and some were already drunk, only minutes after arriving.

The Bishop was delighted to see his guests settling in. At his signal the deacons scattered among the soldiers, and as he began to speak in Latin, they repeated his words in the tongues of the Normans, English, Flemish and men of Cologne.

"Oh, you race of the Franks! People who have come from beyond the mountains of our lands! People loved and chosen by God, as is clear from your many deeds! We welcome you with our hearts open and glad. But we also beg you on our knees to help us resolve a most foul and evil state of affairs."

He had their full attention now.

"I know you are journeying to the East to fight the Saracen but you need not travel so far if you wish to fight the enemies of Christ. They are here; they are here in this land. They destroy our churches and desecrate our altars. They circumcise your brother Christians and pour the blood into the baptismal fonts.

These devils use our people as targets for their archers. They kill our children. They despoil our women. When they take prisoners, they make them stretch out their necks to see if they can sever them with a single blow of their swords."

Pitões paused for breath.

"You go to defend holy places but our churches and shrines, but a few miles from where I stand now, are blasphemously befouled and mocked by the Moor. They carry away all of value from our places of worship and slay the clergy within or make them captive.

"Our Mother Church's arms have been cut off and her face disfigured. She cries aloud for vengeance for the shed blood of her sons, for retribution that you can deliver."

A ripple of murmurs passed through the crowd. The warriors had now ceased eating and drinking as the Bishop's words stirred them. Pitões could sense their growing anger and to ensure this will to wage war didn't fade, he appealed to their naked greed.

"They sit behind high walls and laugh at us. Sit there in their silken robes and covered in jewels and every precious metal you can think of and they mock us. While we eke out a meagre living on our farms and grind through each day till sunset, they drink milk and honey and their storehouses brim with grain and all manner of meat and fish. But all that should be ours. It is the Lord's gifts to those who believe in his risen son and not the property of the Moor. Which one of you will help us throw down those walls and claim what belongs to every single man here today?"

Martins glanced back at the top of the citadel as a huge cheer went up that never seemed to end.

"Damned rabble has decided to stay," the Templar master was utterly downcast as the noise from the secular knights went on and on. "We are finished …God has forsaken us."

William said nothing.

He realised that the vast crusader host could conceivably take the great city of Al-Usbuna. But they would then rape and despoil the city before he could find the True Cross. Some Burgundian knight or English sapper might chance upon the glittering reliquary and steal it. Then it might be lost forever. William had to get into the city first; he had to be in the front line of attack.

Even if that puts my life at terrible risk!

Chapter 33

THE KING OF PORTUGAL'S TENT
NEAR THE WALLS OF SHANTARIN

"Damned Moors!" Dom Afonso, King of Portugal, exploded with his customary volcanic rage. Not yet forty years old, his frame was surprisingly slight for a man whom his loyal Portuguese serfs proudly claimed could lift a sword as heavy as a plough and wield it around his head.

His oiled-back hair had greyed a little at the temples but was otherwise a rich chestnut brown; his face was long, with large eyes and full lips.

"You know what they will be saying in Leon … that impudent scoundrel Afonso … calls himself a king when he is our vassal … now he is back in his proper place … let him try and claim he is anything more than a count."

I was once a mere Count. Other Christian kingdoms thought I was an upstart. The Count of Portugal who imagines himself a king. But this is a kingdom now and Al-Usbuna will be my capital!

"You are a king," came a reassuring woman's voice, that of Queen Maud of Savoy, his long-suffering and heavily pregnant wife.

Afonso picked up the modest crown that had been placed on the small altar in the tent and over which the monks from Santa Cruz in Coimbra had been intoning their prayers.

"I imprisoned my own mother to have this," Afonso reminisced with no regrets at having the ageing Dona Teresa confined to a monastery for siding with her cousins in neighbouring Leon against him. Her hateful cries still rang in his head — *You are no knight! You are no duke! You are no king! Brigand and cattle thief you will always be and nothing more.*

Afonso damned his treacherous mother.

"I have fought for every mile of this new kingdom of Portugal, taking it from the hands of Moorish and Leonense dogs, and when I have the city of Al-Usbuna, the whole world will see I am a king. And my mother will gaze upwards from hell and even she will be forced to recognise my greatness!"

In the shadows, a tall figure drank from a huge Auroch's horn given to him by a German crusader. It never left his side and it never seemed to be empty. The red wine trickled down Geraldo's cheek as he took another glug. Fearless Geraldo, as the Moors and Christians alike called him, was well built, but gone slightly to seed. He'd fought and whored his way through Leon, Castile and Al-Andalus with Afonso. Man and boy, they had known each other, forming a bond Geraldo believed could never be broken.

He rattled an Arab dinar in his mouth, clanking it against his teeth then regarded Afonso's queen with his customary loathing. She was trying to feminise Afonso, turning him into one of those effete French princes she had grown up with in Savoy. But that wasn't what Portugal needed: Afonso had to be a ruler who wouldn't flinch or blink when slicing a Moor in half and killing every last one of his sobbing children.

Maud tried not to look at Geraldo Geraldes Sem Pavor — his full title — directly. She didn't want to flatter the brute. That animal would turn her into the queen of the bandits and drunks if he could. *The stinking whoremonger! I won't let that happen,* she seethed. *Portugal will be as saintly and righteous as my native Savoy.*

Maud shifted uneasily on her throne, the belly bearing her child covered by a light green loosely fitting bliaut gironé, with a belt slung low below her waist. The Queen's hair was long and plaited to either side with a pale saffron veil covering the top of her head. She wasn't the most beautiful princess in Christendom, a little dumpy, but she was impeccably connected as a daughter of Savoy. And if her belly produced a boy, she would have fulfilled her queenly duties admirably.

Maud's father had taken the cross and gone valiantly on crusade. He was a saintly and refined ruler who'd raised vast amounts to fund the crusader cause in Outremer. His court in Savoy had echoed to the heroic ballads of troubadours and the solemn prayers of Benedictines. This refinement, Maud promised herself, will be brought to Portugal!

I will not be queen of some bawdy Gomorrah that tries to dignify itself with the name 'kingdom'. The needless feasting and sinful excess I see all around me in this court will stop!

"Do you remember, Geraldo," Afonso still held the golden crown in his hands, "when I knighted myself in the cathedral in Zamora ..."

"Of course."

"Well, rest assured, I will crown myself on the battlements of Al-Usbuna. And Mother," he stared off into the ether, addressing the dead woman, "you will watch me from hell as I sit on my throne in fine robes and the Archbishop of Braga anoints my head. You will hear the cheers of my subjects like arrows piercing your flesh. And I will rejoice, Mother, to hear your unending howls of anguish."

"First, you must take Shantarin," Maud reminded Afonso of the Portuguese defeat the night before, "and maybe Geraldo will be good enough to fight this time."

"The King did not wish me to go," Geraldo pointed out through gritted teeth. "He was saving me for the attack on Al-Usbuna."

"I hear it was one calamity after another," Maud continued, sticking barbs into her nemesis. "Even the scaling ladders broke."

"That will not happen again," Geraldo assured her.

"How can you be so sure?"

"I had the carpenter's hands removed this morning."

Afonso chuckled while Maud was ashen-faced.

"So now you will put your drinking horn down," the Queen spluttered angrily, "and take Shantarin. Or do you have something better to do?"

Her French accent was grating as ever on Geraldo's ears.

"I will take Shantarin this very night, Mafalda."

"My name is Maud," the dumpy queen bristled with fury at the Portuguese version of her name being used, a deliberate slight, "you know that and I must insist you use my title. And bow your head when you address me."

"Maud!" Afonso interjected, "we have no time for this. Geraldo will take Shantarin, I trust him." He turned to the knight, who was draining the horn of its last contents. "Go now, get the men together and surprise our Moorish friends."

Geraldo lumbered out. Let Afonso stay with his ugly French queen and the tonsured eunuch monks from Santa Cruz praying for his soul – he had a city to take. Afonso sank to his knees and began pleading to God once more for victory. Maud smiled to see this prayerful sight. This was what she wanted her king to be more often – a reverent, God-fearing and truly noble sovereign.

Afonso watched the wisps of incense rising from the swaying censer nearby. His mind went back a few short years to when he'd set out with Geraldo to create this new kingdom of Portugal: two young Iberian crusaders with an overwhelming sense of their own destiny.

They had dreamt of carving out a new realm that would strike at the heart of the caliphate. Maybe they might one day even conquer Morocco! But in their hubris, they had provoked a Moorish ruler, Ali Ibn Yusuf, who had amassed an army too great to number with the intention of crushing Afonso once and for always.

At a place called Ourique, the small Portuguese army had been forced to confront this vast Islamic host. Defeat was certain. The night before battle, Afonso had ridden out into the darkness of the surrounding woods, feeling like a man lost to God. Pride and cockiness had brought him to this field of battle where his life might soon be ended.

As he rode into a clearing, Afonso noticed that the ground around him was bathed in a mysterious, flickering light. It wasn't moonlight nor was it from any fires. He looked upwards to the sky and was forced to shield his eyes from a thousand piercing rays. There, in the heavens, magnificent and radiant, was Jesus Christ. Seated in his throne of glory, the Son of God foretold that the leader of the Portuguese would triumph at Ourique and that the Moors should never be feared.

Afonso snapped out of this reminiscence and turned to Maud.

"I know you despise Geraldo," he spoke gently but firmly to her, "but he has taken many towns for you. No better fighter do I have in my ranks. You will learn to love him as I do."

The Queen held her belly bearing the future heir to the throne. She was convinced it was a son. Her dreams had been full of prophetic signs that the baby would be the second king of Portugal. And for this reason, she wouldn't rest until Geraldo was swinging lifeless from a gibbet. He'd cease to exert any hold on Afonso or his son.

"As you say, dear King, I will learn to love Geraldo."

That malign influence on my husband must be removed!

Within the hour, Geraldo Geraldes Sem Pavor was advancing under cover of night towards Shantarin. Within the town, the citizens had turned in after the curfew. Their walls had repelled the Portuguese and they expected Afonso to slink away like a whipped dog. Guards patrolled the battlements, surveying the dimly lit cornfields beyond for any sign of movement. But their watch was cursory and they failed to note the slight quivering motion among the crops as soldiers with ladders made towards them.

"Keep down!" Geraldo growled to his men.

Over his shoulder, Geraldo carried a curiously stained sack that was empty now but would be filled later on. He signalled towards a stretch of wall that seemed thinly guarded and his small force pounded in that direction. In no time, three scaling ladders had sprouted up against the whitewashed fortifications. Barely pausing to consider his own safety, he began climbing.

Spotting a sentry dozing, the Portuguese knight raised his sword and with one swoosh calmly decapitated the man. He then scooped up the head and threw it in his sack. Geraldo's soldiers silently swarmed over the battlements and methodically slew every guard they could find before the alarum could be raised.

Before long, the main gate swung open and more Portuguese stormed in and began fanning out across the souks and alleys of the medina. Eerie dark shapes gliding silently past doorways and fountains bent on destruction.

Geraldo pointed towards the qasba – the central part of the city that housed the garrison and nobility of any Moorish city. Still there were no cries or alarum.

The Portuguese knight could barely stop himself from laughing out loud: this was far too easy.

His soldiers now tore through the barracks and plunged their swords into the garrison while they still slept. Through sheets, the prone bodies were pierced one after another by the blades of Afonso's army.

From the qasba, Geraldo now made his way to the qasr. This was the fortress and palace at the very epicentre and in here, he'd find the al-kaid – the military governor. Geraldo ran through the main gate, left open and now flanked by two dead sentries. His men had worked speedily and efficiently. There would be a great feast for them when this was over!

Snoring from behind an ornate front door gave away the al-kaid's location. On a quick turn of the handle, Geraldo swung open the door and without bothering to introduce himself, stuck a knife into the throat of the al-kaid's wife as she made to scream. The Governor's eyes blinked open and he turned to find his wife next to him, dead. His grief was short-lived as Geraldo's heavy sword crashed down on his neck, sending a jet of blood over the pillows.

Geraldo picked up his head and threw it into his morbid sack then set to work, hacking off the wife's head. As promised to Afonso, Moorish Shantarin was taken.

Chapter 34

TEMPLAR ENCAMPMENT

Nicholas was to take the horse he'd been given and go find some water and firewood. Pathros was yet again immersed in a medical treatise from ancient times while William, to alleviate the boredom he always dreaded between battles, carved some tent pegs.

This kind of mundane chore he could tolerate, as it was a preparation for war. All soldiers had to sleep in dry conditions if they were going to be battle ready the next morning.

Pathros glanced up from his book and watched Nicholas ride away. The boy had shown no signs of leprosy and William was sure that his turcopole had been wrong. But Pathros was convinced he was right.

He'd observed this hellish condition in the East and it could take years for the victim to finally succumb after being infected. He was sure that when Nicholas had stolen the bread from Jake, he'd condemned himself to an early grave.

Martins joined William.

"Keeping yourself busy?"

"Yes," William smiled. "I've been told that the Devil gets bored when we labour like this."

"Indeed." Martins eased down onto a nearby rock, his badly healed war wound making his descent very painful. "Need to ask you something. Unburden myself."

"Please," William replied, "you can ask anything, Master Martins."

The veteran Portuguese Templar turned to the young English Templar. Unlike his knights drawn from the lands conquered by Afonso, this knight had golden, blond hair that shone in the afternoon sun. The local brothers were from old Galician families and had the typical round faces, brown eyes and were a little short in the leg. In contrast, William towered above these knights with an impressively broad frame and legs that were the height of some of his men!

"Why are you here?"

"To fight for Dom Afonso."

Martins hated being taken for a fool.

"I may be a bluff old soldier and not the sharpest mind in Christendom – but I am not a complete cretin. You are here for something else, I can tell. Be straight with me!"

William stopped carving the small piece of wood in his hands.

"I need to restore my family's honour." The Templar sighed. "Let's just say that it's taken a bit of a battering of late. Partly my fault. My father, my brother ... We're an unlucky family."

"Yes," Martins persisted. "But the obvious thing would be to go to Outremer. Fight Saracens! Defend Jerusalem! Why come here?"

William wondered whether to keep his quest concealed. After all, nobody had been honest to him about the True Cross – least of all his superiors in the Order. But Martins seemed a decent sort of man – a hint of his father even.

"Bernard of Clairvaux has sent me to recover the True Cross. He says it's in Al-Usbuna. I want to be the first over the walls to find it. I'm going to bring it back to our Order and restore it to the Holy Sepulchre in Jerusalem. That's why I'm here."

Martins shuddered.

"My God!" He was as white as a sheet. "That puts me in a pickle."

"Why?"

"Nobody here knows about this – the fact we have lost the great Cross. Not even Pitões or his infernal meddling bishops. Not even our king. Nobody!"

That hardly surprised William. The Order seemed to have made a point of concealing the loss of the True Cross.

"You don't have to tell anybody," William replied. "I'll get it back and its loss will be something known only to a few."

A few hundred or thousand! The Templar mused. Everybody from Dartford to Edessa seemed to be aware that the Lignum Crucis had been stolen. But he wanted to calm Martins down. However, the gruff old warrior wasn't to be so easily stilled.

"Ask yourself, what would Pitões say if he knew this – and all those bishops who hate us? Off they would traipse to the King and tell him – look at those Templars, they lost the True Cross. Let it slip into the hands of the Moors." Martins patted Aleixo, who looked as forlorn as his owner. "Afonso will despise us when now he respects us. Is that what you want?"

"I can get it back before he ever finds out. After all, at some point the Moors will parade it in front of us from the walls of Al-Usbuna to destroy our morale." William watched as Nicholas came back from the woods clasping firewood in his arms. "I can make sure that never happens. We can't keep this a secret forever."

Nicholas threw the firewood to the ground and dismounted, collecting up the scattered branches and preparing a campfire. As he worked enthusiastically for Sir William, he was unaware of being scrutinised by Pathros.

Nicholas reached up to his saddle to fetch the two leather water bottles. As he did so, his tunic rose and Pathros noticed an alarming red patch on the boy's midriff.

I was right.

Soon, Pathros would have to tell William the bitter truth. For the sake of the entire Templar army, Nicholas must be confined to a leper house.

Chapter 35

MEDINA,
AL-USBUNA

The city made a pretence of joy at the arrival of its ruler, the Taifa of Badajoz, Sidray bin Wazir. From every window, doorway and along the winding paths through the medina, the people of Al-Usbuna cried out, proclaiming their loyalty. But Sidray's fury was etched all over his face. He'd been forced out of his capital in Badajoz to come and defend Al-Usbuna from Ibn Arrik, the Moorish title given to Dom Afonso Henriques.

As he made his way through the souks and open spaces, the refugees from Shantarin and Sintra – cities taken by Afonso – cheered him on, though their faces showed no real hope of being returned to their homes.

They had tasted the brutal determination of the Franks. These crude unwashed savages had overwhelmed them, murdered their governor in his sleep and massacred the garrison. They doubted that their refined taifa was any match for the devil that ruled the Portuguese. Sidray cut a dazzling figure in the midst of this deafening tumult. He was dressed in an intricately woven cloak of Damascus brocade and a cream coloured turban with a crescent-shaped emerald at its centre. Perched high on a camel covered in silks and gold tassels, he sailed past his people towards the qasba like an omnipotent godhead.

Behind him came his 'Tangerines' — fiersome African guards from Mauretania, who had been shipped over to Al-Andalus from the port of Tangiers in Morocco, hence their not very affectionate nickname.

Noticeably taller than the crowds around them and hand picked for their formidable physiques and stern faces, they marched behind the Taifa's camel bearing colourful round shields. They were divided into two squadrons sworn to protect the Taifa to the death. In front were the Jackals and behind were the Scorpions.

The Scorpions jealously guarded a plain wooden box that Sidray had been given by his cousin in the East. It contained a magical talisman, sacred to the Knights Templar. This jewel-encrusted object with its innocuous piece of wood within was the city's best defence against Ibn Arrik and his infidel Portuguese. If they dared to approach the city walls of Al-Usbuna, Sidray would take great delight in burning this relic on the battlements in full view of every Portuguese soldier. And he'd cry out — *There is your holy crucifix! Your action has condemned it to the flames!*

Theatrically, the Taifa nodded in reverence to the Great Mosque as he passed it en route to the Bab al-Qasba and the area of the city where the Moorish nobility lived. The dusty approach to the gateway to this very exclusive part of Al-Usbuna had been covered with silk and cotton rugs and carpets. Next to the horseshoe gate, a wealthy landowner called Abbas stood on a raised platform. He had been rewarded with the post of Qadi, the religious judge, charged with welcoming converts to Islam and executing apostates. He raised his hands as the Taifa approached.

"May the peace of Allah be upon you and your sons, great commander of the faithful, descendant of the Prophet, judicious ruler and conqueror of all our enemies."

Sidray's procession halted before the entrance to the qasba. Abbas took a closer look at their omnipotent and munificent ruler. He despised him. Like the rest of the city's nobles, he detested the very sight of this upstart. But he was their ruler — this mercurial despot whose face was layered with powders and creams to hide his ageing features. His spindly legs were padded to appear more muscular. His hair was dyed black and his eyebrows teased into fine points to give his face a more intimidating appearance.

"Where is my al-kaid?" Sidray screamed. "Why is he not here?"

"He is bringing you a gift, great lord," the qadi responded.

"Could he have not brought it already?"

Abbas looked around, hoping another official would offer an explanation but every man held his tongue.

"I am sure he will be here soon, great lord," the judge said nervously.

Sidray was fit to blow.

Qasim ibn Muhammad is doing this deliberately. My al-kaid is being deliberately insubordinate!

The flow of thoughts about all the treachery around him came thick and fast: my al-kaid is making a public display of his displeasure that I am here in Al-Usbuna, the city he is supposed to command. Not that he commands it very well! I have been the lord of generosity and treated my governors well but they have repaid me by losing their cities to Ibn Arrik, so-called King of Portugal.

I'm surrounded by complete imbeciles!

The al-kaids of Sintra and now Shantarin have rolled over like lambs before the Franks but I will not let it happen again. This magnificent city will not fall to them.

I will show them how to fight the filthy Franks!

He beckoned the qadi over to him and spoke down to the official from his high perch.

"Find Qasim. Tell him that I will burn one half of Al-Usbuna to make the other half fight like lions. Tell him that I will hold children as hostages to make their parents fight that much harder. These soft-skinned merchants will be turned into warriors if it is the last thing I do here."

Abbas knelt and kissed the ground. You puffed-up cat that thinks he is a lion, he snarled to himself. You perfumed tyrant! Our al-kaid is brave but you are nothing. If only I had the courage to strike you and suffer a courageous martyrdom. But I have allowed myself to be bought off in order to live a comfortable existence.

Meanwhile, the city's commander, the al-kaid, was busy making a ghoulish choice. In the central courtyard of the city's prison, Qasim looked down into the fetid hole before them. A writhing mass of prisoners clambered on each other's shoulders to suck in some air or see the light. They're like crabs in a pot, the al-kaid pondered, each one struggling to survive but all destined to die.

These Templars had been captured in a battle at Soure, a Moorish town they had dared to try and take. True to form, the Templar knights had refused the choice of being ransomed back to the Franks or converting to Islam. To be ransomed was to put Christian money into Moorish hands and to convert was to betray the Cross.

This left only one path – to the executioner's block.

"That one," Qasim pointed, clasping a silken cloth fragranced with myrrh to his face as the stench was overpowering. The knight was emaciated and his white mantle stained beyond recognition. Barely able to stand, he was forced to trudge behind the al-kaid and his guards as they made their way towards the qasba.

Sidray had slid down from his high perch on the camel and away from the eyes of his subjects; his small and rotund form waddled towards the Hall of the Caliphs. This open courtyard was covered in marble of every shade and curtains woven with gold thread shimmered in the sunlight, hung between the arches. Two large rectangular fishponds flanked a walkway that led to a large divan where the al-kaid normally sat to receive petitioners and make important rulings. With a little help from two of his Tangerines, Sidray was eased up onto the al-kaid's divan.

The Taifa went through the obligatory courtly rituals. He took sweetmeats from a large tray with his bare hands and then handed them to officials, who cherished the food touched by the Taifa. Then a servant poured him wine while his dancers and musicians entertained him.

"Where are my thinkers?"

From behind the Jackals and Scorpions, a group of turbaned scholars emerged gingerly, clutching books, parchments and boxes of scientific instruments. The Taifa needed to have men like this about him, proving that he was a defender of great learning.

"You see I drink wine," he said to them. "There are zealots who have come from the deserts of Africa and are in our lands who say it is wrong to drink the fruit of the grape. They are wrong. They are unwise. They are disloyal to me. I know some of them are in this city." He stared at the gathering of thinkers. "They would burn all of you and your books if they ever took control of Al-Andalus. Your futures and mine are closely bound. Just remember that. If I were to die at their hand, you would die a second after me."

Unknown to the Taifa, he was being watched at that very moment by one of those desert zealots. A tall Berber clad head to toe in black. Many of his kind – Almohads – had sworn to overthrow the corrupt and degenerate taifas of Al-Andalus. Creatures like Sidray! They blamed their decadence for the success of the crusaders in taking more and more of the Iberian peninsula. To halt their advance, the taifas had to die!

But the taifas had responded to the zealots by baring their claws and fangs. Sidray had cheerfully decorated the gibbets of Badajoz with hundreds of these Almohads and knew that his survival depended on wiping out these vermin.

Qasim approached the Hall of the Caliphs with his guards and the emaciated Templar, dazed through hunger and disease, trudging behind. He called a halt to the party and instructed them to wait outside the courtyard. There were countless rooms around the Hall of the Caliphs and Qasim darted off on his own till he reached the small, empty storeroom where Hadid was waiting.

The tall Berber greeted him. Beneath his black turban, the Almohad's green, piercing eyes shone in the semi-light. A deep furrowed scar disfigured his face. That came from the battles in far-off Marrakech, where Hadid and his fellow Almohads had successfully cleansed the city of its rulers.

He'd been scarred after dragging the Emir of Marrakech's sister from her horse and severely beating the woman for her immodest dress and daring to ride. But her brother had retaliated with a dagger slash to Hadid's face – though he had paid very rapidly with his life.

Hadid meant iron – like one of the gates in Al-Usbuna with its iron locks – the Bab al-Hadid. The Berber with an iron soul had two masters – Allah and the newly installed Almohad emir of Marrakech, Abd al-Mu-min. Very soon, that great ruler would also be the emir of an Almohad Al-Andalus and taifas like Sidray could expect to be slain and trodden underfoot.

Qasim protected Hadid and his covert forces. Not for love of their Almohad beliefs, he was quite indifferent to their zealot creed. Qasim's motives were far more straightforward.

I want that wretched Sidray and his lackeys destroyed!

Watching Sidray through the trellis with Hadid, he felt a knot tightening in his stomach.

"Siqlabi," he sneered.

"You hate him for being low-born," Hadid said.

"Yes." Qasim replied. "Great Arabic families once ruled all the way to the Pyrenees and beyond. We were the masters here for four hundred years and swore allegiance only to the caliph in Cordoba. All of us were of the same bloodline as the Prophet." The al-kaid let his mind wander back to greater, more glorious times. "This was an invincible caliphate …"

"But you forgot the Qur'an."

"We did not forget," Qasim corrected Hadid, "men like him did, these taifas who divided up our glorious caliphate. They thought only of their personal gain. And instead of fighting the Franks, they paid them lavishly to go away."

"For that alone they deserve death," Hadid growled.

It was forbidden to tax Muslims to bribe the infidels. Yet that's exactly what Sidray had done. And those dirhams and dinars, delivered in sacks and caskets to the Franks, had only emboldened the crusaders further.

Avaricious Franks like Dom Afonso came to wonder how much more wealth was in the lands of Al-Andalus. Instead of waiting for their regular bribes, the crusader kings had begun to push south to own this gold and silver for themselves. In this way, Allah was punishing his people for enriching the enemies of the faith.

"His grandfather …" Qasim gestured at the Taifa beyond, "… they used to call him Sabur-al-Siqlabi," Sabur the slave in Arabic, "and they said he was bought by a merchant in the slave market at Verdun then resold in Silves. Like a camel, branded on his hide. Yet we let his grandson rise to be our ruler!" Qasim pressed his face against the trellis. "Look at his hair. You can see the red tints, like a Saxon … like a Slav! The grandson of scum! He is a barbarian, for sure."

Hadid could see the pain in Qasim's eyes. It pleased him greatly. He'd little time for the al-kaid's wounded ancestral pride as he wasn't from some great Arabic tribe himself but descended from Berber herdsmen. But fate had flung the two of them together. They both wanted to see the Taifa dead.

The al-kaid sighed.

Every day this taifa is in Al-Usbuna wounds me deeply.

The city's governor had once been strikingly handsome, with the finest of Arabic features, but worry had etched deep lines into his face.

"I feel as if I may go mad," he muttered to Hadid.

"You will rule here soon, my lord al-kaid. All you must do is unseat this unworthy devil."

Qasim watched Sidray continuing to drink wine, dipping his fingers into the food and handing it to courtiers and lecherously eyeing up the dancers, both boys and girls. A shrill laugh rang out at some witty comment from a scholar. Then the Taifa clicked his fingers loudly to the rhythm of the music. Qasim would relish striking Sidray down when the opportune moment presented itself. He turned to Hadid.

"Promise me that your people will support me. I will be a vassal to your Emir in Marrakech so long as I may rule here in peace."

"I promise," Hadid lied.

He was in no position to guarantee such support and the emir might just as well install one of his own men as ruler once the Taifa had been killed. The Almohad leader had no reason to bargain with any of those who had governed in Al-Andalus. They had failed – therefore they were unworthy of being treated as equals. This applied even to Qasim as his hatred for the Taifa was fuelled more by personal pride as opposed to love of the Prophet.

The Taifa giggled as he called for his court astrologer, a Jewish alchemist called Sulayman. Like most Jews and Christians in Al-Usbuna, his family had long Arabised their names and mode of dress. Only a skull cap gave Sulayman's religion away.

The soothsayer made his way nervously to the front of the divan, wondering how to phrase the victories that undoubtedly lay ahead and the glory that the world would bestow on the Taifa. This horoscope would have to be utterly sycophantic to please the swollen-headed potentate.

Behind the grille, Hadid was scandalised by this spectacle.

"He practises sorcery? With a Jew!"

This came as no surprise to Qasim.

"Yes. Now you can see how far this man has parted company with our beloved Qur'an."

Sulayman was soon in full astrological flow.

"Great lord," he began, "He who rules on high has made His will plain through the movement of the celestial bodies. I have observed the heavens and Ibn Arrik walks with Tammuz the crab and like him, he scurries under a rock when a great shadow is cast over him."

"Oh, excellent, this pleases me greatly, Sulayman!" The Taifa rocked back and forth on the divan. "What a fortuitous chart! My arrival here is favoured up above"– he pointed to the sky – "and Ibn Arrik will soon rue the day he took on the Taifa of Badajoz!"

Leaving Hadid skulking in the shadows, hidden from view, Qasim now made himself visible in the Hall of the Caliphs, trailing the dying Templar behind him like a lame dog.

Sidray noted the gift that the city governor was bringing to him. Even in his bedraggled state, the sight of the Templar created a frisson of excitement among the courtiers.

Here was one of those invincible warriors who inspired dread, fear and panic across Al-Andalus. Yet this wretched specimen with an excrement-stained mantle, no longer gleaming white, made the Moors wonder if the Order really was untouchable. Sidray's courtiers pointed to the distinctive cross of the Knights Templar, still just about visible, and giggled at this knight's predicament.

Sidray popped another sweetmeat in his mouth and chewed as the al-kaid approached. He didn't want to betray any emotion at the sight of the Templar but he too was stirred by the presence of this prisoner. All of a sudden, he had a deliciously sadistic idea.

"Bring the box," Sidray ordered one of the Scorpions. "Good of you to join us, Qasim."

"I was bringing you this very special present."

"We appreciate it," Sidray responded with still a hint of displeasure.

The Scorpion returned with the reliquary.

"Excellent!" Sidray clapped his hands in glee. "Wait till you see how the Templar reacts to this. It's their special magical symbol. And I have got it!" The Scorpion lifted the reliquary from the box in which it had been transported from Outremer. Even in the fading sun of late afternoon, the ornate decoration caught the light and the True Cross seemed to radiate a glowing light from within. The Templar immediately recognised the revered object. He reached out to touch it. Then he attempted to moan a prayer but his parched mouth made curious rasping sounds instead.

Sidray plopped down from his divan and shuffled over to the Templar, observing his tortured face close up for his own amusement.

"Oh ... look at him ... That is right, Templar ... it is your magical symbol. The wood on which you think your God was killed ... and we have it." Sidray cackled malevolently. "It is the last thing you will ever see! Kneel!"

But the Templar summoned up enough defiance to stand erect and gaze down with contempt at the ball of spite before him.

"I told you to kneel ... make him kneel ... he's not kneeling!"

The Taifa hollered at the Tangerines, who kicked at the Templar's knees and pressed down on his shoulders until he was at the same level as Sidray.

"I am very angry," the Taifa was close to tears. "I will take his head off myself. Give me a sword."

Qasim watched in horror as the base-born Taifa grabbed a scimitar and made to swing it at the Templar's neck. The warrior monk showed no emotion as his death neared. But Sidray was struggling foolishly with the scimitar, unable to work out how to use it. He held it to one side of his body, then the other — wishing now that he hadn't embarked on this course of action.

The al-kaid couldn't bear to watch this any longer. Drawing his own sword, he swung it high and with one blow, severed the Templar's head. He'd borne the Christian knight no personal grudge. And he certainly had no wish to be a common executioner. But the al-kaid realised that the vain and ill-tempered Taifa would end up hacking and chopping at the Templar as he tried to kill him. The spectacle of a botched beheading would have been very unedifying.

The knight's head rolled near to Sidray's feet and with one sharp kick of his embroidered slippers, he sent it splashing into the fishpond.

"I did not like that present, al-kaid! You have displeased me greatly!"

Chapter 36

DOM AFONSO'S TENT
PORTUGUESE MILITARY CAMP
NEAR SANTAREM (FORMERLY SHANTARIN)

Secluded in some trees nearby and enveloped in the darkness of night, three figures watched William intently. They had come a long way from the plains of Castile, where they traded their mules. Hunrith and Aylmer had stayed away, afraid they would stand out among the Portuguese – whereas the Maragatos might be able to blend in with their fellow Iberians.

The mule traders watched William talking with Martins and accompanied as ever by the Easterner in his gold lamellar armour and black cloak and the little English boy who always seemed slightly confused by his surroundings. The Maragatos had been assured that a great lady in England would reward them handsomely if they could seize the tall, blond-haired Templar.

He looked strong. But they had worked out a crude plan. One of them would club William about the head while the other two held his arms. It hardly mattered if he lived or died so long as his head was identifiable when they brought it back.

Martins was uncharacteristically happy. Trundling towards the Templar party were several packhorses and wagons that groaned under a great weight. Once they stopped, Portuguese Templar serjeants heaved the great chests from inside the wagons onto the ground.

"Careful!" the Master barked as Aleixo went up and sniffed the wooden caskets. "English Templar," Martins turned to William, "watch this."

He opened the curved lid of one of the chests. A flash of light revealed thousands of *livres parisi* – gold bullion that glimmered in the torchlight. "From the Temple in Paris and not before time. Pitões and those bishops preferred it when we took bribes from the Moors. Shameful practice! Taking their tainted money in order not to be in debt to us Templars. But our money is clean. Our money is holy. Our money comes from the industrious work of our preceptories."

William was stupefied by the sheer amount of wealth in the chest. Surely enough to buy the world, let alone fund a siege of Al-Usbuna.

Martins took William to one side.

"You must remain silent on that ... what I've told you not to mention."

"I promise," the knight answered.

The Templars entered the King's tent to be confronted by a scene of bacchanalian excess – feasting on a scale that the Portuguese seemed to relish. Knights and courtiers stumbled round, spilling goblets of wine and devouring chicken legs and pork as they celebrated the fall of Shantarin for yet another night. At the centre of this uncouth feasting sat the pregnant Queen from refined Savoy, wishing that angels would appear and waft her to any other spot on earth but here.

At Maud's side, Dom Afonso clapped loudly to the rhythmic sounds from the tabor pipes and sarronca drums. Behind him was a large battle standard with the emblem of the new kingdom of Portugal – a blue cross on a white background with five small shields inset with eleven silver bezants. Staggering before the royal couple was Geraldo Geraldes Sem Pavor in his element, with the auroch horn to his lips and red wine dribbling down his neck.

Watching Geraldo's performance with aloof indifference were the two most powerful bishops in Portugal – Bishop Pedro Pitões of Porto and superior to him, Archbishop João Peculiar of Braga. The latter styled himself 'Primate of all the Spains' and ruled like a king in his own domains.

Though Dom Afonso found him haughty and disliked the power he wielded, Peculiar had made himself indispensable as he journeyed from Braga to

Rome, repeatedly calling on the Pope to recognise Portugal as a true Christian kingdom.

Geraldo popped his gold Arab dinar back in his mouth then almost fell on the Queen as he moved towards her, showing off the shining coin on the end of his ox-like tongue.

"Aaaaaaahhhhh!!!!!"

With a sickened expression on her face, Maud gripped her distended stomach. Her unborn child's kicks were getting sharper and more insistent as if it wanted to join in the dancing as well. *Truly this is Afonso's child and not mine*, she thought.

"May I drink, Master?" Nicholas had followed William in without him noticing. "Promise I won't drink much. Never do, really. Well, sometimes I do. But it makes me fall over."

"Do you want to be a Templar knight one day?" William asked the boy thief.

Nicholas' eyes widened like saucers.

"Oh yes! Could I be? You're not just saying that?"

"Well …" William paused, "you've got to prove yourself. There's all this sinful temptation here. Drink! Women! So, can you behave like a Templar? Can you compose yourself little, Nicholas?"

"Highly doubtful," Pathros muttered.

"Don't be so cynical," William retorted.

"Yes, always have a go at me," Nicholas chimed in.

"Now," the Templar teased his turcopole, "be nice to Nicholas." Then lowered his voice for the Syrian's ears only. "Let him have some joy before the … before the disease takes hold. He's only a boy. Try and be kind to him."

Nicholas thought the feasting looked more fun than anything he'd ever seen. The Golgotha Tavern had nothing on what was going on here. Empty jugs of wine littered the floor, along with discarded chicken and pig bones, all the meat chewed off them. And there was more food being served from spits outside, with servants rushing around with more wine every second. *I must be good and impress Master William.*

"Hugo!" the King shouted out, having spotted the Templar master. Then his eyes drifted past Martins to the very agreeable sight of the heavy caskets.

Afonso practically drooled at this spectacle. "I like what I see. You Templars have served me well."

Pitões and Peculiar bristled at this compliment to the Order of the Temple.

"However shall we pay you Templars back …" Peculiar's jowls twitched disapprovingly and his bulky frame, covered in stupendously expensive vestments, heaved as he controlled his anger. " … no doubt at a rate of interest that leaves your Order further enriched."

"Not true!" Martins blustered. "Better than taking Moorish dinars, anyway!"

"Quite … quite," the King agreed. "Let us not quarrel, eh? Templar knights … Templar coin … our own good men … and all these fine soldiers come from Flanders and Cologne – we cannot lose!" Afonso squinted as he took in the sight of Pathros. "You an emissary from the Moors? Tell your masters about what you see here! We will crush them!"

William laughed then knelt before Dom Afonso.

"He's my turcopole, your Majesty, not a Moor. His name is Pathros – a man of medicine and healing. He has much wisdom and learning. Never stops reading, in fact."

"Reading? Hmmm …" Afonso didn't seem to approve of such an idle pastime. "Well, I shall soon be king of people like you and people like him. Christians, Moors and Jews shall all be Portuguese! I do not much care who they say their prayers to in Al-Usbuna so long as they recognise me as their sovereign lord. Portugal - that is what unites us all. Christian! Muslim! Jews! All – subjects of the kingdom of Portugal!"

Pitões darted Peculiar a furious glance at these words. Afonso was allowing room for more than one faith in the new kingdom and that was intolerable to the bishops.

Peculiar raised a knowing eyebrow back to his fellow cleric as if to say it was a matter that would be dealt with in the fullness of time. Jews and Muslims had no future in Al-Usbuna or in any of the cities the Portuguese had conquered and would conquer soon. No Jews. No Muslims. And, Peculiar mused, no Templars either!

The tall, blond knight intrigued Afonso.

"You speak Leonense quite well but you are not from these lands."

"From England, your Majesty. Here to serve you and sent by Bernard of Clairvaux himself."

"Why has he sent you to me?"

William paused.

"I was his student. He mentored me as a young monk and then as a knight. I bear him a great love as a teacher and holy man. Bernard believes I may be of service to you in your great cause. He truly believes this kingdom is ordained by God and will strike a death blow at the Saracens from which they will never recover."

"He thinks that?"

"Yes."

"Good, that pleases me."

A large and rather ungainly knight slapped Martins on the back and thundered at the Portuguese Templar master: "By God's bones you should have been at Santarem, Hugo! We slashed and slew those bastards by the hundred." Martim Moniz swayed, a broad grin across his face. "Christ, we gave them a beating!"

"Moniz," Pitões interjected venomously, "I had a man flogged at the pillory before my cathedral for a lesser blasphemy than you have just uttered."

"Ah, sorry, Bishop," the knight affected contrition, "one of the commandments ..."

"The second one," Pitões noted drily.

Moniz raised the jewel-encrusted goblet he'd taken from the house of a merchant during the sack of Santarem.

"Wine will cleanse my sinful mouth!"

Afonso continued to speak with William.

"You look more of a knight than a monk." The King winked. "I bet you could have any woman you wished ... maybe you already have."

"I'm true to my vows, your Majesty," William stifled an impish grin.

"Ha! You hear that, Hugo? You Templars have turned this fine young man into a virgin!" Afonso slapped his knee. "I do not believe you, by the way. You have the look of somebody who has known the pleasures of the flesh ..."

William blushed.

"Before I took my vows."

"Aaaah, of course … before … all different now, eh?" Afonso wondered if he could get William to reject his vows that very evening. "I have something to show you. She is the most dazzling and intoxicating creature you will ever see." Afonso bore the most lascivious of smiles and his eyes twinkled with mischief. "You look worried already. I knew it! You have an eye for the women!"

With that, the King clapped his hands.

"The dancer!"

Out of the murk of a corner of the tent, unlit by torches, a spectacular vision emerged. Slim, curvaceous and bronzed. Raven hair and oval brown eyes, with long painted eyelashes. A body that swayed to the sarronca drum beats like a cobra winding this way and that.

Every movement hypnotised the men in the room and William found his gaze fixed on the jewelled stud in her navel. Hurriedly, he looked away but then, as if pulled by magic, his eyes rested again on her swaying midriff.

She is so beautiful.

Surely God couldn't disapprove of me looking at one of his creations, William tried to reason. I won't touch her. I'd never do that. Just let myself watch her delicate hands weaving patterns in the air above her head.

She is bewitching me.

The expression on her face was one of pride in her art and talent. As she drifted past the knight, his nostrils sucked in the scent of lavender. Traced on her arms and legs in henna were patterns of flowers and William took in every detail as she twirled past him yet again.

I am falling for her and I mustn't.

Some soldiers now urged Geraldo to join them outside the tent. Something had happened. Once outside in the cold night air, the corpulent knight was confronted with three bound figures looking very afraid.

It was the Maragatos sent by the three bounty hunters from Essex to kidnap William.

"They were creeping around the tent, sir," one of the soldiers said.

Geraldo examined their dress.

"A long way from home ... do you even understand me?"

"Yes," one of them answered.

"Maragatos," Geraldo continued. "But you are not here to trade mules, are you?" He slapped the man who had just spoken across the face. "What are you doing here?" He punched another of the Maragatos in the stomach so hard his fist seemed to connect with the man's spine. "Do you mean our king harm? Are you in the pay of our enemies?" Geraldo grabbed one of them by the throat. "Answer me!"

The three men had fallen silent.

"Maybe you got lost." The Portuguese knight produced a small knife from under his belt. "But we cannot take any risks. You," he addressed the man who had spoken, "will convey a message to whoever sent you. And you two," he pointed to the other Maragatos, "will *be* the message."

As the soldiers held the two Maragatos still, Geraldo went to work on their faces, slitting their noses, lips and slicing off their ears. Such was the continued racket from inside the tent as the dancer was cheered and clapped that nobody heard the cries of the mule traders outside. Once Geraldo felt he'd made his point clearly, he permitted the unharmed Maragato to return to wherever he'd come from with his two mutilated companions.

"Tell your paymaster I will do that to him!" Geraldo shouted after them as they hobbled into the night.

Congratulating the Portuguese soldiers on their vigilance, Geraldo entered the tent, nearly falling over a drunken boy sleeping on the ground. Nicholas had succumbed to temptation and collapsed in an inebriated stupor.

"Stupid child!" Geraldo growled.

The dancer was still cavorting to the drums. Geraldo was spellbound, as was every other hot-blooded male. The flickering candlelight made the jewels across her forehead shine like small stars and illuminated the gold and emerald belt that hung loosely and suggestively around her hips. Her lips parted and she mouthed sensual words that any man could interpret as he saw fit.

William was hopelessly bewitched. Maud was appalled. The chubby-cheeked queen, wearied and fattened by pregnancy, watched in despair as the dancer aroused the baser passions of her husband. He was staring at her like a slavering dog.

Afonso kept nudging William suggestively.

The seductive temptress was just a few inches from the King. She crossed her arms above her head, pulsating her flat stomach towards him and edging closer in tiny, imperceptible steps. Her arms then dropped loosely behind her back. Afonso could smell her overpowering scent and felt her body heat. Only Maud's presence prevented him from flinging his arms around this beauty.

Suddenly, the dancer brought her right hand round. In it flashed a small blade. She lunged towards Afonso's neck but before the weapon made contact, an iron hand clamped on her wrist.

William shook her arm and the knife fell to the ground. The Templar hadn't been able to take his eyes off the dancer but his lust had led him to see what was happening just in time.

"Murderer!" she screamed, kicking at William and trying to claw at Afonso's face. "Murderer of my people!"

"Dear God," the King gasped, clutching at his chest, "she will hang from a tree right now. Take her outside and kill the witch."

Geraldo dropped his auroch horn and bounded over.

"Before we kill her – let us find out who sent her!"

He seized the petite figure from William and with one deft movement, turned her upside down. With a free hand, he removed her sandals to reveal the dancer's bare soles. Then, asking for a stave, Geraldo proceeded to beat her feet.

"Bastinado!" he yelled, "Always makes them talk!"

The dancer screamed but said nothing. As the sound of her suffering reverberated around the tent, the Queen could take no more.

"Can she not be taken to a dungeon?" Maud's breaths grew shorter and more insistent, "Must we let this brute interrogate her here, in front of us all?"

Geraldo looked up.

"She tried to kill our king!"

"As if you really care about that … you just enjoy what you are doing … you are an animal …"

With that, Maud tumbled off her throne and fell groaning to the ground. Her ladies in waiting rushed to the Queen. Suddenly, from the crowd of drunken courtiers, Pathros emerged, producing a vial from his leather bag and hurriedly administering it to Maud.

"Great King," the turcopole looked up from his patient, "the Queen will give birth early and you may lose your child. Silence and calm would be the best medicine to prevent this. I beg your Majesty."

"Pathros is always right on these matters," William added in defence of his servant and companion, "Please, your Majesty, I saved your life ... let me guard this woman until she is judged and condemned."

"I have condemned her already," the King replied tersely. "She will hang now!"

William hated this kind of arbitrary justice. The sort of mockery of justice Nicholas had been threatened with, or that poor serf cast off the cliffs of Dover by a mob.

"Please," William begged, "this shouldn't be the way for a great king like you to conduct himself ... the leader of a great kingdom like Portugal. Things should be done properly." The knight flung himself at the King's feet. Once more he recalled the brutal executions he'd been forced to witness in the past – the travesties of justice that led to ferocious and inhuman punishments. "Let me guard her until she can be put on trial and condemned in the proper manner."

"Well, well, well ..." Afonso folded his arms and sat back on his throne, "so you have a cock, after all! Taken quite a liking to the murderous bitch! So be it ... you can guard her ... it will amuse me to see how long it takes before you abandon your precious vows."

The King looked over at the sobbing dancer, still held upside down.

"Geraldo, let her go. Put her in chains. Hand her to our English Templar. When we get to Al-Usbuna, we can give my would-be murderer a little trial as our friend here so badly wants. Then I will take great pleasure in seeing her dance at the end of a rope in front of the battlements, eh? It will be an object lesson to the Moors behind those walls of what I intend for them, if they do not surrender in good time."

Chapter 37

NEAR SANTAREM

The Flemish knight's fist landed square in his opponent's face – crushing his nose and sending a stream of blood jetting out of his mouth. But the other man wasn't going to surrender. Whatever slight or insult had started this grudge match, it wasn't going to end so easily.

Leaping onto his assailant, he dug his thumb into his eye socket till he was thrown off. Then giant fists pounded in all directions. The two giants from Flanders slugged it out while the secular knights cheered them on.

Two northern European nobles stood nearby, watching. Christian of Ghistelles commanded the Flemish knights and Count Arnold of Aerschot was in charge of the men of Cologne. Both had no interest in stopping the bloodshed before them. It was a welcome distraction.

"Have you spoken to Pitões?" Aerschot muttered under his breath.

"Yes," Ghistelles replied. "We will enter the city first. He will ensure that our encampment is to the East of Al-Usbuna, where the walls are weaker. Our sappers should make easy work of it. The Normans, he will ensure, are positioned to the West, where the river flows between them and the walls. Their sappers will come under constant fire."

"What does he want? What do you think he really brought us here?"

The German noble was deeply suspicious of the Bishop of Porto.

Ghistelles chuckled.

"His plan is simple. He wants us to rape the entire city. Not one Moorish man or woman should live — so it'll be like a slate wiped clean. Then these Portuguese can begin all over again. Make the city in their own image."

"And we can take what we want?"

"Yes — every last thing," Ghistelles answered. "I have his personal assurance. There will be three days when our men can do as they please." The Flemish noble watched his two soldiers as their fight grew ever more savage. "Then the men won't be bored anymore. Fighting! Raping! Plundering! We'll have a very happy army when we get back on our ships."

Nearby, Pathros tended to their prisoner's swollen feet but as he smeared some ointment onto her soles, she kicked out at his face.

"That is not very civil, dear lady."

"It hurt!"

"I am trying to heal you."

"You think you are a doctor."

This stung the turcopole as much as the medicine on the dancer's feet. He was forced to consider this for a moment. Was he a doctor? What was he? A mere turcopole whose duties were to prepare his master's horse and fire arrows in battle?

"I know some medicine … I have taught myself. If my father had lived …"

"You are their slave," the dancer derided his pretensions in her heavy Moorish accent, "nothing else. Do not pretend to yourself that you mean anything more to them. You are ridiculous. Leave my foot alone!" Suddenly she was aware of being gawped at by Nicholas. "Why does that boy look at me? Is he simple?"

"He is English. It is more or less the same thing, I have found."

Pathros had started to feel guilty about his initial hostility towards Nicholas now that he knew the leprosy was taking a grip on the boy's young body. But liking him was out of the question. He turned back to the dancer.

"You may say what you wish about him. He does not speak Arabic."

"Unlike you. A traitor to your people."

"I did not betray my people," Pathros hit back, "we were conquered by the Seljuks. They destroyed my family. I have nothing to be ashamed of."

"That is not what your eyes say," the dancer replied.

"My eyes say nothing," the turcopole's voice quavered.

"The Franks," she mused poetically, "are like jars filled with bitter aloe and a little honey dabbed around the rim. A fool like you who tastes them is deceived until the real content is shown beyond doubt."

Pathros pursed his lips — the comment stung.

"We are both creatures of the caliphate, dear lady. I from Aleppo and you from Shantarin."

"Yes — but I know where my loyalty lies. And unlike you, it did not have to be bought."

William appeared.

"Are her feet better?" he asked Pathros.

"I can answer for my own feet," the dancer snapped back in perfect English, "And they are still in agony from that Frankish brute. But you are all brutes! All of you! And this one," she sneered at Pathros, "thinks he is civilised because he has a bag of herbs. He is a traitor to his own people ..."

"Well, you *sound* better," William smirked. "And you speak English very well."

"Because, like my people, I am cultured — not like you beasts!"

"I didn't do this to you," the Templar replied, "and I wish it hadn't happened. But I'm also glad you weren't strangled at the end of a rope unless you want to die. And I can always hand you back to the King. He's very keen to execute you."

The dancer fell silent.

Suddenly, William scooped up the manacled woman in his strong arms and carried her off towards a wood situated on the fringes of the military camp.

"Put me down!"

"No, we need to talk in private."

"You are going to rape me more like."

William dropped his excitable captive. They were now out of view of the military encampment.

"You see this ..." he pointed to the cross on his mantle.

"Yes, I know ... you are a Knight Templar. That would not stop you. You are also a man and a Frank. And that means you are a beast whatever clothes you wear. That scarlet cross means nothing."

"I don't attack women," William answered softly. "What's your name?"

"Why should I tell you?"

"Because I saved your life."

She paused then relented.

"Orraca."

"That's a nice name. I'm William." He heaved his broad chest and clasped Orraca by the shoulders with his firm hands. His light blue eyes gazing into her face, he asked: "Why did you try to kill the King?"

"You ask me that after what his savages did to my people?"

She fought back tears recalling the lament of a great poet:

The white wells of ablution are weeping with sorrow,
As a lover does when torn from his beloved;
They weep over the remains of dwellings devoid of Muslims,
Despoiled of Islam, now peopled with Infidels!

Orraca turned to William. She began to recount the grim sequence of events when Geraldo and his soldiers had taken Shantarin. The city had been her home. Gleaming white buildings, with the mosque and church sitting contentedly side by side, a fine bathhouse and library, squares with gurgling fountains that provided fresh water and refreshing breezes on a hot day.

All that had been wiped away when Geraldo clambered over their walls and began his orgy of slaughter. Those of the Muslim faith knew that their time had come. Geraldo the Fearless would drown them in their own blood and even massacre their children. But as a Christian, Orraca naively thought her people might be treated more leniently.

"We woke up to find the Moors gone. We were alone. We held up the cross of Our Lord and icons of the saints. Look, we cried out to the invaders, we are Christians like you." Orraca paused, turning away, her hair covering her face as the tears ran down her cheeks. "They killed everybody. They said we were all Moors."

"So you're a Christian?"

"Yes," she replied, "but the blood of my Muslim neighbours was equal to ours. We did not regard them as filthy animals the way you do."

William flinched. He was no Geraldo, intent on murdering anybody who got in his way.

"My turcopole is a Christian as well. He's a good man. And like you he's suffered. This is a cruel and foolish world but some of us are trying to make it better."

Orraca snorted derision.

"How? By coming here on crusade? By destroying our beautiful cities? My people lived for centuries in Shantarin and you have turned it into a graveyard. And now you are going to do the same to Al-Usbuna! How are you making things better? Go home – leave us alone! That would make things better!"

"I'm here for a greater reason. There is something in Al-Usbuna I must retrieve …"

"I am sure," Orraca retorted sarcastically, "you will be retrieving as much gold and jewels as you can to take back to England. Our gold! Our jewels!" She ran her delicate fingers through her ebony hair. "You should have let me kill Ibn Arrik. That man will wipe out thousands of men, women and children before his lust for power is sated. You have no idea what you have done by stopping me."

Orraca toyed with a small flower. The words of an Andalusian poem echoed in her head:

A palm tree stands in the middle of Russafa,
Born in the West far from the land of palms.
I said to it: How like me you are, far away and in exile,
In long separation from family and friends.
You have sprung from soil in which you are a stranger,
And I, like you, am far from home.

William placed his hand under her chin and lifted it up so he could see her face. As she looked back at him, he was lost in her seductive stare.

"I've seen my fair share of massacres and killing," he whispered. "I know how terrible it is. It's even affected my senses. I'm torn apart inside by what I've seen and done. But I'm not a beast."

The Moorish captive shrugged.

"If only you knew what misery the Portuguese have brought wherever they conquer," Orraca rested her head on William's shoulder. She was so tired and exhausted. "Fields once irrigated are barren and the fruit shrivels in the trees. Our palaces are smashed and looted till all that is left are bare walls. They take our fine silks but do not know how to fashion such exquisite garments themselves. Our way of life is being strangled."

"I believe Dom Afonso will learn to be a better king," William said.

Orraca pulled away from him.

"You are a fool then!"

William surveyed this temperamental Moor, entranced by her exquisite scent, dark eyes and slim curves. She in turn felt increasingly hypnotised by the Templar's bright gold coloured hair, his broad and square jaw and those inviting pale-blue eyes.

I cannot fall in love with this man. I must not. He's a Frankish devil. Yet he is youthful and tender. His mouth exhales perfume. I must sip this rosy wine of pleasure until its liquid bliss comes to an end.

She stroked his light beard with her henna-painted hand. William could no longer resist the smooth olive skin and delicious aroma of her body. He kissed Orraca. Then kissed her again.

I've never wanted a woman more than you. I'll protect you with my life!

The couple then locked in an embrace, Orraca flinging her chained arms around his broad shoulders. He drew her ever closer, clasping her slender torso. Afonso had been right: the Templar was too weak to keep his vows.

Chapter 38

NEAR SANTAREM

The Archbishop of Braga possessed a sumptuous tent larger than that of the King and more heavily guarded. His accommodation was heaving with some of the finest reliquaries ever fashioned. They had all been brought on this crusade to ensure the intervention of the Trinity and the saints in securing Al-Usbuna for Christ. Pitões watched João Peculiar wander among his priceless treasures, stroking and admiring them.

An enamelled box contained a fragment of the skull of John the Baptist, as well as his right arm and some locks of his blood-clotted hair. The hand of Saint Margaret of Antioch was displayed under a rock crystal cover with a gold backing. The holy lance that had pierced the side of Jesus on the cross was contained in a silver sleeve while a nail from that cross was contained within a reliquary covered in gold filigree and precious stones.

"I'm very proud of this one." João Peculiar placed his hand on a golden portable altar with a carving of a foot on top of it. "The sandal of Andrew the Apostle. Six months' tithes from my estate near Braganca to obtain it." Then he moved on to what appeared to be a walking stick but was covered in pearls. "The staff of Saint Peter."

He paused at a box of ivory and wood carved in Al-Andalus for a Moorish nobleman but now topped with a crucifix. The workmanship was something Peculiar hoped could one day be replicated in Christian Iberia. Then he patted the head of Saint Blaise, fashioned at great expense in a combination of silver and copper gilt.

"I've given the King permission to take the finger bones of Saint Blaise and place them round his neck in battle. It was quite a feat obtaining them." Peculiar had the feeling that Pitões wasn't admiring his relics sufficiently. "You're making my head throb, Pedro. If you have something to say, please say it, but don't just stand there and smoulder. I find it a very unattractive character trait."

"You heard what he said."

"Yes." The Archbishop had been fully aware of Afonso's idiotic reference to ruling three faiths in the new Portugal. "The King says these things without thinking, that's why he needs bishops."

Pitões moved round a large painted bust of one of the companions of Saint Ursula.

"I think you underestimate the danger of such comments," Pitões insisted. "It's bad enough that in Castile, the King there says much the same thing. And in Aragon – that de facto heretic boasts of ruling three faiths all the time. It's unacceptable. Surely we must stamp it out."

Peculiar picked up a reliquary arm of Saint Luke and admired it.

"You fret too much. Afonso will bend to our will." He put the reliquary down. "I travel more than you do. I attend many Church councils. And all over Europe, kings are bending their knees to us. Not the other way round. More and more, Rome has the whip hand over secular monarchs. The Pope can even excommunicate a man like Afonso, if he so chooses. At the mere command of our great pontiff in Rome, the Portuguese people would be ordered to rise up and overthrow Afonso. Things are moving our way, I tell you."

Pitões glared at Peculiar.

"I hear different things."

"Really? Like what?"

"That the Pope's word does not run everywhere in Europe – that there are rebellions against our church."

"And what have you heard?"

Peculiar was unsettled by this conversation. He didn't like talk of any threat to the authority of well-heeled prelates.

"Cathars!" Pitões all but spat the word from his mouth. "Men from France who have journeyed far to spread heresy in our villages and towns. They say Christians don't need bishops. They say it's a sin that you mint your own money." Peculiar flinched. "They say you care more for earthly riches than the salvation of souls." Pitões continued. "I have heard the Templars shelter these French heretics and together they scheme to create a church where there is no Pope and his princes are overthrown. They believe their time has come and ours is past."

Peculiar's jowls twitched again with discomfort and his heavily hooded eyelids lowered over his watery, oyster-like eyes.

"Afonso would never listen to such evil."

"He is a co-frater in the Templar Order, your Grace, as you well know." Pitões pulled his black cap tighter round his white-skinned face and continued: "And he's beholden to them financially." Peculiar looked a lot less complacent now, which pleased the Bishop of Porto immensely. "Afonso respects what they have achieved in *nullis diocesis*."

Pitões was referring to the no man's land between the Templar and Moorish domains, where no prince or bishop wielded authority. Only the courageous Templars guarded the villages against constant incursions by the forces of the caliphate.

Pitões decided to hit Peculiar where he knew it would hurt – his purse!

"Surely they could turn to the King and say that in return for their courageous service against the Moors, they should receive the lion's share of the riches within Al-Usbuna. And we would be powerless to object."

Peculiar glared angrily at a silver casket containing the bones of Saint Adrian and Saint Natalia.

"What do you suggest then?"

"We make sure the secular knights get the riches before the Templars. I've already spoken with the nobles from Flanders, Cologne, Normandy and England. I've promised them everything that lies within Al-Usbuna. Each one believes he has the advantage over the other. So they'll descend on the city and ravage it like locusts, believing they're getting more than the other. I've harnessed their greed to our purpose."

Peculiar held up a splendid talisman once owned by the Emperor Charlemagne: "And you think that will work?"

"Those foreign crusaders will turn Al-Usbuna into a vision of hell itself. No Jew, Muslim or heretical Christian would ever want to live there again. The wall of every house will be smeared with the blood of infants and men will watch helplessly as their wives are defiled. We must convince the King to give them three days to take what they want and then the shell of Al-Usbuna will be handed over to us."

Peculiar nodded in agreement.

"We'll then re-fashion Al-Usbuna as something very different," Pitões concluded. "There won't be a trace of the Jewish or Muslim faith, not one stone set upon another. The city will be Christian alone. One faith. One church. One king."

Peculiar was impressed by the Bishop's logic.

"You're a good man, Pitões. And as you say, that should put an end to the kingdom of three faiths."

"And to the Templars, your Grace," the Bishop of Porto added.

Both men left to celebrate mass before the company of knights. As they exited the tent, a small figure popped up and began feverishly applying a knife to the bust of Saint Amandus. He hadn't understood a word of their cynical conversation, not speaking their strange language. Nicholas stuffed two precious stones in his pocket and then, like a fox in the night, crept out on all fours.

Chapter 39

ON A HILL ACROSS THE TAGUS ESTUARY FROM AL-USBUNA

The Templar squadron had halted and William peeled off with Pathros, Nicholas and his captive, Orraca, to climb the slope of Monte Fragoso and take his first glimpse of the Moorish city of Al-Usbuna. All around them were the deserted munyas of the Moorish nobles, the immaculately laid out orchards and farms they had fled on the news that Ibn Arrik was heading their way. As they paced over the brow of the hill, William gasped in astonishment. Before them was the white bride that Dom Afonso had pledged to take in marriage without her consent: the gleaming city of Al-Usbuna – more dazzling than the Templar could have imagined.

The Moorish metropolis spread over a large hill and if the city was indeed an unwilling bride, as the King had described it, then the qasr fortress at its summit was the wedding tiara. Surrounding it was a broad platform covering the hill summit. This was the qasba, where the nobility lived alongside the chancery, mint and barracks. Then the gleaming white veil extending downwards towards the River Tagus was the countless flat-roofed houses and bleached walls of the medina with the great mosque that Pitões longed to see demolished. This was all hemmed in by the steepest of fortifications.

"It will not fall as easily as Shantarin," Orraca murmured to William.

"We'll see," he replied.

She bit her lip.

"You should just board a ship with your two friends and leave now" She looked out at the Atlantic Ocean beyond the city, a vast sheet of blue water. "I would think of you from time to time, Templar, You have laid claim to a small part of my heart. You have fettered it like a herdsman ties up a camel. But then the memory would fade. We would resume our lives as before. And you would return to your people."

"I'm not going anywhere except here." William was full of resolve. He knew that the siege would be unpleasant. All sieges were unpleasant - but God had ordained this one. "I'm so close to my goal ... what I came all this way to achieve. Back in England ... my father," he gulped at the vision of the lead casket in his head, "my father awaits on the success of this mission."

Orraca didn't know what he was talking about. He hadn't confided in her about the old Earl's disgrace in death.

"You would kill men, women and children to please your father?"

"No," William twisted the point of his sword in the grass. "My quest just involves retrieving a great object ... a priceless relic. And it's in there somewhere."

He looked across at the mighty city and its impenetrable warren of alleys and streets, which he could just about make out. Goodness knew where the Lignum Crucis might be concealed.

Orraca murmured a poem contemplating her beloved Shantarin and what the great city before them was about to endure.

"Even the mihrabs weep though they are solid, even the pulpits mourn though they are wooden. Today, William, there are people who live like kings in their own homes but you will reduce them to slaves who must grovel before a drunken barbarian."

"That won't happen," William demurred.

"And the king's pet monster will hang me." Orraca began to sob a little. She realised that the dinar-chewing knight Geraldo Geraldes Sem Pavor would relish hauling her struggling body onto a prominent gibbet as an early warning to the people of Al-Usbuna. To hang a young woman would convey the Portuguese intention to slay every citizen of the city if they refused to surrender. "That creature will stretch my neck in front of the walls unless you stop him."

"I won't let him touch you. Believe me, I'll cut him into pieces if he comes near you."

Pathros sidled up to William.

"My friend, you cannot take the boy any further. What happens if he spreads this debilitating disease among the soldiers or even into the city? You will have brought defeat to this great cause by your attachment to this child." The turcopole tugged at his goatee. "You are a kind person, this has always been obvious to me. You have great honour. But he will bring havoc to our side simply by his touch."

"He's shown no further sign of the leprosy," William glanced at Nicholas.

Pathros shook his head in dismay.

"I have seen something … on his stomach. To me it looks like a clear sign."

"You could be wrong."

"Please, my friend, do you not respect my powers of healing?"

"Yes," William relented, anguished by a decision he'd have to make very soon. "Keep watching him – all the time. When you see the sickness on his fingers or his face, then we'll part company with Nicholas – but not before then."

The Templar knight watched as the different crusader armies positioned themselves for the onslaught on Al-Usbuna. The hill where William was standing, Monte Fragoso, was being turned into the Norman and English camp. In the valley below flowed an inlet of the Tagus, a fairly shallow but broad stretch of water separating Fragoso from the imposing city walls.

On the far side of Al-Usbuna and out of William's view was another hill, Monte de Sao Vicente, where the Flemish and men of Cologne were preparing for their onslaught. Pitões had secretly promised them that these walls were more vulnerable to being undermined by the sappers.

Humiliatingly, Dom Afonso was forced to occupy a hill furthest from the city – giving his foreign allies the promised right to sack the city first before he entered. Disgruntled and swallowing their pride, the Portuguese camped on the more distant Monte de Sant'Ana.

Even from the top of Monte Fragoso, Nicholas could hear the teeming activity within Al-Usbuna. Thousands of voices conversing, arguing and selling created a permanent hum emanating from Al-Usbuna. Streams of ant-like figures poured in and out of the city's main gates. Nicholas couldn't help but wonder how many purses he could snatch and market stalls he could steal from, were he ever able to get within those walls.

The inlet at the base of Fragoso fed into the huge River Tagus estuary in front of the city, where trading vessels continued to disgorge their opulent cargoes from the markets of Benin to the Greek entrepots of Trebizond – seemingly unaware of the crusaders closing in on them.

Al-Usbuna must be three times the size of London, William thought. Somewhere in that huge metropolis is the True Cross and I must have it. But the task seemed overwhelming. The medina was a maze of alleys and the qasba looked even better defended than the main city. Its walls were clearly built to ensure that if the crusaders broke through, they would never infiltrate the inner sanctum where the Moorish elite lived and governed.

"A city like that will have enough grain and water to withstand a siege for many months," Pathros noted, trying not to sound proud of another Eastern achievement. It reminded him of Damascus or Cairo in its immensity and perfection. "There will be streams feeding wells and cisterns as well as sealed vaults full of grain no rat or cockroach can enter."

"Listen to him, William," Orraca interjected. "He is right. You will never take Al-Usbuna … never! It is a city of lions surrounded by base Frankish jackals. They will roar and scatter you back to the lands from whence you came."

Outside the walls were large settlements on either side of the city, thousands of houses like those in the medina. Orraca explained that they were called the Arribaldes. The western Arribalde, nearest to Monte Fragoso, included the Judiaria – where the Jews of Al-Usbuna lived. There were no high walls to protect them but they would be the first line of defence against the Franks. Knowing defeat meant certain death; they would fight like lions to repel the invaders.

William turned to Nicholas.

"If something very precious was in that city – the richest object in the world – could your nose sniff it out?"

The boy beamed.

"Yes, Master – I'd find it!"

Of course he could, William thought. That's why he's with us. God means me to find the True Cross and I will not betray my quest.

I was meant to rescue Nicholas – he will lead me to the Lignum Crucis!

Down in the valley, Moorish men and women were busily searching for gold in the waters of the Tagus with bronze and iron sieves. It was said that gold dust coated the lower reaches of the city walls, where the river lapped against the great stones at high tide. The hills around them were pockmarked with silver mines and even the humblest citizen of Al-Usbuna was said to drink from shining vessels and wear rings and buckles crafted from precious metals.

Suddenly, one of the gold hunters looked up to see thousands of helmets and shields gleaming in the morning sun and to hear the sound of thousands of Christian feet. Picking up their sieves, they hurtled towards the city gates for refuge. The mighty doors slammed behind them.

"So it begins," William whispered.

Chapter 40

DOM AFONSO'S TENT

"Forty days!"

Dom Afonso couldn't believe his ears. Before him stood the leaders of the secular knights: Count Arnold of Aerschot leading the men of Cologne; Christian of Ghistelles leading the Flemish and the leaders of the Normans and English – Hervey de Glanvill, Simon of Dover and Saher de Archelle. The latter was a ruddy faced, ill-tempered Norman who had little time for the pretensions of the Portuguese king.

"Yes," Saher replied. "You heard correct. After forty days we go. Our men will not stay for false promises ..."

"How dare you!" Afonso screamed.

Martins patted Aleixo on the head – both looked in better spirits than they had done for quite a while. At long last, the foreign secular knights were showing their true colours. They were fair-weather friends after all. The rabble brought to Portugal by Pitões consisted of nothing but thieves and scavengers.

"Rest assured, Dom Afonso – we Templars will not be scurrying off on the forty-first day," Martins purred, a grin on his face. "Here to the end! Victory or death!"

Pitões couldn't permit the Templar master any advantage and he stepped forward, accompanied by his attendants holding the black canopy over his head.

The bright morning sunlight bathed Monte de Sant'Ana and threatened to bring the pale-skinned bishop out in blisters and rashes.

"Your Majesty, there is a solution to this problem – I have been considering it at some length." Afonso sneered, feeling that Pitões had badly let him down. It was going to take at least eighty days to break into the city, but the secular knights the Bishop had brought lacked the patience for a long siege. Pitões continued to outline his solution. "There are two things my friends here want – booty from the city and to sail on to Outremer before winter sets in."

"Booty?" Afonso perched angrily on the edge of his wooden throne. "What booty do they want?"

"It is only reasonable, your Majesty, that they have their share of what lies within Al-Usbuna. These good men from Flanders and Normandy have, after all, forsaken their crusading in Jerusalem to stand with us. We are surely obligated to reward them."

"Never heard such a thing!" Martins howled. "Outrageous! You want them to strip the city first before we get a look in. What do we get, Pitões? The bare bones!"

"Surely the bare bones should suffice?" Peculiar interjected in support of his fellow bishop. "After all, you Templars are not seeking financial gain, are you?"

All parties glowered distrustfully at each other: secular knights, Dom Afonso, Martins and the bishops. Pitões resumed where he'd left off.

"I was going to say that we should exchange hostages between us. This way the knights who have come from afar will stay eighty … ninety … a hundred days – until we take Al-Usbuna. But after we breach the walls, they must be allowed three days to take what they want. Then the city will be handed over to you, great king, to make your capital."

Afonso was horrified. He felt deceived by the wily Pitões. He must have known these knights would only join the King's battle on condition they could strip every ounce of gold and silver from Al-Usbuna.

All I will end up conquering is bricks and mortar!

But he had to take Al-Usbuna. The city must be his! Every Christian king and Moorish taifa on the Iberian peninsula was watching Dom Afonso. Could he win this battle? Was he more than just a bandit? If he lost the siege, they would close in on his kingdom and snuff it out.

"So, what do we do then, Pitões?"

The Bishop couldn't resist a thin-lipped smile.

"I will go as a hostage to the Normans – a guarantee that we will give them the spoils they want in return for staying as long as it takes to win Al-Usbuna."

"That's very generous of you," the King answered, not trusting the Bishop an inch. "You seem to have struck up quite a rapport with them, eh?"

Pitões bowed. Nothing more needed to be said: he had got his way.

Shortly afterwards, a glittering procession emerged from Dom Afonso's camp on Monte de Sant'Ana. Two podgy, jewel-encrusted fingers were raised and traced a cross in the air, blessing the Portuguese troops.

João Peculiar's dazzling cope of scarlet and gold was an awesome spectacle, even to the bemused Moors lining the top of the city walls. The Archbishop of Braga and Primate of All the Spains huffed and puffed his way to the largest gate in the walls of Al-Usbuna, which overlooked the broad Tagus estuary. He eschewed a closed carriage for the short journey, wanting instead to dazzle the Muslim heretics with the opulence of mother church.

After what seemed like an eternity he reached the city's grandest entrance. The Bab Al-Bahr consisted of two huge slabs of oak that could easily resist the onslaught of a battering ram. Before it was the thin strip of beach where the crusaders would have to position their siege tower. Doing this would be nearly impossible, given the position of the watchtowers looming above and brimming with archers and catapults.

Peculiar arrived to deliver the proclamation from the Portuguese king. Protocol demanded that his person was inviolate and the Moors wouldn't attack him. Flanked by priests bearing relics and Pitões lurking behind, the Archbishop raised his white-gloved hands not in benediction, but as a final warning to the Moors.

"We have come to you with a message of conciliation as we are all of the same substance and created by the same God. It is not our intention to subdue you or rob you of your goods, that is not our way. But we must insist that this city you have illegally taken is restored to us. And you Moors must return to the lands whence you came."

The al-kaid could scarcely believe his ears. Next to him his Almohad companion scoffed at the insolent cheek of this jewel-encrusted infidel. Only the etiquette of war prevented him skewering the Archbishop with a well-aimed crossbolt.

At an even greater height, the Taifa took in the unfolding scene from the battlements of the qasba, surrounded by his courtiers. The Archbishop was merely a colourful pinprick far below and anyhow, whatever the leader of the Christians in the realm of Ibn Arrik had to say, Sidray knew it would be just infidel lies.

The Taifa slapped his hand on the shoulder of a timid, elderly man next to him.

"What need do I have of another bishop when I have you?"

He smiled at Abrah, the Mozarabic bishop of Al-Usbuna, whose flock were Christians following the Greek rite of Constantinople and were almost indistinguishable in dress and manner from their Moorish and Jewish neighbours. Given a choice between the civilised comforts of the Taifa's rule and the barbaric uncouthness of Ibn Arrik, the Mozarabes were not about to fling open the city gates to the advancing crusaders. Better the turban of the Taifa than the tiara of the Pope and his Frankish attack dogs.

Like the rest of the medina, they would watch the besiegers slowly starve while they dined and drank as they always had.

"Your Christian subjects wish you a magnificent victory," Abrah replied obsequiously.

"Good! I may have a gift for your church when this is all over," Sidray smiled.

Abrah's eyes widened.

"The Lignum Crucis?"

"Why not?" Sidray chuckled. "I could hardly put it in the great mosque now, could I?"

Anticipating the onslaught of the Franks, the muhtasib of Al-Usbuna had ordered every household to store plentiful supplies of grain, fruit and olive oil. Shibli was a pedantic official whose main role was to regulate the weights and measures in the markets. But now, the muhtasib's most urgent task was to fill the vast subterranean silos that stretched under the qasba with enough food to last for months. These lime-mortar-coated caves had been dug long ago and once the supplies had been placed inside, they would be sealed for protection against rodents and insects.

"You took the cities and villages of Lusitania under false pretences," the Archbishop continued, "and have been here for over three centuries in violation of God's law. These lands were ours before they were yours. You have converted using the sword where we won over souls through the love of Jesus Christ."

The al-kaid listened to these words as he stared out at the small forests of tents sprouting up on every hill surrounding the city. To the East were the men of Cologne. To the West were the Normans and English. And behind the qasba on the hill furthest from the city camped the Portuguese forces of Dom Afonso Henriques. Qasim recognised the various standards that were fluttering above the tents.

"How dare they say we are strangers in this land," he snarled to his Berber companion, "look at those flags. Barely a man among them comes from this side of the Pyrenees."

The Archbishop now reached the climax of his address.

"If you wish to keep your fields and crops from being put to the flame and your wealth being distributed amongst our soldiers, then leave now through the gates in your walls and take to the seas. If you spurn our offer of peace, your days will be few, your children will be fatherless and your wives will be widows. I tell you the end is coming for you. Heed our word now or you will suffer most terribly."

With that, João Peculiar dropped his hands and a deacon handed him his dazzling mitre. Qasim could think of no response to such brazenness. He turned to gaze up towards the qasba to see if Sidray would give him a signal. But the Taifa had retreated with his courtiers, snorting at how they would flick these Franks away within days. This analysis was greeted with fawning agreement from his thinkers, servants and advisers.

As the Archbishop waited in a tense silence, the city's attitude was made clear by a trader in the souk who lobbed a half-eaten orange over the wall, narrowly missing the great cleric. Regarding the orange peel by his velvet-shod feet, João Peculiar decided that he'd treat this insult as the official response of Al-Usbuna. Raising his mitre, he bellowed apocalyptically.

"The earth will shake Al-Usbuna! The heavens will fall upon your bloodied heads!"

With that, the man of godly peace turned away from the Bab al-Bahr. He returned to Dom Afonso with the gladdest of tidings. The Moors had agreed to have their heathen throats slit.

Chapter 41

WESTERN ARRIBALDE AND JUDIARIA

Word had got out in the Portuguese camp that the knights from overseas would take all the booty, leaving them with nothing. The disgruntlement spread like a forest fire till a group of young slingers, farm boys with catapults, could take it no more. They refused to return to lives of poverty in the villages they had left behind. Al-Usbuna contained the riches of the world and they, as Portuguese, would get their share right now.

Hungry for combat, they slipped away from the Monte de Sant'Ana and headed towards the exposed western Arribalde. Those houses would have fine things inside them. All they had to do was kill or scare away the residents and grab what they could before their absence from camp was noticed.

As they neared the whitewashed houses, the youthful figures stretched every sinew to unleash their stones at the citizens of the Arribalde, who either fled into their homes or towards the nearest gate, the Bab al-Hadid — so-called as it was strengthened with huge bands of iron. Behind it was the safety of the medina but to the alarm of those banging their fists and begging admission, it remained shut.

"Al-kaid! Let us in!" they screamed and hollered. "Great Taifa, do not let us be killed!"

The sound of screams and shouts alerted the nearby Judiara, the Jewish quarter, that something was amiss and they too slammed their doors shut and barricaded themselves in as best they could. The relentless hail of stones from the Portuguese slingers was bloodying many heads and the dead and dying lay in the alleys of the Arribalde.

Sidray surveyed the human sea far below, their hands outstretched.

"Cowards, look at them! This is what Qasim has done to these people. They won't fight or defend their own houses."

The Taifa sipped on an apple tea. He was going to leave the residents of the Arribalde outside. It would toughen them up – force them to confront the Franks. One of the Taifa's attendants pointed to some trees near the high walls that bordered onto the qasba. Men and women from the Arribalde, some holding babies, were shinning their way up the trunks in a vain attempt to escape from the slingers.

They had no chance of leaping over the battlements from the branches as even the very tops of the trees were at least twenty feet lower, but their actions infuriated Sidray. He called to some of his Jackals standing to attention nearby.

"Shoot those apes down!"

The Templars were still preparing their camp on the same hill as Dom Afonso when a messenger arrived, badly out of breath. He fell to his knees before Hugo Martins.

"Master, they have begun to attack the city!"

The Templar master bristled. "Who?"

"The slingers. They are attacking the Arribaldes!"

"Idiots!" Martins thundered. Then he turned to face his men. "To horse, all of you! There is no time to lose. Pick up your weapons, we must go now!"

William told Nicholas to stay with Orraca. Though he'd tried to impart some military skills to the boy on their journey from Clairvaux to Portugal, he wasn't yet ready for combat. Pathros mounted his silky black steed and checked his quiver contained every kind of arrow. Each could inflict a different type of wound and travel at varying distances.

"I won't need your elixirs," William said.

But Pathros had heard this already in Mogadouro and then seen his friend crawl back for more of the medicine after the incident with Caretos and their frightful pagan dancing.

"As you wish, my friend."

In the Arribalde, residents watched as their kinsfolk fell from the branches of trees, shot down by their own side. The Jackals were making swift work of those trying to enter the qasba. Now realising they were caught between the Frankish slingers and their own ruler, the mood turned swiftly from fear to anger.

A few with military experience huddled together in an informal council of war then they bolted back towards their homes, yelling instructions at their neighbours. Each family was to lock themselves in as best they could and then stand on the flat roofs of their homes.

Gather as much slingshot as is fired at you and hurl it back at these monsters. All was not lost! The Arribalde could be defended!

A band of Norman and English slingers watched the action unfold from the other side of the Tagus inlet. They weren't going to miss out on the action. Boarding small boats, they hurried across. These youths had no armour, just their stone missiles and small pouches sewn to the middle of cords. Swinging their slingshots, they filled the air with a constant cracking of stones against walls.

Qasim watched the new arrivals land on the shore. It was one thing to be attacked by crusaders on horseback and in full armour but to be assailed by boys with pebbles was insulting. He'd slay every last one of them. Calmly, the al-kaid lined his archers along the top of the battlements and told them to pick off the slingers. It would be like hunting deer or rabbit.

"I will personally pay a dirham for every one that is shot. The reward will be divided up amongst you."

Down below, the Arribalde residents had retreated indoors, collecting as many of the stones as they could in blankets and sheets. The slingers would soon feel the force of their own missiles. Carrying the heavy loads, they slammed the doors shut, piling furniture up to prevent entry from outside.

The trap had been set.

"Come on, lads," an English slinger cried, "let's get the heathen bastards!"

Qasim watched from above as another wave of slingers entered the Arribalde. All over the suburb, the residents emerged on to the flat roofs of their houses, hauling the stones up with them. Then they stood and waited. They didn't have to wait very long. The narrow alleys were soon filled with

Norman and English voices full of bravado, egging each other on, but confused that the alleys were now empty apart from a few corpses.

All of a sudden, one Norman youth clasped his head and toppled to the ground, dead. His skull was fractured. Then the residents of the Arribalde exacted their revenge in a deadly shower of stones that rained down on the youths from above. As the Franks began to fall, the people of the Arribalde slipped into a killing frenzy, laughing as they felled one slinger after another.

Qasim raised his arm and the archers drew their bows above. Then, taking careful aim, they unleashed their arrows. A Suffolk slinger gripped his throat as an arrow embedded itself in his windpipe. Panic gripped the youths as they realised too late they had been sucked into a maze of alleyways. It was impossible to find the way out. As they ran round in confusion, the Moorish archers picked off their prey from above. It was almost a game to them.

"There's one!"

"Two over there by the granary!"

As an English or Portuguese slinger darted fearfully from the shelter of one building to another, the Moorish archers would stick an arrow into the target and whoop with glee as they did so. Qasim shared his men's delight. He'd been appalled that Sidray would bar the gate to his own subjects but now that the threat had been dealt with, he was proud that his people had fought so well. But his jubilation was short-lived.

"Look!" one of the archers shouted.

From Monte Sant'Ana, a line of white-mantled knights cantered towards the Arribalde. As they hurtled along the sand, the knights intoned prayers for victory. William was exhilarated. If only Wulfric could have seen him now — not planting seed or milking cows but back on crusade. How that would chew the old Saxon up!

Up in the qasba, a panicked servant ran across the cobbled platform surrounded by high walls, screaming at the Taifa. He'd just seen the ghostly white cloud of mantles and caparisons that every Moor feared. Dressed for his evening audience with petitioners, the Taifa peered over the battlements, wrapping his elaborate gown tighter around him. A small shudder passed through his body but he put it down to the cooling temperature as the sun set lower in the sky.

"You see this dragonfly on the wall." The Taifa pointed to the metallic-green insect that was slowly scaling the edifice. "It can get up here easily. But a Templar knight has no wings; they cannot fly. Look down yourself."

He ordered the servant to stare down the wall from where they were standing. The man humbly obeyed. The vertiginous drop made him giddy.

"Could you climb it?"

"No, great lord, I could not. Please forgive me." He sank to the Taifa's feet and kissed them repeatedly, half expecting to be tossed from the battlements as evidence of their impressive altitude.

"My Jackals and Scorpions will make short work of them if they ever get close to us," Sidray continued. "It will never happen, though. All our mighty gates are barred and there is no way they can enter."

"Great lord," one of the thinkers interjected, "what about the people down there?"

The Taifa gave the Arribalde an irritated glance.

"They seem to have learned how to fight. Now they can practise a little more."

The sight of the Templars had also been registered in the Norman and English camp on Monte Fragoso. Saher of Archelle ordered his men to arm themselves. He barked at his squires to get a move on. And as the surviving slingers crept back, he contemplated having some flogged or hanged. Their stupidity had goaded the Templars into early action.

"Glory-seeking celibates are not going to steal my booty! Ready yourselves. Mount up, damn you! Let's go!"

It had been one thing to see off the slingers but the residents of the Arribalde and Judiaria had no intention of taking on the Templars. Once more they swarmed to the Bab Al-Hadid and banged their fists against the iron gates. Others gathered at the Bab Al-Khawkha and screamed for admission. They held up their children and babies and implored the Taifa to save them. But he was now seated on Qasim's divan, calmly eating, drinking and dealing with the mundane chores of ruling.

Abbas, the qadi, approached Qasim on the battlements.

"We must let them in."

"We cannot," the al-kaid replied glumly. "Our great lord and taifa has informed me that whoever opens the gate will be flayed alive. I have no wish to suffer such a fate."

The qadi looked back at the press of humans, the anguished faces staring up and the clamour at the gates.

"Why not order out the garrison to defend them?"

"Sidray has forbidden any soldier to leave the city. He seems to think that wine sellers and fishwives can soften up the Franks first. They are left to their fate."

Abbas shook his head.

"Our people deserve better than this."

"I know," Qasim answered, "and one day they will be ruled well." He placed his hand on Abbas' back. "But not today, I am afraid. Today, many of them will die. I will save as many as I can."

As William and Pathros drew closer to the Arribalde, they could see the corpses of slingers lying all about. Pathros looked at the immobile young faces locked in their final expressions. They had expected an easy victory but instead death had claimed them on the first day of the siege. The Franks might be strong fighters, but they were poor thinkers, he mused.

Hugo Martins halted the squadron. At his side, Aleixo – the ever-faithful dog and battle companion – seemed to relish his first taste of conflict at the walls of Al-Usbuna. Hugo gave the Templars their orders.

"You do God's work here. When you kill, it's not Moors you kill – it's evil. The shedding of blood will not blacken your souls, the angels will rejoice to see it. But one thing – all of you take note – we do not kill women, we do not kill children – leave that to the whore mongers Pitões has brought to Portugal. And we never loot for booty." Martins raised his sword. "Do not sheath your sword or retreat from battle till you see our standard drop!" Then he intoned the *Non Nobis Domine*. "Not unto us Lord, but unto your name is the glory!"

The Moorish archers tried in vain to slow the Templars down but with shields raised, they deflected the few arrows that strayed near. On the battlements of Al-Usbuna, a mother pointed to the white mantles and told her child that those ghostly forms were the servants of the devilish Shaitan and that simply by whispering the word 'death', they could slay their opponents.

William could hear his own excited breath behind the apron visor that masked his face as he approached the Arribalde. The arrows were closer and the destrier he was riding sustained a mild flesh wound, staining the white caparison red. But these aggressive horses were trained to withstand pain till the battle was concluded. At a signal, the Templars dismounted and fanned out on foot into the alleyways of the Arribaldes.

As the stones rained down from above, they stepped over the bodies of slingers and began methodically kicking down doors and slaying their assailants on the rooftops. Those who hid in cisterns, wells and under animal troughs were soon found and put to the sword. As William entered one house, a man lunged at him with a dagger. His eyes were wild with fear and hatred as the white-mantled figure entered his home.

William had been trained to deaden his thoughts and harden his heart in battle. With no room to use his sword in the one-roomed abode, he drew out his mace and struck the man dead with a single blow. Then calmly, he moved to the next house. Bit by bit, the Arribalde was being seized by the Templars as they moved with grisly precision, snuffing out all opposition.

Saher of Archelle and his Norman knights disembarked from their boats and charged into the Arribalde, keen to ensure the Templars didn't claim all the glory – and booty. One of Saher's men ran towards a house intent on dipping his sword into some Moorish blood as quickly as he could. After the first killing, the rest were always so much easier.

He encountered some foreigner dressed head to toe in black.

"You Saracen bastard!"

He raised his sword to slice the man in two but suddenly found a dagger to his Adam's apple.

"I am not a Saracen," Pathros curtly informed him, "I am a turcopole."

Pathros was standing in the doorway of a small house. Inside, a Moorish woman cowered against the wall, covering her child's face. Her hand was raised as if it could deflect a sword blow. The Norman licked his lips.

"Right – out of my way, turcopole! I've got work to do."

But Pathros dug the tip of his dagger blade a tiny fraction further into the man's throat.

"Not her – or I will kill you."

The Norman gritted his teeth in anger.

"You're like them, you're not one of us – I'll come back for her – the moment you're gone, I'll slit her throat – you'll see!"

With that, he broke away and went to find his comrades.

To Martins' dismay, the ill-disciplined Normans began setting the houses ablaze. He knew the combination of fading sunlight and smoke would make it impossible to see what they were doing. Sure enough, in no time the knights were stumbling into each other, blinded by the black haze. William tried to protect his eyes as flickering pieces of debris floated past him.

The Arribalde had become an inferno. Great flames leapt upwards from everything that was combustible. William tripped up over a body that could have been a slinger or a Norman knight. From above, the al-kaid's men released more volleys of arrows, but it was impossible for the archers to aim through the thick grey fumes wafting upwards. They no longer knew if they were hitting friend or foe but the prospect of the al-kaid's reward kept them firing.

Encased within his helmet and surrounded by plumes of ashy smoke, William could hear the constant pounding at the city gates as the Arribalde residents begged for admittance. The Templar's head was filled with their howling and wailing. *Take our children! Take our babies! Don't let us die like this! Have mercy!* A woman yelled to her cousin in the medina to open the gate. A merchant threw money up at the archers and insisted he'd pay much more if they could only enter.

William felt light-headed. He could see so little. The heat from the flames sent rivulets of sweat down his face and the acrid fumes stung his eyes. He felt heavy, almost unable to walk. His arms swung uselessly at his sides. I must get out of here, he thought. I must leave. Where is the way out? But the alleys looked identical and none offered an obvious exit. Then he caught sight of what he most dreaded.

The large scaly form snaked from one house to another. Barging past a Templar serjeant, William chased after the Basilisk only to see the scarlet tip of its tail disappear round a corner. For a moment he saw its head devouring a prone body but, without turning to look at the Templar, it slid off, discarding the mangled corpse. Soon its capacious jaws seized on another victim but, again, threw it aside on spying William in pursuit.

"Where are you?" William shouted, but the monster didn't acknowledge him. His breath choking with ash, the Templar stumbled from one alley to another.

It had vanished.

The only way that William could tell where the monster had been was by the trail of lifeless men and women left in its wake, with their throats cut or bellies sliced open. William steadied himself in a doorway. A family stared blankly back at him in death.

"Basilisk, leave me! There are other souls for you to torture. Leave me!"

Saher of Archelle felt his men had done a good job in the Arribalde and turned his attention to the Judiaria. The synagogue was crammed with people who believed – falsely – that the Normans would respect this sanctuary. But Saher had been told that if he coated the streets with Jews and Muslims, as Prince Tancred had done in Jerusalem, his soul would know only eternal glory. Pitões had assured the Norman leader that he'd personally absolve all his soldiers of sin if they did their work well. All the pagans – every last one of them – had to die.

"Block the doors!" Saher barked.

With the Jews trapped inside, the Normans set alight anything flammable they could find and tossed it through the small windows high up in the walls. At first this seemed to have no effect as the crowd inside threw the objects back out. But then plumes of smoke began to billow out and cries for mercy gave way to the singing of psalms as they resigned themselves to an agonising, fiery death.

But salvation came in the form of Hugo Martins as he charged round the corner with several Templars, including William.

"How dare you desecrate their temple! They are the children of Israel. We have no right to murder them!"

Martins ordered his knights to unlock the doors and a mass of coughing and spluttering forms, blackened by smoke, surged onto the street. As some of Saher's men moved to feast the blades of their swords on the escapees, the Templars blocked their way.

"What the hell are you doing?" Saher screamed at Martins, his ruddy, apple-fed Norman face looking as if it might explode.

"Not the Jews!" The Templar master howled and then with uncustomary eloquence quoted the words of Bernard of Clairvaux. "They are punished for their enormous crimes every day but their existence reminds us of the passion of the Lord. At the end of time, they will be asked by the Lord to convert. Those who do will be forgiven. Those who do not – damned! Until then, they are not to be harmed."

"What rot! You are out of your mind, Templar! Your humours are unbalanced."

William bounded over to Saher – his eyes reddened by smoke and bearing a maddened expression. He'd seen Basilisk and this had shaken him to the core. His voice shuddered as he threatened the Norman.

"You will not kill women or children, or I will open you up from your groin to your chin."

Saher was furious. Inside him a storm raged and his face turned a disturbing crimson. Damn these Templars! Damn them all! One day we will exact our revenge on these arrogant monks pretending to be soldiers. The Norman turned to his men and gestured for them to leave. The day's fighting was nearing its close and the booty had been paltry – cooking pots and iron sieves.

Martins watched them go. Pitões really had brought the scum of the world to Portugal. There was no chaplain among the Templars to say the Divine Office but by the position of the sun, he guessed it was time for prayers. He ordered all the knights to remain exactly where they were and to recite thirteen Paternosters. Amid the carnage and smouldering houses, the Templars dutifully praised God.

"Pitch our tents here in full view of the Moors!" Martins ordered.

As everybody began to prepare the new camp, Pathros found William leaning against a dwelling. He'd sunk into a kind of delirium and his mantle resembled a butcher's apron.

"Give me a vial, Pathros."

The turcopole handed William the healing medicine without demur.

"I saw him again." The Templar knight threw his sword to the ground. "I saw the Basilisk. I thought I'd left him in Jerusalem but he's followed me here to Portugal." He glanced at Pathros. "Do you think I'm mad?"

"No, my friend."

"I think I'm mad. I think I'm totally out of my mind."

"When you have achieved your quest," Pathros noted calmly, "your mind will be restored."

"I must slay Basilisk if I'm ever to be whole."

"You will, my friend. You are a great warrior," Pathros consoled him.

William held up the vial to his blood- and filth-streaked face.

"I don't wish to spend my whole life seeking solace in this damned elixir! One day I want to be free of it, I want to be able to think straight."

With that, he downed its contents.

Chapter 42

BEFORE THE BAB AL-BAHR

Nicholas had finally found his mission. He was going to help build the massive siege engine that would be hauled up to the Bab al-Bahr. It would offer protection for a battering ram that would smash down the formidable gate while knights clambered out from the top level and took the battlements. It was a race between the Normans and the Flemish to see who could build the first siege engine. Nicholas was working on the Norman construction while the men of Flanders and Cologne were erecting another engine by the eastern Arribalde.

As it gradually took shape the simple boy from Witham was mesmerised.

Never seen such a great machine!

Most of the parts had been built elsewhere and just needed fitting together. But this was easier said than done. It had to be constructed as close as possible to where it was going to be needed, particularly because the ground was sandy and, with the sea so nearby, waterlogged and unstable.

Nicholas had a few basic carpentry skills: in the past he'd constructed rudimentary furniture for his mother and mended fences and pens in exchange for bread from landholders back home.

He did the best he could to help out and the older men were by turns amused or admiring of his boundless enthusiasm. He may not have been the finest sword fighter in Portugal but he could hammer in a nail and plane a surface smooth.

All this was at a safe distance from other preparations being made to actually get the siege tower up the beach and next to the gate. Right up against the Bab al-Bahr, short posts were being driven into place, around which thick ropes would be placed. One end would be attached to the completed siege engine and the other to oxen driven in the opposite direction, towards the estuary. That was how the tower would be pulled towards the gate.

However, this was a dangerous task. The Moorish guards on the battlements knew exactly what the Franks were up to and hurled rocks down as they tried to approach. This onslaught had already claimed one life: a young Norman felled with a jagged rock embedded in his spine. But the work had to continue and the ordinary soldiers used shields and boards to protect themselves as best they could.

Norman and English archers and crossbowmen provided the workers with some cover from behind a fence of felled tree trunks that had been built along the beach near the Judiaria. But it was difficult to reach their Moorish targets so high up.

"I'm finally a man," Nicholas murmured to himself.

If he met his father again, he'd be so proud of the boy. I might have just ended up a thief or even a murderer. But no! I'm going to be something now. I might even become a Knight Templar like Sir William. Why not? I'm good enough; I could do it.

Nicholas beamed with pride.

"What are you smiling at?"

Pathros had suddenly appeared with his large leather bag. It was bulging more than usual, full of fresh herbs that the turcopole had picked on the nearby hillsides. Nicholas, full of a new confidence, turned his back on him.

"Where've you been?"

"Are you addressing me?" Pathros replied incredulously.

"Yeah."

"As if I have to answer to a village idiot!"

"More use out here than you," Nicholas chirped back.

"Oh really, how do you deduce that?"

"I'm making a siege engine. I'm doing something that'll make a big difference. What are you doing? Messing around with plants."

Pathros dropped his bag.

"When you build your siege engine and get fired on from up there," Pathros pointed to the battlements of Al-Usbuna, "you will be screaming for my elixirs and potions. Oh, help me, Pathros! I'm in so much pain, Pathros! But I will remember your comments and do nothing."

"Won't need your magic."

"Yes, you will – you will see."

Their increasingly petty exchange came to an abrupt halt. A great crashing sound echoed across the beach as one of the gates opened, the doors slamming against the city walls. African swordsmen disgorged from the opening and soldiers beating octagonal-shaped drums and blowing long slender horns. This ugly cacophony was intended to strike fear into the enemy. And it was working! Nicholas and Pathros were rooted to the spot as the armed warriors ran towards them.

"Get out of here!" Pathros screamed at the boy thief. "Move as fast as you can!"

But Nicholas was frozen with fear. The music! The howls of the swordsmen! And Africans! He had never seen an African before.

He turned to Pathros. "Are they human?"

"Human like you and me," the turcopole answered, drawing his scimitar.

Sidray watched from above. It was time to destroy these siege engines before they were fully operational.

None of these Franks will scale the walls of Al-Usbuna! Not one of them!

Arrows and crossbow bolts from the ramparts drove the Normans back and allowed the Jackals to get close to the siege engine. Unwilling to see his labours destroyed, Nicholas foolishly ran forward before Pathros was able to grab him by the collar. One of the Jackals produced a curious green glass ball and threw it onto the engine. A liquid splashed over the front of the half-built contraption but nothing appeared to happen.

"Your magic doesn't work!" Nicholas screamed in delight.

One of the Jackals rode forward with a lit torch and threw it in the same direction. It made contact with the liquid and combusted, creating a powerful orange explosion, which sent the boy flying.

"*Allahu Akbar!*"

Satisfied by their work, the Jackals wheeled round and flew back towards the gates. High above the Taifa clapped his hands ecstatically. The Franks were a pathetic phantom of an enemy. Sulayman had read his horoscope rightly. Ibn Arrik didn't stand a chance against what Al-Usbuna, under the Taifa's wise direction, could unleash against him. And this was just child's play, a small taste of what was to come.

Nicholas looked down at his forearm, realising in horror that he'd been splashed by the Jackals' demonic potion as it ignited. There was a long painful blister on his arm.

"Ouch!"

Pathros quickly searched his medicine bag and in no time at all was rubbing comfrey leaves into the wound. Then he told Nicholas to chew on some dried thyme to speed the healing.

"Having second thoughts about my medicine?"

"Yes," Nicholas whimpered.

Chapter 43

FROM ALL SIDES OF THE CITY
AL-USBUNA

Donning the finger bones of Saint Blaise around his neck, the King set out with his forces from Monte de Sant'Ana to launch a full-frontal attack on the city. William, Hugo Martins and the Templars had decided to approach the Bab al-Bahr by water and storm up the beach behind the siege engine. The machine had now been repaired after coming under fiery attack from the Jackals. To make it more fireproof, it had been covered in leather skins that had been soaked in seawater before being fixed on that morning.

Nicholas was on the second of five towering levels, thrilled at the prospect of this great wooden beast moving up the beach. The teams of oxen were already in place, ready to be driven towards the water, and a group of knights and archers were at the highest level, ready to fire into the city and then storm the battlements.

The Flemish and men of Cologne had their own siege engine and also five huge Balearic mangonels. These catapults would spread terror within the city as their great rocks smashed into rooftops in the medina. They might also put some dents in the walls, although there was little chance of actually demolishing them. That would be down to the sappers and it could take a month for them to tunnel the required distance.

Qasim watched the Frankish preparations closely. He studied their every move and sought to anticipate the tactics they would adopt. The experienced military commander consulted with other senior officers on how to deploy their forces round the battlements to maximum effect and the location of their weakest defence points.

The Taifa, in marked contrast, appeared to have slept late after a bout of drinking the previous night. He yawned loud and long. The Frankish beetles could scurry around the walls of Al-Usbuna but they could never get over them. Allah was on their side and they would surely win. The loss of Shantarin had been down to the incompetence of its governor. Now that Sidray was on the scene, things would go very differently.

And anyway, he brooded, if this crusader scum get too close, I will parade their magical cross along the battlements. They cannot take my city when I have their magical talisman. How those Franks will groan in anguish when they see it!

A thousand blessings to my great cousin Zengi for delivering the Templar's most holy relic into my hands!

Hadid prowled in the shadows, stealing glimpses of the Franks on the beach and Qasim barking orders at his men. Allah had turned his back on Shantarin and Sintra and maybe even Al-Usbuna would fall. Only the cleansing wave of the Almohads could protect these cities from the infidels.

Sidray is a corrupt apostate – not a true Muslim. He must be slain!

Qasim would have to kill the Taifa. The people would then acclaim the al-kaid as the new ruler. The body of this decadent devil with his painted face and god-denying philosophers would be thrown into the sea. Then Hadid would emerge from the shadows.

He and his Almohads would rebuild Al-Andalus. They would reverse the gains made by these Christian princelings and crusaders at the expense of the caliphate. The house of Islam would once more stretch to the Pyrenees – and this time, the Qur'an would be obeyed to the letter. Maybe Qasim would be allowed to live, if he obeyed his Almohad overlords. Or maybe he might have to die. It was immaterial. All that mattered was that the law of Allah would once more prevail.

The al-kaid paced the walls of the medina, alternately encouraging and cajoling his men. Archers were ready to unleash a blizzard of deadly arrows. On top of the watchtowers, the ballistae and huge catapults had been erected to rain down iron projectiles that could skewer many men at once and boulders that could sink approaching sea vessels. On the ramparts above the city gates, huge braziers heated up sand from the beach till it glowed white-hot. Then there was the most potent weapon of all, a mysterious fiery liquid that could be projected over many yards as if by some supernatural force.

Sidray had finally emerged from his slumber. From on high in the qasba, his view of the situation was very different to the al-kaid down on the main battlements. The enemy seemed that much smaller and insignificant.

He watched the Templars approaching in their tiny boats in the estuary. There was the Flemish with their little wooden machines by the eastern Arribalde. With his poor eyesight, he could barely see the armies camped on the three hills. Their tents and flags were a blur from his vantage point.

"Just like insects," he cackled to a servant. "And we will squash them!"

A military officer approached and saluted the Taifa.

"The al-kaid would know your orders, great lord."

Sidray waved his hand.

"Tell him that I wish to see the horizon ablaze with fire."

The officer stood his ground, waiting for something more specific. The Taifa scowled at the man.

"What are you waiting for?"

"Yes, great lord." He saluted again. "I will tell him."

Sidray was offered his customary morning apple tea and strained once more to view the Frankish activity. They could throw their rocks and stones and fire their arrows and crossbow bolts but it would avail them nothing. Al-Usbuna wouldn't fall so long as he was in the city. He turned to one of his Scorpion guards.

"Bring the Templar cross to me, just in case we need it."

In one of the Breton boats bobbing in the Tagus, Martins stood up a little shakily to speak to both the Templars and the Breton boatmen with them.

"We knights of the Temple fight alongside you men of Brittany today not for booty or vain glory, but for the sacred truth. You will not see us looting. You will not see us despoiling. That is not what Templars do. We are the first to wield our swords and the last to put them away."

He faced Al-Usbuna with the flat of his sword held horizontally, pointing at the Bab Al-Bahr.

"We do not leave till those gates yield!"

A great cheer resounded and hundreds of men began rowing with all their might to power the twenty or so boats forward. But as they did so, the very walls of the city seemed to come alive, pulsating with waves of deadly missiles that spewed out over the seaborne crusaders. Three Bretons on the deck of William's boat were skewered together by a ballista bolt, while to the side of the Templar an oarsman gripped his arrow-pierced throat.

Like giant oars, the Moorish catapults snapped forward and discharged their heavy burden from high above. A great boulder crashed through one boat and its mail-clad knights toppled into the Tagus, sinking without trace.

"Keep rowing!" Martins shouted.

"You heard him!" William yelled, eager to get closer to the True Cross. If they could get to shore, he'd force those titanic gates open himself. The young Templar knew his quest was on the verge of being accomplished. All he had to do was get into that city.

"Come on, lads! Come on! Row! *Row!*"

By the western Arribalde, King Afonso and Geraldo had erected long scaling ladders near the Bab Al-Hadid and Portuguese infantrymen hurriedly made their way up, followed by some knights. But as at Santarem, the ladders began to buckle. Afonso screamed in fury at his old battle comrade.

"I thought you said that carpenter had lost his hands!"

"He did," Geraldo yelled back, "but he must have had an apprentice!"

The ladder began to crack and the rungs broke one after another. Qasim couldn't believe what he was seeing as the knights and infantry crashed to the ground in a great pile.

I didn't have to raise a finger — they have destroyed themselves!

He beckoned for a brazier to be brought over to the spot quickly. The sand within was now sizzling at an incredible heat. Guards lifted the iron vessel up to the edge of the battlements and poured its boiling contents onto the scattered heap of Portuguese below.

The air filled with howls and shrieks.

Scorching granules blinded. The sand incinerated the faces of its victims. It penetrated chainmail and helmets as it was intended to do. Knights were cooked inside their armour. Vainly, the wounded struggled to reach the cold water of the sea but fell down on the beach and died.

"God spare me!"

A Portuguese archer discharged an arrow into his comrade to bring his agonies to an end. A knight drove his blade through a friend's throat to dispatch him that much more quickly.

Inside the Norman siege tower, Nicholas was rocked backwards and forwards by its uneven progress over the soft ground. Two teams of oxen were being beaten hard in the opposite direction as the ropes around the posts by the walls moved the great contraption towards the Bab al-Bahr. On the levels above him, he could hear the knights yelling at each other while below, a group of slingers had volunteered to operate the battering ram. There must have been fifty crusaders inside the tower as it struggled to negotiate the sand and the oxen groaned at their enforced task.

As Nicholas stared through the wicker covering, a dart of flame hit the twigs and a small fire broke out. Using just his hands, the boy patted it out, burning his palms.

But then came small thudding sounds as tens of fiery arrows embedded in the wicker under-frame while even more deflected off the ox skins covering the wicker. The occupants of the machine struggled to put out the multiple outbreaks of fire, unaware that this was just the first stage of the Moors' incendiary assault.

The smash of glass and a scream from a level above chilled Nicholas to the bone. These were the strange weapons that released the magic liquid. He looked down at his still-healing blister.

I don't want to be burnt alive! Master William stopped my hand being burnt. And that Pathros healed my blister. Surely I'm not meant for the fires!

But a conflagration was now engulfing the left-hand side of the tower. The ox skins were ablaze. All of a sudden a barrel of flaming pitch crashed into the top of the structure from a watchtower ballista and the whole siege engine shook as if it might fall.

The top of the siege engine was an inferno and each level rapidly collapsed onto the other. Finding his way blocked by fleeing knights, Nicholas could see the menacing flames approaching and felt the incredible heat on his face. A knight transformed into a freakish glowing figure staggered round helplessly till he dropped and his charred body fell through the hole to their level.

Voices screamed all around him.

"Get out! Everybody get out!"

Having seen more than his fill, Nicholas leapt over the heads of the adult knights and bolted out of the death trap as fast as his legs could carry him. This wasn't a day he intended to shake hands with King Death. Looking back, he watched as the machine toppled over to a cheer from the Moors.

Qasim now ran as fast as his legs could carry him to the other side of the city walls. The Flemish mangonels couldn't be allowed to spread panic in the medina or damage the battlements. He ordered out the regular city garrison. Pointedly, he also commanded that the Taifa's Jackals and Scorpions stay put inside the city. They weren't going to be given the credit for any victory that day. His cavalry dipped firebrands into vats of fat and pitch next to the eastern gate known as the Bab Al-Maqbara. Then with shrill cries, they stormed out to deal with the men of Flanders.

Cowardice seized the crusaders. Seeing what was hurtling towards them, the Flemish soldiers fled their positions.

"Get back there!" the Flemish commander Christian of Ghistelles barked from a safe distance.

But the mangonels were deserted. Taking their time, the al-kaid's soldiers lit up their firebrands and tossed them onto the catapults. They then threw their magic liquid onto the blaze and reduced the weapons to useless, charred sticks.

"Do we build some more?" a knight next to Ghistelles asked.

"No, we build gallows. I'll hang every man who deserted his post today."

Beaten back from the shore, Martins continued to urge the boats forward. The catapults along the walls flung their heavy loads down on the Templars at great velocity but still they came forward to attack the gate. Martins could see that everywhere else the secular knights were being beaten back, largely owing to their own incompetence. This was the opportunity for the Templars to show what they were made of. If they could break the Moorish defences now, then King Afonso would be forever in his debt.

On the beach in front of the Bab al-Bahr, Pathros found Nicholas wandering in a daze, his face covered in soot and ash and his hands badly burnt. He took hold of him and sat the poor boy down on a rock, then fished inside his medicine bag.

"There was a man ..." Nicholas spoke dreamily in his shocked state. "He was all black and had no eyes or mouth or ears and couldn't talk. He walked towards me, he did. Then he fell. I think he was dead."

Pathros dabbed a syrupy concoction onto the swollen palms.

"Do not talk, you need to rest now."

Qasim had returned to the ramparts above the Bab al-Bahr and was dismayed to find the Templars hadn't retreated. Their boats were still trying to land on the beach in spite of a sustained onslaught from the watchtowers. It was time to employ Greek fire.

"Send them to hell!" he hollered at the Moorish sailors standing ready behind the gates.

The huge bolt across the Bab Al-Bahr was slid open and a force of Moors stormed through, pushing two boats on wheeled platforms out of the great entrance. In no time the vessels had plunged into the waters of the Tagus and made for the Templar boats.

"What are they doing?" Martins watched in some confusion.

On top of both boats were large wooden tanks attached to a funnel pointing forward. The tanks had levers on both sides at which two Moorish seamen now pumped hard as they neared the Bretons. A lit firebrand was held in front of the funnels as both spewed out a great luminous tongue of fire that shot over a great distance. Where it hit the sea, it continued to burn.

"What is this?" William asked.

"Greek fire," Martins replied with unease.

William's mouth was agape.

They mean to incinerate us!

With the eerie whining sound of a banshee, the funnels spat out their combustible liquid. The Moorish crew swung the funnels left and right, setting vessels and the very sea itself ablaze.

William could feel the searing heat on his face. All around was a glow of destruction as boats were consumed and their timbers went up in smoke. A Breton sailor screamed as he tried to put out the fire on his body but it stuck to him like glue, much as the glowing sand had attached to the knights.

The flames licked their way up sails and masts crashed down onto the crews below. The incandescent jets reduced one boat after another to a wreck until the Templar knight found himself looking into the barrel of one of the funnels, which glared back like an evil eye.

The dark hole suddenly illuminated as yellow curls emerged out of the pipe. A searing discharge leapt over the prow of the boat and coated the oarsmen; those in the front were charred beyond recognition in an instant. William was only aware of white flashes all around him as the combustible mixture inflamed all it touched.

The boat tilted as burning oarsmen dived into the sea in a vain attempt to save their lives. Losing his balance, Martins toppled overboard. Weighed down by chainmail and his heavy sword, he sank like a stone.

"*No!*" William screamed.

He knelt at the side of the boat, staring at the murky waters for a sign of the great Templar.

"Where are you?"

He plunged his hands down to search its shallow waves but the master seemed to have been drowned.

You can't die now!

William couldn't give up; he continued to thrust his gloves into the cold depths until, suddenly, they were gripped from below. Pulling with all his might, William stood up in order to haul the Templar master back to the land of the living. His head appeared above the surface of the water and, spluttering, Martins was dragged on board the boat by William. The master clutched the young Templar's arm and looked sternly into his face.

"Order a retreat!"

Dom Afonso wasn't prepared to give up the fight so easily. Santarem had fallen; Sintra had fallen. He was here with his best knights, Geraldo Geraldes and Martim Moniz. It was impossible this day should slip out of his control. Frantically, he regrouped his men and ordered another attack.

He sent messengers for assistance from the Normans who had been useless thus far. And those cowardly Flemish could come and join him too. They would storm the Bab Al-Hadid and break those iron bonds beyond which lay the qasba.

"I will not be denied my capital!" he screamed at his nobles. "I am a real king! I am as good as those bastards ruling in Leon and Castile, Aragon and Navarre. I am not some bandit! I am a king!"

From above, the Taifa squinted to observe Ibn Arrik.

"That is him, is it not?"

"It is, my lord," one of his officials replied.

"He really should know when he is defeated."

"I think," the same official added, "that he intends to attack the Bab Al-Hadid. That would lead him straight to us."

Sidray felt a tremor through his body. He glanced down at the Lignum Crucis.

"You are sure the King of the Portuguese does not know I possess the most marvelled object in the Christian world?"

"He does not, my lord."

"And how will he feel when he sees this?"

"He will realise that all is lost, my lord."

The Taifa turned to his astrologer.

"Sulayman ..."

"Lord," he bowed.

"Are these Christians really so superstitious that they would lose all hope by seeing this thing paraded along the walls of my great city?"

"It will destroy their will to fight," the astrologer replied.

"Astonishing!"

The velvet altar cloth that Besnik had placed around this most holy of relics when he stole it in Edessa was now removed. The sun reflected off its gold and enamel surface and it seemed to shine of its own volition.

"Show it to Ibn Arrik!"

With that, the Taifa's servants paraded it along the ramparts. Down below, Dom Afonso regarded the divine reliquary. At first he couldn't make out what the object was. With mock reverence, it was waved at the armies below.

But then the Moors began shouting at the Portuguese monarch:

Behold your True Cross! The Templars have lost your most treasured possession! We have the wood on which your false Messiah was nailed! You can't take this city while we possess your magic!

As Bernard of Clairvaux had predicted, the sight of the Lignum Crucis displayed by the Saracens sapped the resolve from the crusader armies. It was as if God was punishing the Christians below for having mislaid the wood of the crucifix.

One of the Moorish soldiers dropped his breeches and to add insult to injury began urinating on the Lignum Crucis. His boisterous disrespect was short-lived, however, as an arrow soared into his groin. Pathros dropped his bow to the ground as the Moor tumbled from the battlements to the sandy beach below. It was the least the turcopole could do in the circumstances.

Dom Afonso fell to his knees and blubbered like a child.

"Stop the fighting," he moaned to Geraldo. "We are defeated."

Chapter 44

CAMP OF DOM AFONSO
MONTE DE SANT'ANA

"It's there after all!"

William was over the moon. Orraca frowned.

"You will never find it."

"Oh yes, I will." The Templar regarded Nicholas. "I've my own secret weapon."

"The boy?"

"A thief's nose! If anybody can find the Lignum Crucis, it'll be Nicholas."

Orraca despaired at this insane Frankish logic.

"That city is a maze, William." She glanced at the chains still binding her arms. "If you let me out of these bonds, we could go and find it together. I know the layout of a Moorish city, where the Treasury is most likely to be and where the guards are posted."

The Templar considered this for a moment.

"I can't free you. You'd be hanged. I'd probably be hanged next to you."

"I am going to be hanged anyway!"

"Don't say that," William placed his arm round her shoulder. "I won't let them execute you."

"As if you have a say in such things." Orraca shook her head. "Your boy will not find your great cross, I will. But if you prefer me chained like a dog, then I will say nothing more."

William regarded her chains. It pained him to see her like this. But those chains were the bargain he had struck with Dom Afonso to be her jailer. It was the only thing keeping her alive. Orraca moved closer to the Templar and stroked his chest with her fingertips.

"Please. I love you with a never diminishing love. So do not chain me up like a wild animal."

"And I love you too," he replied softly. "But the chains must stay for now."

A familiar booming voice interrupted their exchange.

It was Martins ordering William to accompany him to Dom Afonso's tent. This wasn't going to be a happy exchange with the King of the Portuguese. As they entered, the defeated leader cut a miserable sight.

The knowledge that the Moors had the True Cross had driven him into a hair shirt and he knelt at a small altar, surrounded by Benedictine monks from the monastery of Santa Cruz. Hugo Martins grimaced at this spectacle.

He will blame us Templars for losing the True Cross.

Archbishop João Peculiar could barely stifle a broad grin as the Templars entered.

"We should have seen the signs, of course," the Archbishop began. "It was obvious something was very wrong. God was not on our side. The Templars had angered him with the loss of that most sacred and holy of relics."

"He is right!" Dom Afonso barked from the altar.

Peculiar continued.

"The chaplain to the Flemish nobles told me that when they held up the host to their soldiers and tried to tear it in half during the sacrament, it resisted. And when he pulled harder, it bled like flesh. You see, the signs of God's discontent were there, had we chosen to see them. We are being punished for Templar vanity."

"Quite right!" Dom Afonso agreed.

The King leapt up from his knees and bounded towards Martins, prodding the old man in the chest.

"You knew it was there! And you said nothing to me? Nothing! How did the Moors get their hands on the crucifix of Our Lord?"

Martins opened his mouth to answer but Peculiar's voice wafted across the tent once more.

"These great objects of faith should always be guarded by the Church, your Majesty."

"You hear him!" Afonso screamed at Martins. "You Templars are not fit to guard the cross of our Lord! And yet I put my future in your hands, I trusted you."

As he raged, Maud clutched her stomach but the King ignored her pain. This was far more important than the Queen's twinges.

"I supported your Order as my mother did before me. We have always stood by the Templars but you deceived me. You said nothing about having lost the Lignum Crucis, let alone it being in Al-Usbuna!"

Dom Afonso tore at his hair.

"What are we going to do? I cannot attack Al-Usbuna if the True Cross is at risk of being destroyed. Just imagine if they burnt it before the faces of our army!"

"Oh come, come!" Geraldo objected drunkenly, not sharing his king's piety. "Are we really packing up and going just because of that thing?"

"That thing" — João Peculiar glared at the boorish knight — "is the cross upon which Jesus Christ died."

"Well said, João!" Afonso darted his old comrade an acid look.

Maud suddenly screamed and then fainted. Pathros appeared, directing the ladies in waiting how to carry the Queen to her tent. Afonso observed the turcopole as he carefully transported her away.

"Who is that man?"

"My turcopole," William butted in. "He's expert in medicine. Your queen is in safe hands."

"He is a Saracen."

"A Christian," William assured Dom Afonso.

"Probably make a better job than our midwives," the King relented.

He regarded midwives as nothing more than witches. Meanwhile, inside the Queen's tent, Pathros ordered the midwives to lay a sheet and some pillows on the ground.

"These are contractions," he informed them.

"Yes," one of them replied a little tartly, "we know what they are."

"There's nothing you can tell us, foreigner," another chimed in.

"You know what you are doing then?" Pathros asked.

"Of course!" The first midwife pursed her lips angrily. "We have prayed and untied knots and unlocked every chest in the room."

"Why?"

The midwives looked quizzically at the turcopole. Did he really know anything about medicine?

"To unlock her womb, of course."

"I see."

He lifted Maud up from her bed and amid a cackle of protests from the midwives, placed her on the floor. Then he put a pillow under her hips. By propping her up and then easing her down again, he steadily eased the heir to the Portuguese throne out of her womb.

"This is undignified," sniffed one of the midwives.

"He will bring out the child back to front," another added.

The baby was in no hurry to emerge. This will be an obstinate ruler, Pathros thought, as he moved his patient backwards and forwards. But finally, a pink head slipped out.

"There you are!"

Pathros asked for a ewer and a bowl of water. The baffled midwives watched as he washed his hands before touching the emerging prince. The stubborn future ruler was trying his best not to leave his mother so the turcopole placed his dark-skinned hand inside the Queen and pulled it out, much as a foal would be delivered.

"There is no need to push, your Majesty," he assured Maud.

One of the midwives attended to the umbilical cord and placenta while another bathed the newly born child in slightly warmed milk. After clearing the baby's mucus, she then dabbed a tiny amount of honey onto its palate. Suddenly, a great cheer broke out in the camp outside.

This confused the turcopole. The baby was a boy, he would be king – but nobody could have known that yet. Pathros went over to the entrance flap of the Queen's tent and peeped out. To his amazement a vast column of Templar knights was filing into the camp at Monte de Sant'Ana. They had come from far-off to join Dom Afonso.

Hugo Martins rushed out, relieved to be away from the King and the Archbishop, and warmly embraced Gualdim Pais, a Templar hero revered in all of Portugal and beyond. His army of knights had ridden from *nullis diocesis*, the lands where no Christian or Muslim ruler fully held sway.

"Thank God you are here!" Martins gushed.

"What is wrong?" Pais enquired as he dismounted.

"The King knows we lost the True Cross."

Pais scoffed.

"That chip from an old barn door! A church forgery! We Templars should be exposing these lies, not protecting them."

Martins pressed his finger to his lips.

"Not so loud, eh? People still believe in these things."

"People," Pais answered disparagingly, " who do not understand scripture."

William overheard these blasphemous comments.

What kind of a Templar is this man?

He didn't believe in the Lignum Crucis; he said it was just some old piece of wood. This was blasphemy. William had never witnessed a Templar uttering such pagan opinions. But there was something else unusual about Pais: it was the ring on the index finger of his right hand. On it was a symbol that William had last seen displayed by a Templar in Tiberias.

It was the demon Abraxas.

Chapter 45

WESTERN ARRIBALDE

A great cheer was going up from Dom Afonso's tent as Pathros, kneeling before the King, introduced his new son and future leader of the Portuguese. While the rejoicing continued, Geraldo took the opportunity to skulk away. He headed towards the now solitary figure of Orraca.

Geraldo had almost forgotten the murderous captive but then he saw the petite figure lying on the sand in the Templar camp near the western Arribalde. She really should have been dead already. He scoured the area for a suitable gibbet, noting the charred remains of the siege engine as one possibility or he could use one of the Flemish mangonels, now that they had been repaired, to catapult her over the walls. That kind of brutality always rattled the nerves of a besieged people.

He strode up to Orraca.

"Time to die, I fear."

He was about to grab her by the hair when an Eastern voice intervened.

Geraldo turned to find Pathros aiming an arrow at him. The knight leered, putting up his hands in mock surrender.

"You are going to kill me, Turkish dog?"

"Yes," Pathros answered. "If you touch her again."

"How amusing," the portly knight considered calling the turcopole's bluff and charging at him with his sword. But there was something about Pathros' demeanour that suggested he might actually release the bowstring. "I thought your master was copulating with her, but it seems he is sharing her with his servants. *Very* generous of him! You better stay awake, Turk, because the moment your eyes close, I will string this bitch up!"

Irritated at being unable to carry through the long overdue execution, Geraldo went off to perform some military duties – his sort of military duties. These involved using every kind of underhand tactic to make a city run up the white flag. Fighting clean wouldn't win Al-Usbuna any time soon but using fear and disease might open its gates.

As Geraldo disappeared, Orraca turned to Pathros.

"I will confess that I was not ready to die just then. But do not expect me to forgive you for your misplaced allegiance to the Franks."

Pathros stiffened, fed up of these admonishments: "I ask for no forgiveness from you, dear lady."

The sun was setting and Geraldo had an appointment to keep with some of the secular knights near the eastern Arribalde. As night fell, Geraldo was to be found crouching behind some rocks with a group of Flemish soldiers. They had discovered a new game to play.

The Taifa was still refusing the residents of the Arribalde entry to the city and their food supplies were running dangerously low. For several nights, Geraldo and the Flemish had put bundles of figs and peaches out in the open and some of these residents had crept out of their homes and taken the offerings, wondering what kind souls would have left such provisions for them. But tonight, a different fate awaited the famished people.

There was little light, with heavy clouds above, and a waning moon. A group of about twenty tiptoed out from the Arribalde and made for the fruit. In no time, the sound of metal vices snapping shut and the screams of victims rang out. Geraldo fell on his back, laughing and rattling the dinar in his mouth. They had managed to capture eight people in the animal traps while the others had scampered back into the eastern Arribalde.

Geraldo stood over them and informed the injured Moors that half of them would be kept hostage while the other four performed a very important task. They were to break into the city and smash the seals to the granaries, letting in the insects and rodents. If they refused to do this, the four left behind would die. Fortunately for Geraldo, he'd managed to capture an extended family and they obligingly agreed to this arrangement.

He handed them a bag of coins.

"Use this to bribe the gatekeeper. Do not return without having done what I have asked. If you lie, I will know it."

Geraldo then bounded off to meet some Breton oarsmen who'd agreed to row him and a small group of Portuguese infantrymen to a small village he'd noticed on the far shore of the Tagus estuary.

It was called Almada and in the dead of night, Geraldo paid some of the Moors there a very unwelcome visit. Hours later, he returned with a very large and bloody sack. As he did so, his boat chanced upon another vessel departing the Al-Usbuna shoreline.

He ordered the Bretons to row with all their might and in no time caught up with the much smaller boat. There were only two people on board. Without pausing to ask who they were and what was their business, Geraldo slew them and picked up a bundle of documents one of them had been carrying. Unlike many of his social class, Geraldo could read.

"Must be important to be delivered in the dead of night."

The knight punched the air as he hungrily scanned the contents of the letters. The nervous qadi had penned a series of begging missives to the rulers of Evora, Silves and many other Moorish towns further south, pleading for assistance.

"We are shut up within this city and the Franks will not leave," he wrote. "We have destroyed their siege engines and catapults but yet they have not gone. These barbarians will be the ruin of us if you do not come to our aid. Tell all our cousins throughout Al-Andalus that this city must not fall. Pray to Allah and beg him to intercede for us. We have our supplies but I fear a great calamity ahead."

Geraldo wondered what to do with the qadi's correspondence. Something to really dishearten the defenders of the city! As the sun rose, he sat on the beach and nailed each letter to a different severed head acquired from Almada. Lucky there were enough heads in the sack to cover all the items of correspondence.

Then he ordered a team of soldiers to catapult them into Al-Usbuna, one by one. He listened with satisfaction to the wails within the city as the ghoulish missiles landed.

Returning to the Flemish camp, he found the four hostages and their four relatives now reunited.

"Keep them all," he said. They remonstrated that they had done exactly as he'd asked, but he shouted at them to be silent. "I need all of you to perform one more service for me." He turned to the Flemish, whose language he spoke fluently from past mercenary expeditions to northern Europe. "Bring them to me as the sun sets this evening."

Not having slept at all didn't tire Geraldo; the prospect of shedding more blood powered him forward. With a rope in his hand, he now looked forward to executing the bitch that had tried to kill Afonso.

He'd do it from the remnants of the destroyed siege engine. As he neared the spot where Orraca had been hours before, he noticed that the Templar knights, serjeants and their squires and retainers had all shuffled off to say early morning prayers before a chaplain in the Portuguese camp. This time, the dancer would be alone. There would be no turcopole to stop him with his arrows.

"Where is she?"

But Orraca was nowhere to be found.

"That hypocrite Templar is probably having his way with her," he muttered.

Then something caught his eye a few feet away: manacles and leg irons but no prisoner. His blackened heart sank.

Orraca had escaped.

Chapter 46

BAB AL BAHR
AL-USBUNA

The moment had come. Dom Afonso's fury at discovering the Lignum Crucis was within Al-Usbuna had created an opportunity for William to convince the Portuguese Templar master to get him safe passage into the city.

Under the pretence of negotiating on behalf of Dom Afonso, William would be taken before Sidray in his palace. He'd dangle fake peace terms before the Moorish ruler while Nicholas would scamper away to find the True Cross. Once in their hands and spirited out of the gates, it could be displayed before the crusaders' armies to restore their morale.

And then I will take it back to Outremer!

William glanced at the clear sky. Very soon, he'd be able to guide his father's soul upwards into heaven. With the holiest of relics recovered, surely the King of England and his clergy would have to forgive the late Earl of Essex.

I will dig the burial plot myself and lay that casket and the bones within to rest.

Suddenly, there was a grinding and squealing noise as a great bolt was heaved back to open the mighty Bab Al-Bahr.

"Don't let me down, Nicholas," William muttered under his breath.

"I'll find it," the boy replied. "Don't you worry!"

Pathros thought this an insane scheme. We will be tossed over the battlements when they realise our purpose, he mused.

The trio moved forward.

"Today you will see the Taifa of Badajoz," William grinned at the boy.

"Try not to pick your nose when you do," Pathros added.

Beyond the heavy gates, the medina appeared: the main part of the city with its innumerable alleys, streets and squares. Tiers of white-painted houses seemed to be piled one on top of the other. As they passed through the gate, ululating women in brightly coloured, vibrant silks showered flower petals down on the city's guests, from where archers had fired arrows just days before.

Shibli – the bureaucratic muhtasib – stepped forward.

"You are very welcome. May the peace of Allah shine upon you."

Sidray had ordered Shibli to present a show of the abundance and prosperity of Al-Usbuna, to prove to these Franks that it could never be starved into submission. Women offered up sweetmeats, dates, almonds, figs, oranges and slices of melon.

"We have every type of produce from all over the world, as you can see." The muhtasib indicated to different stalls. "This wood for sale here is used to make the bows on musical instruments. Our Jewish merchants bring it from India. Perhaps you have heard of this place?"

He moved them on.

"These cheeses are from Cordoba and I insist they are sold in these leather bottles to ensure they retain their freshness. It also seals in their pungent aroma."

He shook hands with a butcher.

"I have a rule that different meats cannot be sold on the same stall and entrails must be removed before weighing to make sure the buyer isn't cheated. I am sure that Frankish butchers are not so honest as ours! I remove the hands of any trader who disobeys me."

Pathros regarded the many market stalls with interest, in particular the one with countless baskets of dried and ground herbs. Each basket specified the condition its contents could relieve, such as 'circulation of the blood', 'difficult menstruation' and one that simply declared 'liver'.

A drink with allegedly magical properties was being boiled in a large vat made from beans imported from the land of the Ethiopians. The rotund vendor served this delicacy from a ladle into small wooden cups. His sign in Arabic claimed that a single cup would cure an "overwrought disposition".

At other stalls, stews and stir-fries were being cooked and sold in exchange for dirhams and quirats, silver coins minted in Cordoba and Badajoz. Olive oil, figs, pomegranates, dried fruit and sweets such as the Arabic qayyata were in plentiful supply, filling the air with an intoxicating mix of aromas.

Butchers scraped meat from the bones of horse, rabbit, chicken, cow and goat; on the stalls run by Mozarabic Christians pork was available. No fair in the Frankish north could compete with the quality of the produce on offer.

"I must congratulate you," William turned to Shibli. "This really rivals Jerusalem's markets for choice."

"Oh!" The muhtasib looked discomfited for a moment. "You've been to Jerusalem."

"Of course," William continued. "We Templars are at the forefront of defending that great city."

"Indeed."

Pathros regarded the shutters of houses above them. Something was stirring in his memory. Then he realised what it was. Just every now and then, he caught a glimpse of a face etched with fear and apprehension.

They are like the Franks in Jerusalem. They are waiting for the end.

The muhtasib directed the trio towards the bathhouse.

"Please bathe and prepare your bodies before meeting our great lord."

This wasn't a suggestion but an order. The Taifa couldn't bear the stench of malodorous Franks. They'd have to be perfumed before being admitted to his presence. Nicholas was appalled as Pathros translated to him.

"Bathe? Are you mad?"

"There is nothing wrong with bathing." Pathros eyed the alarmed boy. He had the look of a cat about to be dropped into a river. "You should try it – it might improve the way you smell."

"No time for that," William intervened to save Nicholas from his fate. "You've got other things to do.

They were now passing the great Mosque. The building was covered in painted tiles with symmetrical designs intended to pull the soul away from the distractions of the world outside and towards consideration of the unknowable creator. The faithful of the medina flocked through its gold-leaf covered doors. They washed their feet in marble troughs, water flowing endlessly from silver taps.

Within the mosque, the floors were entirely obscured by intricately woven rugs; each one must have taken years to make. Columns of jasper, onyx, marble and granite supported the entire edifice. Above them were arches of equally sized red and white wedge-shaped stones. The illusion was one of a never-ending sea of pillars beneath which the supplicants bowed their heads to Allah.

The outside walls were covered in exhortations to prayer and, more tellingly, information on the victory against the besieging Franks. These messages were either on parchment pasted to the walls or painted in large black Kufic script. Beyond the mosque, the gradient of the path got that much steeper as they approached the centre of power in Al-Usbuna.

Shibli escorted the trio into the qasba – the city quarter where the nobility resided behind extremely high walls. They passed through an imposing ornate horseshoe-shaped gate called the Bab Al-Qasba. Here were large houses built round courtyards, cooled by gurgling fountains. William cantered over to the edge of the wall that enclosed the nobles' compound and gazed down the hillside at the medina below. No wonder the rulers of Al-Usbuna felt secure. It was like a fortified city within a city.

Dominating the qasba was the qasr, the al-kaid's fortress-like yet opulent palace now occupied by the Taifa. Shibli bade them farewell and the palace servants escorted them to their rooms, a sumptuous chamber for William and more modest accommodation for his servants. But Nicholas had never experienced smooth sheets or a canopy over his bed before in his life. He stretched out on the bed and rested his head on the feather-stuffed pillow, grinning with delight.

"Don't fall asleep," William remarked at the door before leaving him. "We must bathe now but you've got to get on with your mission. I'm relying on you, Nicholas. Don't let me down."

"I won't."

"You're sure that thief's nose is working?"

"It's never failed me yet, Master."

"Good!"

As night fell, William was summoned to appear before his host, the Taifa Sidray. Lanterns of glass and iron lit up the Hall of the Caliphs. Seated on the divan, the ruler of Badajoz was clapping away to some music and watching some dancers. The Templar knight approached along a walkway flanked by pools full of large tropical fish gliding round lilies floating on the surface. The fish were better fed than many of Sidray's subjects in the Arribaldes.

The al-kaid scrutinised William. Nearby, Hadid lurked as ever in the shadows.

"This is no envoy of peace," Qasim growled. "What is he really here for?"

The Almohad's eyes flashed in the moonlight.

"You are right, Ibn Arrik wants this city. He will not rest until he has it. This Templar has been sent to trick your fool of a taifa into doing something that will bring about the defeat of Al-Usbuna. And I have proof of this."

The al-kaid was intrigued.

"What proof?"

"Great al-kaid, let me show you something."

With that, Hadid led Qasim to the palace stables. They approached the horse that Nicholas had been trained by William to ride over the last few weeks. The mule he'd been forced to ride on the first part of the journey had been sold. Nicholas was so proud of his new steed that he'd added a treasured item acquired during the journey through Castile.

"Look!" Hadid pointed to the bridle on Nicholas' horse. The boy had rubbed off the gold leaf that had once traced the Qur'anic script. "This belonged to one of my fellow Almohads!"

The boy thief had purloined the bridle from the Almohad whose head he'd smashed in with a mace, back on the Iberian plain. It was a kind of trophy. He'd stuffed the item into his bag without mentioning it to William or especially Pathros. The latter was bound to disapprove.

"Whose horse is this?" Qasim asked.

"The Frankish child servant the Templar rode here with."

"I did not see him with the Templar."

Qasim reflected for a moment. The fog of confusion in his mind was lifting.

"I know why they are here." He turned to Hadid. "They have come for the True Cross. They think if they get it back, they can restore the spirit of their armies."

"But how could they steal it?" the Almohad asked.

"I am sure they are stealing it now," Qasim replied.

It was obvious. While the Templar flattered Sidray and indulged in mindless small talk, the boy had been sent to take back the holy relic. Then they would simply disappear like a puff of smoke.

"What do we do?"

"You go to the Treasury," Qasim instructed the Almohad. "Smash the superstitious object to pieces so it can never be rescued. Stamp on it with your boot a thousand times!"

"The Treasury is guarded by your men, surely?"

"Yes," the al-kaid cast his eyes downwards. "Kill the guards. There will be only two. I posted them there myself. We can blame the boy for their deaths afterwards. Then destroy the relic. If you catch the Frankish boy, tear him limb from limb."

Hadid bowed, then rushed into the darkness.

As Qasim entered the Hall, the Taifa was exchanging gifts with William. The Templar gave him wool from England while he handed over a brass astrolabe. William passed it on to Pathros, knowing he would make far better use of it.

With the gloom of night enveloping the qasba, Nicholas too was on the move. He opened his bag full of ropes and grappling hooks. The boy didn't need a map, which he wouldn't have been able to read anyway. All he needed was his thief's nose to find the sacred item.

Once it was in his hands, all he had to do was make a pre-arranged signal, a bit like the owl-hooting sound that Izani had used in the Pyrenees. That had seemed to work well for the Basques so he would use it too. Then William and Pathros would make an excuse and leave the Taifa. And all three would escape from Al-Usbuna.

He opened the shutters to his bedroom window and gulped at the drop to the ground far below. Even the church roofs he'd robbed lead from had never seemed as high as this. Failure in this quest wasn't an option, though: Master William was going to look after him forever if he got the Lignum Crucis.

Hadid had already reached the Treasury and approached the guards.

"You are dismissed."

The guards glanced at each other.

"Who are you?" one of them retorted. "Where is your authority to issue such an order?"

With one short step, the Berber plunged two daggers deep in their abdomens. Then he swiftly retracted the weapons. The two men gazed at their killer in shock. Pools of blood formed on their uniforms. As they remained standing, the Berber plunged the daggers through their hearts.

"That is my authority."

He took a key from one of them, unlocked the door and then entered. Meanwhile, Nicholas skipped from one room to another with no light to guide his way but suddenly halted as he passed a room where an oil lamp was burning brightly. An open casket lined with folds of red and green silk held a shimmering collection of rubies, sapphires and diamonds.

"Oh!" the boy thief gasped.

As he made to enter, Nicholas halted abruptly as a large Moorish woman of noble birth shuffled across the room, picking up a necklace from the casket and placing it on her neck. One servant held a small mirror to her face so she could take in her reflection while another fastened the jewellery from behind.

That booty was clearly beyond his reach. But in the corridor, Nicholas spied a very bright and shiny row of taps. Must be silver, he thought. Get a good price for one of those in Witham. He unscrewed the tap and, after a couple of determined yanks, pulled it out of the wall, landing on his backside with his treasure.

William was making all the required small talk with the Taifa, who was becoming progressively drunk.

"None of this had to happen, you know," the Taifa confided to William. "Your Ibn Arrik could have been bought off with some bribes." Qasim bore a look of disgust at this kind of talk but the Taifa continued. "But my al-kaid decided to play tough with the Portuguese and now look where we are. Your armies camped outside our gates. And I have to leave my beautiful Badajoz to put matters right." Sidray edged closer to William. "And the food here is terrible! I cannot wait to get home."

Suddenly, Sidray kicked one of two almost identically dressed scribes seated cross-legged at the foot of his divan, writing down every word he said for posterity.

"Are you writing everything I say? I swear you missed that last bit."

Sidray giggled.

"My two scribes look exactly the same, do they not? I dress them in the same clothes as it makes me laugh. But this one is a Muladi." He tapped him hard on the head. "His ancestors were Christians from these lands but they converted to Islam. In spite of that, they still hate us. We will always be conquering Arabs to them irrespective of our shared belief. This one," he said, tapping the other scribe on the head, "is a Mozarab. He is still a Christian but he dresses and speaks exactly like us. And, strange to say, I trust his people more than the Muladis. What do you make of that?"

William could see nothing but hostility towards their ruler in both of the scribes' faces.

The Taifa clapped his hands for the banquet to be served. Pathros was seated close to the Taifa's thinkers and began eavesdropping on their conversation. They moaned at length that there was a poor choice these days between the brutal Almohads and the uncivilised Franks. Knowledge was being sacrificed to narrow-mindedness. Pathros couldn't resist introducing himself.

"I am called Pathros. A man of medicine and philosophy."

The young Moor before him in a long grey flowing robe was less than convinced.

"I thought you were a squire to that Templar knight."

Pathros blushed.

"I am not a squire, I am his turcopole. Circumstances have led me to this position in life. But first and foremost, I am, as I said, a man of medicine and philosophy."

Now the young Moor felt a little chastened. He extended his hand.

"I have offended you. Please, accept my friendship. My name is Ibn Rushd."

It was as if a thunderbolt had hit Pathros.

"The great Averroes! I bow before you and honour you, great teacher."

"That is very kind and I am flattered you know my name but please do not say you have read The Incoherence of the Incoherence as I will not believe you."

Pathros beamed.

"But I have …"

"And you are still awake," one of the other philosophers guffawed. But Averroes was warming to his new acolyte. He pointed to a very old man in their group, his head covered in a black-and-white chequered veil that reached to his knees.

"This is my friend Ibn Zuhr. You will have to shout as he is as good as deaf."

Pathros now lay prostrate in veneration before the geriatric.

"Great Avenzoar, never would I expect to meet the finest doctor of this and any other time!"

Averroes shouted into his ear.

"It seems this Syrian has heard of you and reveres you even more than me, which I find distinctly annoying. I was starting to like him."

Clutching the hem of his garment, the turcopole spoke breathlessly.

"You discovered the creatures who live maliciously off others."

"Parasites," the geriatric chortled, "yes, I found them. But they are not malicious. Allah created them to live by their wits, that is all."

Pathros wondered if he'd died and gone to some kind of intellectual heaven where those men who had written the books in his medicine bag resided.

Damn this foolish quest for the True Cross!

Imagine what he could learn from them if he remained at the Taifa's court! Then a terrible thought occurred to him.

If the Franks win, will they destroy all this learning? Maybe it would be better if they lost.

In the moonlight, Nicholas scampered across the tiled roofs of the palace, sending a slate smashing to the ground far below. Some instinct convinced him he was above the right courtyard. He fastened a rope to a chimney and lowered himself down.

On the first floor was a colonnaded corridor and he swung himself through an opening and landed with a bump on a floor of terracotta tiles.

Bolting through the darkness, he passed one unfurnished room after another till he thought he'd located the Treasury. He entered, only to be confronted by a row of latrines.

"Saint Barbara — help me!"

His instincts were failing him.

But I can smell it. I can smell huge amounts of wealth!

Nicholas dashed down some stone steps whose walls were covered in azulejos with intense floral designs. Entering the room below the one he'd just been in, he was confronted by yet another row of latrines. How many toilets could a palace need?

He darted off again. Hurrying across another courtyard, this one with a cage full of exotic birds in the middle, he found himself in front of the Treasury door.

This is it, I'm sure of it! This is the door!

To his relief, there was no sign of life.

In the nocturnal obscurity, Nicholas didn't spot the great smears of blood on the ground where the Berber had dragged two bodies away. All he could make out was the door before him, which amazingly opened without any effort as he turned the handle.

That was odd.

The rich always look after their wealth better than this.

Sidray had completely bought into the idea of William being with him for a genuine peace parlay.

"Tell Ibn Arrik that we wish to resolve our differences with him," the Taifa pronounced to William. "Tell him to give me back my beloved cities of Shantarin and Sintra. He has no need of these places. And their citizens are crammed within the walls of this city. Surely he can see this is unjust."

At this he kicked one of the scribes.

"Make sure you write this down!"

"I'll tell him," William answered.

The qadi appeared at the other end of the Hall of the Caliphs and bowed to the Taifa.

"You must excuse me," Sidray said to William, "but I have to address a matter of great importance. It is a judicial thing. A criminal who must be punished! I am sure you understand."

He beckoned to Abbas, who brought the prisoner forward. It was a woman. Of slight build, her head was bowed and long black hair covered her face. Two guards were almost carrying her. The Taifa climbed down from his divan and went to where the group from the prison were standing.

"Aisha," Sidray addressed the prisoner. The woman looked up. The Taifa ran a finger under her chin. "You are alive."

"Yes."

"Ibn Arrik is also alive."

"Yes."

"One of you should be dead by now." Sidray sighed. "I find this very disagreeable. And you know, I find failure very tedious. I paid you good money to perform a simple task and yet Ibn Arrik still breathes."

William shot to his feet. It couldn't be … It was.

Orraca! Why was Sidray addressing her as Aisha? How did he know her?

The distraught Templar was about to cry out but a flash of her eyes, now more weary than sultry, was enough to indicate that he should remain silent. It began to dawn on William that Orraca was not who she claimed to be.

Sidray was oblivious to William's heartache.

"How did Ibn Arrik intend to punish you, my dear?"

"He was going to hang me before our walls …"

"By this pretty neck?"

"… to show his resolve. The pig!"

"We must likewise show *our* resolve," Sidray smiled and then turned to his guards, "Take her away! Hang her from the ramparts at dawn. Let the infidels see what I am made of!"

As she was dragged from the hall and back to prison Orraca screamed for mercy.

Sidray returned to the divan to resume his peace parlay. But William was now wrestling with two missions: to rescue the True Cross and to rescue

Orraca. The Templar darted a glance at Pathros, who shook his head. The turcopole could see now that her account of being a Mozarabic Christian from Shantarin bent on revenge for the murder of her family was a tissue of lies: Orraca was really Aisha and a mercenary assassin. His master had to get wise to the truth and forget her.

But William couldn't allow her to hang.

In his mind, he saw her slender form being dragged before the crusader armies. The rope placed about her neck. And then her body would be flung from the walls.

I won't let them do this to you!

Sidray kicked one of his scribes for some minor infraction. Then he laughed and called for more dates. In the heat of the summer night, his black hair dye ran a little onto his cloak and the powder on his face was sweated away, revealing a tired old man. Not just old, but corrupt too.

William had taken a marked dislike to this serpent and even if Orraca, or Aisha as he now called her, was in his pay, he'd rescue her as well as taking the True Cross.

Chapter 47

INSIDE AL-USBUNA

Nicholas entered the Treasury. Piled two-thirds of the way up the bare granite walls shone gold items of every shape and size mixed with ceremonial weapons studded with precious stones. The boy wanted to carry it all out with him, every last bit of it. There must have been more gold here than in London or the rest of the world. All that fuss about a cross when there was all this treasure here that would make the three of them rich for the rest of their lives!

But then William's words came back to him. How much the Templar would be in Nicholas' debt if he retrieved the True Cross. That it was the greatest quest any man could be asked to undertake. He'd have to make do with the silver tap then. If Master William wanted the True Cross so badly, he'd get it for him. He owed him his life, after all.

Only one object in the room didn't glisten and shine. It was wrapped in a velvet cloth and indicated the unmistakable shape of a crucifix. Nicholas clambered up a small mountain of gold dinars and silver dirhams to reach it, the coins giving way under his feet. He clasped it to his chest much as Besnik had done long ago in Edessa. It felt good to do as Master William asked, even though it pained him to leave all the other richness behind.

As he slid down the hill of coins holding the cross with his right arm, he failed to see the figure closing in on him.

Suddenly, a muscular forearm grabbed him across the throat from behind. He was lifted from the floor and dropped the Lignum Crucis. His feet kicked and he tried to pull the arm away but slowly it pressed down until Nicholas could barely breathe. His mouth opened wide to gasp and his eyes watered with the pain.

The silver tap, it's in my hand. Do what I did with the mace in Iberia. Do it now. Hit him!

Nicholas swung his hand back and slammed the tap into his assailant's face. Then again! And once more for good measure! The arm weakened as the man howled in agony. Picking up the True Cross, Nicholas didn't pause to find out his assailant's identity but sped out the door.

Hadid held a hand to his face and continued to cry out but he had to follow the boy. The Almohad drew his scimitar and did his best to ignore the sickening pains in his head. One eyeball was crushed. Manic with rage, he powered after the little Frankish devil.

With the heavy reliquary under his arm, Nicholas ran from room to room, jumping over indoor fountains and skidding on polished floor tiles.

How do I get back to my master? I don't know where I am now!

The Berber Almohad cursed him loudly in his native tongue. To the boy, it sounded like the harsh, rasping voice of Lucifer himself. He spotted the latrines he'd seen earlier and slipped inside. It smelt no worse than Witham on market day and he stayed there until the deranged figure of Hadid hurtled past the room, wondering where the boy had gone.

Hadid stuck his head through one door after another. He shouted out what he intended to do to him when he captured Nicholas. How he'd tear him limb from limb, gouge out his eyes, rip out his tongue, castrate and eviscerate the evil little Frank. The boy would pay for his deeds!

Pathros was immersed in discussion with the thinkers. He never wanted to leave them. All his life he'd read the works of men like these and now he was able to sit among them and discourse. This was how he'd imagined his future while still a youth in Aleppo.

I will be learned. I will be wise. I will teach my wisdom to others.

But none of these things had come to pass. Instead, he'd ended up a servant to a Frankish knight. Now, however, in the Hall of the Caliphs in Al-Usbuna, he could at least indulge his dreams for one night. He could pretend that he too was a great philosopher fit to keep the company of scholars and the wise.

But as he made to ask Averroes another question, Pathros heard the unmistakable hooting of an owl. Not a very convincing owl, actually. It was a Frankish owl from England that had found the True Cross. The turcopole despaired that he'd have to leave and resume his mundane existence.

Qasim also heard the hooting. That wasn't any bird in his aviary. It wasn't even a bird native to Al-Andalus. And as it sounded again, the al-kaid became steadily convinced it might not be a bird at all.

William picked up the signal. It was time for him and Pathros to make their excuses and escape with their prize.

"My lord taifa," the Templar raised his golden chalice brimming with the finest wine, "may I wish you health now and always. You have the strength of ten men and I see you could talk in a learned manner till dawn but I'm far weaker than you ..." William yawned. "I must go to my bed. I humbly beg your pardon."

Sidray was pleased to know that his constitution was more robust than that of a Templar.

"You may go. We will meet again in the morning."

But Pathros wasn't ready to leave. He had one more question for Avenzoar. Ignoring William, he launched into another subject.

"So you do not believe in the four humours?"

"No," Avenzoar began, "and let me explain why ..."

It would be a lengthy answer. William glared at Pathros but the turopole ignored him.

I never want to leave this place. I want to be among these great men always.

"Damn you, Pathros!" William cursed to himself.

Determined not to lose the True Cross, the Templar left the Hall of the Caliphs without his turcopole. He made repeated bows down the walkway to the Taifa on his divan and then belted off into the dark to find Nicholas. At least the boy had performed his task to the letter. As agreed, they met at the stables and Nicholas held up the reliquary.

William took it.

"You're a smart boy, well done! God guided you, I'm sure of it!" William kissed the holy reliquary. "Thank you, thank you!"

He looked back to the Hall of the Caliphs.

"Make your owl sound one more time."

"Is Pathros still there?" Nicholas asked.

"Yes, I had to leave him."

But Pathros was hanging onto every word from the scholars and ignored the fake owl. There is nothing to run to, he thought. No reason to leave the company of these unrivalled minds!

I will simply be reduced again to being an inconsequential servant. William is not a bad man, he has treated me well but I am more than he realises. I will stay here and learn from Averroes and Avenzoar and in time, I will be as great as them.

Qasim looked in horror as the badly injured Hadid staggered into the Hall of the Caliphs. Sidray leapt behind his divan at the sight of the Almohad with his easily identifiable black garb. This was an attempt on his life! He called for his Scorpions and Jackals. The Almohads are coming! They are going to kill me! But then the Berber raised his hand, exposing a hole gouged in his face.

"They have stolen the Templars' cross!" Hadid screamed. "And they are escaping!"

"Impossible!" Sidray yelled.

The Berber sank to his knees with a trembling pain.

"They have it," he insisted. "Your Cross is gone!"

The Taifa turned to his Jackals and Scorpions, who had massed at the other end of the hall.

"After them!"

Sidray was suddenly aware that Pathros was still in the courtyard. The Templar had seemingly left his servant behind. How careless, Sidray mused. Well, if the cross really had gone, then the Taifa would have this man's skin flayed from his body and displayed from the walls alongside Orraca at dawn.

"Take him to my dungeon," the Taifa ordered.

With the alarm raised, the whole of the qasba burst into a frenzy of activity as nobles and soldiers set off after the Templar knight. The Jackals and Scorpions led the search.

From the Hall of the Caliphs, a group of guards escorted both Orraca and Pathros to the prison. Their torchlit procession passed near to where William, Nicholas and their two horses had concealed themselves by the city's mint.

The Templar handed the boy Pathros' bow and quiver.

"Take it and aim as well as you can."

Nicholas had shot many birds, rabbits and hares with the most primitive of English bows and arrows but this Turkish weapon was a devilish contraption: so taut that it cut into his fingers and with different-shaped arrowheads that totally confused him.

But Master William says I can use this, so I can use it.

"We must go now," the Templar whispered to Nicholas, "be brave!"

They stormed out of their hiding place on horseback. Grabbing a barbed tip from Pathros' quiver, Nicholas, riding hands-free, drew the bow back. It shook briefly in his small arms but fear seemed to give him power and the boy whooped with glee as his first arrow flew successfully through the air.

Pathros ducked just in time as it hit one of his guards in the thigh.

William threw him a dagger and the turcopole stabbed with wild abandon at his jailers. Orraca produced a dagger of her own and followed suit.

The Templar split a head open and trampled another guard before running him through on the ground. Nicholas reloaded the bow a little faster this time with a chisel tip and, finding his form, sent this projectile hurtling into a guard's face. Pathros' horse, upset by the carnage, tried to bolt but Nicholas grasped its bridle and tugged it towards its owner, who mounted and took his bow from its inexperienced user.

As Pathros sent two more barbed arrows flying into the sixth and final guard while from above, the watchtowers resonated with cries for assistance as soldiers spied the gory scene below.

"Through the gate!" William shrieked.

He swept up Orraca, who straddled the horse facing the Templar. Together they turned and galloped at full speed out of the qasba. However, the labyrinthine warren of souks and alleys in the medina immediately confronted them.

"Where now?" William asked.

"That way!" Orraca pointed to the left.

The medina was a picture of calm compared to the chaos of the qasba above. The ordinary residents were still fast asleep, observing the nightly curfew, but it would be only a matter of time before the Scorpions and Jackals encircled them.

"We should just keep going downhill, my friend," Pathros said, "that will surely lead us to the river and one of the gates in the wall."

But as they turned a corner into a narrow alley, an ominous figure loomed before them, bawling like a madman. Hadid was shouting in his native Amazigh tongue, the ancient language of the Berbers. He swung his sword at the trio, daring them to try and pass.

"He attacked me," Nicholas whimpered, "I got him back, though. Good and proper. Tried to stop me taking the Cross but I didn't let him."

William dismounted. Hadid swung his scimitar at William's head. The Templar avoided decapitation by a hairsbreadth, jumping to one side.

"You attacked a boy," William said. "Not much of a warrior, are you?"

The Berber lunged forward and struck the Templar in the face with the pommel of his sword, bruising his cheek and drawing blood from his mouth. William grabbed the handle of the sword with his left hand and yanked it from the Berber's grasp. The weapon clanged to the ground.

"You fight dishonourably," William scowled.

He raised his sword to deliver a death stroke to Hadid but the Berber rushed towards him and grabbed William's calves, pulling hard and toppling him to the ground. This gave Hadid time to to retrieve his sword. William rolled and bounded to his feet again but scarcely had he done so when the Berber thrust his sword at the Templar's abdomen, hoping to spill the young Frank's guts onto the ground.

William deflected the blade by clasping it halfway down in his mailed glove. Only the last few inches were razor-sharp. This brought them face-to-face. Hadid's damaged eye was nothing but an empty socket and he'd lost his front teeth from the second blow of the silver tap. The Berber was breathing heavily, his nostrils flaring and his mouth locked in a grimace.

The Scorpions and Jackals were coming! The thunder of hooves was pounding through the medina. William was running out of time. He pushed Hadid away and attempted an upward strike with his sword, which the Berber blocked successfully. Once more they grappled at close quarters and Hadid could taste victory as he pressed his blade against William's neck.

This was a fight for survival. No rules! The Templar rammed his knee into Hadid's groin. The Berber slipped and fell flat on his back. Without pause, William rammed the tip of his sword through Hadid's ribcage and placed his full bodyweight behind the pommel. He then calmly extracted the blade from the dead man's body.

"Come," he told Pathros and Nicholas, "they are getting near."

Leaping over piles of baskets, pots and amphorae discarded in the various market places, they caught sight of a horseshoe arch that would lead them out of Al-Usbuna. A guard by the gate opened his mouth but an arrow from Pathros rendered him silent. Leaping from their horses, the three struggled to open the entrance and with a gratifying heaving sound, succeeded. Clambering back onto their horses, they flew out of the city.

William stopped once they felt out of harm's way. He instructed his companions to return to the camp. Both knew why their presence wasn't wanted. As they disappeared into the night, William turned to Orraca.

"I do not know why he called me Aisha," she blurted out, "my name is Orraca."

"It's not, is it?" William murmured. "It is Aisha. Or maybe it's not even that. Who knows?"

"William, I did not lie to you."

The Templar looked away.

"You're lying now. I'm not sure if every word you ever said to me was a lie. Are you a Christian? Are you a Muslim? Did you come from Shantarin? Who knows!"

She frowned.

"You are rather sensitive for an uncivilised and boorish crusader."

"Maybe I'm not uncivilised. Maybe I liked you."

Orraca found this slightly disconcerting. She was not Orraca, she was not Aisha, but it was nobody's business to know her real name. That was how she survived in a world that was turning on its head. Chaos ruled and she had to make a living.

I have used my beauty to kill those who deserve to die. I am serving my people. So — what of it?

Orraca's expression hardened.

"I was paid to kill Ibn Arrik. And I wish I had done it." She gestured to the walls of Al-Usbuna behind her. "I told you the truth when I said your king would destroy a great civilisation. I told you the truth when I said he was a brutal animal. I would have killed him for no reward. But Sidray offered me money and I have a family to feed, like anybody else!"

William dropped her gently to the ground and turned his horse away.

"Will I see you again?" she asked. "Or am I now your enemy?"

"You will see me," the Templar replied, "at the side of King Afonso when he's crowned King of the Portuguese on the battlements of Al-Usbuna."

Chapter 48

CAMP OF DOM AFONSO
MONTE DE SANT'ANA

Not a word was spoken as the ropes were cut and the velvet cloth from the altar at Edessa fell away to reveal the True Cross. Hugo Martins beamed with pride at William's achievement. He was even more overjoyed at removing a source of discord between himself and King Afonso.

He'd lied to him in order to conceal the poor judgement of the Grand Master in Jerusalem. This sacred relic should never have been sent to the front line against the Saracens. It had been a terrible mistake for which the Order could have paid grievously.

But now it was once more in the right hands.

We Templars once more enjoy the confidence of Dom Afonso!

João Peculiar tried to look overjoyed. He knelt before the large crucifix-shaped receptacle and noted the dozens of inlaid rubies and diamonds, as well as the squares of deepest blue lapis lazuli. The figure of Jesus Christ was painted in the Greek style and the Messiah bore a demure expression. The Archbishop felt quite intoxicated by the heady mix of vivid colours, jewels and bands of gold and silver that traced up and down the arms of the cross.

Raising himself with difficulty, Peculiar circled the reliquary and, removing the rings from his right hand and taking off his glove, opened the delicate little cabinet containing the piece of the crucifix. The lock was at the back of the relic and proved a little resistant. As he pulled at the small glass door, the Archbishop couldn't help but notice that a jewel had been hacked off the back of the reliquary. That was Besnik's doing – but Peculiar suspected Nicholas.

As if that wasn't bad enough, the great Prince of the Church suddenly found something even more disagreeable: there was a fresh break where a piece of the cross of the Lord had been snapped off.

"Outrageous!" he stormed. "The boy has stolen part of the Lignum Crucis!"

Nicholas found the eyes of Dom Afonso, his knights, courtiers, monks and the Templars boring into him.

"I took nothing, just the tap! And that was a good thing because I hit that man with it. Took his eye out, good and proper!"

But the Portuguese were in no mood for his excuses. The True Cross should assure them of victory but if it had been defiled, then God would punish them severely.

"I didn't touch it!" Nicholas whined. "Could've taken lots of treasure. That woman's jewels, she had loads! But I left them. And the gold coins. Honest!"

João Peculiar knew the boy was attached to the Templars. This might sully their little victory over him and the Church.

"He should be subject to ordeal to prove his innocence," Peculiar bellowed.

Nicholas tucked his right hand under his shirt and wailed.

"No! Did nothing! Don't make me hold a bar."

William was about to defend Nicholas when a commanding voice seized the attention of all those present.

"My lord Archbishop" – Gualdim Pais looked at Peculiar with hatred blazing in his eyes – "you could spare a gem for this reliquary. That yellow one on your mitre would do." Everybody laughed, including Dom Afonso, though he placed a hand over his mouth to hide his mirth. "Let the boy alone!"

"This is outrageous!" Peculiar raged.

But Pais was enjoying his bating of the prelate.

"Who will I need on the battlefield tomorrow?" Pais snarled at the cleric. "An Archbishop in his best vestments or a courageous lad with a sword?"

The secular and Templar knights cheered in unison.

"Enough!" Afonso interjected. "That is enough, Gualdim. You insult the Archbishop's person and I cannot permit that." The King looked over at Nicholas. "This young English child brought back the Cross. I could not sleep at the thought of it being in the hands of the Moors. Now we have it back, I know we can win Al-Usbuna. That is all that matters."

Chapter 49

BAB AL MAQBARA

The Flemish troops and men of Cologne stood observed the nightly ritual, a little bemused by this grotesque spectacle. Nearly a month had passed and still thousands upon thousands of people clamoured at the Bab Al-Maqbara gate. The entrance to the city from the eastern Arribalde faced onto the city's cemetery, which was now clogged with makeshift wooden tombs side by side with the stone tombs the dead had received in happier times. Harried every day by Flemish crossbow bolts and arrows, they had reached the end of their tether. The great groaning mass begged the Taifa to hear their voices and let them in.

A commander from Cologne approached Christian of Ghistelles.

"Do we attack?"

"Why should we?" the Flemish lord responded. "They are trampling each other to death. They are doing our work for us."

Qasim watched the pitiful spectacle but the ruler of Badajoz had forbidden him to admit a single one of them. These had once been proud people, he recalled, fishing in the Tagus, selling their produce in the city's souks and trading with the merchants from every corner of the world that came here in their ships. Now they were reduced to savages living off scraps. There were even rumours they had begun to eat human flesh, the meat of those who were wounded or dying.

An officer rushed to the al-kaid.

"Something terrible has happened, my lord!"

"What is it?"

"The people of the medina have thrown open the Bab Al-Hamma."

He referred to a gate flanked by a hot and cold spring, from which it took its name. Qasim panicked. With that gate open, not only could the people of the Arribaldes flood in, the Frankish crusaders might seize their chance if they saw the opening.

"Get it closed!" the al-kaid ordered. "Do whatever you have to do, but close those gates now! I will be with you shortly."

As the officer ran to implement the command, Shibli the muhtasib shuffled into view.

"Qasim, you must see something."

"I have no time," the al-kaid responded. "One of the gates is opened. This one here" – he pointed to the Bab Al-Maqbara below – "could give at any moment. If you need me to enforce market regulations, I am afraid that will have to wait!"

Shibli fumbled nervously with his garments.

"You must see it. And you must tell the Taifa what I am about to show you."

Qasim relented and followed the official to one of the food silos burrowed deep into the hard rock of the city. The muhtasib had filled them with grain and oil to last many months of a siege and then sealed them from the depredations of rodents and insects.

But as they approached, the al-kaid could see that something had gone badly wrong. He ran a finger along the broken seals. Then as he entered, the air rang to the scuttling of cockroaches and the sound of thousands of rats feasting on Al-Usbuna's supplies.

In his shock, the only thing that came to Qasim's mind was a verse of the Holy Qur'an.

A township that dwelt secure and well content, its provision coming to it in abundance from every place, but it disbelieved in Allah's favours, so Allah made it experience the garb of death and fear because of what they used to do.

The muhtasib, so proud of his organisationational skills, watched his siege preparations disappear into the mouths of ravenous rats.

"Who would have done such a thing?"

Qasim knew only too well.

"This is the work of Ibn Arrik and his devil, Geraldo Geraldes. This is how they fight. Not like warriors, but like scheming dogs."

Shibli was distraught. He was a man who loved order and this was chaos. As they left the cave, Shibli told Qasim that the wells had been polluted with rotting carcasses and the pipes supplying water to the city from outside its walls had been stopped up or broken. There was nothing to drink or to cool the air. Already, he said, he'd seen the red patches appear on the bellies of many of the Taifa's subjects.

"The plague is spreading. People beg to die as their bodies roast from within. It is all over the medina. I fear it will soon spread to the qasba."

"Do what you must to deal with it."

"Where shall I put the bodies?"

There was only one large space inside the city walls that could accommodate such a grisly heap of humanity.

"Pile them up in the Great Mosque," Qasim responded.

The al-kaid took his leave and rode up to the qasr. As he entered the Hall of the Caliphs, the high-pitched laughter of the Taifa rang out around the courtyard and over the fishponds. Surrounded by his courtiers, they still feasted as if nothing was happening at the very gates of Al-Usbuna.

"Well, Qasim," the Taifa propped himself up on a divan, a little merry from several goblets of wine, "what do you have to report?"

The city's governor strode down the walkway of his palace and fixed his gaze on the corpulent and corrupt ruler.

"Disease in the city, my great lord. The granaries sabotaged by the Franks. The wells poisoned, the streets full of fear and rumour. The Arribaldes clamouring to get in at our gates."

The Taifa seemed only to have heard the last point. He leant forward.

"They have not broken in, I hope, Qasim?"

"At one of the gates they have, great lord," the al-kaid replied.

"This is your fault! All of it! Not mine!" Slipping off his divan, Sidray waddled rapidly towards Qasim. "This is how you make amends, al-kaid. You double the Jizya." This was the tax paid by non-Muslims. "Not only the men among the Jews and Christians, but the women and children must pay it as well. And you make sure they hand it over. Brand and whip them if you must."

The Taifa didn't care if the Qur'an said that only men should pay, nor that it should be collected with mercy.

"You recruit every beggar and stallholder in the souks into your garrison. And you get that useless qadi up here and tell him to bring every last dinar from the Bayt mat al-Muslimin with him."

He was ordering that the Great Mosque's chests of gold be emptied out into the Palace Treasury.

"Will that not displease Allah?" Qasim asked.

"Oh, of course," the Taifa's face screwed up in anger, "you are such an expert on what Allah wants!" He wagged his finger at the al-kaid. "I saw that man who came into this hall with the bloodied face. I know what kind of person that is – I hang them in Badajoz. But what do you do, Qasim? Do you consort with these Almohads? Maybe you plot with them. And they tell you that one day they can make you ruler of Al-Andalus, that Qasim ibn Muhammad will sit in a palace in Cordoba and rule like the great Abd al-Rahman himself."

The Taifa screamed with laughter at the al-kaid's pretensions.

"I see it in your face, Qasim, that is what they have told you. Fool! You will not even rule here. When I have vanquished Ibn Arrik, I will celebrate my victory by executing you after Friday prayers."

He began waddling back to his divan.

"Now get out of here!"

Qasim rode to the qadi's house in the qasba. In one of the courtyards, the wives of both men had been chatting apprehensively about the future. At the sight of her husband, Qasim's wife ran to him and kissed his hand. Abbas appeared, looking thoroughly miserable, and the two couples did something they hadn't done since they were betrothed so many years ago: they walked their wives along the walls of the qasba and took in the vista beyond. In the cool evening air, it was almost possible to ignore the Frankish encampments that scarred the three hills nearby.

"You are proud," Qasim's wife said to him. "And you are sometimes stubborn." The al-kaid had married a strong-minded woman who didn't hesitate to express her opinions. "Pay the bribes to the Franks again, husband. We are a rich city. We have children who will grow up here, think of them. Pay the Franks, make them go."

Qasim looked out at the tents and campfires dotted around them.

"No, I will not hand the infidel a single dirham."

"This is not your voice speaking," his wife persisted, "all I hear is the voice of the Almohad."

"It *is* my voice," he reproached her sternly. "It is the same voice that commands you to be silent on these matters. Return to our children, you have displeased me."

As she left, the qadi dismissed his wife and the two men stood together on the battlements. The al-kaid stroked the great stones of the wall. Qasim's ancestors had dwelt in this place within a hundred years of the Prophet's death. So many generations had enriched and served Al-Usbuna.

You are my city, he thought, and you belong to nobody else. You will obey my command alone, and not that of any taifa or Christian king. I will not let any other enslave you.

"How do you think this will end?" Qasim asked Abbas.

The religious judge had given up hope. It was too late to put anything right now. The Dar al-Islam was being overwhelmed by the Dar al-Kufr. Belief was giving way to disbelief. The city would soon be unrecognisable under new rulers, who would tear down the mosques and replace them with their churches.

"This is the fitnah," the qadi murmured, "when heaven shall be stripped off and hell shall be set ablaze. When the sun shall be darkened and the stars shall be thrown down. It is the end of everything."

The two men were interrupted as one of the al-kaid's guards rode up to them.

"Lord al-kaid?"

"Yes."

"The Bab Al-Maqbara ... it is broken, lord. The people have swarmed in like a sea. They are everywhere. We can do nothing."

Chapter 50

BEFORE THE WALLS OF AL-USBUNA

William sat by one of many campfires along the beach, unable to sleep. He'd brought back that most sacred of relics from the heart of Al-Usbuna. Now he would take it back to England and then on to Outremer. The Portuguese might want to hold onto it but he'd try and convince them otherwise. It should be restored to the Holy Sepulchre in Jerusalem – that was its proper place.

The future was looking a lot brighter. His return to England wouldn't be enforced and in disgrace but of his own volition and in triumph. William pictured himself entering the preceptory garden in Holborn and taking down his father's coffin, then burying it with his own hands. He'd return to Pleshey Castle and confront his brother and mother over their wickedness and deceit, and with the support of the people, he would take the earldom. The people of Essex didn't deserve the depredations of Edward.

He poked at the fire. Maybe this was a madman's fantasy.

I'm stuck here in this foreign land, he mused. Edward is still the earl in Essex. My mother has paid men to kill me. And Hugh of Argentine might never forgive me for bringing death and destruction down on Cressing.

Maybe Wulfric had even died in the fighting against my brother.

William felt a pang of remorse. Whatever he thought about the old Saxon, he never wanted him to die — and certainly not at the hands of his brother's hired thugs and vagabonds.

Another Templar settled himself next to William. He turned to find Gualdim Pais sharing the warmth of the fire. The hero of Tomar and vanquisher of Moors in nullius diocesis stretched out his hand and they shook as Templar brothers. As they did so, William noticed the ring that Pais wore. It was the same as the one he'd once seen in Tiberias.

Abraxas!

"Why do you wear that ring?"

It bore an image of the strange deity that Pathros had spoken of that had existed in the darkness before time. The fire picked up suddenly — maybe roused by a passing breeze off the Tagus making the embers glow more fiercely.

Pais answered with another question.

"What do you think of those who raid gallows for bones and skin and then claim they are from saints?"

"I despise them," William declared. "They're charlatans. They deceive the common people."

"Look at that devil from Braga," Gualdim continued. "Peculiar travels with bejewelled cases of mule bones he says belonged to saints. His vestments are covered in emeralds and pearls when his own serfs starve. I tell you" — he lowered his voice — "I will not rest until I see his vestments stripped from his bloated carcass and distributed to the poor."

"That's heresy, surely," William lowered his voice. "You're preaching the overthrow of Christ's Church."

"If we do not overthrow them, then they will overthrow us. Men like João Peculiar will not rest until all our preceptories are in their hands. For now we are tolerated as their foot soldiers who bear the brunt of everything the Moors can throw at us. But when Al-Usbuna is taken, they will move to wipe us out." Pais rested his hand on William's forearm. "They repel you too, I can see it. Do not deny it."

Pais then discoursed at length on his vision for the kingdom of Portugal, that it would be a beacon for all Christians and the Templars would be its militant and pure priesthood. Portugal would be a dagger that would stab into the heart of the Moorish realms, not stopping at Al-Usbuna or even the southernmost reaches of the Al-Gharb. It would continue into Morocco and lay waste the heresy of Islam for once and for all.

William listened with growing impatience. He wasn't convinced by Gualdim's apocalyptic vision.

"I don't like rich priests who ride on the backs of the poor either," William declared. "But I don't want to drown them in their own blood. That's too much, it's madness."

"It's not madness, it's what we must do! They will burn us at the stake one day – you or your children will see it happen. They mean to annihilate us."

William poked the fire again, wishing Pais hadn't come to join him.

"I'm not up for killing priests. And I don't even want to kill all the Jews and Muslims as you do. You would turn our seas red with all your slaying."

Pais rose.

"You are not fit to be a Templar."

William regarded the ring of Abraxas again.

"I'm a Templar," he responded. "But I've no idea what you are."

Chapter 51

THE ROAD TO SINTRA

"When that maiden caressed me
I swear she undressed me
Now I has the pox ... the pox ... the pox
A burning ... a burning
For I'm never learning
To leave them fair maidens alone ..."

The song brought William to his senses. His head hurt. Putting his fingers to his forehead, they appeared before his eyes covered in blood. Gazing at them with confusion, he gradually recalled the walk from the campfire to re-join Pathros and Nicholas after his strange conversation with Gualdim Pais. After that, nothing: there was simply a dark void in his mind.

William found his wrists were bound with cords.

What?

Looking round for a dagger or sword, he found that his weapons had been taken off him. Fear shot through his body and he rose quickly. This was a signal to his captors to begin moving. They whipped their horses and William found himself forced to run behind one of them. He fell and was dragged a little in the mud. Somehow he got back on his feet and resumed running.

I have been taken prisoner, he realised. The two men had their backs turned but he knew who they were: the bounty hunters sent by his mother.

"Where are your friends?" William yelled.

Aylmer and Hunrith didn't appreciate his reference to the Maragatos. After Geraldo had mutilated one of them, they had demanded payment to return to the Castile. Things had threatened to turn ugly for the two Witham men and they had paid off the hot-tempered mule traders. Despairing as their money ran out, they had looked for the first opportunity to grab William and now they had their prize.

"What kind of a mother does this to her son?"

"Countess of Essex," Aylmer answered. "Fine woman!"

The two bounty hunters chortled.

"No more siege for you!" Hunrith shouted.

William gazed at the ground passing rapidly under his feet as he struggled to stay upright. He was still giddy from the blow of the club and could taste blood in his mouth. The bounty hunters had taken not only his weapons but everything of value he had, including his belt and a ring bearing the seal of the Order.

"I'll cleave both of you in two when you untie my hands," William promised.

The bounty hunters slowed their horses as Hunrith began speaking in whispers to Aylmer. Maybe it wasn't a good idea to try and take the knight back alive to England. He might well overpower them.

"Let's just take his head back," Hunrith said.

Aylmer pointed to the wound he'd sustained to his arm in the Pyrenees.

"I'm not strong enough to fight him if he broke free," he told Hunrith, "so I reckon you're right."

"Would his mother be alright with just his head? We'd get the same money, right?"

"Course she would! You saw the look on her face when we asked did she mind him dead or alive. Reckon she's not bothered either way."

Those words pained William: his mother really didn't care about him at all.

"Let's get to the boat," Aylmer advised. "Can't wait to be in the Golgotha Tavern ..."

Both men guffawed.

"Oh, this'll be a tale to tell alright," Hunrith chimed in.

As they rounded a corner in the path by a small copse of trees, the two serfs ground to a sudden halt. Two armed men, swords unsheathed, were barring their way. One, from whose mouth came a strangle rattling sound, scythed his weapon through the air. With a swishing sound, Aylmer's head flew sideways while his neck belched out a crimson fountain.

After a few frenzied metallic clanks of swords crashing against each other, the second knight, blaspheming all the time, felled Hunrith. William ran forward to find Martim Moniz trying to get his blade out of Hunrith's still-quivering body.

Geraldo Geraldes held up the blacksmith's head.

"You English are incredibly ugly. Look at this!"

Moniz was now standing on top of Hunrith to extract his sword from the Witham gong farmer's chest.

"By the fanny of Saint Euphemia, this one is gristly!"

Geraldo cut William's ropes with his dagger. Moniz had finally retrieved his sword and joined them on his mount.

"That one was dead and yet continued to fight me!"

Geraldo offered his sack of wine to the others. Moniz took a swig and passed it to William, who also had a glug. His throat was parched from the enforced jog behind the bounty hunters.

As he handed the wine back, Geraldo explained that roaming round the military camps and beyond, killing Moors, poisoning the city water supply and intercepting messengers, he'd noticed these two bounty hunters. He could tell at once they weren't soldiers and, by observing them closely, realised they seemed focused on only one thing: William.

"What did they want with you?"

"To take me back to England," William answered.

"Why?" Geraldo asked.

"My mother wants my head."

"Aaaaah," Geraldo answered, "mothers. Afonso had a mother too, you know. She was a monster as well. But he imprisoned her in a convent till she died. Maybe you should try that with your mother."

The Portuguese knight put Aylmer's head into his stained sack.

"What are you going to do with that?" William enquired.

"Oh," Geraldo seemed slightly thrown by the question, "I just keep them for a while. Reminds me who I have killed."

William had seen many crusaders collect mementoes and trophies from the dead, but never their heads. As they rode back to camp, he found it hard not to cast occasional glances at the sack carrying Aylmer's head.

It clearly wasn't the first head that the Portuguese knight had collected. In that sack now was the man who had heated up the iron bar to torture Nicholas and had taken his mother's payment to kill her own son.

Good riddance to you, Aylmer, and may the Devil take your soul!

"Did you release that bitch?" Geraldo asked the Templar.

"If you mean Orraca," William answered, "then no, I didn't."

"Good," Geraldo patted William on the back with the hand not holding Aylmer's head. "Because I am going to hang her, rest assured of that." He cackled in a coarse manner. "You had your way with her, I know you did." William avoided Geraldo's stare. "Good to know some of you Templars have balls. I mean, what is the point of having them if you never use them? Look at those monks that trail after Afonso. Eunuchs, all of them!"

William reminisced on that brief passionate fling he had enjoyed with Orraca: the feel of her skin against his, her lips, her eyes and her lustrous black hair.

Will I ever feel such love with a woman again?

Chapter 52

UNDERNEATH THE WALLS OF AL-USBUNA

"Does it get hotter as we near hell?" Nicholas asked one of the sappers. They were deep below ground, in the dark beneath the walls of Al-Usbuna. The miners were hacking furiously at the rock with their pickaxes. Nicholas had joined them eagerly, even though he had no experience of digging a tunnel.

They bellowed uproariously and then, remembering where they were, quietened down in case the walls collapsed on account of their laughter.

"I never met Old Nick yet, but if we do, he can help us make a fire under the walls, eh, boy?"

Nicholas's face screwed up disapprovingly at being called a boy. The King of the Portuguese had praised him for bringing back the True Cross. All the big men in the King's tent had said nice things to him, except that archbishop. He wasn't a boy anymore! He was Master William's companion, squire even. A future knight!

"Stop daydreaming, boy!" one of the sappers shouted. "If you want to stay down here, put your best shoulder into the job."

News had come that the Flemish and men of Cologne were digging their own tunnel. It was said to have five entrances and was already twenty feet from the city walls. The Normans had to dig fast if they weren't going to be beaten.

"Aedelbald would have loved this," Nicholas said, grabbing a pick and hacking away. "Best sapper ever! Brought down whole castles on his own." The other sappers grinned at the boy's nonsense. "But the Earl chopped his hands off so he can't dig no more."

It was getting hotter below. So as not to be seen by the Moors, a vertical pit had been burrowed downwards behind a row of embedded tree trunks. They were supposed to look like a defence work to repel sorties, but really they masked the activities of the sappers.

They had burrowed deep while others had spirited away the debris. Once at the right depth, the lead sapper followed the vein of the rock with his keenly trained eyes while another guided him in the right direction. Knee-deep in water, they battled forward in the dark, praying to their favourite saints that the walls and ceiling wouldn't collapse and entomb them.

The walls surrounding the qasba were built on a huge rock formation but nearer to the Tagus estuary, they met the sandy beach. The sappers were heading for this inviting stretch of wall. Once at the correct point, they would undermine the foundations with a mighty subterranean explosion.

"I think we're nearly there!"

The sapper frantically swung his pick at a last piece of rock and then with his bare hands pulled away at the remaining earth and stones. There it was, the foundations of the city walls were clearly visible by torchlight! Every man cheered and crossed himself. Nicholas jumped up and down for joy.

"Shit!" the lead sapper exclaimed.

"What's wrong?" Nicholas asked, impatient to see the walls blow up and fall. "We're here, aren't we?"

"This isn't like our castles," the sapper responded.

Sitting down with the other men, he conferred for a few minutes. Unlike the flint walls of Norman castles, these were built of massive stones of a great thickness that had been moulded together with immense precision. Ordinarily, the sappers could scoop away the loosely packed flints and mortar, replacing them steadily with a short corridor of wooden posts, till a small part of the castle sat on these insecure props. Then a fire of wood and pig fat would be created underneath, bringing the walls tumbling down.

Faced with such formidable masonry, they would either have to dig even deeper to get beneath the wall or simply build the fire here and now and hope for the best.

"An explosion here won't do nothing, no matter how big," one sapper moaned. "Got to go deeper, much deeper."

"Show of hands then," the lead sapper suggested. The majority opted for a new vertical shaft from their current position.

He turned to Nicholas.

"Seems like we might meet Old Nick after all. We dig deeper, everybody!"

Way above their heads, Qasim stood by the walls and pointed to the ground. One of his guards placed a glass of water on the spot indicated by the al-kaid. Then they watched intently. Nothing happened; the surface of the water remained motionless.

"Move it here!"

Once more they regarded the innocuous object and waited. Qasim was about to move further along when something caught his eye.

"Look! Did you see it?"

Sure enough, there was a small ripple on the surface of the water. It was barely perceptible at first but then there was a sudden jolt.

"There again. Yes!"

Everybody agreed that directly below their feet, the Franks were up to no good.

"Begin here!" Qasim ordered.

Below ground, the new vertical shaft materialised very slowly as the sappers struggled with the lack of headroom to swing their picks and make their way into the bowels of the earth. The clinking of their axe heads against the stony mass was so loud that Nicholas covered his ears.

"Never heard such a din!"

It went on for several hours until aching muscles and exhausted hands could work no longer.

"Right, lads! Stop and rest yourselves."

The group of sappers halted but the clinking didn't.

"Where is that sound coming from?" Nicholas enquired innocently.

As he spoke, one of the great stones in the wall before him, which their tools had failed to budge, began to slide forward. Then another next to it did the same. The lead sapper prodded Nicholas sharply.

"Run, my friend! Like you've never run before!"

He sprinted through the tunnel that had taken so many weeks to dig with the other sappers, bent double to avoid bumping their heads on the jagged ceiling, with Arabic war cries filling the space behind them. The footsteps of the petrified and unarmed sappers mingled with those of the city garrison bearing down on them. Behind Nicholas, the lead sapper tripped and fell, twisting his ankle on a rock. As Nicholas turned to help him, the man screamed.

"Leave me, boy! I'm done."

In the darkness, all that could be seen approaching were the eyes of the hideous warriors; the rest of their heads were covered in black turbans and scarves. Still staggering forward, Nicholas cast one last backward glance to witness them swarm over the sapper, chopping his flesh with their scimitars. The boy's feet barely touched the ground as he powered towards the speck of light in the distance. He splashed through the puddles, feeling the water rise to his middle as his clothes became soaked and heavier.

"*Allahu Akbar!*"

In their long black cloaks and scaly armour, the Moorish guards were a terrifying presence in the confined space. Nicholas froze as they screamed their oaths and killed every Frank they got close to.

"*Allahu Akbar!*"

The older sappers were having a tough time of the escape and another fell. This time Nicholas didn't look back to view his fate. A scream, cut short, told him all he needed to know. The panting of the sappers grew hoarse with fatigue and fear and one turned with his pickaxe to make a stand.

"Keep going, boy! I'll keep them at bay."

The stand proved to be brief and futile as a scimitar curved into his torso. The pickaxe had barely been raised in its owner's defence as, still conscious, the sapper fell to the rocky ground. His intestines spilled out. A guard paused to take in the spectacle before decapitating the man.

The light from the tunnel exit was now much bigger and the guards halted, not wishing to emerge in the Norman camp. Nicholas burst into the daylight and promptly collapsed, gasping, on the grass. He clutched the green shoots and held them against his mouth, vowing never to go beneath the earth again.

As he rolled onto his back, a tremor shook the ground accompanied by a great explosion.

"We did it!" Nicholas exclaimed.

But turning to face the city, he saw that the great tumult was on the other side of Al-Usbuna. Along the ramparts, guards and citizens were hastening to the now-demolished section of wall facing the eastern Arrabalde and the Flemish camp, from where plumes of smoke and ash were rising.

The men of Flanders and Cologne had succeeded where the Normans had failed.

Chapter 53

THE BAB AL-BAHR

A ghoulish spectacle presented itself before the gate where João Peculiar had declared war on Al-Usbuna. Standing proud and tall was the reconstructed siege engine. Nicholas was inside, with knights and infantry ready to overrun the Moors. The battering ram was primed and ready to smash into the gates and open up an entrance to the medina for the Templars and secular knights. Ox skins had once more been placed all over the engine to protect it from fire. But Geraldo Geraldes had added another ingredient to make the siege engine a much more fearful sight.

Along the top were placed some unused heads acquired in Almada – those that had not been lobbed over the walls with the qadi's correspondence nailed into their foreheads.

Tied to the front of the siege engine begging for mercy was the extended family of eight Geraldo had captured outside the eastern Arribalde, lured to their fate by free gifts of food. In four rows of two, they spanned the engine from top to bottom, spread-eagled and screaming to be let down or for their own people to grant them a quick death.

This gruesome scene was sanctified by the presence of Archbishop João Peculiar. Resplendent in his most spectacular chasuble and wearing a hulking pectoral cross that heaved with amethysts set in gold, he blessed the siege engine with a liberal sprinkling of holy water. It splashed on the faces of the Moors fastened on the front of the contraption.

Behind the Archbishop, a group of Templar knights held up the Lignum Crucis. King Afonso and Hugo Martins rode behind it with the combined might of the Templar Order and the army of Portugal.

Afonso felt as if the True Cross was radiating a power across his soldiers that would make them truly invincible. Its presence meant victory was an utter certainty. God had delivered it into their hands and whatever they did that day had His divine sanction.

We protect the True Cross! God must therefore protect us!

Gualdim Pais had brought his vast Templar army of knights and serjeants to the fray. They had fought so long and hard in nullius diocesis that peace was a mystery to them, a long distant memory. War was their only reality and today, Qasim and his men would face an enemy whose zeal could easily match any Almohad.

If the Moors of Al-Andalus thought for one moment that they could regain their lost lands, then Gualdim Pais would teach them a lesson that they and their children would never forget.

From Monte Fragoso came Saher of Archelle and the Norman and English armies to join forces and make the great breakthrough into the city. Pedro Pitões, Bishop of Porto, stood proudly next to the Norman leader. He'd used his time as a hostage among these people well and convinced them that they could pillage with the complete backing of the Church. Pitões had one particular target in mind for destruction – the heretical Mozarabic Christians whose Greek and even largely Arabised rite of worship was an offence to Rome.

Notably absent were the Flemish and men of Cologne. Christian of Ghistelles had succeeded in getting his sappers to create a two hundred foot breach in the wall by the eastern Arribalde. The gap revealed the streets of the medina and the large dwellings further up in the qasba, as if the skin had been ripped off a portion of the city's body to reveal muscle and sinew beneath. The city's people and soldiers were hurriedly filling the gap as best they could.

But Christian of Ghistelles could see his opportunity to get into Al-Usbuna before the Normans and sack the city first. He'd forbidden all the other armies to come near and threatened them with force if they did.

Qasim watched the Franks assembling. The siege engine rolled up the narrow stretch of beach before the Bab Al-Bahr. On its front hung Geraldo's hostages, crying pitifully. The al-kaid signalled to his archers to end their suffering.

"Aim well, kill them now!"

With tears running down their faces, the archers dispatched the eight martyrs. Their bodies, pierced by arrows, now hung limp over the ox skins. But the sight had struck terror into the hearts of the Moorish defenders as Geraldo Geraldes had intended.

"Prepare the Greek Fire," Qasim ordered. "Archers – fire!"

Once more the walls of Al-Usbuna pulsed into life as a hail of arrows spewed out, followed by heavy rocks and stones from the battlement ballistae. Every watchtower hurled down great missiles that demolished rows of Franks. An arrow struck one of the oxen towing the siege engine and its progress stalled.

"The tide is rising," called a Norman knight, pointing to the estuary. "The wheels need support!"

The dead ox was cleared and a group of serfs from Ipswich in Suffolk volunteered to go in front of the siege engine and lay down wooden planks that would give the wheels a purchase. To do this without being killed by the Moorish archers, they hid under a large wicker roof that resembled a small house.

This strange house hurtled along the beach, dodging arrows as it went. Working at speed as rocks and boiling sand were dropped on top of the roof, its inhabitants dug away at the sand and laid down wooden planks. Then the wicker-roofed contraption moved away.

"Welsh cat got here in time," an English knight said to Nicholas.

"What?" the boy answered. "I see no cat."

The company inside the siege engine laughed.

"There it is." He pointed to the house now moving at breakneck speed to get away from the Moorish missiles. "That's a Welsh cat!"

Sidray squinted to view the unfolding battle from the qasba. The calm detachment with which he'd observed the conflicts before had gone. As an apple tea was brought to him, he sent it flying across the cobbles with a furious sweep of his hand.

"I have no time for that!"

His thinkers had been caught trying to leave the city under cover of night and he'd placed them under arrest in some rooms in the qasr — not an uncomfortable prison.

For others, the punishment for treachery was worse.

Market traders and their customers in the souks had been overheard disparaging him.

Disparaging the Taifa!

The Taifa is weak, they said. He is proud and godless. Allah has forsaken him. He isn't of noble blood. Sidray is of slavish stock.

These wagging tongues were now nailed to the door of the Grand Mosque as an example to anyone else who might think of expressing dissent.

Sidray had forbidden his Scorpions and Jackals to enter the fray. These African warriors, the Tangerines, were to stay in the qasba for his own personal protection. Not that he wished to countenance the idea of the Franks bursting into the medina but that possible eventuality was covered.

"Sulayman."

The Taifa's astrologer bowed low before him.

"Yes, great lord."

"If your recent horoscope proves to be in any way wrong, I will have you crucified on the walls of Badajoz. And I will force-feed you your charts."

William watched, unable to help Nicholas, as Qasim unleashed Greek fire onto the siege engine. Screeching jets of fire arched out of the city's watchtowers. The great plumes of hot yellow filled the air with an acrid, sulphurous aroma. Nicholas gasped as the curling, liquid flames howled out of the city walls and spread over the front of the siege engine, instantly cooking the eight bodies.

The Welsh cat reappeared, only this time to pour water over the flames.

"Get that engine moving before it is destroyed!" Hugo Martins yelled.

"I want to be inside that damned city," King Afonso chimed in.

Whipping the oxen and crusaders pulling the ropes themselves got the siege engine moving once more. There were pockets of flames all over the front of the machine but Nicholas could see the walls getting ever closer.

One more heave and we'll be there!

Qasim ordered more Greek fire. His soldiers fired seemingly endless volleys of arrows at the deathly contraption as it lumbered ever nearer. The top of the siege engine was now visible within the medina and the terror-stricken womenfolk joined their husbands with burning material to throw at it.

Boom!

The first thud of the battering ram against the Bab Al-Bahr resounded, but the formidable wooden doors barely moved an inch. Frustrated, a group of Norman soldiers burst out of the siege engine and pushed against the doors. But being out in the open, they were at the mercy of the al-kaid, who signalled to his guards. In no time, boiling sand coated the over-enthusiastic infantrymen, cascading over their brimmed kettle hats and sticking to their bodies. Agonised screams chilled Nicholas' blood.

The sudden loss of their comrades stunned the Normans and at all levels in the tower, nobody moved or said anything. The ram fell silent and the wheels of the siege engine ceased to turn.

Till one voice piped up.

"Come on … we're that close, aren't we? Don't let them drive us back now! We're nearly there."

The seasoned battlers regarded the small figure in his borrowed soldier's tunic, which was slightly too big for him. Nicholas waited for the dismissive aside that would put him back in his lowly place.

"He's right, lads! Put your backs into it."

Boom!

Shock had turned to fury as the men within the siege engine sought to avenge their comrades. They pounded the gate over and over.

Boom!

The splintering of wood and groaning of an iron bolt as it buckled under the strain raised morale. The siege engine was like a maddened giant pounding at the entry to Al-Usbuna.

Boom!

An almighty crack resounded as the thick iron bolt broke and the doors slowly swung open. Behind them, the soldiers and citizens of the medina frantically tried to close the Bab Al-Bahr, but it was as if the gate itself had surrendered to the inevitable. As the ram burst through, the drawbridge from the top of the siege engine lowered onto the ramparts and knights scurried up the wooden stairs within the engine, clambering onto the battlements and slaying the waiting guards.

"Charge!"

The Templars stormed in through the gate first, followed by the Portuguese. The Moorish guards struggled to push them back but the warriors in white mantles scythed them down. William's sword flashed this way and that, killing all around him. Martins felt a great inner strength as he felled one guard after another. Gualdim Pais and his men spread at lightning speed across the battlements and finished off every sentry and archer they encountered.

Qasim could see the medina was falling to the Franks and pushed his men back towards the qasba. They would fight house by house but he could tell the forces of Ibn Arrik had the advantage. As he retreated, the al-kaid ran straight into the Flemish and men of Cologne. They had entered the city hours before the rest of the Franks and set about looting. They were so pre-occupied with seizing wealth that they ignored the Moorish military governor and with his men he fled in another direction.

Dom Afonso was dismayed to see the Flemish stripping the city when it had not yet been taken. Sword in hand, he fought alongside his men and they advanced slowly across the medina. But as he turned towards a deserted souk, a familiar figure staggered into his path with a large, stained sack in his hand.

"Geraldo, I have not seen you for hours." He looked at the sack, sadly. "Please, old friend, do not say you have been looting as well."

"No. Well ... a kind of booty. Not gold, something I like to collect."

"What?"

"Oh," Geraldo shrugged, "you know what I have in here."

"I do not," the King persisted.

This was something the knight hadn't shown his king before. Not that Geraldo was ashamed, but Afonso could be such a prude at times.

"It is nothing important."

"Show me what you collect, Geraldo."

Slowly, he opened the bag and Afonso peered within. Several sets of eyes stared back. Decapitated heads, both male and female! No wonder the sack was stiff with blood.

"My queen is right," Afonso remarked bleakly, "I keep bad company. I really should mix with better people."

"Ha!" Geraldo scoffed. "Would those people take Santarem? Sintra? Attack Moorish towns with no care for their safety? No! But that's what I do for you, Afonso, while that French *bitch* sneers!"

Afonso reeled from his words.

"You have shown me your true worth today, Geraldo. We are no longer friends. Leave my sight and never return to court."

The dinar rolled along Geraldo's lower lip. Picking up his sack, he turned his back on Dom Afonso and stomped off. Refusing to look back, he turned into an alleyway in search of another head. But suddenly, Fearless Geraldo realised he was fighting back tears. Drunken tears maybe, but tears nonetheless.

"I will make you pay, Afonso," he sobbed to himself, "I will make you pay very dearly!"

Chapter 54

MOZARABIC CHRISTIAN
CHURCH IN THE QASBA

Pedro Pitões entered the church.

These pet Christians of the Moors! Their travesty of Christianity disgusts me!

Pitões seethed as he regarded the horseshoe arches, painted tiles and decorative stone tracery of leaves and flowers. This looks more like a mosque or synagogue than a church, he thought. Behind him filed a line of Norman knights eyeing up whatever they could pillage. But one of the knights had been promised a particularly handsome reward by Pitões.

At the altar stood Abrah, the Mozarabic Bishop of Al-Usbuna. He held up a Visigothic bible made by the last Christian rulers of the city many centuries before.

"I am the Bishop of Al-Usbuna. Come in peace, my children."

"We do not come in peace," Pitões corrected him, "we come in war!"

"Surely we are brothers in Christ."

Abrah shook with fear.

"I am not so sure," Pitões replied.

The leader of Al-Usbuna's Christians seemed as ancient as his bible. Wisps of white hair clung to his head and heavy jowls hung over a sagging neck. The cleric had to squint to view his unwanted guests. There was the chainmail of the Normans and in front of them the forbidding figure of Pitões, head to toe in black. Now he recognised the infamous Bishop of Porto.

"*Dominus Vobiscum*," he greeted Pitões weakly.

"Oh, you know some Latin then?"

Abrah regarded the severe-looking prelate from the North with trepidation. He'd heard that Pitões had skin as white as snow, that his eyes were dead like those of a shark, and that his smile normally presaged some vicious outburst. His reputation had preceded him as a sworn enemy of both Islam and those strands of Christianity that didn't adhere closely enough to the rites of Rome. Abrah was not enjoying the encounter.

"Tell me," Pitões stared coldly into Abrah's watering eyes, "do you speak Arabic more often than you speak Latin? Do you recite Moorish poetry more often than you read scripture? Do you celebrate the Muslim holidays as well as our own?"

"No ... no," Abrah protested.

"We are told that the Moors come to your church and treat it as a tavern because their faith forbids alcohol."

"This is not true," the old Mozarabic bishop was lost for words. "Nothing like that happens here."

This place stinks of Greeks and Arabs, Pitões thought. I sense the influence of schismatic Constantinople here when I should feel that this is part of Catholic Rome. That pulpit looks more like the minbar in a mosque. Those icons belong in Byzantium, not in Portugal. This is not a house of Christ, this is Islam masquerading as Christianity.

Saher of Archelle bobbed up and down behind Pitões impatiently. The latter had been his hostage officially but in truth had been egging the crusaders on to comprehensively sacking the city.

"My men would like to start now, if your Grace doesn't mind," Saher addressed Pitões, who nodded his consent.

With that, the Normans set about removing every precious object they could find. Silver and gold fittings were torn from the painted walls, statues robbed of their jewels. A chest of silk vestments was flung open.

"Oh, no!" Abrah sobbed. "What are they doing?" He turned to Pitões. "Please, you must stop them desecrating this place."

"They cannot desecrate what is not holy," Pitões responded.

Saher of Archelles stood in front of Abrah.

"What did you say your name was again?"

The ancient man held up the bible.

"I am the Bishop of Al-Usbuna."

"Yes," Saher said, "that is what I thought you said."

With one deft movement Saher slashed the man's throat and then wiped the dagger clean on his tunic. The Bishop crashed face down onto the tiled floor.

"Thank you," Pitões nodded as if a minor inconvenience had been politely dealt with. "As I explained to you all earlier," he continued, as he pulled Abrah's episcopal ring from the dead man's finger, "these are not Christians but Moors. They have mingled for far too long with the infidel. Slay them as you would anybody else. And," he made a sign of benediction, "you have my blessing, needless to say."

A Norman knight by the name of Gilbert of Hastings stepped forward.

"You promised, your Grace," he beamed.

"Yes, I did," Pitões answered.

He slipped the episcopal ring onto the knight's finger – then regarded the corpse of Abrah.

"There never was a bishop here because there never was an Al-Usbuna. This city is called Lisbon from this day forth and Dom Afonso is its king. Everything is born anew! Whatever happened here for three centuries past will be erased from the chronicles." Pitões raised his hands in a blessing to all present. "Gilbert of Hastings, I anoint you the first legitimate bishop of Lisbon!"

Gilbert bounced in full chainmail up to the altar and sat in the late Bishop's throne.

"How do I look?"

"Like a bishop," Saher guffawed.

"Here's my first pronouncement as a bishop!" He raised two fingers in mock benediction. "You're not a Christian if you don't obey me! You'd better eat like a Norman, drink like a Norman and whore like a Norman!"

That should make life difficult for those infidels who decided to stay in Al-Usbuna, Pitões grinned. He'd make sure that Gilbert enacted some particularly draconian laws to re-shape the population in a generation. Any Moor bedding or marrying a Christian woman would be hanged. Only Christian babies would be tolerated from this day forward.

The Bishop of Porto left the newly consecrated Bishop of Lisbon. As he wandered out of the church door, the searing sunlight burnt his skin. Where were his attendants? They were nowhere to be seen.

My face feels like it's on fire!

He swung round to re-enter the church but was seized from behind. A mailed hand clamped over his mouth to silence him. Helpless, Pitões was dragged towards the steep wall that surrounded the qasba. As he and his assailant turned a corner, the Bishop was horrified to spy the bloodied bodies of his attendants nearby, his canopy discarded next to them.

I need my canopy. The sun is scorching. My eyes are in agony!

Some distance from the church with the sound of fighting still raging down below, he was flung onto the top of the qasba's battlements. He was faced with a vertiginous drop. Pitões' hat was torn from his head and his arms restrained. Now his entire head felt as if it were ablaze.

"I beg you – stop this!"

The sunlight was blistering.

"I saw what you did in that church."

Pitões recognised the voice.

"Gualdim ... Pais. The Templar?"

The Commander of Tomar chuckled sadistically.

"The Cathar. The Gnostic. The heretic. Whatever you are not, I am!"

"Devil! Let me go!"

"You would like to burn me – but I will burn you first. Pitões, you will roast in this heat for your sins. God has given me the means to finish you off without having to strike a blow. All we need to do is to wait for that yellow ball in the sky to do its holy work."

Soon Pitões' head was erupting in ulcerous sores. Rivers of stinging sweat pored down his face. His breaths became ever shorter as his lungs grew clogged.

Curse my body! Curse you, God, for bringing me so feeble into this world! You have left me powerless to defend your faith. And now I die at the hands of this demon.

Pais maintained a vice-like grip on his victim. There were so many of these wicked creatures to snuff out. A world of venal and self-serving ecclesiastical scum! All they cared about was screwing tithes from peasants and erecting fine palaces and cathedrals. Pitões struggled to break free.

"Love not the world," Pais intoned some heretical sentiments to him. "Love not the things that are in the world. You have loved the world, haughty priest, so the Father does not love you anymore. You have lusted with your eyes for the riches of this world and forgotten the riches of heaven ..."

"Heretic!"

"I am no heretic. I am God's judge!"

At which point, the blade of a hefty sword appeared under the Portuguese Templar's throat. The tip touched his throat. William glared at Pais.

"Let him go!"

"Or what will you do, Sir William de Mandeville?"

Typical of this swaggering Englishman with no understanding of the great wars that lay ahead between the forces of papal avarice and those Templars sworn to build God's kingdom on earth. Pitões was one less adversary. One less cleric to cut down when Christ's true church came to rule.

"Go in that church!" Pais thundered. "Go and see what he did!"

The Norman knights were still looting as Abrah's body stiffened and cooled.

"Just let him go," William responded. Pais was fighting the wrong enemy. He was beating up a defenceless weasel. There was nothing honourable in his action. And he risked offending God. "We're set to win a great victory today — don't ruin it."

Chapter 55

QASBA AND QASR

Qasim and his men flew through the gate to the qasba and locked it quickly. But already, the Franks were pounding at the Bab al-Qasba and setting their ladders up against the walls of the nobility's compound. All along the steep fortifications of the qasba, once thought impregnable, the Templars and Portuguese were massing for the final onslaught.

"Where is the Taifa?" the al-kaid panted, trying to catch his breath.

"He has barricaded himself in the qasr," Shibli the muhtasib replied, "and taken as much food and supplies as he could. He said you are forbidden to enter, that you and your men must fight and die out here."

"Anything else?" Qasim asked.

"Your skin will be flayed from your body when he celebrates his victory over the Franks," Shibli added. "If it is any comfort, he has not allowed any of the great families who live here to enter the qasr either."

Sure enough, the qadi and all the officials of Al-Usbuna were assembled nearby with their families waiting for the Frankish onslaught. The women and children wept as they realised very soon their lives would be lost and their beautiful houses smashed to pieces. Maybe Abbas was right after all, Qasim thought, and this was the fitnah, the end of days, when all things are brought down, including the stars and the sky.

Qasim watched as his men toppled scaling ladders that were sprouting up all along the walls. Frankish arrows were thinning out their numbers and soon the qasba would be defenceless.

He turned to address the nobility.

"The qasr is my palace – not that painted son of slaves! Follow me, I will not allow you great nobles to be cut down like the rabble. How dare that worthless siqlabi leave us to be slaughtered like this? Remember, all of you, that our forefathers saw the very face of the Prophet. They were amongst his companions. But as for that painted monster's ancestors, they stared at a branding iron."

Leaving their servants behind, the nobles were led by Qasim into the qasr fortress along with most of the guards, who peeled off the walls and fled to the last solidly Moorish position in Al-Usbuna. Everything else was now falling to the Franks.

Outside the Bab Al-Qasba, William, Pathros and Nicholas joined hundreds of other knights in slamming the iron-tipped tree trunk from the siege engine into the gates. The only people left to defend the compound were the nobles' servants, and they did what they could, throwing furniture and stones onto the Frankish heads. All they achieved by this was to guarantee their own deaths.

Smashing their way through, the secular knights made a beeline for the richest pickings in Al-Usbuna. From the Bab Al-Bahr to the qasr, every thief and murderer that had taken the cross and joined the Normans or Flemish was now combing the city for loot and carnal satisfaction. Screams and moans of victims in countless houses rang out constantly as every item of worth was taken, the men were hacked to pieces and the women raped. Pitões had promised the secular knights that they could despoil the city before handing it over to King Afonso and they had taken him very much at his word.

Geraldo was roaming the wealthier houses of the qasba, seeking booty and heads. He scoured the finely decorated riads with their internal courtyard gardens and spacious living quarters but was disappointed to find the scum from other kingdoms had got there first. In one house, he chanced upon the body of a dead eunuch splayed across a dry fountain and staring at the blue sky above.

"I am sorry," Geraldo apologised to the corpse, "but I only include heads I have killed myself."

He was about to move on when the sound of a vase breaking rooted him to the spot. Somebody was inside one of the rooms, a knight or common infantryman taking what he could. Geraldo waited for the man to emerge. Suddenly, a figure bounded out, holding a knife.

"Is this your house, my dear?" Geraldo found himself addressing Orraca – or Aisha, as Sidray knew her.

"These humble stones ..."

Geraldo raised his hand.

"No! No Moorish poetry! I hate your poems as much as I hate you. I would cut out your tongues not to hear your rhyming doggerel."

"You are a brute!"

He looked around, rattling the dinar in his mouth.

"So you were a wealthy woman?"

"From one of the finest families of this city."

"I am *so* impressed," Geraldo bowed. "Though I suspect you made your money on your back or using that silvery tongue of yours!"

"Get out of here!"

Geraldo shook his head. He couldn't possible comply with that order.

"I have a different plan. I have decided to behead you in your own home. Then one of your Moorish poets can pen a lament. The Headless Dancer!" He dropped his sack and drew his sword. "Did that lovestruck Templar ever figure out who you were?"

Clattering the dinar against his front teeth, Geraldo could scarcely believe this moment had finally come. This would be his most enjoyable decapitation ever.

"Stop. Please," she implored him. "I can offer you great riches!"

"I can take them myself," Geraldo responded, the blade of his sword now touching her waist.

"Something far greater than you will ever find in this city," she added breathlessly. "I promise you, upon the souls of all my ancestors. On the life of my mother! You could be al-kaid of Marrakech. Think of it. You would live like a sultan. My family can arrange it. We are very powerful."

Geraldo shook his head.

"What people will say to avoid death."

"It is true," she implored him. "Pledge your allegiance to the Almohads and Marrakech would be yours."

"So now you are claiming to be an Almohad!"

"Leave with me! Come to Marrakech! It would be a great body blow to your king."

"He is not my king anymore," Geraldo snarled.

"Then you're a traitor," another voice interjected.

William had walked into the riad. The Portuguese swung his sword away from Orraca and jabbed at the Templar.

"I saved your life once, Englishman, but now I shall take it."

Orraca could have escaped there and then. All she had to do was retrace her steps through the house and out to the open streets, where she would be free of the dinar-sucking monster. The canny spy and assassin knew places to hide from the Flemish and Normans until they had finished raping Al-Usbuna.

But standing before her was William – the dashing English knight who had selflessly stopped her from being executed. Even in these dire circumstances, poetry flooded her mind. It was the disease that afflicted every Moor – a love of mournful verses. She regarded the tall Englishman before her and was overcome by strong emotions.

I wish my heart were split by a knife,
And you were put into it, and then my bosom were closed tight again:
And you would stay in it, not dwelling in any other,
Until the arrival of the Day of Resurrection and the gathering of the dead;
Living in it as long as I lived, and when I die,
You would live in the inside of the heart in the darkness of the grave!

Orraca knew that for reasons she had to keep to herself, she was bound to save his life. He couldn't be allowed to die.

"Stop this! Geraldo, I promise you Marrakech!"

"Oh, damn your false promises!" The Portuguese knight brought his sword back to decapitate the mistress of fabrications and falsehoods once and for all. "You have nothing to offer me."

Then suddenly she screamed:

"I am pregnant!"

Even the heartless and cynical Geraldo had to stop in his tracks. His head swivelled towards William. This was priceless. When the blond-haired baby eventually emerged, how would the Templar explain his less-than-righteous conduct?

"Did you forget your Templar vows, Englishman?" The Portuguese knight burst into uproarious laughter. This was hysterical. It was far more amusing to let Orraca live than die. "Bet you wish I had killed her now, eh?"

William stood silent, his jaw dropped in disbelief.

Chapter 56

QASR

Sidray waddled along the line of nobles who had burst into the qasr, defying his orders. Qasim placed himself first in line. He had no apology to make to Sidray over shepherding his fellow nobles to the security of the qasr. Only a man of slavish stock like Sidray would leave Muslims from good backgrounds to be butchered by the Frankish wolves.

But the Taifa saw things very differently.

"Him," Sidray pointed at Shibli.

One of the tall and imposing Scorpions bounded forward and grabbed the slight figure of the muhtasib. Qasim made to object but Sidray placed a finger on his lips, ordering silence.

"Say nothing, al-kaid. Simply watch."

Sidray nodded and the Scorpion placed his large hands around Shibli's throat and began to squeeze. The African's face was entirely dispassionate as the Moorish nobleman choked and then expired. He cast him down on the ground.

"The qasr will not fall," Sidray explained. "We will all fight. And when we have defended the qasr, we will re-take the qasba and the medina. I saw the way in which the people welcomed me here." He remembered how they had lauded him through the streets only two short months before. "They love me and when we emerge from here, they will rise up and strike at the Franks!"

Qasim gulped.

Sidray is a deluded madman.

It was over, and defeat was all that awaited them. All the dreams the al-kaid had formed of renewing the caliphate in this small part of Al-Andalus with the help of the fearsome Almohads had been a cruel fantasy.

Tomorrow, the Franks will stand in the qasr and raise their standard above it.

The great families would be expelled, along with the common people of the medina, and the mosques would be dismantled and their stones used to build the churches of the infidels. This was already happening in Shantarin and Sintra and it would come to pass in Al-Usbuna, but on a much more devastating scale.

The Taifa continued hectoring his nobles.

"You will see me up there" – Sidray pointed at the battlements – "cheering you on and giving you hope at all times. We will be victorious! Ibn Arrik's body will be cut to pieces and fed to wild dogs! Now, fight or you will face the same fate as this fool!"

Martins and Pais were surveying the walls of the qasr to find an entry point. The secular knights had already declared victory and weren't interested in risking their lives to take the palace. When the Templars have seized it, they reasoned, we'll come in and strip its treasures. Until then, we have the medina and qasba to keep us busy!

"How will we get in?" William asked Martins, the two men keenly surveying the qasr.

"The main gate," Pais answered bluntly, giving him a hate-filled glance. "No clever tactics. We go in the same way those Moorish dogs did."

As they resolved on their direct course of action, the Templars were joined by a group of Portuguese knights including Martim Moniz, whose blasphemies, as ever, preceded him.

"Feel hotter than Saint Anthony's arse sitting in the desert fighting in this armour! Can't wait till we're finished here and I can rip it off."

The prospect of taking the qasr thrilled him and, with a group of Templar knights, he made for the main gate. Archers provided cover from the defenders on the ramparts as the knights heaved against the final entrance they had to smash down. The ram was brought up and yet again it began thudding until the sound of wood splitting and bolts shearing inspired a cheer.

"In Christ's name, come on!" Moniz shouted as if commanding the gate to open.

On the other side of it, Moorish defenders now pushed equally hard to keep it shut. But the momentum was on the Frankish side. Suddenly, a gap opened up between the two gates and with characteristic but fatal rashness, Moniz placed himself in the opening.

"By the balls of Saint Botolph – think I am stuck!"

Straight away, the Moors had begun a concerted shove back. William pulled at his arm to try and release Moniz but he was caught between the two great slabs of wood. The portly Portuguese knight realised he'd blundered. He tried to utter a last blasphemous battle cry as his bones were crushed and a trickle of blood ran from his open mouth.

King Afonso arrived just in time to see his friend slumped between the gates.

"For Moniz! For Saint James!" he shouted to his men. "For Portugal! Open those damned gates!"

Inspired by their king, the Portuguese and the Templars heaved one more time and overwhelmed the Moors, who gave up and scurried to the next line of defence. What remained of Moniz slumped to the ground and was carried away by some Templar serjeants.

"Follow me," William yelled. "I've been here before."

Pathros watched as the mop of blond hair and billowing white mantle disappearied once more into the centre of a battle. This was William's way. Impetuous. Brave. Foolhardy. But would his insanity return with a vengeance once he emerged from the fray? Was the Basilisk lurking within the qasr, waiting to torment him?

Please be strong, William – my dear friend.

William led the Templar and Portuguese soldiers through the gates and towards the Hall of the Caliphs. As they entered, they found the Jackals and Scorpions had formed a welcoming party. The formidable warriors drew their scimitars and stormed down the walkway between the two fishponds towards the Franks.

Sidray had ordered them to exterminate every crusader who dared to enter his palace.

"Courage!" Pais shouted at his men. "They are devils! We are God's chosen! Slay all of them!"

The clash of steel rang out around the courtyard. In the upper corridor, behind the wooden grilles, Sidray watched his elite guards fighting the Templars.

He bit his nails furiously. His eyes twitched. How had the crusaders ever been allowed to get this close?

One Jackal was knee-deep in the fishpond, slashing at a knight who finally succumbed to his wounds and ended up floating, face down, with the lilies. A Scorpion drove his scimitar with incredible strength through the chest of a Templar and brought it out through his shoulder. But Sidray's Tangerines were badly outnumbered. Little by little, they retreated across the Hall of the Caliphs.

The Taifa could scarcely believe what he was seeing.

Cowards!

Sidray held a bundle under his arm and with two servants he scuttled into a room.

"Get this off!" He tore at his fine silk clothes and turban.

William left the Hall of the Caliphs with Pathros and Nicholas and went in search of the ruler of Badajoz.

"I don't want him to be tortured," he told Pathros. "If we get to him first, we can hand him over in chains to Dom Afonso."

Pathros knew how sadistic the Franks could be in these circumstances. The wrong kind of knights would toy with Sidray. They might strip him first. Then cut him over and over again with their blades. The Taifa would yelp and howl, but that would only encourage his tormentors.

We must find him first!

But he was nowhere in sight. Three servants scuttled past, trying to avoid the fighting and escape the qasr. William shouted after them, asking if they had seen the Taifa, but they didn't stop.

"Bet they been stealing their master's things," Nicholas observed. He knew how the poor took advantage of the heat of battle to fill their pockets. His mind strayed to that fat lady he'd seen with the heaps of jewels If only he could remember where her room was.

The trio of servants now entered a small courtyard. They were desperate to quit the qasr but to their dismay, a voice boomed out at them.

"Stop!" Qasim had spotted the servants. "Where are you going? Go back to your posts."

They stood perfectly still.

"I said, go back to your posts."

One of them – rather short and plump – turned to Qasim. His face powder had been removed and his hair dye washed out. Its real colour was quite reddish, as the al-kaid had always suspected – a sure sign of slavish stock. His eyebrows had been trimmed and his beard shaved off. The Taifa was dressed as a menial and attempting to slip away.

The al-kaid regarded the ruler of Badajoz.

"How appropriate, Siqlabi," Qasim muttered.

The plump servant – his identity revealed – exploded.

"How dare you call me that!"

The al-kaid struck the Taifa firmly across his flabby face.

"Be silent, Siqlabi!"

Drawing out his scimitar, Qasim prodded the Taifa's capacious gut.

"A servant who would betray his master by running away deserves only one punishment."

With that he slid the long steel blade into Sidray's stomach. The Taifa's mouth opened wide in astonishment as he clutched at the gaping wound in disbelief. His two scribes, who had accompanied him in the attempted escape, whipped out their styluses and gleefully stabbed at his face as the disgraced Taifa fell to the tiled floor.

No more being kicked for copying things down wrong!

No more petty insults from this puffed-up excuse for a taifa!

Qasim turned his back on the undignified scene. Now he chanced upon yet another trio.

"Templar," he addressed William, who glanced briefly at the bloody mess that had once terrified the population of Al-Usbuna.

"Is that who I think it is?"

Qasim refused to answer William and ignored the scribes hacking at their hated master. He wasn't much interested in the mutilation of the dead Taifa. Instead, his attention was squarely on the man who had been the architect of the city's doom. That wretched Templar!

If the True Cross had remained within Al-Usbuna, then the superstitious oaf Ibn Arrik would have slunk away. The barbaric and backward Franks really believed in its sacral power. Look at how they had carried it before them at the final siege and through the impenetrable walls of Al-Usbuna.

Qasim was consumed by a bitter hatred towards the powerfully built, tall and handsome knight from a cold kingdom far to the North.

"You came here to destroy a great civilisation."

"Somebody else told me I'd do that," William responded, reaching for his sword.

"Who?"

"Orraca."

"You mean our spy, Aisha. I suspect she bewitched you. Poor, stupid Frank." The al-kaid raised his scimitar. "If you want my city so badly, you will have to take it from me. It is not yours! It is mine! It is the city of my ancestors!"

Qasim swung at him but William evaded the sharp blade.

"You think this is about honour, Templar. This is about my home!" This time William was forced to parry a strike from the al-kaid. "You Franks saw our city for what it was: a jewel. And you came to steal it." Qasim struck at William with greater ferocity. "Greed, that is all that motivates you barbarians! Innocent men are slain in their homes, women and children murdered by their side."

William ducked just in time as Qasim's blade tip swept past and smacked the wall, sending sparks flying.

"This city lived in harmony, and with beauty." He hit out at the Templar once more. "So many precious objects that your king wants to steal." He cut William's forearm, drawing blood, and the Templar realised he had to find the strength to win. "So much wisdom and learning and proud history. When you have finished, it will be as if we never existed. You Franks are only satisfied when you have humbled proud peoples and reduced us to beggars."

Qasim stopped talking. William's blade had run him through just beneath his ribcage. He'd said all there was to be said. His city was gone. And now he would die with it. Qasim's heart stopped beating.

Chapter 57

MEDINA OF AL-USBUNA

"Will they stop soon?" Nicholas asked.

The boy who had been an incurable thief now witnessed larceny on an unimaginable and bloody scale. Every alley was cluttered with bodies. And the secular knights still had two more days under the terms of their oaths sworn with King Afonso to plunder Al-Usbuna. It seemed their lust for violence and possessions was insatiable. For the first time in his life, the sight of stealing repelled Nicholas.

"Why do they do this?" Pathros was equally disgusted. "The people have left all their belongings in front of their houses as they were ordered and still these barbarians go in and kill them."

Not only were the Moors dead in their homes but also there were bodies that had died clutching crucifixes and Christian icons, as in Santarem. The Jews, so easily identifiable by their garb and the Mezuzah nailed to the right-hand side of their doorways, hadn't been spared either.

"I wish the noise would stop," Nicholas clasped his ears.

The trio arrived outside the Grand Mosque. They reached the main entrance but within it was now completely dark. No candelabras lit up the gloom and instead of voices in prayer, there was an eerie humming. William clasped his hand to his face.

"Death!" the knight gasped.

The stench of bodily decay was everywhere, and the buzzing of thousands of flies.

"Their bodies have given birth to a million winged creatures," Pathros noted.

If the dead were left unburied, Pathros knew from his reading that these vile creatures erupted spontaneously from the rotting flesh. Qasim's order to put the plague dead in the Great Mosque had resulted in a spectacle that horrified the three companions. Hundreds of corpses were piled on top of each other in different stages of decomposition. The rich and poor mingled and clasped each other in a deathly embrace.

Pathros dipped three pieces of cloth in lavender oil and urged his companions to press them to their faces.

"What happened to these people?" William lamented.

"Plague and hunger," Pathros explained.

The trio turned to leave when William became faintly aware of a ghostly murmuring. Could the dead be talking? The voices grew a little louder. It was a mixture of Arabic and Portuguese.

"We should leave," Nicholas quaked. "They've not been taken to hell yet. These dead'uns will rise and attack us any moment."

"No," Pathros looked around to identify the source of the sound, "not everybody is dead."

William trotted past the many columns and around the pile of dead till he found a cowering multitude attempting to hide behind the rotting plague victims.

"Are you going to kill us?" a woman sobbed.

The sight of Pathros, an Easterner by appearance, calmed the terrified families. Hesitantly at first, but then tripping over each other to speak, they introduced themselves as Mozarab Christians, Jews, old Arabic families, Berbers and others whose heritage was so confused and remote they had given up wondering what they were.

Some had been blacksmiths and others were once merchants. There was a masseur from the bathhouse and a barber who cut hair by the river. One man sold eggs in the market with a bowl of water in front of his stall to show that they were fresh, while another had been a joiner, making furniture for the elite in the qasba.

"What happens to us now?" one old woman asked. "I do not care for myself but my children and grandchildren. I fear for them."

"They will kill us all," moaned a man who had baked bread for years at a stall near the qasba. "We are strangers in our own city. We are nothing to them. They want to murder every one of us."

Yesterday these people had known who and what they were. Their lives had been governed by familiar routines of work in the city or fields, Friday prayers in the Grand Mosque, afternoons in the bathhouses and walks in the gardens with their aviaries and refreshing fountains. But now they had nothing: the city was not theirs anymore. And these invaders had no taste for the delicate refinements they had always enjoyed.

Pathros' heart ached.

"I will stay and help you," the turcopole fought back tears.

This pathetic scene reminded him of something and suddenly he recalled what it was. The survivors of that great earthquake in his native Aleppo crawling in the rubble-strewn streets, begging for help; the wounded dying slowly and no grave for them; the newly pauperised begging but nobody having anything to spare. Great Aleppo devastated. Houses reduced to wreckage. Fortunes built up over generations lost in a second.

I still see my mother's anguished face and her voice imploring me to leave.

Pathros turned to William.

"Go back to England, my friend. I will join you soon. But let me stay and help these people."

William was suddenly gripped by a terrible fear. Pathros couldn't leave him!

"You mustn't – I need you!"

"William," Pathros dropped his medicine bag and pulled at his goatee, "my family in Syria had twenty servants. My father was highly regarded by the caliph. My mother was literate and well-born. Yet look at me. I am nothing better than a shiner of boots and polisher of bridles." He glanced at the sick and dying and on to the hideous pile of corpses. "Let me be more than that. Let me bring my knowledge to these people."

William was devastated.

I should have treated Pathros as a friend — I always treated him as a servant.

He clasped the turcopole by the hands. Long ago, when his friend Robert lay dying after being poisoned at the well, Pathros had appeared, offering his potions and elixirs. William hadn't believed in his powers. He'd been prepared to dismiss him as just an insubordinate local menial but he was so much more than that.

"I'm glad we met," William's voice broke. "I'm *so* glad we met."

He embraced the Syrian.

This man had stopped the wicked Augustinians boring a hole into his skull. He'd pulled him back from the verge of a terrible madness. And he'd pointed the way on to this great quest that would restore the name of de Mandeville and let William bury his father.

"Stay here then ..." William caved in. "But not for good."

"We will meet again, my friend."

Then suddenly a thought hit the Templar like a thunderbolt: "But what about Nicholas?"

Pathros took a deep breath.

"Call it a miracle, if you must," the rationalist Pathros almost choked on those words, "but since we discovered the Lignum Crucis, all signs of his grave illness have disappeared."

William glanced at the boy thief.

"He's cured of leprosy?"

"Somehow, yes. In defiance of anything written in my books."

The Templar beamed. But then his expression darkened in an instant.

"And what about me?"

Pathros reached into his medicine bag and brought out a single vial.

"Only one left. Dare yourself never to take it, dear friend. Free yourself of the shackles of the poppy. And when we meet again, the Basilisk will surely be slain!"

Chapter 58

THE BATTLEMENTS OF AL-USBUNA

An hour later, William and Nicholas stood on battlements over the Bab Al-Bahr and watched a steady stream of people leaving with what modest belongings the Normans and Flemish had shown no interest in. They were like the swarm of refugees the trio had encountered in Castile led by the sole Templar. Only these people were fleeing Christians and not Muslims.

If William had looked hard, he'd have seen a figure wrapped in a plain cloak and a hood over his head, hoping not to be recognised. He was throwing in his lot with these Moors, expecting to get on the right side of the Almohads, whom he'd help to fight back against Dom Afonso. Every so often, a dinar rattled in his mouth.

I will be avenged against you, Afonso. Rejecting an old friend — that is unforgivable after all I have done for you. All those towns I took. You and your bitch of a queen will come to rue the day you treated me like a cur!

In just three days the whole city would have to be cleared of its Muslims and Jews. Those who stayed would be forced to convert or burn at the stake. They would have to bow to a new king and genuflect before a new bishop. If they tried to find their old mosques, they'd come across ruins being quarried for masonry to construct new churches and a splendid cathedral.

Martins sidled up to William.

"I have asked the King. There is no question of you having permission to take the True Cross."

William ground his teeth in anger.

"My boy got it for Dom Afonso. There'd have been no victory without him."

"You have to understand," Martins responded with a voice full of sorrow for the young Templar's predicament, "we are a new country and we need this symbol. It led us to victory."

"So I return to England empty-handed – as if nothing happened."

"Nonsense!" Martins bristled. "I will flood your superiors in England with letters detailing your courage and bravery. Dom Afonso has assured me he will do likewise. You will achieve your quest."

William wasn't so sure.

The monks from Santa Cruz now processed with Afonso, João Peculiar and Pedro Pitões on to the battlements. Behind Pitões stood the new Bishop of Lisbon, the Norman Gilbert of Hastings. To a deafening acclamation, the clerics held aloft the True Cross – sacred symbol of a new Portugal. The Te Deum was sung and Peculiar placed the kingly crown onto Afonso's head.

Hugo Martins took pride of place but Gualdim Pais absented himself from this ceremony. He'd no wish to stand in the giant shadow cast by that insult to God, João Peculiar.

Let the Archbishop have his day of celebration because soon, sinful and wealthy prelates like him will be dethroned and cast out.

William became aware of a familiar presence. He pivoted round to find Orraca standing behind him. She was glum.

"You must be very proud. Not many men can say they have decimated a great city."

William watched the exodus.

"I'm not proud of this."

"But you got your True Cross."

"Not quite," William tousled Nicholas' hair. "The boy did very well. But I don't get to take it home. The Portuguese insist on keeping it. Think I've failed in my quest, actually."

"And the Eastern Christian ... your servant?"

"My turcopole has decided to stay and help."

"How noble of him," Orraca paused. There was something she had to get off her mind. "I am carrying your child, William. But I know you are straining to get back to your Templar masters in England and bury your father. For you, the dead come before new life." She adjusted her dress as if her belly was already swollen. "I do not think that journey would be wise for a woman in my condition. Maybe it is fortuitous that your turcopole has stayed here. I hear he delivered Ibn Arrik's son so he can deliver mine as well."

William placed his arm gingerly around Orraca's waist.

"When I bury my father, I will come back for my son."

She pointedly broke away.

"Leave the Templars! They are murderers of my people! Do that and I, with your turcopole, will bring your son to you in England. Then we can all live together happily ever after!"

She smiled with a trace of delicious malice. William's expression was utterly conflicted, as she had hoped.

"So," Orraca twisted the emotional knife into the Englishman, "you put your beloved Templars before your future wife, son and dearest friend."

The Templar ran his fingers through his hair then stroked his chin.

"Let me bury my father first — then look out for a message from me."

Part 4

ENGLAND

Chapter 59

BAY OF BISCAY

The waves reared up as if determined to beat the ship's crew and its passengers to death. Walls of dark green water fringed with foam smashed down on the vessel. The sea was lashing out with an inchoate fury. Some believed that to take to the oceans was an offence against the spirits that controlled the waters. While William knew this was mere superstition, there was no doubting the sea was very angry.

Suddenly the cog heeled over so steeply it seemed impossible it could right itself again.

"I saw the monster," an oarsman screamed, "There! I saw it there!"

Grasping the gunwale, William peered into the storm, but could see nothing. The Basilisk has departed me, he assured himself.

Maybe this is Leviathan.

All godly people knew that Leviathan was the great monster that ruled the sea and only on Judgement Day would it be slain. Its flesh would then be served to the righteous under a tent made of its skin.

"It's definitely Leviathan," William felt curiously consoled while all others around him screamed to God for mercy.

Basilisk is dead. The Devil has gone. My quest has vanquished the beast.

Another wave crashed onto the other side of the cog and William found himself gaping at a watery abyss that threatened to consume him. Its jaws opened up but before they could snap shut, the cog slammed down again, flinging him against the mast behind him.

He clung on with his arms and legs as fiercely as an English soldier nearby was clinging onto a chaplain to make his last confession. The infantryman was in some distress and struggled to get his words out.

"We murdered a child ..."

The confessor yelled in his ear.

"In Al-Usbuna?"

"No, we did the foul deed in Norwich. It was in a forest. Just a boy he was."

"Why would you do such a thing?" The confessor shouted over the storm.

"We were paid well. Very well indeed! And the lads from the Golgotha Tavern convinced me to get involved. I helped hold the poor boy down." The soldier sobbed. "I must know I'm shriven, Father. My poor soul ..." The soldier clutched at the confessor's cloak. "I don't want to go to hell! You can get God in heaven to forgive me ... a wretch ... a sinner!"

The priest wiped his face of seawater.

"How was the boy killed?"

The soldier couldn't speak for a few moments.

"You must tell me," the priest shouted over the violent storm. "Else I will not confess you."

"We crucified him like Our Lord. We nailed him to a cross and blamed the Jews."

The priest crossed himself.

"Who paid you to do such a monstrous crime? What devil would mock our Lord like this?"

"The Earl of Essex."

William, overhearing the exchange, felt as if lightning had just struck him. He no longer sensed the storm around him in what the Moors called the Sea of Perpetual Gloom. The tempest could turn the ship upside down and immerse all aboard and he wouldn't notice it.

So this is what my brother is capable of.

Not content with burning the feet of peasants, he was now crucifying them as well. Slipping across the sodden deck, William opened a door and threw himself into a sheltered space where several passengers, including Nicholas, were trying in vain to sleep.

"Sea's gone mad," Nicholas clutched his guts to stop being sick.

"It's alright," William responded. "We'll be in England soon. Just be brave."

The knight reflected on what the boy had been through since he'd rescued him in Witham: the chase through France and Castile and the hand-to-hand combat with the Almohads, the siege of Al-Usbuna and the daring theft of the great relic. The boy deserved to become a knight one day, he'd experienced so much.

The Templar found a damp corner and slid to the ground. A day of reckoning back in England was fast approaching and he needed the strength that several hours' slumber would give him. Damn the storm and damn Leviathan! If God wanted to take him now, he could do so. But he doubted the Lord would deny him the chance to confront his brother.

That murderous wretch! I'll punish Edward on behalf of all those he's tortured.

Sleep overtook William quicker than he could have imagined. But with it came a vicious renewal of the images of battles fought long before in Outremer. It was as if they resented being ignored or shouldered aside by his new crusade in Portugal and demanded his attention.

William convulsed in his sleep until his eyes opened with a start.

My father made my brother from base material. Clay and water, while I was made of fire! But he worshipped the son made in his likeness and spurned me.

Before William the Basilisk reared upwards, its scaly hood fanned open and scarlet crest pulsating.

I would not worship my brother. I am of fire, I said. I will set my throne against his and be greater than him.

The Templar's sword emerged slowly from its scabbard as the demon's mouth opened to reveal a ghastly darkness that seemed to stretch forever.

You are mine and I am yours. Our fathers spurn us! We only have each other.

Leave me, Basilisk. I am not of your kind.

William's sword was readied at his side and he waited for the monster to draw closer. He'd sever its monstrous head.

I cannot leave you. I am with you for all time.

The Templar's hand grasped the hilt of the weapon and he prepared to swing the blade with all his might.

We are cast down into the void. Thrown from heaven into the pit.

Not I, Basilisk. Not I.

The sword blade swooped through the air and severed the serpent's head in one blow. The body continued to writhe and William hacked at it till it finally slumped to the ground.

"Hey, watch yourself!"

Another Norman rose, prepared to run the Templar through. Was he mad, to be wielding a sword like that for no reason?

"Been having a bad dream, have you?" one of the other soldiers sneered. "You want to be more careful."

Roused by the commotion, Nicholas saw the mood was turning ugly. Stumbling in his haste, he put himself between William and their fellow voyagers.

"Master William has strange dreams. It's nothing to be concerned about. Well, sorry about the sword and all but it's just his mind. So everybody sit down and go back to sleep."

Nicholas turned to William and reached into his pocket.

"Know I'm not supposed to steal …" He produced a vial of elixir he'd taken from Pathros' medicine bag. "But I got it just in case. So here you are, Master William."

"No," he replied. "I'm not going to take those infusions anymore. I want my own mind back. I really believe the Basilisk is dead now. I've got to prove it has gone."

Suddenly, Nicholas' luggage drew his attention. He'd set out on this long journey with nothing but was returning to England with what seemed to be some sizeable and recently acquired possessions.

"What's in that large sack?" William pointed. "It's almost as big as you."

"Nothing," Nicholas lied.

The Templar despaired.

"Don't make me open it. Just show me what you've taken." He looked down into the rapidly blinking eyes of the mendacious boy. "Better if you own up to me now. That's the sign of being a man – admitting the bad things you've done."

Nicholas shuffled uneasily.

"I only took it so as to please you."

"What did you steal?"

With that, the boy staggered to the large sack, opened it and pulled down the coarse hemp cloth. William could scarcely believe what he was seeing. He clasped a hand over his mouth.

Somehow, Nicholas had stolen the Lignum Crucis.

Chapter 60

DARTMOUTH

"I thought'd you'd be angry," Nicholas skipped down the gangplank.

"No," William replied. "The True Cross helped me kill the Basilisk – I'm sure of it."

The cog had docked at Dartmouth. Now he'd make straight for the preceptory in London. The True Cross would be handed over and he could cut his father's coffin down and bury it in consecrated ground. But as his feet touched firm ground, William became aware of three burly men heading towards him.

"Keep hold of the cross, Nicholas," he whispered to the boy. "Whatever happens now, never lose it. Take it to London."

"I don't understand."

The watchmen were upon the Templar. One of them produced an official-looking parchment replete with two impressive wax seals.

"You must come with us to the Tower, William de Mandeville," one of the watchmen commanded. "You are hereby arrested for treason against your brother and thereby our lawful King Stephen. You have also absconded with a thief and fomented revolt against the Earl of Essex."

Behind the three watchmen was a group of similarly built men – hefty enforcers of the King's law. William turned to tell Nicholas to run but he'd already melted into the dockside crowd.

"I'll answer for everything I've done," the Templar responded.

"Oh, you'll do that alright!" one of the watchmen leered.

The knight submitted to the authority of the watchmen and three days later found himself in chains in a grimy cell in the Tower of London. Through a small window in the Norman keep, he was able to look across the city to the Templar preceptory at Holborn where his father was unburied still, and to Newgate, where his head would soon appear on a spike.

William's jailer was a drunken barrel of ale on legs. Covered in food and drink stains, he delighted in goading his better-off prisoners.

"Martinmass now," he reminded the Templar that summer had gone and it was the blood month when livestock were slaughtered and many pious folk fasted as they had done in Lent. "You'll be fasting here ... May not want to, but you won't want to eat what we got!"

William ignored the brute. Instead, he cursed himself for having been so deluded to think he could return a hero, when his brother was still earl and he'd challenged him so openly before the common serfs.

Edward wants me dead. I won't see Christmas.

There was a jangle of keys outside his cell door.

"Visitor for ya," the jailer announced before making a string of obscene comments to the stout old lady who had come to see William. She wore a simple dress and placed some barley cakes on the small table in the cell.

"Bit old for ya, that one, ain't she?" the jailer continued.

The door slammed behind the prisoner and visitor.

"Never thought I'd see you like this, Sir William."

The Templar recognised her.

"It's been a long time. How is your husband?"

She broke down and wept.

"Ageric is dead."

The steward's widow then recounted a grim tale to William. Not only did Edward connive to have an innocent youth murdered in Thorpe Wood, rousing the mob against the Jews and seizing their wealth for himself – but he'd then pressured the Church to have the victim canonised.

The Earl had turned up at Norwich Cathedral to greet the still-furious skinners, tanners and cordwainers who felt a special affinity to the crucified boy on account of his trade. And Edward had greeted them oozing pious grief.

Ageric had found the whole display repellent.

He realised that all those involved would be crucified over and over again in hell for this most heinous of sins. Their limbs would be burnt and branded by demons and their backs repeatedly scourged in the manner that our Lord suffered.

"And while my husband was torn apart by all this, that dog Blacwin sucked up to the Earl something rotten."

"So you knew the Jews had nothing to do with this," William said.

"Of course! They came up with all those lies about their rituals – but Edward planned it all! And he roped in my husband to hire the thugs to go find some people to ..."

She could hardly bring herself to say it.

"... poor child. They pulled at his arms and legs while he screamed for them to stop." Ageric's widow gasped with the enormity of the crime. "They fastened him to the cross with the blacksmith's nails. Other things were done to make sure the common folk were enraged. Symbols carved onto his body."

After the service in Norwich Cathedral to canonise the dead boy a saint, Ageric, Blacwin and the Earl had gone for a stroll in the cloister. Eventually they'd found themselves in the monks' cemetery. The steward had noted a freshly dug grave, with the sexton leaning on his spade still sweating as his task had only just been completed.

"The Earl started talking in his usual riddles. Said that my husband was like a crocodile that needs to eat but when it kills and consumes a human being, it's filled with remorse. But the Earl said he was more like a fox that could gorge on chickens – by which he meant his own serfs – till his face was covered in blood and would still be smiling."

That was certainly typical of the way in which Edward spoke. He'd taken great learning and twisted it in his mind. The works of great philosophers were employed to legitimise his insane cruelty.

"Then he starts accusing Ageric of being disloyal. Said he thought my husband had been in league with you against him. And then ..."

The widow's breast heaved as she struggled to breathe. William took her hand.

"Oh lord, such a beast! That Blacwin creeps up behind my poor man and runs him through with his sword. Then he falls headlong into the newly-dug grave." She turned to William. "They had it all planned. To kill him there and then."

"How do you know all this?"

"A monk was hiding behind a pillar in the cloister and saw it all. Then he came to me …" – she reached for a document under her cloak – "he had this with him."

She handed it to William.

"It's your father's last will and testament."

"Leaving the earldom to my brother," the Templar noted gloomily.

"No, not at all, William. He wanted you to be earl."

William's eyes widened as he read.

"The two monks that drafted that document were murdered," she explained. "And then those men who witnessed it, they got done in as well. There was Thomas Draper, Ben Mercer and those two harmless souls, the brothers Odo and Alfred. All just disappeared off the face of the earth."

"And my brother did that?"

The widow winced.

"No, William – your mother!"

Chapter 61

PLESHEY CASTLE

The Earl crouched in his mother's bedroom, occasionally daring to look out of the window to the snow-covered fields beyond. They were still there, motionless and determined. Countless rows of mantles as white as the falling snow, steel helmets that flashed in the winter sun and kite-shaped shields bearing the red eight-pointed cross. In front of this menacing host, the black-and-white piebald standard of the Knights Templar, gripped firmly by the gonfanonier, fluttered in the breeze.

The Countess lay quite still, lost in thought.

"Remind me, Mother – whose idea was it to attack the Templars?"

Her head rolled on the pillow.

"This is because you crucified that boy!"

This boy has brought heaven's wrath upon our family!

Maybe he should just surrender. He might not face the executioner's axe. The Templars might make him do penance, in chains crawling on his knees from Witham to Cologne, Santiago and possibly even Jerusalem.

But he could never be earl again after that. Nobody would respect him.

The monstrous act in Thorpe Wood was all her son's doing. That, above all else, was why fate was acting against them. He'd killed a simple child in mockery of Christ's crucifixion just to squeeze some money out of the local

Jews. This was truly unforgivable. Edward had stepped over a line that even the Countess in her most calculating schemes would never have done.

God will never forgive me unless I take action.

"You've still had no prayers said for my immortal soul," she hissed at her son.

"Not one prayer, Mother. Nor am I going to. Why on earth would anybody bother? We all know where you're going."

The Countess shut her eyes.

So it's up to me to save my own soul.

I can't let our great family fall from grace. It's always fallen to me to ensure the dynasty continues, she mused. A mother must make all the painful and dreadful decisions. The men are always so foolish or cruel. I must do something now to put things right and do it swiftly before I breathe my last.

"What a wretch you are!" she wheezed at Edward. "I thought William was the waste of space in my womb, but it was you. Your father was right. I should have listened … should have listened to my husband."

Edward slammed his goblet down by this mother's bed.

"I really don't care for this, Mother. If you've got something to tell me that will help, then say it. Otherwise, please get on with dying. I'm finding the long walk to this room exceedingly tiresome."

Rohese was consumed by hatred.

I have nothing more to say to you, my son.

A killer of children! A robber of Templars! The King of Snakes! Rohese summoned up a fading wisp of energy and reached for Edward's goblet and then quickly withdrew her hand.

The Earl took another glimpse at the Templars massed outside his castle and grabbed his goblet back. The Countess watched him.

Drink, my son.

He drained its contents. Rohese counted in her head. One and two and three and four and …

Edward clasped his throat and sank to his knees. How obliging of that physician-cum-abbot to supply her with some poison! He'd taken a huge dislike to Edward and been surprisingly amenable to having the Earl bumped off – by his own mother. She'd paid him well for the deadly concoction.

He is dead. Let William rule in his stead!

I have redeemed myself before God. He will wipe my slate clean. The Devil's sentinels, whom Rohese had seen around her for weeks before, departed sullenly from the bedside, returning to hell's deep.

You will not have my soul!

Suddenly the entire room was illuminated with shafts of golden light and a great staircase, like the ladder of Jacob, appeared with angels ascending and descending. A tall and youthful man walked down the celestial steps towards his wife. Angelic voices whispered all around him.

It was Geoffrey, the first Earl of Essex, and he looked as handsome as he had done on their wedding day. Rohese glanced at her own hands, no longer wrinkled and gnarled. She wore a fine gown of silk trimmed with ermine; her hair spilt down over her shoulders and her complexion was as pink as peaches.

"How is our son?" the Earl asked.

"He's in good spirits, I'm told." She referred to the only son she now recognised. "He's been on crusade and fought bravely."

"Good," the Earl responded. "I hear he's going to bury my mortal remains. That's very decent of him, don't you think?"

"Well," Rohese answered, "he always was the honourable one."

As the Countess ascended the staircase to her heavenly reward, two stiff and cold bodies of a mother and her eldest son lay in a dank room at Pleshey Castle as the candles around them spluttered out.

Chapter 62

GALLOWS NEAR THE RIVER CAN

"No … please, God … No … such pain … no …"
The almost-naked man covered in filth and blood was tied to a hurdle. The once well-dressed and mighty servant of the Earl was being dragged through Chelmsford. His destination was the gibbet by the River Can. Already the condemned man's eyes had been put out and the mob had castrated him.

The public torture had gone on for many hours. Villagers from the highest to lowest rank had wanted to inflict their own distinct wound on this hapless individual – to carve their revenge into his flesh.

Hiding in a barn, Blacwin had begged for mercy as the avenging crowd gathered outside. Many had lost friends to Edward's viper pits. Others had seen men like Daegmund disfigured for being unable to pay onerous taxes. The incessant raids on the holy men of the Knights Templar and Benedictines had appalled every soul in the county. So the barn doors had been kicked down and the terrified chamberlain hauled out and stripped.

His fine garments had soon disappeared into the howling mob. Tied to a post, Blacwin had been beaten and whipped like a common criminal. His wispy beard was pulled at savagely and his teeth knocked out of his head. His increasingly incoherent moans for mercy had been roundly ignored.

Blinded, he knew even in his delirious state that he was close to the gibbet. The peasants surged all around him, kicking and spitting. Then one woman, shrieking some unintelligible curse, poured a pot of boiling water over his face. He screamed in agony as it scalded and burned away his flesh.

It was almost a relief to be untied from the hurdle and carried up the ladder by the side of the gibbet. A rope was then placed about his neck and Blacwin was tossed into mid-air. As he struggled and writhed, nobody stepped forward to pull at his ankles.

Instead they cheered as the chamberlain danced.

Chapter 63

TOWER OF LONDON

The cell door swung open with a clang. For a few seconds nobody stood at the entrance and the knight made to bolt for his freedom. Then the jailer suddenly appeared, blocking his way with his bulky frame.

"Free to go," he declared in a matter-of-fact way.

"What do you mean?"

"Go!" the jailer yelled. "Traitors need this cell!"

Not quite believing this turn of fortune, William walked hesitantly towards his portly captor. The man stuck out his hand for a shilling.

"Cost of your upkeep."

"If you want to keep that hand," William snarled, "put it away now!"

Peeved by this, the jailer spat out one bit of bad news that would sting his former charge.

"Your mother and brother are dead, by the way."

William was rooted to the spot.

"The power of the Lignum Crucis," he said softly.

Leaving the White Tower, the Templar blinked in the wintery daylight. It was bitterly cold and the ground was coated in snow. William was offered a sorry-looking nag to make his way to the preceptory at Holborn.

The dilapidated beast could barely muster a trot and it took an unendurable length of time to cross through London. William shivered and beat his hands together for warmth as they made a snail-like progress down Cheapside.

Eventually, the low walls of the preceptory presented themselves. Not bothering to tether the animal – and rather hoping it would slope away – the knight bounded off it and made his way in through the main gateway. He was immediately confronted by a variety of mouth-watering aromas.

Game birds coated in butter and saffron were roasting. Pots of frumenty bubbled over a hearth and pies were being baked, stuffed with venison and blackbird. Cinnamon and nutmeg, cooking apples and gooseberries and a plump goose sailed past on a tray carried by a scullion. A boy chased after the tray, unable to take his eyes off the soon-to-be roasted bird.

"Nicholas!" William shouted.

He stopped and turned to face his master. As he did so, Hugh of Argentine appeared behind him. The English Templar master held two maple cups of wine and handed one to William.

"Come into the chapel," he beckoned.

As they entered the circular building modelled on the Holy Sepulchre in Jerusalem, all eyes fixed on the most cherished possession of the Knights Templar on an altar in the middle. This revered relic had led a people to victory and who knew what other miracles it had performed? In front of it, a redheaded, well-built Norman prince of medium height was praying fervently.

"Who is he?" William asked in a hushed tone.

Before Hugh could answer, the man rose to his feet.

"I am Henry of Anjou. Son of the Empress Matilda! Future King of England! And," he outstretched his hand, "a loyal friend to you poor fellow-soldiers of Christ and the Temple of Solomon."

By which he meant the Templars by the full title of the Order.

"Matilda's son," William gasped.

"The Empress Matilda!" The Prince had a temper to match his red hair. "I know what your father did, but I also know what you've done. And I see it here," he gestured to the Lignum Crucis. "You have my blessing to take him down and grant the late Earl a Christian burial. Do what a son must do, honour your father. And we'll speak later of other things."

William was stunned. Hugh raised an eyebrow and tipped his head towards the orchard outside. It was time to make things right. The soon-to-be third Earl of Essex pushed open a half-rotten door in the stone wall and crunched across the snow-covered ground to that accursed tree.

Nicholas ran over to him.

"You know," William looked down, "you're all I've got left. My family are dead. Pathros is in Portugal. And ..."

"Don't worry, Master William, I've got nothing else to do."

The knight laughed.

"Well, that's good to know, I suppose."

The trees were now denuded of leaves, presenting an even starker sight than his last visit, nearly three years before. There, through naked branches, he could clearly see the lead casket. The bleak grey vessel contained the rotting remains of the man who had moulded his second son into a fine warrior.

Then William noticed a group of familiar figures. The white mantles! The cross of the Order upon them!

Could it be?

He belted towards them. Not since his madness in the infirmary had he seen his old battle comrades. William had half-expected they wouldn't want to speak to him again.

"Ralf – dear and loyal friend! Sorry I hit you! Walter – haven't changed a bit! Thomas – that's an ugly scar some Saracen blade cut there but it suits you!" He shook hands with each of his dear companions. "Roger – good of you to be here. Richard – thought I'd never see you again."

Ralf looked up at the apple tree.

"Shall we get him down then?"

William drew his sword. Nobody would stop him this time. He sent the blade slicing through the ropes. His fellow knights had only the briefest of moments to catch the coffin as it fell to the ground. The tree bough, which had been bent over by its heavy load, sprang upwards and sent snow flying over the knights.

Rearranging the ropes beneath the coffin, the assembled Templars eased it into a plot they had already dug. Ralf, a chaplain, sprinkled holy water on the lead surface and blessed the body as it at last found eternal rest.

Requiem aeternam dona ei, Domine.

Each knight took it in turns to drop a fistful of soil onto the lid of the casket. William knelt down likewise. As he did so, he reached beneath his mantle and, out of sight of his fellow brothers, inserted a small but very sacred shaving of wood into the soil he held in his hand. Then he cast it onto the lid that bore the embossed crest of the Earls of Essex.

He was sorry Nicholas had been accused by João Peculiar of breaking a piece of wood off the Lignum Crucis but William had determined to come back with at least a small part of the sacred relic. Fearful the Portuguese would insist on keeping the True Cross, he'd wanted to retain a tiny portion to help his father on his long journey in the hereafter.

"All of you," he tearfully beseeched his fellow Templars, "pray for my father. He committed acts against the Church that were wrong but I'm sure that noble reasoning drove him to such madness."

Accept his soul, William prayed, because I defeated the Prince of Hell. And I rescued your Son's cross from the hands of pagans. I have served you well, Lord, let the first Earl of Essex enter paradise.

Slowly, the coffin was consumed into consecrated ground.

I am everything you wanted me to be, Father.

Stout-hearted and dauntless, a warrior for the truth! In battle, I have slain the Saracens and the Moors. I have laid low the enemies of Christ. I have wielded my sword to stop the powerful abusing the meek. To you, Father, I will be a worthy successor.

William's blue eyes glinted with happiness. His fellow knights gathered round and Ralf privately cursed those Augustinians who would have drilled into his friend's head. There was nothing wrong with William – bit of a fever in the thick of war, that was all.

The third Earl of Essex looked down at the fresh grave. He would rule wisely and strive to be loved by his people. The name de Mandeville would no longer be feared and cursed.

Farewell, Father – God take your soul forever.

CHRISTMAS DAY, ANNO DOMINI 1147
THURSDAY 30 RAJAB 542
ANNO HEGIRAE

ENDS

ABOUT THE AUTHOR

Former BBC producer Tony McMahon is an award-shortlisted author living in south London. After working for twenty years as a news journalist for the *BBC*, *Sky News* and the *Financial Times*, he now pursues his avid interest in politics, religion and history by writing books and has already published two biographies: *Original Rude Boy*, the story of legendary vocalist Neville Staple, and *No Place to Hide*, about middleweight champion boxer Errol Christie, which was shortlisted for best UK sports biography of 2011.

McMahon manages the medieval blog thetemplarknight.com and has travelled extensively in Europe and the Middle East to research the sites featured in his first historical novel, *Quest for the True Cross*.